THE
PRISM

ANETA TORCHIA

THE
LUMINARY
PRESS

"Imagination is more important than knowledge. Knowledge
is limited. Imagination encircles the world."

"Imagination is everything. It is the preview to life's coming
attraction."

— *Albert Einstein*

THE PRISM

Copyright © 2023 by Aneta Torchia

Written by Aneta Torchia
Edited by The Luminary Press
Cover design by The Luminary Press
Illustrations by Aneta Torchia

The story, all names, characters, and incidents portrayed in this book are fictitious. No identification with actual persons (living or deceased), places, building, and products is intended or should be inferred.

ISBN: 978-1-7387687-3-8, 1st edition paperback, 2023
ISBN: 978-1-7387687-5-2, 1st edition hardcover, 2023
ISBN: 978-1-7387687-4-5, 1st edition eBook, 2023

Published by The Luminary Press
Mississauga, ON, Canada
info@theluminarypress.com
www.theluminarypress.com

Other books in THE PRISM series:
EMERALD PASSAGE (Book 2)
FINDING AEONIA (Book 3)

Dedicated to my husband who has supported me on every journey; my mother who always encouraged me to write; and every soul searching for truth, purpose, and deeper connection – I sincerely hope you find it!

Reviews

"Aneta Torchia creates a powerful story of a game-changing world gone awry, and a girl's difficult options... *The Prism* sets the stage for what looks to be an extraordinary trilogy steeped in life-changing decisions and glimpses of life's meaning and purpose."
Senior Reviewer, Midwest Book Review

*

"*The Prism* intersects fantasy, thriller, and paranormal themes so seamlessly…readers are treated to a vivid tale that sparkles with unexpected angles and encounters…

[R]eaders seeking fantasies that intersect nicely with thriller components, interpersonal relationships that teeter on the edge of disaster, and explorations of spiritual and metaphysical influences on the world will find *The Prism* a compelling adventure and a thought-provoking journey."
D. Donovan, Editor, Donovan's Literary Services

*

"*The Prism* is an immersive book that will transport you to another world. Beautifully descriptive. It is a perfect blend of fantasy and mystery. It sucks you in from the first page and keeps you guessing. Can't wait for book 2!"
Amazon Reader

What if there's more?

Prologue

There wasn't much to do in Greenland, or many people to do things with, 14 floors beneath the ice. But that was exactly the way the Order wanted it. After all, anonymity had proven an effective strategy for thousands of years.

It was why the four-person teams of analysts who took turns manning the Cyprus Project arrived unconscious – and hooded in case the drugs wore off too soon. The security measures and lack of obvious exits made escape a fool's errand. Not that the analysts gave it much thought. It wasn't the holograms of azure beach water and lush jungles, or the abundance of delicacies and video games that kept them in line; those were only distractions to alleviate the inevitable boredom.

No – what ensured their compliance was a vague promise of what they would receive after 90 days once they completed their assignment.

The promise of the Prism.

A world of limitless possibilities, or so they'd been told. Not seeing the light of day for three months seemed a small price to pay for such an alluring reward; and compared to carrying out desensitization sessions on new initiates, being cut off from the outside world and manning a secret bunker sounded like a walk in the park.

The ear-piercing buzzer of the Arachna startled Sarah away from her 145th sudoku puzzle. She abandoned her cushioned pod and joined Mason in the hallway outside the kitchen. He had arrived at the Cypress Project only a few hours before, not that he or Sarah knew it was called that. The newbie pressed his palms tightly to his ears as he shadowed his mentor, both dressed in their mandatory black jumpsuits with a red "V" across their backs.

"You'll get used to it," Sarah told her trainee as they maneuvered the artificial jungle plants towards the Web, a dome-like structure in the center of the facility. "There's stockpiles of earplugs in the storage room."

"Couldn't they make it quieter?" Mason complained. "Then again, they are a sadistic bunch."

"Aren't we all?"

"So, any idea where we are?"

"Nope. They knocked me out well before we reached the airport. This is all very need to know. I'm skipping out a few days early, by the way. They'll come for me in a few hours – early recruitment by the Paris chapter, which is why you're here."

"Paris, nice!" Mason replied.

"I'm not complaining. Although my parents won't be too thrilled that I'm not coming back to Michigan."

"Uh…I trained with a team…"

"Yeah, they should be here within a week. Robby will take over your orientation before turning over the keys. After that, it's just you newbies in this pressure cooker." Sarah grimaced a little, then let out a chuckle. "Do yourselves a favor — don't spend too much time together."

Typically, she would offer a wink or a smile of reassurance to go along with her usual wit, but after nearly 90 days she couldn't stomach being phony.

Once inside the Web, they joined two other analysts whose fingers furiously typed code and flipped switches to identify the exact coordinates of the frequency that was the cause for all the commotion. The charcoal walls were lit up by a reddish glow coming off several archaic-looking computer monitors.

"The Arachna's named after the ability of spiders to sense their prey using vibrations," Sarah explained, giving Mason some context. "It can track significant energy emissions on an individual level anywhere in the world, down to the frequency of a single thought. Even the NSA doesn't know about it!"

"At this decibel, that won't last long!" Mason grumbled.

Sarah tied back her curly black hair in a short ponytail. "When a frequency comes in, we use the Arachna to translate it and figure out the source location, then phone it into the nearest chapter house. They use the coordinates to locate the targets and send the info back, so we know who the frequency belongs to going forward. See, each frequency has an original signature — like a fingerprint." She motioned behind her at an impenetrable floor-to-ceiling steel door, guarded by a thick wall of glass. "Whatever they're trying to hide down here, that's where they keep it."

Mason studied the intimidating containment chamber, accessible only by biometric scan. "How big is this thing?" he asked, inching closer to it.

"Don't!"

"What?"

"Get any idiotic ideas. Even if you manage to get through

the glass without clearance, try to open the main latch and the lasers will slice your skull in half."

Some color vanished from Mason's thin cheeks. "Really?"

Sarah smirked and shrugged. "Maybe it's just a rumor, but I'd rather not find out."

"Hey, it's definitely her again," one of the other analysts called out once he'd finished analyzing the fingerprint of the frequency.

Sarah reached for the landline telephone. "I'll call it in."

"A landline? Seriously?" Mason asked. "There's a biometric scanner on that door over there, and you're using a landline?"

"I guess it prevents interception – maybe helps keep this place off the grid."

Mason's cheeks got another shade whiter, and he looked uneasily around the Web. "So…if we die down here…"

Sarah chuckled. "Just…try *not* to die. And maybe stay away from the jellybeans in the vending machine. I swear, they taste like bleach."

She finished dialing the Paris number and waited for a voice from the world above the ice. "Cleary, Everest. 50241. Episode 3 in 24," she advised the contact, snapping her fingers at her associate to pull up the data logs, "so…that's 17 so far for the week. Her pattern's amplifying quickly – 7.96 today. Yup…ok."

When the line went dead, Sarah froze. The phone felt like a cold concrete block against her ear, and it shook slightly thanks to her trembling hand. Before anyone could notice, she returned the phone to its cradle and busied herself brushing two days' worth of hollow peanut shells into the trash, imparting a disgusted glance on the culprit.

"Gross, Robby!"

"Don't worry; if we can't get out the rats won't get in,"

Robby teased, chewing another peanut loudly and smiling through his unruly beard. "You'll be rid of me soon enough."

Not nearly soon enough, Sarah thought to herself. Her pupils scanned the other red targets on the main monitor for a surge, secretly hoping not to see one. "Hey, can you look up that kid in Singapore we've been tracking? His marker went missing the other day."

Robby pulled up the latest status report as he scratched at the unkept stubble on his chin. "Chua, wasn't it? Uh…EXTINGUISHED. Yeah… two days ago."

"They had no use for you either, huh?" Sarah mumbled to herself. A sadness gripped her chest momentarily as she recalled the target's age and photo – he still had that baby fat on his cheeks…

She pushed the emotion aside. The Order didn't tolerate empathy. It was counterproductive, they said. A weakness, they said. They said a lot of things that left her sleep deprived.

Still, she was born into this world. Her choices were limited. For now…

"Extinguished. Does that mean –"

"Yeah," Sarah confirmed for Mason as the buzzer finally stopped.

Mason shook out his hands which had remained pressed against his ears over the ear plugs. "It's about time! All this for a frequency? What's the big deal anyway?"

Sarah smirked. "You'll have to earn that knowledge, like the rest of us. Somehow, I doubt we'll find out for a very long time."

She continued to scan the targets. All seemed steady and within parameters.

All but one.

This 'Paris Girl.' The frequency waxed and waned, but it was always significantly higher than the others, and often unpredictable and erratic, making it look like the tracking screen had an abnormal heart rhythm. Sarah cracked the only remaining intact peanut shell between her fingers as she analyzed the pattern, wondering why this target was allowed to intensify to such levels when the Order didn't give a second thought to wiping weaker ones from existence.

That burning question nagged at her once again: what was the Order's agenda?

Everest Cleary, why are you still alive?

* * *

"Crétin!" The towering bald man twirled his thick granite ring with his thumb, his leather jacket still intentionally blood-stained from the previous week's assignment. He could easily wipe it off but allowed it to remain for the same reason he never let hair overgrow the scar that ran down the back of his shaved skull. They served as reminders in case anyone ever doubted what he was capable of.

His unimposing and shorter associate was hunched over the motionless body of a homeless man who seconds earlier livened up the Paris Abbesses metro station with a battered accordion.

"Irra! He is not moving! Irra," the shorter man hissed, careful not to let his overpriced charcoal suit touch the homeless man's clothes. Unlike his mentor, he still had some semblance of a conscience, although the desensitization sessions were slowly rectifying that problem.

"Too much Basile, you drained him too long," the tall man replied, the whites of his eyes darting around the tunnels which were beginning to look less deserted with the steady onslaught of commuters. "Killing them is not the point."

Basile straightened up, then buttoned and adjusted his suit.

"Come on," Irra instructed, "we have to get back."

"Right. To the Eveline girl again."

"Everest."

"Whatever…the old man really wants a lot of eyes on her."

Irra's face tightened. If the Order allowed him to indulge his compulsions, there would be no need for surveillance of the stupid girl. "The Ertu's obsession with the prophecy clouds his judgement."

"But if she can find it —"

"*If* she can find it," Irra sneered. "A game of telephone can change a sentence beyond recognition in under a minute, and we are supposed to believe a 3,000-year-old myth!"

Basile shifted uncomfortably. He knew the Order didn't take well to members questioning its methods. Those who didn't toe the line paid the price or vanished.

"Don't worry, the old man is well aware of my dissenting opinion," Irra reassured his nervous partner. "For now, we do what he wants: we see what the girl sees, hear what she hears, monitor her frequencies. Only time will tell if she's worth the trouble."

The body at their feet began to stir.

"He'll live," Irra said, turning on his heel and leaving the musician's donation box untouched. "Let's go. And try not to draw too much attention. Remember, we don't exist."

CHAPTER 1

Chasing Time

EVEREST CLEARY

I've done the math a hundred times: by age 75, the average person spends close to 9,000 days asleep – 9,000 days doing absolutely nothing while the universe expands into a billion more particles a second. Seems like a massive waste of time, doesn't it?

Time. It's kind of all a cruel joke. We try to count it, fill it, save it…make it stand still. We make movies about defying its laws, while in the same vein allowing it to dictate how we spend our days. We race against it, forever coming up short. And despite it making us anxious and crazy, we work our entire lives in the hopes that we'll finally get to enjoy it when it's no longer on our side.

It's kind of the definition of a toxic relationship.

I seem to have a few of those relationships in my life, Tristan Sarazen being one of them. I'm fortunate, I suppose. At least I've found little ways to beat Time at its own game when it comes to Tristan.

Well, sort of.

See, I've figured out through trial and error – through countless restless nights and premature awakenings – that by the early hours of the morning I'm mostly free of him, and that his hold on me diminishes, like a toxin that loses its potency. Then, even if only for a few hours, I get back a small piece of myself before I lose it again. I guess you could say I've figured out a way to make Time work for me. That's why the alarm jolts me awake at 4:30 sharp, every single morning. Those few extra hours, sitting awake in the darkness of my room have been a lifeline – a daily reminder that I'm not lost for good.

But it's also why Time has become an adversary I can never beat with any lasting satisfaction, because I know eventually it will slip away. Again.

I run a finger over the purple bruise on my wrist and my stomach twists. The nausea returns as I silently kick myself. They say you should listen to your gut, but I seem to let mine down every time. It's always the same routine after I see Tristan — feeling paralyzed for reasons I can never quite articulate, like I'm struggling underwater with a chain around my ankle. The key is in my hand, but no matter how much I struggle I can't bring myself to use it, even if it means I never see the surface again.

Why do I allow it? I'd love to know myself. I know I'm capable of removing him from my life. It should be so easy – we barely know each other after all.

So why do I fail? It's the question that nags at me day after day as I stare out onto my night cloaked Montmartre street.

I've gotten to know the comings and goings of the early risers pretty well. The police sergeant who lives above Emile's Patisserie runs past the apartment in her lime green runners that seem to glow in the dark. The walk-in clinic nurses nod to her as she passes them, then take a few more puffs of their cigarettes before stomping them into the pavement and heading inside. Like clockwork, Monsieur Goulet emerges around 5:30 to walk his puffy white Pomeranian, moving rather briskly inspite of his hip replacement and fused spine.

And then there's Hulk and Shorty. You can probably guess why I named them that. Shorty isn't really that short – Hulk just towers over him with his giant-like stature. They first appeared a few months back. Since then, their black Mercedes sedan maintains an almost constant vigil under the crooked streetlamp. Heavy tint on the windows, a red sticker on the license plate – a bird, maybe? I can't help but wonder about the meaning of their presence in our picturesque Parisian corner. Tourists don't exactly hang out on the same street at all hours of the day.

The two men lean lazily against their car, sipping their first of many tiny cups of espresso coffee (I've learned that's a European thing). Shorty dabs at a spill on his ill-fitting suit while Hulk glares at him in disgust, arms crossed over his leather jacket.

I ran into Hulk once at Emile's. I remember his massive hand reaching out to take the change from the barista, a tattoo of a "V" on his wrist. I remember the dirty leather jacket he wore over his broad shoulders and the unsightly scar that ran down the back of his hairless head and got lost in the skin folds above his neck. He's even more of a beast up close, and he stared down at me for an intimidating second before striding off. I'd be okay with not running into him again. There's something about his permanent scowl and cold energy that makes my bones rattle. Still, for some strange reason I'm drawn to him, or rather to the notion of figuring out who the hell he is and what he wants from Rue Marienne.

Hulk pops the trunk and leans into it, pulling at something that appears stuck inside. The streetlamp reflects off a shiny black surface, and the two men get to work manhandling it. It's too dark to tell what it is, but for a terrifying second, I convince myself that they'll suddenly whip out a hand or other body part.

Don't be ridiculous!

Still…would it be that surprising?

Mr. Goulet and his walking powderpuff round the corner and are quickly followed by a loud thud as Shorty slams the trunk shut.

Time's up.

I end my reconnaissance, shimmy off the window ledge, and reach for the lamp switch.

"Ahh!"

Without warning, the light bulb shatters and falls in a shower of glass onto the bedside table, a sharp shard grazing my fingertip on the way down.

"Are you…kidding me!?"

My eyes narrow to examine the fresh cut, the blood now outlining the labyrinth of ridges on my fingerprint. I grimace at the metallic aftertaste as I apply pressure with my lips. *Why do the small cuts bleed so much?*

Up until a few years ago, I had always thought light bulb explosions were a rare phenomenon. How things change...

I stare at the remnants of the last explosion. A piece of glass rests on a letter from Cambridge which offers me the college admission I can't accept. It's like the universe is taunting me, rubbing salt into another kind of wound. I try to push down the resentment and head out of the room to find a band-aid.

The old hardwood creaks on my way to the living area where the smell of cinnamon and vanilla incense tickles my nostrils. My aunt is on the phone, probably complaining about how the world is going to hell to whoever will listen. That's usually the gist of it. She pokes pointlessly at a couch cushion as she speaks into the handset, the coffee table littered with bottles of nail polish and manicure tools.

"I don't know why she can't just go to a school around here in a few years. She's almost 19. When I was 19, I certainly didn't go galivanting around the world! And after everything –"

"I'm right beside you," I remind her as I rifle through a cluttered drawer to unearth the last band-aid. I'm tired of hearing her twist the truth and absolve herself of any wrongdoing.

Catherine brings the handset to her chest. "It's your aunt Michaela," she fills me in. "She asked about your studies."

"I'm sure you left out a few things."

We haven't spoken much since I stepped off the plane in Paris four years ago. I think we both like it best that way. Uncle Tim was the buffer that made it all bearable. But now that he's gone, being in the same room with her can be torturous.

"Michaela!" Catherine says sternly to my other aunt over the telephone. "Michaela...now don't start with that again! No one's found you! Micha –" She huffs at the sound of the line going dead and stretches out dramatically on the couch. "She is utterly impossible!"

You could say that again. "Must run in the family."

"I hate to break it to you Everest, but you're part of that family too," she reminds me.

She says that a lot, tries to make me believe that I'm just like her because we share some DNA. It's probably in my top three worst fears – to end up like her, with no purpose, confined to an apartment, waiting for the next mushroom cloud to send us to oblivion. As far as I'm concerned, the only thing we share are a pair of blue-green eyes, warm blonde hair that tangles far too easily, a few freckles, and my mother's stubbornness. Sometimes I think we may share Mom's smile, but Catherine never wears one long enough to make a proper assessment.

Mom. My eyes fill with tears at the thought of her. *Mom.* That word haunts me, forever a reminder of what I had and what was ripped away. That sweet, comforting word that I'll never get to say to anyone again.

She was getting out of a cab when the car hit her. One moment of inattention, a second – a split second – and she evaporated from my life. Her smile, her warmth, her embrace…she took it all with her. If I knew that morning what Fate had in store, I would have never let her leave the apartment.

The pain of that day is difficult to revisit, and I've locked my memory of it away in a dark corner room in my brain where I pretend it doesn't exist. Maybe someday I'll have to face it. But for now, I don't allow myself to go anywhere near that room, always turning down another hallway when I feel myself veering toward it. Truthfully, I'm afraid of what I'll unleash if I open that door.

My grandparents offered to take me in after Mom passed. Ironic, considering they couldn't have cared less about us while she was alive. They had a tough time, you see, explaining their single-mother daughter and granddaughter to their ritzy New York country club friends. It was always nauseating hearing about their charitable donations to progressive causes on the evening news. I saw them for who they truly were – the gold medal champions of hypocrisy. I boldly told the lawyer that I'd rather end up in foster care than stare at their phony faces every day. That's when Uncle Tim thankfully stepped in and offered to have me live with him and Aunt Catherine…in Paris!

Paris. Sounds pretty great, doesn't it. Except…well, Catherine. I half-heartedly agreed, having no better options, and hoping that maybe leaving Chicago would help me box up my pain and forget about it for a while – like putting it on lay-a-way.

But life doesn't work like that.

Catherine was never happy about my presence, and she made no attempt to hide her feelings. I could hear her quarrelling with Uncle Tim constantly, telling him I'd be better off in America, that I wouldn't "fit in", that I didn't speak French, that I had "American manners" (whatever that meant). Uncle Tim never seemed to mind my manners, and he was as French as they came.

"*You'll* have to support her then!" Catherine had ordered.

"You mean, how I support you?" Uncle Tim had fired back with a chuckle as he continued reading the newspaper. I watched with satisfaction through the crack in the door as Catherine's face burned up. That was the last fight they had about me. Uncle Tim must have seen me peeking down the hall because he winked and smiled before moving onto the sports section.

I find the band-aid just as Catherine speaks again. "She's in a bit of a state, you know," Catherine says, referring to my aunt Michaela. Michaela's the third Cleary sister – an odd-ball who lives in the middle of the woods on the outskirts of Brussels. How Mom could have been so different from her siblings still amazes me.

"She thinks someone's 'watching her'," Catherine continues. "I should visit. Just for a few weeks, before she goes totally mad. I'm sure you'll be fine here without me."

I'm sure I will.

"Have you considered having her see someone?" I suggest. "I mean, she keeps accusing 'strange birds' of being drones. That can't be good."

Catherine shoots me a look of disdain. "Have some compassion Everest!" she retorts, taking my concern out of context. "Don't be so insensitive!"

"I didn't mean anything...." But explaining my point is useless. Once Catherine thinks she knows something, she'll die on that hill and gaslight you until you believe it too.

I shuffle into the kitchen, wringing my sweaty hands together. "I guess you'll be leaving soon then?" I ask.

"Tomorrow, probably. I'd like to be there by Wednesday."

"How long do you plan on staying?"

"That depends on whether Michaela lets me stay at all. But if all goes well, a few weeks, maybe three."

I keep pacing, hands sweatier by the minute.

Just ask!

No, now's not a good time.

It's never a good time!

"Before you leave, can we just talk about..."

"The money again?" Catherine interrupts, staring at me accusingly.

And...we're not off to a great start. I can feel what little hope I had evaporating at lightning speed. "The school year starts in a few weeks. I know Uncle Tim wouldn't touch that money. Cambridge may still have my spot. If you could just check..."

"It's gone, Everest!" Catherine insists. "Timothy didn't have a clue how much it cost to have you here. He may have made the money, but I managed the house. It cost money to feed and clothe you, you know. School uniforms, all those books you wanted...Timothy could never say no. Anyway, I'd much appreciate it if you just stopped bringing this up. What's done is done!"

What's done is done. Ever tried telling someone that? Spoiler alert – no one wants to hear it. They want to hear that you have a magical time machine in your attic that can fix everything while it spits out puppies, unicorns and hundred-dollar bills. And no one ever does.

Catherine's gaze seems to soften, the dark circles under her eyes becoming more visible under the light of the dining room chandelier. I know she hasn't slept much since Uncle Tim's death either.

"What happened?" she asks, pointing to my hand.

"Nothing. Just a bulb. I'm fine."

Catherine huffs. "Again? That's the second one this week!"

It's more like the eighteenth, but I keep that to myself.

"This can't be normal," she huffs again. "There has to be some explanation to these bizarre explosions!"

There is. The explanation is me, only she doesn't know it.

No one does.

CHAPTER 2

Nineteen Lightbulbs

The "incidents" began shortly after I arrived in Paris. Light bulb explosions, sometimes twice a day. Occasionally, it was glassware. We'd just find it shattered in the cupboards, which drove Catherine mad. That part was amusing, I must admit.

Catherine was convinced the apartment was possessed and brought in a woman dressed in layers of flowing fabric to stink up the place with smoky leaves that smelled like burning rubber. Uncle Tim and I laughed our pants off, but Catherine stood stone-faced and glared directly at me.

"This is you!" she had screeched, pointing her long red fingernail at my face. "Ever since you came…you've brought a curse into this house!"

The funny thing is, Catherine was actually right about something for once. I just didn't know it yet.

The incidents started to settle after some time. I'd try to replace the bulbs quickly to prevent Catherine from boiling over, and Uncle Tim was far too busy with his work at the Louvre to give it much thought. But it was the calm before the storm.

It was the end of spring. A damp rainy Thursday, the kind that makes you want to bury yourself in a blanket for days. I'd just returned from school when Catherine got the call from the hospital.

Everything was about to change.

They told us it was a type of blood clot in his brain, that it was "severe", and that they had "done all they could." Catherine crumpled to the floor and sat there motionless and silent like a sack of potatoes for what seemed like hours. I sat stunned on my bed, staring at the wall for what seemed like hours.

In the flash of an instant, without any warning, Uncle Tim was gone too. Just like Mom. And everything that reminded me of her, everything that was warm and decent and kind had vanished with him.

Uncle Tim made Paris feel like home – his stories, his off-colour jokes, his light-hearted nature and animated expressions. I don't know how he ended up with someone as cold and self-centred as Aunt Catherine, but I could forgive him that one lapse in judgement since he made me feel like a piece of Mom had come to Paris with me.

And then, suddenly, I was back at square one.

As I sat staring at that wall, the pain and anger became unbearable and unleashed something in me – something dark and terrifyingly intense. That was the day I realized that I was the one responsible for all the trips to the hardware store and growing piles of shattered glass in the trash bin. Because the pain and the rage that fueled my scream turned our entire building dark that evening.

Not one intact light remained in our flat, or for a two-block radius.

Not one.

The electric company was baffled. The blackout and even

made the news. And I finally figured out a piece of the puzzle that had been staring me in the face.

It's unsettling, knowing I'm affecting my reality in a way I don't understand. I'm in denial about it most of the time. But denial is easier than feeling powerless to stop it.

Catherine busies herself by blowing on her fingernails. "I'll call another electrician after work," I lie, knowing full well that the only person capable of fixing the problem is me, and I have no idea how to do it.

"Speaking of work…" Catherine adds, "how fortunate Tristan got you into Peterson. And I just love that new doorknob he got us. He's such a gentleman!" she gushes. "I'm surprised the tabloids haven't picked up on the two of you yet."

I roll my eyes at the irony of her statement. 'Fortunate' or 'gentleman' aren't words I'd use to describe Tristan Sarazen. And staying out of garbage tabloids is ok with me.

"I hope you're still not upset with me," Catherine continues, referring to our earlier non-discussion. "It'll be good for you, putting off school for a while., working a little. You're so young Everest. You're not ready for college, and in another country to top it off! Oh, I almost forgot, could you run by the grocery store on your way home? I've made a list…"

Catherine's voice becomes muffled and slow as I stare at her with disbelief. There's an unwavering pattern to our interactions. It starts with indifference – that can last for days. That progresses to annoyance at some point, followed by a triggered rage. Then release, relief, guilt, repeat.

I've just entered phase three.

"Seriously?" I raise my voice to her. "You're pretending to care about what's *best* for me?"

Catherine looks at me like I'm a confused amnesia patient. "Everest, what's wrong?"

I can feel my blood pressure rising through the veins in my neck as I unleash on her.

"Mom worked two jobs to put aside that college money! How much did me being here really cost you? How much did I really eat or need? I've given you nearly every penny I've earned since I've been here. You never once said anything about needing more. I know you still have it! *Why are you doing this?*"

The anger consumes me and expands in me like an all-consuming cyclone. My hand reaches toward the fruit bowl and takes hold of something spherical, and before I realize it, I'm launching an orange across the room. It decapitates a giraffe statue before falling to the floor and rolling out of sight. It's all too much for one of the chandelier lightbulbs, which shatters and litters the dining table.

That's 19.

"I can't believe you're still justifying what you did," I go on, my skull hot and throbbing from the anger, "like it's no big deal and I'm just supposed to…get over it. That was my future!"

Catherine sends the couch sliding back as she rises to her feet. "So, I'm the one that's keeping you from living your life, is that it?" she yells back. She jostles my shoulder on her way to her bedroom, wrapping the robe she'll spend the day in tightly around herself. "You're just like Joanna!" she says, comparing me to Mom, "entitled and irresponsible, with your head in the clouds! No idea about how the real-world works. I've done everything for you – gave you Paris, damn it! And this is the thanks I get?"

Catherine lets out what sounds like a sob and slams the bedroom door. I know that's the end of that conversation and the last I'll see of her for a while. She'll milk this for as long as she can, playing victim and trying to get me to feel guilty enough to apologize.

Darn it! I've let my emotions take the reins, again. *Why can't I control myself?*

I retrieve the fractured statue and put it in the buffet drawer where it joins a growing pile of broken things I need to glue back together, then clean up the glass fragments from the dining table.

Phase five: relief.

My breathing evens out and the coldness sets in. It always follows the release – a sort of emptiness, like when everyone at a crowded party leaves and takes their upbeat energy and body heat with them, leaving a hollow, lonely space. But if I can put off the creeping guilt, it does bring a quenching tranquility, even if it's only fleeting.

I change quickly, grab my scooter helmet and head for the door, taking the grocery list on my way. My hand grips the doorknob, a constant reminder of *him* – Tristan. I feel it momentarily – that dreaded sensation. It's like he's there in person, taking me apart slowly and getting rid of all the good parts.

And just like that, in a devastating instant I'm back to the muted version of myself I despise.

CHAPTER 3

The Alley

The Champlain Building looks like a glass capsule spaceship that's made a perfect landing in the Paris financial district. I drag my feet through the front doors to the cylindrical coffin that will take me to Peterson Securité. It's an awkward and crowded ride to the 32nd floor as people try inconspicuously to wipe beads of sweat off their foreheads on this humid August morning.

"Bonjour Claude." I greet the veteran security guard with a smile at the Peterson doors. He returns the gesture with less teeth. He's not very thorough as he goes through the motions of checking my purse, but he's one of the only things I like about this place.

"You coming to my retirement party?" he asks, his eyes twinkling with excitement over his upcoming freedom.

I nod confidently. "Wouldn't miss it! I'm on pastry duty, so I wouldn't mind some hints about your favorite sweets."

"Oh, I have too many. That's the problem," Claude says grinning as he motions to his protruding belly, then waves me inside.

Peterson caters to an elite clientele, primarily English-speaking millionaires who require private security or private investigation services. I don't do any of the fun stuff. My job is to be on intake and input basic data and run reports and try my best not to pass out from boredom. Occasionally I get a juicy detail or two when a potential client reveals too much up front. That's followed by instructions to "be discrete" and creates a whole chain of events that never make the news. But generally, it's not very exciting. At least I have a job and I can save for college.

Peterson employees are expected to keep their heads down and their voice boxes on *mute*. Whoever designed the office probably wasn't much fun. Almost everything is grey, and the blinds are usually drawn, hiding the magnificent city view. I guess they don't want the staff daydreaming too much (not that it stops me). An unpleasant antiseptic odor shoots up my nose when I approach my monochromatic cubicle, like someone was busy all night covering up a crime scene. I cram my legs under a desk designed for a horse jockey and wave to my neighbor, a petite brunette with shoulder-length hair and a fierce straight bang across her forehead.

"The hawk is circling," Nina warns me through her teeth about our supervisor Vincent while her eyes remain glued to a data spreadsheet that makes me go cross-eyed.

I crinkle my nose from the smell, turn on my charcoal monitor and groan. "You mean the Hades to our Underworld? I'm still not sure if the complete absence of movement on his face is from excessive Botox or because he's not entirely human." *Maybe he came down on the glass spaceship.*

"He is going to hear you one of these days," Nina warns under her breath as she tries to unstick one of the keys. I move her full coffee mug further away from her keyboard, suspecting there's probably a picture of Nina's face next to the word "clumsy" in the dictionary.

Vincent's down the hall but looking the other way, so I'm good for a few more sentences. "Hey, would you be free for dinner tonight? You could join me and Tristan at Pinot Noir. It's short notice but…"

"Pinot Noir?" Nina gushes, suddenly forgetting Vincent's proximity, her long eyelashes touching her bangs and her rich hazel eyes glowing with intrigue. "I've been dying to try it!"

"I know. So, you'll come?" I know the slightly higher pitch of my voice must betray my pleading, and Nina's eyes narrow as she immediately takes notice.

"What's going on Everest? You never seem to want to be alone with this guy. What am I missing? I mean, it's Tristan Sarazen!"

"Shhhh!"

I want to tell her but fail as usual, too embarrassed that I'm such fool. "It's just more fun with you around," I half-lie.

"How did you even meet a Sarazen?"

Unlike me, Nina follows all the latest celebrity gossip. Tristan is Parisian royalty essentially, one of *the* Sarazens and heir to his father's banking empire at Crédit Guerrin. When Nina saw us having coffee one day she nearly fell on her face. And then almost fell on her face again once she realized I had no idea who he was.

"It's not like he told me his high society status right away," I answered her. "He was just nice…it was a job fair; we were talking about internships. I said I needed a summer job before I left for college, which I still thought was happening at the time, and he said he might know of an opening. That's pretty much it. He got me an interview here that same week."

"Right…he got you that fancy doorknob as a present for your first day." Nina laughs under her breath. "Who gives someone a doorknob?"

"Yeah, must be a rich-people thing," I chuckle. Catherine had our neighbour install the ugly thing right away and tells anyone who'll listen that Tristan Sarazen gave it to "the family." It's hard to keep a straight face or hold back the eye roll. "Anyway, we just meet occasionally. That's all."

"And…"

"And nothing. It's not what you think."

"But you see him at least twice a week, and you sound like you hate every minute of it. What's up with that?"

I sigh. "I don't know. I really don't like him, Nina. But I guess I feel like I owe him? I really don't know…"

Truthfully, I just don't know! And I'm getting tired of that pathetic non-explanation.

"Anyway, can you come?"

Nina pouts, still eyeing me skeptically. "I can't. My family's visiting from Lebanon so I'll have to babysit my cousins when my parents go out for dinner tonight. But keep me in mind for the next time – if there even is one."

There's always a next time, unfortunately.

I turn my attention to my own uninspiring data spreadsheet, a sensation of dread twisting my stomach into a pretzel. I could cancel, but he would just keep asking.

Just get it over with and tell him it's the last time.

* * *

Five after six. That's the time I arrive for my six o'clock dinner with Tristan. A sharp pain travels through my bruised wrist like a conditioned response because I know all too well that 6:05 is unforgivable. The same way 5:35 was the other night, and 5:17 the week before.

Tristan taps his fingers on the white tablecloth as I approach, nausea gripping my stomach. "It's like you do it on purpose to aggravate me," he chastises me without getting up or lifting his hazel eyes from the menu. "American manners." His dark brown hair is cut short, and his skin is tanned from his recent "business" trip to Turkey – a way for his father to groom him to one day take over Crédit Guerrin after graduating from the Sorbonne business school.

"Honestly Tristan," I reply, settling into the chair, "you won't starve to death if you wait five minutes." *Maybe if I annoy him enough, he'll never want to see me again.* It's always fun to watch his temples twitch when he grinds his teeth. "You know, I read once that lateness was a common problem for optimistic people, so it can't be the worst of all my flaws."

"You should stop reading so much," he replies, his temples twitching as expected.

I open my menu, smiling to myself. "Actually, I might take a part-time course while I save up for Cambridge. Positive psychology. It's all about how positive thoughts and emotions can improve our well-being. It sounds fascinating!"

Tristan grimaces as if he's just watched a centipede crawl out of a drain. "It sounds like hippy bullshit. Proves that too much education is not always a good thing."

I roll my eyes. We really couldn't be more different. *What am I even doing here?*

After our first few encounters, Tristan's presence became a routine nuisance: dinners and coffees slowly escalated into him telling me what to eat and how to dress. Then came the rudeness, the berating…the arm twisting.

It was like a switch had flipped and Mr. Hyde was at the table. I'm not entirely sure why he's so determined to be around me because he doesn't seem to like me all that much either. In fact, I'm pretty sure I grate on his last nerve.

But for whatever reason, no matter how much I want to be rid of him, no matter how many times he bruises my wrist or belittles me for doing or saying something he doesn't approve of, here we are again. Something always pulls me back, against my better judgement. Moreover, the idea of resisting fills me with dread, dread over how Tristan would react and whether there's a new layer to Mr. Hyde he hasn't yet revealed.

All I know is that in the middle of the night I feel I could do it – finally tell him to leave me alone. But the feeling usually only lasts until I'm out the door. That's why I live for those few hours before the sun rises – they're all mine.

Yet even then, the ticking clock reminds me that my freedom is limited, which stirs up a subconscious anger over feeling confined in my invisible cage.

And that's usually when the glass starts shattering again.

The waiter arrives, and my predictable dinner partner orders his usual steak and frites. Part of me wants to just leave and be done with it. But the smell of delicious food reminds me that I'm starving. "The shrimp linguini pour moi, merci," I tell the waiter. My French is passing, at least for the purpose of ordering food and asking for directions, but I still mix in English here and there.

"Not the best choice for your, uh, waistline," Tristan hints under his breath at my selection. The waiter eyes me with confusion since I'm rather slim, but I'm used to Tristan's asinine comments.

"I'll take my chances," I assure the waiter before he runs off. I look around the restaurant. It's modern and expensive looking, but nothing overly impressive. Looks like every other over-rated, over-priced new restaurant in Paris. It feels cold and lacks soul. *Reminds me of someone.*

"So, how was your trip?"

Tristan has moved on to reviewing his emails. "Fine."

"Are you going to have time for the company, with business school?"

"Yes."

Our conversations are as fun as watching paint dry. For my own sanity I keep trying. "I found out Peterson lets us take time off to volunteer. Couldn't have been their idea. Probably tax-break related. There's a house build —"

"God!" Tristan interrupts loudly, slamming his hand on the table and startling the smartly dressed guests at the neighboring table. "Do you ever shut up? Every week it's something else with you. Some new hobby, new book or whatever…why can't you just be normal and go…shopping, or something?"

Shopping, or something? Seriously, what am I doing here?

To my own surprise I feel the cyclone building, almost choking my breath, and for a moment I believe I'll finally do it – finally tell him to screw off!

He places his right hand on mine as he so often does, the weight of his cold ring numbing my fingers. It's so odd that stone, that band, with those weird etchings — an "A" or a "V", or whatever it is. It's clearly too big for him because it's always facing the inside of his palm. I can never figure out the creature on the crest, or why the band is made from granite…

I suddenly feel it – that dreaded sensation, like the one I feel every time I leave the house. Like someone's jamming a vacuum cleaner down my throat, turning me inside out. I lose track of time, imprisoned in a foggy purgatory. Goosebumps blanket my skin, and a numbness spreads from my fingers to the underside of my arm. My skull becomes heavy, like it's been inflated with helium and the rest of my body is pulling down on it to prevent it from dislodging from my spine and floating away…

Tristan retracts his hand and slowly the suction switches off. It feels like hours have passed but I know it's been only 30 seconds, tops. Whatever the duration I know I'm somehow changed: the suction has removed something intangible, something I won't reclaim for several hours – a sense of purpose, a sense of empowerment.

A sense of self.

He's taken me apart again somehow, and I shudder at the thought of what I'd be left with if he ever cranked up that suction even a little bit.

My water glass begins to vibrate as if a small earthquake has hit it. Tristan is unsurprisingly oblivious.

Seriously? Why am I here?!

Is it not enough that I deal with Catherine? Must I also have my soul sucked out of me by this stranger?

I rest my palm on top of the shaking glass and motion to the waiter, somehow managing to find a sliver of strength. Something has changed in me. Something has calmed the storm and given me the courage to break through that wall.

"Pardon, I'll take my order to go, si vous plait."

Tristan's eyebrows shoot up as he meets my gaze for the first time since I've arrived. "Wonderful. First late, now running off. She is not going anywhere."

"No, yes…I am," I insist, placing money on the table and inhaling a measured breath. They say that's supposed to calm you down, but it never quite does the trick for me, and today is no exception. I can't hold it in any longer and snap at Tristan the second we're alone again. "Is there no decision that can be my own? 'Don't eat that Everest, don't wear that Everest, don't act like a fool, you'll embarrass us Everest, stop smiling, stop laughing, don't run, don't read, don't think, don't speak…' Anything else I should know so I can conduct myself according to your ridiculous standards? I mean, who the hell do you think you are? Look, thanks for the job and all, really, but, seriously, what do you even want from me? You don't even *like* me. Let's both stop this charade and just be done with it!"

When the last syllable leaves my lips, I almost cheer. Until now, standing up to him has been confined to my fantasies. But my new-found courage brings equal amounts of exhilaration and apprehension as I realize Tristan won't like losing. It's the absence of anger in his eyes and the flicker of a subtle smirk on the right side of his mouth that scares me the most. It's like I've given him exactly what he wanted, and he's already devised a way to punish me.

"I'm not your jailer," he says slowly. "If you want to leave, you're free to go," he dares.

I stare at my opponent in the hopes that he'll reveal whether my non-compliance is worth the price I'll pay. But he gives me nothing.

When the waiter returns with my order I stick to the plan and take the dare without looking back, holding my breath on the way to the door, my body stiff from the nervous tension. From the corner of my eye, I see a wall sconce crack in half as I pass the hostess stand and bolt out of the restaurant.

I keep moving, relishing my freedom and the humid air hitting my face. *I did it! It's over. I don't have to see him again…* I begin to breathe again.

But within seconds I realize my victory is short-lived. When I turn into the alley to take a shortcut to the metro, the moment I've been dreading becomes a reality.

A hand clamps around my arm. The next thing I know my body is being hurled into a wall, my head bouncing off the jagged plaster. The pain shoots excruciatingly through my cranium like a splitting fault line.

"I bet you wish you had stayed now!" Tristan snarls, pinning me back with his forearm.

I cry out, flinching from the throbbing headache.

"Stop it!"

But he's not finished and unleashes his fist into my ribs. Then again. And a third time.

And with each painful strike the suction resumes its momentary extraction.

I feel myself being violently catapulted against a dumpster and fall hard onto the concrete, a layer of skin tearing from my knee and the other knee landing onto an open container of pasta. He pulls me back up to my feet by the collar of my blouse.

"Don't ever speak to me like that again. Don't ever walk out on me!" he hisses in my ear before pushing me away like I'm a worthless punching bag he's done with.

"*AGAIN?*" My head's still pulsing as I try to find my equilibrium. *Is he insane?* "You arrogant bastard! As if there's going to be a next time!"

I start to run back to the street, praying my trembling legs won't fail me before Tristan strikes again. To my relief, a sidewalk full of witnesses comes into view and I try to avoid the odd stares as I fix myself up and brush pasta sauce off my knee.

But I notice to my own dismay that my anger towards Tristan starts to dissipate a little as I walk further away.

Why? No! Damn it Everest, no! Don't let it go!... Did I push him to this? I blame myself, and let the tears fall.

* * *

When I enter the apartment, Catherine is still in her robe, glued to her laptop and entrenched in another news story.

"There was some kind of flood in Indonesia," she announces, getting right to it and avoiding any discussion of this morning. "20,000 dead. What is this world coming to? And did you hear about that serial killer in Marseilles? I don't even want to live in this world anymore!"

Catherine has an unfortunate superpower – killing joy in all its forms. I squint my eyes, trying to fight the vertigo from my injuries while I block out the intel. If I allow it to, her negativity will burrow its way into my brain like a parasite. "I see you've scoured the internet for proof of the impending apocalypse again," she says.

"You need to know what's going on in the world, Everest. You can't just exist in your fairytale bubble all the time."

"Can't I? Beats your miserable bubble."

"You're not informed! The world isn't as alluring and innocent as Timothy's stories and magazines made it out to be. Do you want to grow up to be stupid and ignorant?"

I set down the glass of water I've poured myself on the kitchen counter with a little too much force, then find an answer: "I'm informed enough to know that the media pounce on the bad like ravenous vultures, skew the truth to suit their agenda, and ignore all the good that happens every passing second. That makes a lot more sense than believing we live in a bucket full of crap!"

Catherine's face is so close to the computer it looks like she'll be sucked into the screen at any moment, like in an episode of the Outer Limits. *Wouldn't be the worst thing.*

"You're so insolent…" her voice drifts off. "How's Tristan? Such a nice boy…Did you get the groceries?"

I roll my eyes as I grab a bottle of Tylenol. *No, I was a little busy getting beat up.* "I'll get them tomorrow. I'm going to bed. You can get depressed all on your own.

"And…for the record, Tristan's not what you think."

"What?" she mumbles with disinterest.

Sigh. "Nothing." Just don't even bother…

"No music!" Catherine orders loudly. I slip into the hallway and grab a pair of headphones from the console table, then pause at my bedroom door to study my roommate. She looks more like my grandfather than Mom, but sometimes I see Mom in her for a fleeing moment, like when the light catches her face just right and softens the permanent scowl on her face. There must have been a part of her that was fun and happy once upon a time. I need to believe Uncle Tim – the smartest man I've ever known – thought this major life decision through and saw something I'm missing.

I'm standing there, praying for that Newton moment, when I glimpse it: that stupid doorknob, taunting me from down the hall.

No! No more Tristan!

I tie my long hair up in a pony, then head for the storage closet to retrieve the screwdriver set. I find the old doorknob resting on the shelf next to it. Catherine's too busy with the news to hear me swapping them out. I feel that cursed suction as I hold it in my hand. When the job's done, I store the stupid thing away in the storage closet, vowing to throw it in the dumpster in the morning and erase the last reminder of Tristan and his strange power over me from my life for good.

I refuse to think of him as I head back to my room, but our encounter has left me predictably drained – unmotivated, like a mushy bowl of oatmeal – and confused most of all.

I notice my Cambridge acceptance letter again and lunge at it with tear-filled eyes, crushing it between my palms before angrily tossing it into the trash bin. Mom watches over my tantrum from the silver photo frame on my dresser, the words

"In Memory" etched at the bottom – the two of us on a rollercoaster at Six Flags, screaming our faces off and enjoying every minute. It was the last trip we took together. A stack of bracelets lies beside the frame. Mom started making them for me for my birthdays before turning it into a side business. She saved every cent... for me. I can't even bring myself to wear them now.

The tears spill out, and I look back at the trash bin, embarrassed and defeated.

Catherine's words play over in my head. *What's done is done...*

I glance up at the ceiling – at God. He must be there, right? Somewhere? Somewhere there must be something or someone balancing the scales and making things right. I say a silent prayer and fall back onto the bed.

Maybe it's time I finally accept my fate and move on. "There's no such thing as a time machine."

CHAPTER 4

La Libération

Hulk has barely emerged from the Mercedes in the last four days. He's always there when I get home from work and sits so still, he resembles a corpse. I'm beginning to imagine all sorts of things about his line of work. Drug dealer comes to mind. Maybe he's Interpol, hunting a nemesis that's eluded him for decades. Whatever his story, I try to avoid making eye contact with him as I pass the sedan on my way to the posh bistro a few doors down. I walk past the velvet drapes and hostess stand and take my seat across from Tristan for hopefully the last time.

I never thought I'd see him again after Monday night. But when the voicemails and text messages didn't stop, I realized that he probably couldn't conceive of the possibility that I had finally grown a backbone. So, here I am, ready to lay it out for him in black and white.

From the kitchen escapes the aroma of overpriced meat that will soon arrive on plates in minuscule portions. I stand out like a sore thumb among the stylish guests, and Tristan eyes my t-shirt and jeans in disgust. I expected no less.

What he doesn't know is that for the past four days I've been collecting fragments of myself and gluing them back together.

They come creeping back in a rather scrambled way, like pieces of a puzzle floating in the obscurity of my mind. Occasionally, I'm able to hold on to a few and put them back where they belong.

Best of all, there's no more life-draining suction, no paralysis of my mind or my voice. And I can't wait to let Tristan know it.

He leans back in his chair, chest puffed out, and raises his wine glass. "I'm glad we can put this all behind us," he toasts.

I don't reciprocate.

"Too soon. Okay." He returns the glass to the table after taking a long sip. "How many times do I have to apologize?"

I remain silent, too busy fantasizing about going back in time, turning him into a miniature stone statue and swapping him for the giraffe my flying orange decapitated. I chuckle, slightly concerned about my sociopathic thought process.

"Something funny?" he asks.

I let my inner grin spill out. "You wouldn't think so."

The meal I never ordered arrives – duck – smaller than I would have guessed and covered in a lake of burgundy syrup and green confetti. I push it away. "I'm not here to eat."

"It's a Michelin Star meal. You'll like it. And it won't make you fat."

He reaches across the table to rest his hand on mine. My fingers stiffen. I wait for the goosebumps, the helium filling my skull, the suction...

But they don't come.

I let out my breath slowly, noticing a tan line where Tristan's ring used to be. Maybe he finally lost the ugly thing.

"How about next time we go for dinner it can be your pick," he offers. "We can eat some disgusting American food."

How generous.

I quickly remove my hand and lean back in my chair. "There won't be a next time," I tell him firmly. There's no catch in my breath, no shakiness in my tone. "I never want to see you again," I continue. "I don't want you to ever come near me, contact me, look at me, ever again. Whatever this little game was, it ends. Today. Now!"

He looks up from his plate. "Look, I know you're angry Everest, but there's no need to be impulsive."

"*NO!*" I insist. People turn to stare, and I check my volume. "I want you out of my life Tristan. That's why I came – to make myself clear. In fact, I should have done this a long time ago. I don't know what you want, but I don't want any part of it."

He shifts uncomfortably in his seat and the temple twitches begin. "Shut up! You're making a scene!"

I start to rise from my seat. "Just stay the hell away from me!" I feel beyond relieved, proud even. But one look at Tristan and I'm grateful the restaurant is crowded.

"Don't make me angry again, Everest," he warns in a slow, measured manner as he glares at me from under his thick eyelids. "Or have you forgotten what happened the last time?"

I lean in to stare him dead in the eyes with an invigorating lack of fear. Finally, the chain that's chaffed my ankle has slipped off and sunk to the bottom of the pool, the water pushing me to the surface. "I haven't forgotten a thing," I tell him, my palms clutching the napkin lying on the table. "And if you so much as look at me again I'll have you arrested, you sadistic son of a bitch!"

I start to feel it – a storm whirling violently around my bones until my body can't contain it. I know what's coming – I've felt it before, and there's no way I can stop it. It escapes with such a force that it leaves me feeling exorcised of a demon, and as if in slow motion I watch as the tempered glass panel that divides the dining room from the kitchen shatters, thousands of tiny glass particles exploding like fireworks and then loudly crashing to the floor. The stunned chefs stand frozen as food burns, their faces mirroring the shocked expressions of the guests and wait staff.

Oops.

Tristan yanks my arm back as I try to walk away, his nails digging into my skin like the claws of a predator as he draws me closer. "Bravo Everest. Enjoy your little victory. But one day you'll realize you have no power other than what I allow you to have."

I rip my arm free and study Tristan's pleased expression with puzzlement. I've imagined my liberation so many times and it's always ended with him writhing in his fury, engulfed in flames, and shriveling up in front of me like a piece of birch bark tossed into a fire. His reaction leaves me wanting, and I feel uneasy about the ugly hunger growing inside me – a hunger to give him a taste of his own medicine, even if just a small dose.

I spin around before he can touch me again, weaving with determination between the stunned faces and broom-wielding waiters.

"What a mess," I say to the hostess and point at Tristan. "He generously offered to take care of it."

* * *

My legs seem to have a mind of their own as they carry me in the opposite direction of home. Whatever I'm feeling, there's repositories of it pouring through the now open flood gates. I don't care how crazed I look, so long as I can feel the night breeze through my hair, feel the muscles burn in my legs, hear the impact of my feet against the cobblestone as I run.

I follow the swarms of tourists making their way to Sacré-Coeur and arrive at the cathedral breathless, the majestic structure looming above me like a symbol of all that's possible by mankind. I walk up to the railing which separates the hilltop from the city below and gaze out onto the scene that still takes my breath away. The city lights begin to appear as the sky transforms into a pastel watercolor painting, and I relish an unparalleled high.

Hours pass and night falls before I finally rise from the steps with a profound sense of inner calm. From inside the cathedral escape the haunting voices of a Gregorian choir. Mom used to love listening to that kind of music - soothed her soul she said. As I allow a Latin hymn work its magic, I can understand the appeal.

I take my time walking home, coming in through the back entrance out of an abundance of caution and checking behind me every so often. Catherine left Tuesday morning, so after checking the locks twice I crank up the volume on my uncle's old radio and make for his study. His stack of National Geographics sits on his antique walnut desk, surrounded by uneven piles of dusty books. I haven't even scratched the surface of his world. Just like that little box tucked away in my brain, the idea of opening the door to his study had been too painful. Now it calls to me insistently, like a ravenous lion, pulling me in to that world I yearn to know so much about.

A cardboard box lies next to the Nat Geos; Catherine must have started packing some things to prepare for turning the study into a large closet. They lie there, ready to be disposed of along with everything else she deems trivial and unnecessary — like my travel journal, which she said I must have 'misplaced' months ago. The journal is more of a wish list really, of all the places I long to see before I die. I flip through the pages, the grainy texture of the paper awakening something in me that I had neglected for a long time. Before I know it, I'm pulling out my uncle's white board and an old red marker that's so dried up it squeaks more than writes. My hand works furiously, transferring the contents of my journal to the board. The scribbles are soon joined by magnets holding up the postcards my uncle sent me when I was young from his expeditions and archeological digs, and my grief returns with a vengeance, clenching my heart and sending a sob to my throat.

I recall all the times I lay awake imagining what it would be like to scale an Icelandic volcano or unearth a lost artifact that would end up in the Metropolitan. He was my inspiration, my real-life Indiana Jones – the reason I spent hours in the history section of the library while my friends chilled at the movies with boys and caught up on the latest make-up trends. He's the reason I set my heart on a history major at Cambridge – his *alma mater*. I almost let that desire become drowned in that mushy bowl of oatmeal.

Almost…

I push down the sob. I'm filled with a renewed determination now, with nothing holding me back or taking the wind out of my sails. The postcard I've selected for the center of the board seems to pop out like a three-dimensional illusion: a photograph of the Helix Nebula, a quote by Einstein tucked away in the bottom right corner:

The most important decision we make is whether we believe we live in a friendly or hostile universe.

I repeat the words over and over in my head, trying to decide for myself. There's no way Catherine-the-Miserable could be right. The universe can't be just some meaningless void full of black holes and deadly meteorites waiting to wipe out humanity. It's too hopeless.

There must be more, and it has to be good. It just has to!

Mind made up, I step back to examine my work. It's perfect in its chaos because for the first time in years I feel a sense of control over the future, like the future is something tangible I can mold with my hands instead of a vague, abstract, and unattainable "what-if." Mom would be proud. She was always hopeful. Always in awe of the possibilities of the future.

I turn off the 4:30 alarm on my phone and make my peace with time, the rhythmic tick of my uncle's 19th century desk clock no longer filling me with dread.

Finally, I remember what freedom feels like, and I can't imagine giving it up again.

* * *

Besides allowing the body to restore, the main perk of sleep is the ability to dream. The only downside is that dreams all too often slip through our fingers despite our best efforts to hold on to them. And once again, they've eluded me as my consciousness rejoins the waking world.

A light breeze tickles my cheek, and the air that fills the room seems to chill my insides as I inhale an exaggerated breath. I'm relieved to find that I've managed to hang on to that unparalleled sense of pure contentment that rocked me to sleep. My body feels like gelatin on my perfectly soft mattress, which on every other night is a touch too firm. The sunlight hits my face…from the wrong direction…?

Wait a second…

I hear something…like water trickling down a cliffside. Then rushing water. *Strange.*

Is there a leak? What's going on? What time is it?

Time…

"Crap!" Vincent's overtime weekend assignment completely slipped my mind. My eyes shoot open as I prepare to race through my morning routine.

But instead of tearing out of bed, I freeze. The gelatin in my legs hardens to concrete and panic sets in, hard.

This isn't my room. This isn't my apartment.

Where on earth am?

CHAPTER 5

Not Dead

"What the…"

What's going on?

Why isn't this my apartment?

Only my eyeballs can move, and dart around like little ping pong balls to the beat of my quickening pulse.

I'm in a bedroom…empty and quite plain. Ivory curtains flutter in the draft that flows in through ajar French doors. There's a puffy white duvet on the bed that rises like a cloud over my lap and feels so light I wait for it to drift away before my eyes.

But it's not *my* duvet. It's not *my* bed.

The smells hit me next: juniper, oranges, hazelnuts? Everything is foreign, yet at the same time, in an odd way strangely familiar…

"What is this place?" I ask foolishly to no one as I look around the blank room.

It's hard to pin down the emotion that pulses through me – it's not quite fear…well, maybe a bit of fear, mixed with a whole lot of anxiety and worry for my sanity.

Is this what happens when you lose your mind – you exist in an empty colorless world? *Would Tristan do this?* Kidnappers wouldn't do this, would they? And if they did, wouldn't they pick a room with a more menacing wall color and some blood stains or mold on the walls, like in the movies?

You're fine. Don't jump to conclusions. It's fine…

Fully aware that everything is 'not fine', I manage to gather my wits and set out to find life, because what other choice do I have. A ray of light distracts me, and I follow the dazzling patterns it casts around the room like a cat chasing a beam. No clock. No telephone. The only other things in the room are a wardrobe and a bedside table with a lamp base and no bulb. The welcome irony makes me smile. *Thank goodness for that at least.*

Hopeful for clues, I step through the French doors onto a small balcony, and gasp as my legs turn to gelatin again.

As I rest my awestruck body on the balcony railing, a vast sea of water comes into view, sparkling like an ice rink in the sunlight. It stretches out in front of me like a gateway to infinity, so vast and breathtaking I wish I could immerse myself in its mesmerizing tranquility. A lilac scent overcomes me next reminding me of a vague memory from my childhood that cruelly teases me from that inaccessible part of my brain – like an itch I can't scratch.

I peer over the balcony and glimpse a long wide staircase leading from the building I've found myself in. Something resembling a boardwalk meets the end of the staircase, dotted with people and colorful umbrellas, with a cobblestone road that wraps around the perimeter of the water and disappears into the horizon.

Ok…there's people. At least I'm not alone.

I can't make sense of it. *What is this place? Why am I here?*

I keep expecting a logical explanation to dawn on me. *There's always a logical explanation.*

The trees seem unusually tall, some reaching higher than my floor. *I'm on what, the 15th, maybe higher?* The soothing sound of crashing waves echoes through the crisp air, and to my right, lush green peaks jut up from the surrounding landscape. Cliffs pour out foaming waterfalls. I can't see them all, but the mist rising above the tree canopies suggests there are countless more hidden from view.

I inhale two deep breaths to calm myself. But the exercise proves pointless, as dropping from the sky and onto the cobblestone is not an airplane or glider or anything I would normally expect to be airborne, but a creature with elaborate and expansive wings!

I stare at it until my eyes dry up, then rub frantically at my face before allowing myself to accept the obvious conclusion that it's a winged horse. A winged horse – an actual Pegasus! It prances and neighs, its hooves performing a graceful dance on the ground. A man dismounts, and just as suddenly as it descended the animal takes to the air again, vanishing into the horizon.

Seriously, what is going on??? "I'm hallucinating…I must be! This isn't possible…"

I enter a sort of manic state as I try to recount all the things I recently ate, all the occasions I could have been poisoned. Was it the stew I had for lunch? Was Tristan responsible? But I didn't eat that stupid duck…

It must be Tristan…Is this some island for the super-rich where they can fly animatronic mythical creatures?

Or is this all just a dream? An insanely realistic incredible dream? That would be the simplest explanation…

Yet my intuition tells me this is no hallucination, and no dream. This is different; not hazy and fleeting, but clear and permanent, and I don't have to chase it down. Moreover, there's something inexplicably pure about it, which means it couldn't possibly have anything to do with *him.*

What if I'm dead! Did I die in my sleep? I could be dead!

"Stop it!" I yell at myself. *You'll figure things out. Just breathe.*

Nerves calmed slightly, I allow myself to take in the world unfolding before me and momentarily forget how much I'm freaking out on the inside. I'm simultaneously awestruck, confused, and terrified, but whatever I'm feeling I can barely pull myself away.

The building I'm in is architecturally stunning, like something out of a fantasy novel – bright white masonry bricks cover the exterior. It looks like an expensive hotel but 100 times taller. I can't see the end of it as it pierces the clouds like the Tower of Babel. Rows of balconies peek out from archways and stretch out on either side, and lush emerald vines and hanging flowers cascade gracefully from each floor, giving the place a Hanging Gardens of Babylon vibe.

Incredible!

The more I take it all in, the more I'm determined to explore this magnificent and fantastic world I've mysteriously found myself in.

But just how exactly do I get out there?

A string of bougainvillea hanging from the balcony above grazes my forehead as I turn to go back inside to look for another way out. It's easier than I thought; a large wooden door now stands to the right of the bed. It wasn't there before, or at least I didn't see it. Then again, I was slightly distracted by the possibility of abduction or death.

Something glistens from the center of the door. When I get closer, I realize it's a gold envelope, held closed by a wax circular gold seal with the symbol of a triangle and some lines imprinted on it. It means nothing to me, and I don't remember ever seeing it before. But there's a rush of excitement through my body as I realize whatever's inside the envelope could answer all my burning questions.

I break the seal frantically, remove a piece of thick stamped white paper and read the text aloud with a slight tremble:

Everest Cleary,

Welcome to the Prism, where life is meant to be lived, not limited.

The Prism. I repeat the name to myself, hoping to trigger a memory, any detail that could put everything into context… Nothing.

Please enjoy your personal dimension during your stay.

An elevator awaits on the other side of this door. Take it to the Forum where someone is waiting to guide you on your journey. All will be revealed.

Trust your mind, and anything can become reality. The power lies within you.

I stare at the paper, mouth gaping open, and whisper the same question my mind keeps playing on repeat: "What is happening?"

The Prism?

How do these people know me?

How did they get me here?

Where is this?

Am I still even in France?

Am I going home today?

I think about that last question for a second.

Do I even want to go home?

As I prepare to place the card back in the envelope, I notice more text on the reverse side.

Don't worry, you're not dead.

Well, at least whoever wrote this has a sense of humor.

But even as I allow a faint smile of relief I'm not entirely reassured. Before I can ponder the message further the text begins to move, the letters scrambling and fading. The paper then evaporates like a ghostly mist before my eyes, slipping through my fingers like stardust and leaving only a brief afterimage of the Prism's seal and no other evidence of its existence.

And just like that, hallucination is back on the table. *Great!*

I understand the symbol now — at least I think I do: an abstract representation of a prism, breaking up white light into the color spectrum. But that's about all that makes sense.

All will be revealed, I remind myself. *It better be!*

The draft grazes my bare legs. I'm still wearing the pajamas I fell asleep in. Not exactly elevator attire. Fortunately, a standing wardrobe contains a convenient selection of perfectly fitting garments that couldn't just be a coincidence.

After all, there are no coincidences. That was something Uncle Tim and I both agreed on.

I pull out a pair of velvet-like jeans and a pale-yellow t-shirt that cools my skin like a refreshing shower. Then, with equal amounts of anxiety and exhilaration I step through the wooden door and into the unknown.

The hallway outside is finished from floor to ceiling in ivory paneling like you see in fancy mansions, with the Prism's seal imbedded along a beige marble floor. *'Everest Clearly'* reads a gold nameplate on the room I've just left behind. And I have neighbors running down one side of the hall – lots of them, in fact. I can't reconcile the incredibly short distance between the doors with the layout of my own room – only a few feet separate the door frames, which makes no spatial sense at all. What I assume to be elevators are spread out on the other side of the hall. I approach one and let my palm depress an oversized silver button in the center of the doors, which signals them to split apart.

Here goes…

Once inside the box, my reflection stares back at me in a gold-framed mirror that hangs on the maroon walls. I reach up slowly and start to poke and pull at my cheeks and skin. They feel so smooth…My un-brushed long hair falls in manageable waves over my shoulders, untangled. I don't *look* dead. *What does 'dead' look like anyway?* At least there isn't flesh peeling off my face. That's promising.

There's no way of instructing the elevator where to go. No

panel. Not a single button. Only one option remains – I feel foolish and look around for a camera, wondering if I'm on a prank reality show.

"Forum?" I ask absolutely no one, expecting crickets.

But the doors glide back together instantly and seal me inside. I brace myself for the usual duration of an elevator ride, yet the trip takes a mere few seconds, and before I have a chance to take a second breath I've arrived at the next checkpoint.

I inhale nervously as the elevator doors begin to open and a blinding light pushes its way through the widening gap…

CHAPTER 6

Far From Normal

Just breathe…you're not dead…just breathe…

I exit the elevator into a long rectangular room, finding to my surprise that my legs feel fine, and my nervousness has subsided, at least for now. The center of the ceiling is cut out, revealing a mesmerizing cyan sky dotted with wispy clouds. My eyes focus on a set of massive wooden doors standing opposite me, at least 20 feet high. Treacherously heavy looking things, with a sliver of light outlining them and trying to break in from the world beyond.

Triangular pillars hold up the perimeter of the enclosure with incredibly realistic murals tucked between them – four on each side of the room, each depicting a different landscape. I begin to walk up the rectangular marble hallway, placing my feet lightly as if afraid that I'll fall through it if I step too firmly and shatter this remarkable illusion. I recognize the Great Wall of China on the mural marked *Estra,* the name engraved in a stone plaque above it. As I study the mural's life-like detail, a young girl approaches it, probably no older than 13. One minute she's standing in front of it, and the next…it swallows her up like some sort of wormhole! She appears a bit fuzzy as she passes through it, the whole mural wobbling like Jell-O until it finally regains its stillness. And just like that, she's gone!

I can't look away, utterly paralyzed. "What just…"

I make my way toward the mural in a sort of trance, nervous about what it could do to me yet desperate to see it, touch it. *What on earth is it?* This can't be real…

"Everest Cleary, by chance?"

The mural-wormhole-human-eating thing is fascinating, but someone here knowing my name is slightly more important now.

I turn reluctantly to stare into the face of a young stranger. Early to mid 20's probably. His short light brown hair is slightly wavy and looks incredibly soft, like the fur of a puppy. I almost have to stop myself from reaching out to touch it. His eyes are an icy blue yet warm and inviting. They turn up at the corners as he smiles at me like everything is totally normal.

Everything is not normal! I want to scream at him. But his smile stills my tongue, and his sympathetic gaze sends a shot of warmth to my cheeks.

I snap out of it and finally manage to speak. "That's me. Everest. Um…I don't know where I am, exactly…"

The stranger extends his hand. "No one who walks out of that elevator for the first time does. Pleased to me you Everest! I'm Erik."

He has a firm handshake and holds my hand for a few seconds longer than I expect him to. "Sorry, your eyes," he says, explaining his delay, "what an interesting color. Reminds me of the sea."

I know I'm probably blushing. My discomfort over compliments always betrays itself in bright pink on my cheeks. But thankfully, Erik remedies the awkwardness by speaking again.

"Anyway, Everest, welcome to the Prism!" He lets go of my hand and smooths out his pale blue t-shirt and grey slacks. He's a half-head taller than me, with an unusual accent. *British maybe? Nope, that's not quite it.*

"I'm your magister," he adds, making absolutely no sense.

"My what?"

"It's really just a fancy term for 'guide.' You don't have to use it."

Magister. "Sure. Um…can we back up a little bit? Why do I need a magister or…guide? What is this place?" I whip around toward the mural again. "I just saw someone disappear…she was there, then she walked into it and it, and it…it got like…I don't know…It ate her. It literally ate her!"

I press my rattling lips shut as I watch two more people get swallowed up by the mural. "Like that! See! Sorry…I'm just freaking out a little bit!"

Erik laughs. "I'd be worried if you weren't! Trust me, I was in your shoes just over two years ago when I first got here, and I nearly passed out!"

I turn back to face him and allow myself to smile back nervously, glancing around the Forum once more before turning my attention back to the handsome stranger. His presence soothes me.

"I can explain everything," he offers. "Well, almost."

He's easy on the eyes. Whatever this place turns out to be, I don't mind having to look at him while he explains it all.

Erik's head is slightly tilted as he appears to study me. "So, Everest, is that what you go by?"

"Yes," I reply. "Or Ev. Whatever suits you." I begin to pace around Erik, eyeing my surroundings with increasing intrigue. A row of elevators faces the wooden door. There are people moving about everywhere. *Who are they?*

"Like the mountain?" Erik asks again about my name.

If only I had a quarter... "Yes, like the mountain."

"I imagine everyone asks you that. It's different. How did you come by it?"

My anxiety comes creeping back a little, though not as much as it usually does when I get asked this question. "Uh, my father…he was a climber apparently. Always wanted to climb 'The Big One.'"

Erik relaxes his stance and leans in, all ears. "Fascinating! And did he?"

I stop my pacing and shift my weight uncomfortably, not willing to go into any further detail about my absentee father with a total stranger. I barely discuss the topic with people I know.

"I honestly haven't a clue," I reply a little coldly, then immediately regret it.

Erik seems to sense my hesitation and doesn't press me, offering a quick smile instead. "Right, back to business then. First off, you'll be relieved to know that you're not dead, which I'm sure has crossed your mind at least a few dozen times."

"At least!" A wave of relief rushes over me as I resume my pacing. The fact of my status among the living is more convincing coming from a human than a disintegrating piece of paper.

"Death is naturally the first assumption most newcomers make. That or alien abduction, which probably wouldn't be much fun either," Erik jokes before his smile suddenly fades. He puts his hands behind his back and clears his throat, as if he's getting ready to give a big speech.

"Look, Ev, what I'm going to tell you will challenge everything you have come to accept as reality. I need you to try to keep an open mind. Can you do that for me?"

I stop my pacing and stare at him. There's a desperation in his eyes that's hard to turn down. I simply nod, hungry for the answers he can provide, even if I'm not sure I can handle them.

"All right then, here goes," my magister begins. "The Prism is a world that exists in parallel to our own on Earth. It may surprise you to know that you are, at this very moment, sleeping. You haven't physically left Earth, but your conscious mind has entered an altered state, a reality that only a fraction of the world's population can access, and it's every bit as real as if your Earthly body was here with you."

Sleeping? Altered state? Seriously? Okay, wasn't expecting that. "I'm sleeping? Like…a dream?"

The corners of Erik's mouth lift higher. "Oh, it's much more than that! This is all real! Hard to get in, but once you do, there's no unseeing it, no going back. Only a fool would give it up."

"Sleeping?" I mumble. "Might take a while to wrap my head around that one."

"I wouldn't waste time on that. Not sure it's really possible to wrap your head around most of what you see here, and some brilliant minds have given it their best shot, trust me!"

Erik's words deliver a disappointing blow; aside from the TV show, I don't like unsolved mysteries. I'm too curious for my own good. "So, I haven't physically left my bed or anything?"

"No. You're still there."

"Like, just lying there…sleeping? Eyes closed and all?"

"Yup."

"Is this like a parallel reality, or something?"

"You could say that. Honestly, I'm not entirely sure myself. Some believe it is."

Great, more non-answers. "Okay. Well, who built it then? And how am I even here? How are any of us here?"

Erik inhales and scratches his head, as if worried that I won't buy what he has to say next, then puts his hands into the pockets of his slacks. He lifts his broad shoulders, raises one eyebrow and answers. "You did."

"I did…I did what?"

"You built it, Ev. You built the Prism. Along with me and everyone else that visits here in their altered state. We call ourselves Wakers.

"You see, the Prism is an amalgamation of all the things that we all find beautiful, exciting, desirable; experiences we want to have, places we want to see. Here, you won't find sickness, destruction, run-down buildings, or anything that isn't the best version of itself. No discord or hunger…Like an actual prism, it takes our input and creates this amazing spectrum of experience that's always changing, always being transformed to reflect the desires of our population."

What the heck is he talking about? A parallel world that *I* created. *And he makes it sound so normal!* He's right; I'm *not* going to grasp it. This is *so* far from normal!

"Think of it as a democracy," Erik continues. "The Prism reads the desires of its people and forms a reality that reflects what the majority wants, so long as it comes from a good place. In the end, it becomes a world made up of many smaller ones, based on a collective desire."

I can't bring myself to utter a single stupid word. My lips feel glued shut even though I know my mouth is gaping open.

"But it wouldn't be a perfect reality if you always had to share your wish list with everyone else, would it?" Erik asks rhetorically, not giving me time to answer. "See, where we are now and where the amalgamation takes place is the Nucleus. It's the part that we all have shared access to. But there's another perk." He motions around us. "This building is known as Castellum. And each Waker has their very own personal dimension within it, a dimension in which they can create absolutely anything they want."

Anything? "Anything? Really? No restrictions in the fine print?" I finally manage to speak, challenging him to check his facts.

But Erik nods firmly without breaking eye contact, his gaze holding me and piercing me in a way that blankets my skin with a welcome set of goosebumps. "Absolutely anything," he assures me. "You can create inventions, relive memories, visit Jupiter if you let yourself believe you can…It's *your* canvass."

His blue eyes brighten again with a naive child-like enthusiasm. It's one I've seen before, in the eyes of my mother, in the eyes of Uncle Tim. I stare at him hungrily, desperately trying to hold on to the exhilaration I'm feeling and turn it into something real that can never slip away.

"As cliché as it sounds," Erik adds, "here, anything truly is possible!"

CHAPTER 7

Geography 101

I'm trying to process it. But no one prepares you for being told you've just entered a parallel dimension in your sleep where you can alter reality with your mind. There's no playbook for that – no checklist for how to feel or what to say without sounding either completely insane or…completely insane!

Erik's studying me again, his head tilted to the other side now. "Have I lost you? You think I'm a mad man, don't you? Damn, you've lost the ability to speak!" He leans in to stare at my pupils. "I've heard of this happening."

I manage a laugh. "No, I…I think I'm following you. It's just…this is crazy! It's just really overwhelming and…" I sigh loudly and give up on finishing the sentence. *What is there to say?*

"Oh absolutely," Erik affirms with a chuckle. "It's complete lunacy, I totally agree. But it is real, Ev. I promise. And there really is no better way to start believing than to see it for yourself."

I nearly jump out of my skin, forgetting my skepticism instantly. "I was beginning to think you were just going to talk about it all day!"

"I haven't scared you off?"

"Are you kidding? If this place *is* real, then I want to see every corner of it!"

Suddenly, my desire to propel my body through those wooden doors is stronger than any desire I've ever experienced, even my desire to see home again.

But then I remember the wormholes, and my inquisitiveness sidetracks me as I watch more bodies disappear in a blurry swirl.

"Before we do that though, what the heck are those things?"

Erik follows my gaze. "Right! How did I forget that? Sorry, still getting the hang of this magister thing. Pretty cool, aren't they? They're portals, to the Prism's realms. They can take you anywhere you want to go in seconds."

"Portals?!" I run my hands through my hair, which to my astonishment isn't the least bit tangled. My fingers glide through as if my hair is made of silk. "You just said 'portals.' Ok, totally normal…"

Erik lets out a laugh again. "Are you really surprised at this point? It's like this – the Prismatic is our main waterbody. The rest of the Prism is laid out around it and divided into nine realms, most mirrored after the landscapes and continents of Earth. With two exceptions: Senna — that's our fantasy realm — essentially everything the human imagination wants that can't neatly fit into any other realm. And Agora, where we're standing now."

"Meeting place." I recognize the Greek word. "What else is in Agora?"

"Arguably the best part of the Prism; the Luminary. It's a place of enlightenment, like a kind of university. Some Wakers teach there as a hobby. It has an incredible library too; the Lumus. Any book you could ever want. Manuscripts, some thousands of years old, all the comics ever written…"

I stop listening, another layer of excitement setting in. *Any book? When do I see that?*

"I see that caught your attention," Erik observes, no doubt noticing my eyes lighting up.

"Yeah – sounds like something worth seeing," I reply, trying to contain myself and play it cool.

"Behind the Luminary is the Imperium," Erik continues, "built into the rock wall on the Prism's perimeter. It's where some elected representatives meet to discuss, well, Prism things."

"Wait, people actually want a government in their paradise?" I ask skeptically.

"It's not a real government. I suppose people feel comforted knowing there's an order to things. The idea of a ruling body is so deeply ingrained in our civilization, it may be difficult for people to imagine an existence without one, even a dream existence."

"So…the Imperium controls the Prism?"

"Absolutely not! The creative power comes from the population collectively. Aside from that, no one knows who or what truly controls the Prism. Everyone has their own theory about it. A Higher Power always leads the polls. One eccentric fellow I met a few months ago is convinced we're just players in an elaborate matrix."

I chuckle. "I'll bet there's more where he came from. So then, what does the Imperium do, exactly?"

"Nothing too political. There's a chairperson who oversees the Prism's activities and keeps an eye on things generally, organizes elections, that sort of thing; a social rep and committee; a statistician who monitors population and demographic trends; two historians that chronicle changes in the Prism over the years. They keep records of past Prisms in the main floor archives — kind of like a magical photo album of time. Truly fantastic Ev! Rumor has it they're even working on a way to enable time travel through past Prisms! That's where the new physicist comes in. First one got elected last year. She leads a research team of volunteers."

No one prepares you for that either. "Dream world time travel!!? Are they close to figuring it out?"

Erik lifts his shoulders, his giddiness escaping through his infectious smile. "It's only a rumor so far. But you can sit in on the Imperium's meetings if you'd like to learn more.

"Oh, right – Agora also houses Cascada, a valley of waterfalls, and the Climbing Gardens, an enormous maze of every kind of plant life you can imagine. Did I miss anything…no, I think I got it all. Moving on…"

I walk with Erik at a steady pace, listening as he motions to the first portal on the left: the realm of Edenia. Rooftops of chateau towers amid rolling hills. "The most beautiful elements of Europe," he explains. "So much to see there. Next, we have Estra, our counterpart to Asia. That one," he motions to the third mural, "is Azula. Best of the South Pacific, including Bora Borealis. Its close enough to the polar region that you get the beauty of Polynesia set against the backdrop of the northern lights at night. Just breathtaking! And at the back we have Nevar, the winter realm. One of my favorite spots."

For the first time since our meeting, I glimpse a melancholy come over Erik's features and hear a hint of nostalgia in his otherwise cheery voice. But he quickly recovers and moves on to the realm on the right of the large wooden doors.

"Senna," he almost sighs. "There are no words. It's everyone's wildest fantasies come to life — elves and wizards and dragons and flying carpets, all rolled into one fantastic domain. Even a few dinos. Just brilliant!"

I shudder, remembering how Jurassic Park left me traumatized for weeks. "Uh, how big are these dinos?"

"Oh, I wouldn't worry. I've never seen them eat anyone."

"How reassuring. I guess nothing bad can happen in paradise, right?"

Erik continues with his lesson. "That's Oransen: Africa and the Middle East. I promise, you'll never go to a zoo again!"

Only two realms remain. "Arboran and Verding, your North and South Americas," Erik explains. "All the big selling points, including the Jakur islands; basically, the high-def version of the Caribbean." He inhales a dramatic breath and throws up his hands. "And that's it, in a nutshell of course."

It's my turn to laugh. "I'm not sure I'd end with that." His geography lesson has been invaluable, but also overwhelming, to say the least, like peeling away the layers of an onion that keeps multiplying itself.

"I don't even know what to say...the Prism sounds incredible. All of this is...actually real?" I start to tremble as if my body is experiencing a type of supernova, like when you have the flu but can't stop shaking no matter how many sweatshirts and blankets you pile on.

"It's real," Erik assures. "Are you ready to see it for yourself?"

Every instinct I have is screaming at me to run towards those doors. Even if I'm dead, even if this is all some grand illusion or hallucination or fleeting dream...I need to see it. I need to know.

"More than ready!" I answer.

Two almost unnoticeable dimples appear on Erik's cheeks as he gently brushes away a loose hair that's been obstructing my view, giving me another set of welcome shivers. "I'm glad you're still on board."

The remaining distance to the doors seems to take an eternity, and I can hear my every breath and the echo of my every step as I make my way towards them. Every so often they swing open as people enter and leave, but all I can see is a blinding light before they close again. A diamond-shaped map is carved into the wood, the realms laid out exactly as Erik described them, the Prism's seal etched into the center of the Prismatic.

Erik breaks the silence. "Remember, just have an open mind. It's a lot all at once." He places his hands on a pair of large silver rings. "Behold your second life!" he says, then swings the massive doors open effortlessly, as if they're weightless.

CHAPTER 8

A Second Life

It's taking excruciatingly long for my eyes to adjust. Everything's more intense: reds richer, blues deeper, yellows brighter. The scents, the sounds... It brings me back to the room I woke up in, to that sense of confusion and familiarity and unmatched exhilaration.

The blinding light has a face now. Before me stretches the long staircase that I saw from my terrace. Erik calls it the Avenue. It feels like an indulgent cushion under the soles of my shoes and looks like it's covered in an ivory carpet that remains pristine despite the constant traffic.

Erik notices me looking down. "You know, you don't even need shoes here. People wear them out of habit, but you won't really feel physical discomfort at all. Your body temperature won't fluctuate much. You won't experience hunger or..."

I'm only half listening to him. My mind is on fire. My senses, on overdrive.

Astonishingly giant flower beds line the steps, set against a backdrop of flowing grasses that dwarf them in comparison. Someone jostles my shoulder. "Sorry miss!" I hear them call out. I notice the people now and the low hum of their chatter. It's almost unnatural – all the smiles, the energy...

"Is everyone always this…"

"Disgustingly cheerful? Most of the time," Erik affirms, grinning. "I know, it's creepy at first. The goal of the Prism is to create only the good things people want, which has the effect of eliciting positive emotions. In fact, intense negative emotions of any kind are pretty rare here, and often result in the person who's experiencing them not being able to return until they're emotionally ready."

"You're serious? No negative emotions at all?" *I'm in trouble!*

"Oh no, we still get them," Erik corrects himself to my immediate relief. "We are human after all. We all get down or frustrated every now and then. It's still going to happen, but it won't be as extreme. You'll be…inoculated to some degree – if that's even the right metaphor. Your goal will be to only experience the states of being that are necessary for you to thrive and evolve."

"That sounds complicated," I note, wondering if my emotions will get me into hot water. Considering they can make glass shatter and knock out power to entire neighborhoods, I'm not off to a great start.

Erik nods. "It takes work, sure. But too much negativity threatens the stability of this world, and it will only keep you from returning. Your consciousness affects reality, so you need to learn how to control your thoughts and feelings if you want to keep accessing the Prism."

*Because I'm so good at that…*A loud sigh escapes my lips. "No pressure," I mumble as Erik carries on, taking his duty as my magister quite seriously. I hope he's still managing to breathe through it all.

"Most people first arrive here following some catalytic experience, one where they're so deliriously happy that they can't even imagine feeling anything else. We call it 'awakening.'

*How curious…*Was my stand-off with Tristan the catalyst for *my* awakening? It makes sense, although Catherine's absence and lack of doomsday nagging might have been a small contributing factor. Regardless, I silently celebrate at the realization that Tristan could be in some way responsible for me finding this place. *Talk about sweet revenge.*

"What if I'm not that great at reining in the…you know…negative stuff?" I ask. "Let me rephrase that: what if I'm beyond terrible at it?"

Erik just smiles at me. "Well, you got here, didn't you? You must be doing something right. But that's also why you get a magister," he adds. "It's like a support system, to help you navigate this world and facilitate your return." He stops walking and turns to face me. "I know it's a high standard. But Ev, I promise you, if you let me, I can help you live your life to the fullest possible measure."

For a second, I think his gaze seems to intensify. He looks back at the Prismatic, his features softening in innocent bewilderment as if he's seeing it all for the first time himself. "Think about it – it's like having two lives. I don't think you realize yet what an incredible gift that is." He seems far away, as if transported elsewhere in that instant. "An incredible gift," he repeats before resuming our walk and snapping back to his old up-beat self.

"I should mention, time moves much slower here. You'll find that out soon enough. It's about the equivalent of two Earth days."

"*Two* days!!?" I exclaim.

"We estimate. Of course, the actual time you're asleep on Earth is likely a few minutes, at the most. Oh, and don't bother looking for clocks — you won't find any of those."

That's refreshing. No one nagging me about being a few

minutes late…sounds pretty perfect. "Clocks would only make you feel like time is running out. And that's not what people want."

"Precisely!" Erik confirms proudly. "See, you're catching on already. You'll be a magister yourself in no time."

We're almost upon the Prismatic. The waves fold soothingly onto the pristine white sand. Heads bob in the water like apples at a fair while others worship the never-burning sun. I notice children swimming quite far out and worry sets in. "Is it all shallow?"

"This isn't Earth," Erik chuckles, picking up on my anxiety like he's psychic. "We don't face the same dangers here. They'll be fine. Many Wakers are children, in fact. Society changes us as we age, teaches us to fear and doubt. Children still retain that innocence the Prism seeks — that belief in infinite possibility that overtime is etched away."

We stop at the edge of the roadway where those magnificent horses I glimpsed earlier set down gracefully on the cobblestones, one after the next. Their wings are extraordinary, arguably the most magnificent thing about them, with intricate markings drawn on in gold brush strokes – labyrinths, mandalas, and other patterns that hypnotically draw me in. They don't look animatronic anymore.

"Pretty incredible, aren't they?" Erik observes.

But 'incredible' isn't quite the right word. I don't think any word is.

"I'll take you to them later," he promises as the no longer mythical creatures lift off, leaving me completely speechless. "Any idea what you'd like to see first?"

I feel a sense of paralysis set in as I struggle to decide which metaphorical door to open. "I don't know…I want to be everywhere right now…"

Erik laughs. "I wish I could tell you it gets easier. I suppose that's a good thing. After all, we wouldn't want you to get bored."

Something about the waves crashing victoriously onto the sand mirrors the kaleidoscope of emotions within me, and before my brain can employ any form of logical thought process, my legs lunge impulsively towards the Prismatic without asking my permission.

All my inhibitions melt away as I feel the smooth sand under my feet, the individual grains indiscernible. I dig into the velvet texture as I weave through the crowd, finally letting my body collapse into the water. I feel the remnants of my doubt and anxiety obliterated in an instant. The current carries me away from the beach into deeper tumultuous waters, until Erik's face comes into view in the corner of my eye.

"This is incredible!" I cry as I tread the water, exerting barely any effort at all. I look back at the shoreline, Castellum disappearing into the clouds with no end in sight.

Again, Erik just smiles. "Come on, I want to show you something."

I follow him to a turquoise shallow area where the water only reaches our shins. Around the perimeter, the water changes to a royal blue, signaling a significant drop, and foaming waves encircle us like a fortress wall. Erik's t-shirt clings to his athletic body as he removes his shoes and throws them aside.

"Oh, right," he says, snapping his fingers. "The Prism has this brilliant built-in feature of disposing of things you don't need anymore. If you stare at those shoes long enough, they'll just disappear!" I follow Erik's lead and leave my own shoes floating nearby. Sure enough, they vanish within seconds.

Unbelievable!

Erik begins making a series of high-pitched whistling

sounds, forming a subtle enchanting melody that hangs like a frozen echo in the air. He seems to be waiting for something…

Suddenly, a large fish leaps out of the water behind us, followed by another. More join by the second, and swim around us so quickly they begin to blend until I can no longer see the individual creatures at all or the patterns that adorn their scales, just a mirage of endless color with no beginning and end. After a few minutes, the fish begin to scatter leaving behind an afterimage that slowly fades, and the pool reclaims the ripples and returns to its pristine stillness.

"Not bad for the first hour, right" Erik says, looking very pleased with himself and full of that child-like wonder again.

I nod, trying desperately to keep a straight face for once. "Good start. Let's see what else you can come up with."

"Ah, hard to impress. That won't last long – not with everything else I've got lined up."

I feel so content exactly where I am that I haven't even entertained the idea of leaving. When we finally swim back to the beach, something overcomes me, and I can't hold myself back from throwing my hands around Erik's neck and hugging him. "Thank you," I manage to croak, even though I know a large part of my gratitude is directed at whatever mysterious force brought me here.

"Anytime," Erik replies, placing a soothing hand on my back. "But I'm going to need you to keep it together. We're just getting started!"

We remain in an embrace for a few seconds longer, and I can feel the warmth of Erik's breath in my hair. It's not like me to be so vulnerable with anyone, let alone a total stranger. But this feels different. I'm not embarrassed by my gesture. I know Erik's been here before. I know he understands.

He's not a stranger anymore.

* * *

It's uncanny – the sand not burning my feet, the absence of sweat on my brow, the weightlessness of my dry clothes.

Wait…

"It wouldn't be paradise if we had to worry about the small stuff," Erik explains as I pat myself down. "You'll be dry the second you're out of the water."

"Well, isn't that convenient!" We join other Wakers on the Promenade. "Is it always summer?" I ask.

"Mostly. It's always winter in Nevar and some of the mountain regions. You get some variability with the other seasons, but it stays comfortable. It does rain on occasion, but it's nothing like on Earth." A mysterious grin spreads across his face. "You'll see," he adds, without offering any more details.

The bistros and cafes trigger my cravings, but I'm not hungry. I recall what Erik mentioned earlier. "So, no hunger here at all?"

He nods, saluting an acquaintance who passes us. "You eat to be social and pass the time, to indulge your taste buds —not because you need to. Our bodies remain nourished and hydrated at all times."

"Sounds pretty perfect. And my shoes?" I ask again, remembering my bare feet. "Doesn't hurt but…just feels weird."

"You can pick up a pair at one of the shops on the strip."

"But I don't have any money."

Erik tries not to snicker, and I catch on. "Let me guess, there's no need for money in the Prism."

"This is a utopic existence Ev. No need to pay for anything, ever!"

Must be nice. "Right. Well, I guess I could get used to that."

The strip is buzzing with a mosaic of faces of all ages and walks of life. Naturally, I resume my questions. "How many people come here anyway?"

Erik shrugs. "Not entirely sure. The Imperium statistician tries to keep a record based on how many people attend the Luminary for novice courses or vote in the elections every year. But those records are far from accurate. Robert Crawford — he teaches at the Luminary — he estimates it at about 2 million or so."

I stop in my tracks and stare at Erik in disbelief, wondering if he perhaps mixes up his m's and b's like my neighbour's four-year-old mixes up her s's and f's. "2 million?"

"Yup."

"Million? *That's it?* But the world has over 7 billion people in it!"

"I know," Erik agrees, frowning. "It's sad, isn't it? But it's not easy to access this place. Think of how many people live in misery every day. War, poverty — and those are the obvious culprits. The battles we wage with ourselves can be equally devastating. They constantly keep us from accessing higher states of being."

"Our negative emotions?"

Erik nods. "And humans have a ton of them. They give us an excuse to stagnate and accept defeat. Even in the first world, where we have more than most could ever hope for, we're still so unsatisfied, so unfulfilled, so quick to blame others for our failings and the things we lack."

He's got a point. "But if people knew about the Prism, wouldn't they want to leave all the misery behind, so that they could come here?"

A sadness seems to come over Erik again. "I appreciate where you're coming from. But over time you'll realize that people should come here *because* they're ready, not the other way around."

I've heard all that before in some form or another. Happiness should come from within, and so on and so forth. "It just seems so unfair, such an incredible place not being accessible to everyone…"

"Oh, it's accessible. People just don't know *how* to access it. I probably shouldn't tell you this, but Robert's a bit worried about our numbers," Erik confides.

"What do you mean?"

"Well, he says they've stayed more or less constant for the last five decades. With population increase on Earth, you would expect the Prism population to increase in proportion. But it hasn't. He has a theory – well, maybe he'll tell you about it sometime. He's pretty brilliant," Erik adds, betraying his admiration for the man.

"You know him well."

"You could say that. I took his *Foundations* course when I first arrived. We've stayed in touch. He teaches geology at Yale."

"Yale, like New Haven Connecticut Yale?"

"Only one I know of."

"So, people who live on different continents, they come here at the same time? How is that even possible? What about the time difference?"

"I know, it defies logic," Erik responds. "Just another mystery of the universe I suppose. Some of the scientists around here believe that we never actually go back to our old reality at all, but rather transcend into some other parallel existence with only tiny variations. Try to chew on that one! I can't make heads or tails of it."

No kidding! I immediately give up trying to figure out the mind-bending time zone conundrum. Still, the impossible possibility of it annoys me and a small part of me aches to solve it and pat myself on the back for being a brilliant genius.

"And we can all understand each other just fine," Erik adds. "The Prism removes all barriers to communication, like a language app – except the translation is instantaneous and makes sense. You hear everyone in the language you speak."

It seems every time Erik opens his mouth something comes out of it that puts me right back in that dimension room, feeling utterly confused and bewildered.

We walk past a small boutique with shoes in the display window. I've completely forgotten I'm barefoot. Still, earthly habits die hard. I pick out a pair of slip-on sandals and we're on our way in minutes without paying a dime. *Definitely could get used to this!*

Erik motions ahead to a sign of a lobster with comical bulging eyes, its oversized claws holding the word "Stella's" between them. "Are you up for a bite and meeting some new faces? Even if you hate the company, the food's worth it."

"You don't have to ask me twice when it comes to food. Does it taste different here?"

Erik holds open the door like a perfect gentleman and motions me through. "See for yourself."

Inside, the coastal-style eatery is fitted with crisp white tablecloths and large windows overlooking the Prismatic. Erik waves to a group seated on a patio that juts out over the water. A girl in a yellow vintage dress waves back, probably slightly older than me, her black hair gathered into a braid that hangs elegantly over her shoulder and contrasts with a pretty lace collar. She's seated next to a stunning red-headed woman with bright green eyes that seem to glow from underneath her bangs.

Erik approaches the third figure, a guy close to my age

wearing surf shorts. He has straight black hair down to his shoulders. They exchange a quick embrace. "Fox, about time! It's good to see you again mate. Everything alright?"

"Yeah, yeah…just family stuff…you know how it is," Fox replies, waving off whatever "it is" and shutting down that topic of conversation. I instantly assume he must have had trouble returning. That really sucks, for both of us. It's probably just a matter of time before it happens to me too.

Fox ties up his hair in a samurai man-bun. He looks like the free-spirit type – like he lives in a hut on the beach, grows his own mango trees and surfs his carefree days away. "But I'm not going anywhere for a while, I'll promise you that," he insists. "Man, these five days felt like five months! I haven't had a long stretch like that since…well, a while."

Erik pulls me in front of him proudly like I'm a show and tell toy. "Everyone, meet Everest! Fresh off the elevator and lucky enough to get yours truly as a magister." He takes a quick jester-like bow as he pulls out a chair for me.

Fox eyes me with pity. "Well, you have my sympathy Everest! He's not all bad though. If he gets too irritating just give him a quick smack on the head. That usually fixes any bugs."

"And here I was hoping you would all help me make a *good* impression." Erik takes his seat next to me and glances at his friend with pretend disdain. "Not all bad…" he huffs before continuing introductions.

Jenna Delgado from Belize wears the yellow dress, which matches her disposition perfectly. She introduces herself with pep and delves eagerly into more context, her Latin roots coming through her graceful hand gestures. "Erik and I awakened around the same time, so we toured a lot together," she fills me in enthusiastically, her bright smile framed by her red lipstick. I wish I had a miniature version of her to carry around all the time like a personal ray of sunshine, the perfect antidote for those miserable days. "I was terrified! Wasn't I Erik? I mean, until we saw the museums…"

Erik groans and rolls his eyes and if reliving a traumatic memory. "She dragged me to *every single museum*. The mummies haunt me to this day!"

"Yeah, don't go to Edenia with her," Fox warns through a full mouth of pizza while receiving a playful shove from Jenna.

"What?" Fox adds defensively. "You can't argue that you overdo it a little."

"I am an Art History major," Jenna enlightens me proudly.

"Ah," I reply, "that explains a lot."

"This chap was my magister," Erik says, pointing at Fox. "Don't let the surfer-dude image fool you – he's brighter than he looks."

Fox extends his hand. "Fox Kwan. Pleased to meet you."

It seems people still retain their accents in the Prism. "You sound American," I observe as I accept his handshake.

"Your assessment is correct. North Carolina, at least for now. I'm a bit of a nomad. Grew up in a small town in Pennsylvania which had like 12 people in it, and they were mostly Amish. We were the only Asian family for miles."

"That must have been an experience," I say.

"It was amazing!" Fox elaborates, throwing a piece of calamari into his mouth and chewing it loudly. "My best friend from the farm next door was Amish. Taught me how to churn butter. Yeah, that's right! Eighth-grade butter churning champion sitting right here!"

I laugh. I like him. And I suspect he's got more stories where that one came from. He motions to me.

"What about you Everest, where'd you get sucked in from?"

"Uh, Chicago originally. I live in Paris now. When I was –"

"You live in Paris too?" Jenna practically squeals, not giving me a chance to finish. Her face is right up in mine, eyes wide and inquisitive.

Erik laughs. "Probably should have kept that to yourself! She'll try to be your permanent houseguest."

I wink at Jenna. "Well, if you're ever in the neighborhood, I think we could find some room."

"I will hold you to that," Jenna promises.

"Last but not least, this is Maeve." Erik refers to the intimidating woman who to this point has only observed me silently. I find her harder to read than the others, but she smiles warmly. I return the gesture, admiring the flawlessness of her porcelain skin. "Maeve found us six months ago," Erik adds. "Coincidently, she also lives in Paris, to Jenna's utter delight."

Maeve laughs and extends her hand. "It's nice to meet someone from the Prism so close to home. And I can always take over boarding Jenna if she becomes a handful. I work so much the apartment is usually empty anyway."

"What do you do?" I ask, shaking her hand.

"I'm the marketing director at the Salle St. Germain. Do you know it? It's a large event space."

"Yeah!" I reply, "I've been there once. Cool place! You must meet all kinds of people."

"All kinds!" Maeve agrees. "You should all visit sometime," she offers, making eye contact with Erik and adding coyly, "I can get you the best seats in the house."

Fox orders a drink from a passing server and immediately my questions resume. "People actually work here?"

Fox shakes his head. "No. They do look incredibly real though, don't they? The Prism provides them to fill needed roles. They're probably some kind of AI –"

"Oh please! Why is it always a robot with you?" Jenna interjects passionately. "You have no idea what you are talking about! This is a spiritual and metaphysical place, not some video game you play."

Fox raises his hand. "Wait, you study paintings, but the software engineer has no idea what he's talking about?" he retorts with a snort. "Come on, they could totally be robots!"

"Anyway," Jenna says, rolling her eyes, and leaning back in her chair, "Fox's 'robots' give the place a bit of normality. It is so unbelievable as it is, no?"

As I look out onto the Prismatic while chewing bites of mouthwatering lobster jambalaya that Fox pushes my way, I'm overcome with an overwhelming feeling of peace. I've found this place, or it's found me. I still question my sanity a little, and if I deserve to be here when so many others are shut out. But those lingering thoughts become lost amid my intense fascination, and I feel a part of something that challenges me and stretches my mind to its very limits.

"What are you up to now?" Maeve asks Erik as we all prepare to leave.

"That's up to Ev. Now remember," he warns me, "you're not going to see *everything* today."

Darn it! He's read my thoughts, again. I follow the shoreline of the Prismatic past the Agora Marina and can just barely make out the silhouettes of the unmistakable architecture on the horizon.

"How about a gondola ride?"

"To Venice it is," Erik cries jubilantly, downing the remainder of his soda.

We say our goodbyes to the group and head back onto the Promenade, savoring a refreshing breeze that comes off the pristine water.

"This is all still so surreal. Does it feel like an endless vacation?" I ask Erik after inhaling a lung full of air.

"Yeah, a bit like that, I suppose," he agrees. "But Earth's still great too. I couldn't choose one over the other. Believe it or not, you can only take perfect for so long. At least that's been my experience. Still, it's a nice reward to wake up to on a tough day."

With his last words, we suddenly find ourselves under an enormous shadow. A massive, winged creature soars overhead, turning west and disappearing over the tree line.

"Come on," Erik says, "that's where we're headed. Race?"

I laugh. "What are you, twelve?" Tristan would have never approved.

No more thoughts of Tristan, I promise again, and give myself a head start.

CHAPTER 9

A Friendly Universe

My advantage doesn't benefit me all that much, and I quickly find myself trailing Erik as he leads us to an open pasture. In the middle stand five Pegasi. They look me over as we approach, their muscles twitching as they lift their legs in a graceful dance.

I wonder how children must feel, arriving here and seeing these creatures. As adults, we resign ourselves to the fact that certain things we indisputably believed to be real as children aren't. It sucks for a while until you start getting interested in more grown-up things. Still, there's a sadness that accompanies the realization that magic only exists in fairytales.

Of course, children aren't so easily dissuaded. They hold on to that belief in the magical and the supernatural with an admirable determination. *How validating it must feel for them, seeing all this.* If my inner child is doing cartwheels, they must be beside themselves! How do they not wake up and tell everyone, 'I told you so'?" Of course, who would believe it…

Despite their regal elegance, I approach the large creatures cautiously. While I don't think the Prism would allow them to trample me, I've lived in the real world long enough to develop some healthy skepticism.

But there's a serenity in their presence that wipes that skepticism away almost instantly. And if the word "peace" had a physical manifestation, it would be this moment, this valley, right now.

Erik leads me through the herd towards a silver-blue mare with a freckled nose. "Pegasi are deeply connected with those that can see their inner spirit," he says. "Around here, it's believed they dwelled on Earth during a time of human decency. Once humans began to doubt goodness and fear the illusion of darkness, they were no longer worthy of seeing the magic of the Pegasus. Disillusioned with humanity, they travelled to a dimension worthy of their gifts."

Erik pats the silver mare gently on the snout. "The one you choose will serve you loyally, and always come when summoned. This one's mine. Cassiopeia, or Cass for short. She's the most dependable companion I have."

"She's beautiful," I marvel, looking at her and the others admiringly. "Do I pick one now?"

Erik smiles and motions for me to go right ahead, then returns to petting Cass.

Ok. I'm picking a winged horse. Totally normal stuff…

I'm immediately drawn to a Palomino mare with an iridescent ivory mane who prances impatiently on the spot. Her eyes seem to peer into my very soul — deep, insightful eyes that suddenly seem privy to every thought and secret in a way that's somewhat unnerving. She neighs as I approach. My hand finds her velvet cheek and my decision becomes an easy one.

"Hey. What do you say…Juno? Do you like that name? I've always liked that name."

"She's stunning," Erik says approvingly. "Looks like our job here is done. We have some canals to explore!"

"Wait, that's it? Isn't there some training or something?" I notice Juno's bare back. "Or, you know, maybe a saddle at least?"

Erik laughs. "A saddle? No! Nothing like that. You won't need it. Still interested?"

I look at Juno – no halter, no reins, no saddle, no guarantee I'll be able to even stay on her. *Erik wouldn't let me die, would he?* I take a breath and pretend it's all normal. "Okay, let's do this!"

Erik's already begun walking, as if he knew what my decision would be before I even knew it myself. Cass follows him closely.

"How do I get mine to do that?" I call after him.

"You just tell her."

Right. Should have expected that. Juno's massive wings twitch with eagerness. "You won't let me fall right? Please don't let me fall…"

I start to walk, willing Juno to follow, and she immediately obeys.

"How's it like in the air?" I ask Erik as I check back to make sure Juno's still behind me.

"Different. But you'll figure it out. Just trust her."

Further out in the pasture, Juno kneels on her front knees, allowing me to climb up onto her strong back and take hold of her mane, her wings hugging my legs.

"So far so good," Erik says with a wink as he mounts Cass. "Remember, the Prism reads your thoughts. Your mind will tell her where to go."

"You make it sound so easy."

"It is. Oh, and most definitely look down. Might as well enjoy the view!"

Before I can respond or change my mind, Erik darts forward and begins riding away. I hesitate, but I'd rather be with Erik in the sky than alone in this strange world on land.

"All right girl, I'm trusting you. Follow them," I instruct Juno. The majestic animal begins to move. I hang on to her satin mane, hoping it won't slip through my fingers, and urge her to go a little faster. Juno makes up ground quickly and soon we're on Cass and Erik's heels. I see Cass' wings begin to stretch out on either side of her body. Juno mirrors her leader and before I realize it, we're lifting off into the cool air.

This is actually happening! I'm not afraid of heights, but this is a whole new experience.

I take Erik's advice and look down. My breath catches as I take in the incredible scene beneath me: the tree canopies of the Climbing Gardens, the shimmering waterfalls drizzling off the lush Cascada cliffsides, the vastness of the Prismatic. Erik leads us towards Castellum first. We sail past the balconies, the tips of Juno's wings grazing the building's brilliant limestone as I try to curiously peek into open terrace doors. When we reach the edge of the structure, Erik circles back around and heads East, into that refreshing breeze that offers no resistance, only unparalleled calm. Soon, we're leaving Agora behind and sailing over a lush Edenian green countryside. I gaze in awe at a landscape that may as well be lifted out of a fairytale oil painting, with picturesque cottages dotting meadows, and valleys drizzled with sapphire streams, all set against a backdrop of sugar-dusted mountain peaks. I don't even feel the time passing.

The reality of the Prism slowly sinks in as we descend upon the maze-like landscape of a canal city. I want to pinch myself, but I'm afraid of slipping off and falling to my death if I loosen my grip.

Just enjoy this! I convince myself.

This is real! This is so incredibly real!

* * *

I understand now why Venice is found on many bucket lists. I still hope to see the real city one day, with its old-world rustic charm and all the little corners that are missing from the Prism. But this condensed replica has its own appeal — untouched by time, it boasts the most iconic features of its earthly counterpart. It's breathtaking and charming and really, *really* clean. And I assume it's probably not sinking into the sea either.

We've spent the afternoon touring the pigeon-filled streets and visiting the main attractions, and it's left me in shambles. The good kind, that is. The kind you're in when you're completely overwhelmed and overstimulated in the best possible way and you don't quite know what to do with all your feelings – all you know is that you want more, and more and more, and you never want it to end.

With evening nearly upon us, I won't be leaving without checking that gondola off my own bucket list.

"No trip to Venice would be complete without it," Erik agrees.

"Or, we could go to a museum, since you're so fond of them."

Erik pretends to think for a moment. "Tempting, but I think I need more time to recover from the last thirty!"

We find a vacant boat and board. There's no gondolier, no oars. "We just steer with our thoughts," Erik reminds me. "Unless you really want one of those handsome tenors to serenade you. There's probably one around here that I could flag down."

I think I've got 'handsome companion' covered, but I don't tell Erik that. "What happens if two people in the same boat want to go in different directions?" I ask.

"Ah, well that depends on whose desire is stronger. If both are equal, I guess you're left with a stalemate." Erik takes a seat across from me and leans in. "Practice. Focus on something behind me — a landmark, a…pigeon…anything, and I'll do the same."

"And I just simply wish to go there?"

"Well, it's a little more involved than that. The Prism will only grant a true desire. You need to feel it in here, and see it in here," he says, placing a hand on his chest and then tapping his head. "You already did it when you flew here."

"I did do that, didn't I?" I reply, feeling more confident. "All right. Let's try this mind-over-matter thing again." I focus on a bridge up ahead, close my eyes and try and imagine myself moving toward it through the water…*see it…feel it…* But when I open my eyes again our vessel hasn't moved an inch. *Disappointing.* "Well, that didn't work."

Erik grins at me with a sneaky expression. "That's because I'm a bit better at this than you, and I'm really craving a slice of Luciano's Diavolo pizza."

I glance behind me and see Luciano's bright red restaurant canopy. "Didn't you just eat?"

"You always have time for Luciano's!"

"Ok…now I know never to get between you and pizza. So, it looks like we have that stalemate."

"Unless I consider revising my desire," Erik concedes. His eyes focus on me, as if he's trying to read my thoughts again or decipher a secret code. "I now wish to go wherever this inquisitive woman sitting in front of me wishes to go."

As we lock eyes and I cringe at the idea of my cheeks burning up, I realize that the gondola has begun travelling silently through the still waters of the canal in my chosen direction, without anything but my desire propelling it forward. It's moving rather slowly, so I refocus my intention and instantly it speeds up. *Definitely cool.* Erik did say to practice. *Stop.* The boat stops. *GO!* The boat jerks forward, sending Erik flying off the seat. "Sorry!" I correct, taking my mind off the gas a little.

"See," Erik says through a grunt as he awkwardly climbs back into position, "it's not that complicated."

We pass under the bridge then continue down the canal in silence, admiring the old and simultaneously new city. And since I have a captive audience, I set a course for the next checkpoint and resume my questions. "How do you become a magister?"

"I guess when the Prism senses you're ready it lets you know," Erik answers. "It seems to have a way of bringing the right people together."

"Have you been one before?"

Erik hesitates and looks away, and I pick up on that same melancholy I noticed about him before. "Once…but they don't come here anymore." I immediately regret prying and drop it.

The sky is on fire now in hues of pink and orange as if Rembrandt himself has painted a masterpiece above us, and the lights of Venice begin to reflect in the darkening water.

It's Erik's turn to pry. "So, Chicago to Paris. Sound like a fun story."

I cringe. I wish it was. "Not sure 'fun's" the word. I moved to Paris after my mom passed away to live with my aunt and uncle."

Erik's grin vanishes. He looks horrified. "Ev, I'm so sorry! I didn't mean to suggest —"

"It's fine, I know," I reassure him. I let my hand trail beside me in the canal water, remembering all the nights I cried myself to sleep after hearing the news. "It is what it is. I didn't take the move well at first. But it's Paris — there's a lot to fall in love with. I just wish I could have ended up there some other way, any other way really, you know?"

"You shouldn't feel guilty about the way your cards were dealt," Erik says with a look of sympathy.

I pretend to be convinced and return my hand to my lap. "Yeah, I know. So, what about you? Where's home?"

"London, now. My dad is half Norwegian. For a while we split our time between the UK and Norway for my dad's work, then moved to London permanently when I was 13."

"That's it!" I think out loud, then clarify my outburst for Erik. "The accent, I mean."

He laughs. "Yeah, it throws people off. I still haven't told my flat mate, Tommy – drives him mad that he can't figure it out. He bet South Africa once in a poker game and had to hand over his favorite record. You'd like him. He's a riot, though a bit trying at times." Erik chuckles to himself. "That's not a fair description — he can be a downright lunatic!"

I smile at Erik, enjoying getting to know him better. Unlike some of the other interactions I've had lately, it's completely effortless. "I almost went to England," I confide in him, trying to keep the conversation going. "For school, Cambridge. But that might have to wait now." *Ok, enough about that depressing subject.* "Anyway, what do you do in London, when you're not busy extorting records from your friends?"

Erik grins. "Well, the extortion is definitely my main gig, but I also work at a secondary school as a student advocate – try to get through to troubled kids, that sort of thing."

"Wow. Sounds challenging…and rewarding."

He shrugs. "I suppose it is. Most days I feel like I make a small difference. Just maybe not the days they curse and spit at me."

"Right. That part. Still, must be nice, to have found your place," I remark with a touch of envy.

"I'm not sure I've found it, necessarily," Erik replies, lifting his eyes upward and leaning back. "I was a bit aimless and jaded for a while. Then I came across this great quote. I think it was Einstein. 'The most important decision we make is whether we believe we live in a friendly or hostile universe.' That changed everything for me."

I don't believe in coincidences. Never have. I've always felt they were hidden clues to the invisible workings of the cosmos, perhaps even links to past lives…something intangible. And now Erik's just referenced a postcard I'd pinned to a whiteboard in another parallel reality just hours earlier. "I'm familiar with it," I simply tell him, my thoughts racing and a small grin of validation lifting my cheeks.

"It makes you think, doesn't it?" he continues. "Maybe the universe, God, is really on our side, listening, and every challenge and experience is merely a necessity in some master plan to give us exactly what we want. The Prism is kind of proof of that listening, isn't it?"

I'm still trying to dissect what's happening, the meaning of it all. What is the universe trying to tell me, exactly? "Are you always this philosophical?" I ask Erik through a lump in my throat.

"Only when I'm riding around in gondolas, apparently," he teases. "What about your family?"

Darn. It's a fair question. *Might as well get it out of the way.* I draw in a deep breath, the Prism air soothing my nerves.

"It was always just my mom and me. I never met my dad. My mom slipped up and told me I was named after him. He was a climber, a good one, she said. Didn't narrow things down a whole lot though. She was always very tight-lipped about it — never revealed much."

"Do you want to know more?" Erik asks softly. The tone of his voice suggests he seems to sense my insecurity, and I feel he wouldn't be offended if I chose to clam up and keep the rest to myself. But for the first time I want to tell someone.

Not just 'someone' – I want to tell *him*.

"I think I'm too curious not to," I confess. "I know I probably shouldn't want to know him and be all tough about it, because I don't need him, I don't…"

I can't bring my eyes to meet Erik's for fear that he'll see right through me and realize I'm not tough at all, just a needy child who desperately wants to be loved by the one person who will never love her.

"I guess," I continue, "I wish I could accidentally bump into him, share a laugh over spilled coffee or something. He wouldn't even have to know who I was. But at least I would have a face, a moment, a glimpse into a part of me I've never known."

I finally lift me eyes to meet Erik's, losing myself in the glacial pools of his irises. He places a hand on mine. "I get that," he says. "I hope you get that chance."

Yeah, me too. His hand feels like a warm blanket on a cold morning, and I try desperately to hold on to that feeling.

"How's it like living with your aunt and uncle?" Erik continues, withdrawing his hand slowly to my disappointment.

"My uncle died this past spring."

"Oh God, I'm sorry Ev – "

"It's fine."

"No, I'll stop talking."

"Erik, it's ok – these are normal questions. I just have an abnormal ability to attract death into my life, I guess. You would have liked him though, my mom and my uncle. They were…so alive. Never a dull moment, you know."

Erik nods, his eyes full of understanding for my loss. "They sound great. I hope, in time, the grief gets easier."

Everyone always says that. *It will get easier.* It's a sweet sentiment, even if it isn't that simple. "I don't think it really gets better. You just learn to live with it – adapt to your new baseline because you have no choice."

Erik nods, and I wonder if he knows something about that. "Well, I'm glad you still have your aunt."

I laugh cynically and shake my head. "Who, Catherine? You wouldn't be if you knew her! We don't exactly see the world the same way."

"Oh?" Erik says, waiting for the details.

"She lives her life angry at the past and terrified of the future. I don't even know how she and my mother are related. As we speak, she's in Brussels, probably taking bets on how the world will end in my other aunt's off-the-grid bunker. I mean, this place is *literally* off-the-grid. You 'follow the owls' to find it. But that's a story for another time."

"Which I hope to hear!"

"Trust me, it's not that interesting. Not compared to all this. It's so surreal to be here, I still can't believe it!" I smirk to myself. "I might have to send Tristan a thank you card."

Erik tilts his head slightly. "Tristan? That a friend of yours?"

I really need to stop saying my thoughts out loud. "Oh um, just a…" *How do I describe this?* "Let's just say it was a nightmare that finally ended last night."

Erik raises his eyebrows and appears to read between the lines.

"My awakening?" I suggest, lifting my shoulders.

Erik grins, his eyes fixed on me. "Well…I'm glad it's behind you."

The sun has vanished now. Erik draws my attention upward to the most magnificent star-filled sky I could have ever imagined existing, even in the furthest corners of the galaxy.

Blinding, mystical stars, so many that it's easy to forget that darkness exists in the spaces between them. Spiral galaxies are dispersed throughout the heavens, and dozens of massive moons and planets fight for their place on the brilliant night canvas. They seem to hang on the edge of the Prism's atmosphere, as if they've lost their gravitational force and are about to fall into the Prismatic, the intricacies of their craters visible to the naked eye.

"Let me know when you want to head back to Agora," I can hear Erik say.

I can't peel my eyes away from the sky. It looks like something out of a movie. "You're going to have to pull me out of this boat." *Maybe I could just fall asleep right here…*

I'm not sure how long we remain in the gondola in silence as I gape at the sky, but eventually Erik takes the reigns and steers us to a nearby dock where Cass stands waiting.

I look around the cobblestone streets. "Where's Juno?"

"I willed Cass here. You'll have to do the same."

"Actually," I ask nervously, "could I ride on Cass with you? It's been kind of an overwhelming day. In a good way, of course. Still, I don't want to lose focus and fall out of the sky."

"I don't think Juno would allow that. But sure. Come on." Erik helps me onto the silver mare before getting on himself. There's something comforting about having his arms around me as he holds on to Cass' mane – like that blanket on a cold day all over again.

I'm in a daze as we lift off. Venice slowly fades away, and I immerse myself in my first starlit journey of my first Prism night, my life forever changed.

CHAPTER 10

What Happens Tomorrow?

I have no idea what to say to Erik as we ascend the steps to Castellum, and I've officially run out of adjectives and clichés. We reach the wooden doors I'd been so impatient to walk through earlier. It feels so strange now, approaching them with hesitation. What if it really is just a dream? What if I never see this place again?

Maybe I can hold off sleep just a little longer? An hour, maybe? I can do a lot in an hour…

But I can feel it; a dull, strange new echo in my brain – my first Prism day is approaching an end and Earth is calling me back.

Erik seems to pick up on my inner turmoil with that superhuman intuition of his. "You *will* come back Ev," he assures me as he holds open the door. "This is just Day 1."

I turn briefly to look back at the new world I've discovered. "I will come back." I try to sound confident, but even as I say the words my doubt lingers. With a final sigh of temporary farewell, I step into the Forum which is still buzzing with Wakers moving in and out of the portals.

"Right! Eden Hall!" Erik suddenly exclaims, then realizes his words mean nothing. "I knew I forgot something important earlier! What do you say? Do you have enough energy for one last stop?"

Ha! It's not over yet! "Do you have to ask?"

Erik leads us toward the elevators at the end of the hall. Two dimly lit corridors sit on either side of them, camouflaged into the stone wall and barely noticeable. We take the one on the left.

"There's so much to this place," I whisper, running my fingertips over markings etched and painted on the walls, depicting the different Prism realms. Softball-sized orb-shaped lights float throughout the corridor and provide the only source of light. Yet they oddly don't appear connected to any power source.

"There's no need for electricity here," Erik explains. "That's just pure, concentrated energy. You'll find them everywhere. It's our version of the light bulb."

"Perfect! I rather hate light bulbs."

"I take it there's a story there too," he guesses correctly, not that I have any desire to get into that one.

At last, we step out into a large open space. "Eden Hall!" Erik announces, glancing at me periodically to gage my reaction.

And I thought the Forum was grand…Eden Hall gives a whole new meaning to the word!

It's an elongated cylinder the diameter of a football field, climbing at least 50 stories. An open ceiling reveals the diamond sky we just left behind, and a grand spiral escalator hugs the perimeter, with one other option for descent – a wide spiral slide that spits a person out every few seconds.

Erik starts on his tour. "Pool's over here. The second floor has billiards, poker tables, arcades…hobby stuff. Third floor has museums and art galleries. Fourth, a panoramic movie theatre. There are big band halls, restaurants…even an aquarium…I forget which floor now. Arenas, racquet courts –"

Ridiculous!

"It's like a cruise ship on steroids! How could anyone ever see it all?" I ask, baffled.

But Erik seems to take it all in stride. "Just think, how many nights you've slept so far in your life without ever coming here; 365 nights in one year alone. Trust me, you have plenty of time!"

If anyone knows anything about calculating hours, it's me. Suddenly, sleep doesn't seem like a huge waste of time anymore. "I guess when you put it that way…"

"It's an amazing gift, the Prism," Erik says, repeating his earlier sentiment. "A second life." He looks at me intently, his brow furrowing. "Don't let anything ever prevent you from coming back. All the negativity and despair…it's just not worth it if it means missing out on this. This…," he pauses, looking solemnly around the room at the limitless opportunities around us, "is something all human beings should be able to experience."

He seems to shake off whatever's troubling him, and his dimples return. "Sorry, I didn't mean to get so intense or put pressure on you. You're probably mentally exhausted as it is. It would just be a shame not to see you here again."

Yes, it would, I silently agree.

"What happens tomorrow?" I ask Erik as we make our way back to my dimension. There's only one thing I care about right now, and that's guaranteeing my return. "I'm not exactly Miss Sunshine and Rainbows on Earth all the time. What if I have too much baggage to make it back?"

"We all have baggage Ev. Some of us are just better at storing it away from the eyes of the world." Erik stops before we reach my room and turns me toward him gently by my shoulders. "The Prism knows when to bring you back. It's an intelligence we're always connected to, even if we don't understand it. And it's pretty forgiving. You'll know when you feel right and when you don't."

I study Erik's bright eyes, wishing I shared his confidence. "It scares me," I confide, "putting my faith in something I can't see or control. I want to be the one behind the wheel." *And I haven't been for a long time.*

"But that's what I'm trying to tell you," Erik insists, his gaze intensifying. "You are."

Erik's been nothing but honest with me so far, at least from what I can tell. I settle a little, considering that perhaps I have more control than I allow myself to believe, considering that perhaps I'm not destined to completely fail at this Prism thing. "I guess I should try to rest and convince myself I'm not insane."

"Ah, sanity is overrated. Nothing wrong with a little craziness, in my opinion," Erik replies as we resume walking.

My pulse quickens as we arrive at my dimension door. I'm not quite ready for him to go. There's something about his presence…he makes everything feel balanced and calms the storm of thoughts racing through my brain. "Thank you, for today," I tell him. "Thanking you doesn't even begin to cover it."

Our eyes lock and he grins at me shyly. "You can thank me by returning. Then I'll know I did my job well."

"Honestly, you could have totally sucked at your job, and I would still want to come back."

"Yeah, I gave myself too much credit there, didn't I?"

"No," I assure him, trying to still my heartbeat, "you did good…magister." My hand grips the doorknob behind my back, but I can't bring myself to open it, not ready for the night to end.

He smiles back and brushes another wayward hair away from my face before putting his hands back in the pockets of his slacks. The goosebumps return.

"Goodnight Ms Cleary," he says finally, then nods and starts to walk away. "And *when* you're back tomorrow," he adds, turning around and walking backwards to the elevator, "you can find me at the Gastronomique…third floor Eden Hall. The gang, we gather there some mornings. I'll wait for you."

"I'll be there!" I promise.

Erik gives me one last smile. "I know," he says, then turns to board the elevator, nearly colliding with a little boy who skips out and in the opposite direction, holding a swirly lollypop twice his size.

I let out the breath I didn't even realize I'd been holding and let myself into the room. Inside my dimension, the night air streams in through the open terrace doors, and the little orb of energy appears above the lamp base, illuminating the bare walls. *Too bright!* Within a second, my wish is accommodated, and the bulb dims to an ideal intensity. *Fascinating!*

This room is my blank canvass. I recall what Erik said about creating anything within it. *Anything!*

But where to even start?

Baby steps. I need to process the world outside first before attempting to create a brand new one in here.

Stepping out onto the balcony, the Prism steals my breath away again, the lights of nearby realms flickering around the perimeter of the Prismatic, their brightness no match for the star-studded heavens. I just barely make out Erik walking down the Avenue below. A figure approaches to meet him, red hair flowing behind her like moving strokes of a paintbrush. Erik looks up at the balconies of Castellum, and I take a few steps back so that he doesn't see me spying, trying to push aside a little jealous whisper that's nagging in my ear. As Maeve pulls Erik away and they disappear among the other moving bodies, I remember what Erik said about negative emotions and silence the whispers, then retreat into the room and fall onto the bed.

The day replays like a movie in my mind as I stare up at the white ceiling. *How can this be real?* At last, my eyelids give their last warning as I ponder the possibility of a psychotic break for the hundredth time.

CHAPTER 11

No Coincidences

As soon as I hear my ear-splitting alarm I know I'm home, and there goes my brain again for a run on the hamster wheel as the thoughts hit me, one after the next.

Did I dream or hallucinate the entire thing? Was any of it real? Is there something wrong with me?

I expect the Prism to begin fading from my memory like a typical dream. Yet my memories remain vivid and steadfast. There's no need to desperately hang on to them. Not this time.

I stare at the ceiling, Erik's words replaying in my mind.

Don't let anything ever prevent you from coming back… Don't let anything ever prevent you from coming back…

It's Saturday. With Catherine's absence, the apartment is eerily quiet.

Then reality calls. "Darn it!" *Peterson!* And this time, there's no Prism, real or imagined, to save me from it.

Traffic in Paris is as one would expect – irritating and constant, even on a weekend. But today I steer my scooter though the streets with a surprising sense of ease, too preoccupied with another world to notice the annoyances of this one. I step onto the charcoal office carpet with ten minutes to spare and note the absence of my usual nausea. Unfortunately, the antiseptic smell remains.

The day proves expectedly uneventful, the highlight being Nina dropping a case of thumb tacks on the floor which Vincent steps on, to everyone's amusement. He spends the afternoon in his office cursing and trying to remove them from the sole of his $500 shoes.

"Really?" Nina asks when I break the news about Tristan. "Ev, I had no idea!"

"I didn't tell you everything."

"I figured that much. I really wish you did."

"It doesn't matter anymore. He's out of my life now, finally!" It feels so good to say that and actually believe it.

"Guess I should have taken you up on those fancy dinners while I had the chance," Nina jokes, pouting. "Hey, did you hear about those two homeless men they found dead? Close to your neighborhood – Rue Antoine."

"Oh, no…I didn't. How awful. Was it the heat?" August was being nasty this year.

"That's just it – it wasn't. It's unexplained. My cousin told me." Nina had a lot of cousins. Most of them seemed to work in law enforcement or the renovation business. "Ramos said he saw this once before, a homeless teen who died of unknown causes. No trauma, no overdose, no dehydration, nothing like that."

"Did they do an autopsy?"

"Yeah, inconclusive. But then they were told to leave it alone, for some reason. When he tried to access the results again, they were gone from the system. It was very odd."

"Yeah, that is strange," I agree. I can't help but wonder if they ever got the chance to see the Prism before they ran out of time.

The hours drag. On my break I open a search browser to look up the story Nina's told me about, since it's so close to home. The article has basic information, not much more than Nina already disclosed. Found in an alley, poor souls. Young too.

But it's the photo of the taped-off police scene that sends a shiver down my spine. Standing a block away from the police vehicles are two figures I've seen before. Hulk and Shorty. They seem to be observing the scene from afar.

Stop overanalyzing. They hang around the neighborhood all the time. Still…why are they even here?

Five o'clock can't come faster, and I'm a bundle of nervous energy when I finally push the gas pedal on my scooter. As I head up Rue Saint-Jacques toward the Seine, my thoughts inadvertently turn to Tristan. I know his pride is even more important to him than his money and I begin to compulsively check my mirrors.

Stop being paranoid.

But my paranoid alter-ego starts to feel validated when I spot a black Mercedes with heavy tint on the windows two cars back. The car stays with me until I cross the river, but I manage to lose it at a red light a few blocks later. *Don't be ridiculous. There are thousands of black Mercedes in Paris. Thousands.*

When I pull up in front of my building, I notice the black Mercedes is missing from its usual spot under the crooked streetlamp, and a small shiver runs up my arms.

Inside the flat, I draw the curtains and peek out onto the street, finding the same scene as every other day, and another dark sedan now parked in Hulk's spot. Curious timing.

Let it go. Happy thoughts!

The flat is eerily silent, absent the usual hum of the news in the background. For a moment I wish Catherine was home, senseless nagging and all. But the sentiment doesn't last very long.

The dusty grandfather clock in the living room reads 6:03, leading me to compare the experience of time in my two realities. Time was barely a consideration in the Prism. But on Earth, time is everything.

I groan, realizing it won't be dark for hours. A rumbling sound reminds me that hunger is a real thing again. A slice of pizza at a nearby bistro does the trick and kills a whopping 20 minutes. I take my time walking home, at one point passing a familiar restaurant and wondering if the owners replaced a certain shattered glass panel yet.

Still no sign of Hulk or his sidekick…

The sun hasn't yet set by the time I step back into the apartment. I kill another few hours in my uncle's study reading *Mysteries of the Arabian Desert*, a book of artifacts uncovered in the Middle East. One of the pages is marked: a picture of a tarnished silver trinket box, a singular emerald in the center of the square lid. *Discovered by Timothy Dupont, 2002.* A warmth fills my chest and spreads to my fingertips. *I really miss you.*

Finally, my eyelids begin to feel as if made of concrete and I head for my bed where the torturous task of willing my brain to sleep begins. *Turn. Turn again. Get up. Watch TV. Lie Down. Repeat.*

But the harder I try to relax the faster my neurons fire and the louder the second-hand ticks. Once again, I find myself detesting the cruel inconvenience of time.

CHAPTER 12

Seize the Night

I can't remember at what time my brain finally gave in to sleep, but it's all here, just as I remember it! The empty room, the door, the same view from the terrace. A breeze brushes against my skin, and it's enough to make my heart want to burst through my rib cage, my pulse throbbing in my neck from the adrenaline.

I'm back! Those torturous pre-Prism hours paid off. This is no fantasy!

It's real! It's actually real!

And I'm not insane, which is a welcome bonus.

Where did Erik say to meet? The Gastro-something, third floor…

I'm almost out the door when I notice it: a new addition to my room. It's a silver trinket box lying on the nightstand, identical to the one my uncle discovered, emerald and all. I pick it up, a little suspicious of its uncanny resemblance. Has the Prism pulled it out of my mind and replicated it here? I don't know why this particular box, of all things. But through my confusion I begin to glimpse it – the possibilities of my dimension, to create anything.

All in good time. I place the trinket box away in my nightstand

and prepare for my second Prism day, opening the wardrobe to find the shoes I'd left floating in the Prismatic occupying their usual place. I dress in record time and fly out the door.

When I board the elevator, I test a theory…

"Eden Hall, third floor."

My guess is spot on, and seconds later I'm stepping out next to the museum. The Gastronomique stands across from me, flanked by two potted Cyprus trees. I follow the intricate banister of the circular hallway to the café where I'm met with what looks like every variety of pastry or dessert that has ever been created. Tall cylinders filled to the brim with colorful bubbling liquids and mists line one of the walls. The setup seems more suitable for a mad scientist's lab, but it doesn't dissuade Wakers from trying sips of the mystery substances and giggling their faces off.

As much as I want to try it myself, I'm too busy looking for a face in the crowd. Finally, I find it near the back of the cafe. Erik beams at me, his dimples discernible even from across the room. He rises from the table and weaves between the guests wearing a simple white t-shirt and jeans, then immediately embraces me for a few moments I shamelessly don't want to end.

"You did it Ev! I knew you'd be back!" he says, still holding on.

"Did you? That's more than I can say."

He lets go and studies me with that tilt of his head again, his blue eyes just as bright as I remember them. "How do you feel?"

"Um…relieved, to start." I'm surprised to find I'm just as relieved to see Erik as I am to be back. I keep that to myself. "And hungry, in the Prism sense, that is. Look at this place!"

We fill our plates and take our seats by a window that

overlooks a lush green jungle with a path weaving through the brush. My selection of delicacies doesn't disappoint, and I catch Erik observing me with an amused smirk on his face.

"Don't judge me," I defend myself, shoving a pastry puff in my mouth. "These are delicious!"

"Oh, no judgement, trust me. My first time here, I went for thirds!" he admits. "So, um…I thought maybe you'd like to see the Luminary today,"

The Luminary. Right…that place sounded awesome. Then again, what didn't?

"Yeah, sounds great! Are any of your friends coming?" As I wipe some jam from my mouth, I feel a touch of guilt for wishing one specific friend wouldn't make an appearance.

"Not sure. They would usually be here by now. We can give it a few more minutes. They might have other plans."

"How do people even communicate here? It's weird not seeing everyone glued to a cellphone. It's like the twilight zone!"

Erik shakes his head emphatically. "You won't find any of those in the Nucleus. Maybe humanity secretly longs to be free of those time devouring, antisocial things. Or maybe the Prism realizes that they would only prevent us from living in the moment and thankfully bans them for us. Besides, I find most people that get in here realize there's more to life than selfies and tweets anyway."

Interesting. "So, it's back to the good old days of telegrams then?"

"Not exactly. The Prism sorts through the jumble of thoughts and helps you connect when you need to. If you don't make plans, things have a way of just falling into place. You'll run into the right people, at the right time, that sort of thing. It's a little eerie sometimes, but it works."

After about ten minutes (or whatever that amounts to in

Prism time) of no Jenna, Fox, or Maeve, and both of us satisfied with our multiple shots of Persimmon Guava Giggle Mist that leaves us keeling over in fits of unprovoked laughter, we finally head out on our own and enter the jungle we saw from the window. The path leads to a tunnel of interwoven vines and branches.

"The path on the opposite side of Eden Hall leads to Cascada," Erik explains as we navigate the tunnel. "This one…"

"The Climbing Gardens!" I finish for him as we step onto a crisp green carpet and into yet another world. Immediately, we're dwarfed by towering trees and flower stalks as thick as telephone poles and as tall as houses. The blooms themselves are magnificent and magnified tenfold, every vein and variation in hue breathtakingly obvious.

Rows upon rows of plant life form a complex and vast maze. "This is enormous!"

"And confusing," Erik warns. "Not the best place to visit in the dark, speaking from experience."

I'm still mesmerized by the flora when a drop of water hits the edge of my cheek, followed by another. Suddenly, the heavens open without warning and in the flash of an instant drench us relentlessly. It's the kind of downpour that would usually send me running for cover. But as the rain washes over my body, I realize this is no ordinary rainfall. It falls out of a brilliant blue sky, the water encasing me in a sort of time capsule. I watch time decelerate around me, and my heart rate slows to an almost indiscernible pace. A warmth transcends my core like a welcome electric shock, revitalizing every cell in my body. Eventually, I feel the water slipping off my skin, taking the warmth with it until it finally evaporates through the tips of my fingers. The shower disappears as swiftly as it came, leaving no trace of itself – only a memory and a longing. I exhale slowly, trying to hold on to it a little longer and imprint the experience into my brain.

"Does it always feel like that?" I whisper, still recovering.

Erik grins knowingly. "Every time. Told you it was different here."

I'm dying for more of whatever that was, but I'm left wanting for now as the rain shows no signs of returning.

We take a convoluted route through the gardens on our way to the Luminary, marveling at the countless creations that surround us. A striking display of red snapdragons brings something to mind.

"So, are you and Maeve a…thing?" I ask Erik. As soon as the last syllable leaves my mouth, I'm horrified that I've actually said the words out loud.

"Maeve? No," he responds firmly, looking straight ahead. "Why?"

Why did I open my big mouth? But I see Erik's temples twitching ever so slightly, and if there's one thing I've learned from observing Tristan Sarazen it's the meaning of the temple twitch. "Never mind. I must have just misread things," I reply, trying to bury the topic. But in my gut, I'm certain that whatever Maeve wants from Erik is more than friendship, whether Erik knows it or cares to admit it. And Erik's odd reaction tells me I'm onto something.

As I'm about to ask how many more tunnels we're going to have to traverse, Erik finds the clearing he's been searching for. There it looms, in the center of a vast courtyard, its view obstructed by the trunks of massive oaks whose canopies steal away the sky. I find myself in a game of hide-and-seek as I try to behold the entire structure through the trees. Finally, we're close enough, with nothing in our way.

The Luminary.

It conveys beauty and symmetry, yet simultaneously the strength of a fortress that cannot be taken. Its two towers stretch beyond the treetops, a combination of medieval and renaissance architecture. The unblemished exterior is overlaid with ivory limestone, and the grand steel front doors look like they belong on an ancient citadel. Two bartizan towers project from the front of the ninth and uppermost floor, which Erik tells me house colossal energy orbs that light up the front courtyard at night.

As Erik chatters on about facts and history, we head inside to an open interior courtyard. A three-sided display board stands in the center, listing the Luminary's attractions. My eyes follow the balconies as they rise floor by floor to the domed ceiling, where my breath is taken hostage yet again.

Every inch of the dome is covered by a painting — heavenly bodies and galaxies set against a bluish periwinkle haze, the words *Carpe Noctem* written inside the center star. The entire scene seems to move and come alive before my eyes like a live feed.

"Seize the night," I translate under my breath.

"Michelangelo."

"What?" I turn to Erik in confusion. "*The* Michelangelo?"

"Same one. He's one of our celebrity Prism alumni. Not surprising he made it in here, I suppose. You'll find many works he painted while at the Prism in the Eden Hall Museum. The *Galaxia Hyacinthum,* or *Blue Galaxy,* is his most popular Prism work. Mesmerizing, isn't it?"

Still not the right word. "Yeah, you could say that…"

"This is probably a good time to mention that you can't take anything out of the Prism," Erik adds. "Anything you acquire or create here remains in the Prism, indefinitely. There are things here the world has never seen, and that's one of them. It's an odd feeling, knowing you're privileged to behold something most people never will." Erik lets me process the new intel, then adds softly under his breath. "Both a proud and sad moment."

"Doesn't seem fair at all." I begin to sense an angry energy in my gut and barely notice the Wakers streaming into the main floor auditorium.

"Classes will be starting soon," Erik points out. "Let's see…*Foundations* is well worth it if you're interested. And Robert does a much better job at explaining this place than I ever could."

Ah yes! Robert Crawford. The man with all the answers. "I guess more information couldn't hurt," I agree.

I glance up a final time at the painted masterpiece, awestruck for the millionth time.

But as perfect as everything seems, I can't seem to shake Catherine's voice in the back of my head, warning me that the ball will drop at any moment, catapulting my perfect world into ruins.

CHAPTER 13

Revelations

The red velvet chairs make the lecture hall feel more like an opera house, and the room is already half full by the time we arrive.

"Most people attend more than once," Erik says.

"Are you staying?"

"Wouldn't mind. But first, introductions."

I follow Erik to the edge of the lecturer's podium where Robert Crawford stands, sizing up the growing crowd. He's a good-looking man of average height, with a square jaw, slightly greying sandy brown hair, and a matching sandy brown sports jacket. The lifelines on his face reflect an earned wisdom, and his hazel eyes twinkle with a dreamy idealism, much like Erik's do. He appears poised and relaxed at the front of such an intimidating room.

Robert's warm smile widens when we approach. "Erik! Haven't you heard me babble on about this enough?"

"Just keeping you on your toes," Erik teases back.

The professor leans in to ask Erik a question in a quieter voice. "Are you coming tomorrow?"

"Of course."

"Good, good. We have some new developments to discuss."

Erik catches my curious gaze and offers a vague clarification: "A study group some of us attend."

Now it's Robert's turn to notice me. "Are you one of the poor souls suffering through my class today?"

I shake his outstretched hand. "Everest, Cleary. Erik's my magister. He speaks very highly of you. Practically insisted I listen to you speak."

"Did he, now? So, Everest? Like the mountain?"

"My mother said my father was a climber," I explain for the hundredth time, wondering if I should just change my name to Everest-Just-Like-the-Mountain Cleary to save myself some time. "She named me after the mountain he always wanted to climb."

"How interesting. Cleary, you said?" He looks perplexed as his eyebrows come together and form wrinkles above his nose. "So, first impressions of the Prism Ms Cleary?"

"Um…too many! But let's start with 'surreal' for arguments sake."

Robert's smile returns and his wrinkles soften. "Yes. 'Surreal' is about right. It's truly an amazing gift, the Prism."

"Erik's been telling me," I reply, shooting Erik a grateful look.

"You have one of the best magisters the Prism can offer. Erik has been here only a short while but has an instinctual understanding of this world." Robert pauses and looks at me, his wrinkles returning. "You have very interesting eyes," he adds, off topic. "The world is a small place, isn't it?" he whispers, more to himself. "I hope you enjoy the class Everest. Um, Erik…a moment. I have a small favor to ask."

Erik wavers and shoots me a quick glance. "Go on," I insist. "I can survive a few hours without you."

"I'll find you after the class," he promises.

As I take my seat, I see Robert whisper something to Erik again before Erik turns and leaves the room, giving me a wave on the way out. Robert then proceeds to address the class through the chatter.

"Good morning new and returning Wakers to another Foundations. Quick survey – how many of you have sat here before?" A third of the class raise their hands, and I realize Robert probably has ulterior motives for asking the question.

"Still consistent," he mutters. "All right then, new people. You fall sleep, most likely after the best day you've had in years, and then moments later you're wondering if your grandmother put some special mushrooms in that soup, or if your crazy neighbor finally snapped and murdered you in your sleep."

The class chuckles collectively.

"You must be overwhelmed," he continues. "Tell you the truth, I still am. Almost every time I'm here I have a moment or two – or six – where I think to myself, 'this is *absolutely* impossible! This is nuts!' Because it is! And yet, here we are.

"So, what is it? What is this place? Why is it here? Why are *we* here?"

I feel like I'm on the cusp of a great revelation. *All right! This is it! Bring it on – tell me everything!*

Robert begins to draw a rectangle on the chalkboard. "There's still much we don't know, but we've figured some things out over the years. Think of your body as a generator that powers a great door. This generator runs on something special — a kind of energy. It needs a certain amount of that energy to generate enough force to open that door. But only some succeed at producing enough of it. Call it happy juice, joy, love — it's all the same, really. The name doesn't matter so much as what it does, how it makes us *feel*. What we know for certain is that it's generated in moments of extreme, deep-level happiness or emotional release, or as we refer to it here, 'awakening.' It finally opens that door and lets you in here, to the most incredible reality you've ever experienced.

"You probably know all this already, from your magisters, yes?"

The sea of heads begins to nod, and Robert proceeds.

"Well, what you might *not* know yet is that this energy, this special ingredient is latent in every human being. We all have the potential to come here. We're all worthy of it. The Prism doesn't pick and choose who can access it – it just listens, like a mathematician looking for the right variables to solve an equation. And when all your variables line up - presto! It opens a world of possibilities beyond your wildest dreams!"

Robert steps away from his amateur drawings of doors and lines and continues. "So…who created it? You're all wondering. Well…allow yourselves to consider that there is a creative power behind the universe, an intelligence – scientific, spiritual, whatever suits you. If we're part of this intelligence – derived from it – then naturally the part should share some properties of the whole, wouldn't you agree? And what better proof do we have of this than our own imagination. Imagination," the professor elaborates, "is our own everyday magic. It's possible thanks to one of the most powerful things in the universe: thoughts. Thoughts lead to ideas, and there is nothing that exists without an idea that came before it. Not a single thing! It's those ideas that gave way to airplanes and telephones and rocket ships, and perhaps in the future to teleportation devices, and maybe even children who listen to their parents."

More echoes of laughter.

Robert smirks to himself. "I can dream. In any case, if we can imagine and create those wonderful things, who's to say we couldn't create the Prism with the help of some cosmic intangible link — to turn formless energy into something real. It's certainly not impossible. In fact, I'm sure most of you are rethinking your definition of that word as we speak."

You can hear a pin drop as everyone ponders what Robert Crawford's said and hangs on his every word. *A cosmic link. And we're all a part of it...*

"Just theories," Robert says. "But here, our minds influence the landscape of this reality. *Our* minds. Explain that."

I can't stop the words from leaving my lips. "But why us, specifically? I mean…why aren't more of us here?" *Should I have raised my hand? Too late now.*

Robert makes his way to the edge of the podium. He takes a seat on the steps before he answers, a slight tension visible on his face. "Yes, a good question I can't fully answer. But…I believe life is about growth and progress. If we choose to stagnate, we defy that life principle that always strives to be evolving. If you ask me, you're here because on some level you believe in that principle more than others. It's that belief that unlocks your potential, for the desire to progress is inherently good. Stagnation leads to despair and shutting down of mental processes and stifles the will to live. And that state of mind can never bring about evolution. Your belief allows you to operate on a higher frequency, emitting energy that is purer and stronger — the kind you need to open *that* door," he says, pointing to the chalkboard. "You persevere. You use a crisis to create more energy. Perhaps that's why *you're* here."

I don't give myself enough time to process the answer, another question already on its way. "And returning?" I press, "how do we guarantee that?"

"Patience Ms Cleary! I was just getting to that! The formula is rather simple," he goes on, addressing the room, "although not always easy to follow. There *will* be times when we won't make it back, unless we're unbelievably skilled at not letting our worst day get to us. Negative emotions are part of what makes us human after all. However, in excess they're dangerous and can quickly become a contagion from which recovery is slow and miserable.

"One thing is clear," he adds, "whether you succeed at returning or not is all about state of mind. If you believe you can do something, eventually you will. It's a simple law. Many of the negative things we experience — misery, poverty, war, stress, even illness — are the products of hardships and limitations humans place upon themselves. It's a hard pill to swallow, accepting that we are, either individually or as a society, the cause of many of our problems.

"So, to answer your question Ms Cleary," he says, looking right at me, "start by not being the cause of your problems – start by limiting that contagion and remember that good is something we are all entitled to."

A sudden fit of coughing erupts from the front row. Robert jerks to look at the woman responsible for it, who's busy blowing her nose. I expect Robert to ask if she's ok, maybe offer a glass of water or a replacement tissue. But he simply eyes her with an unexpected coldness. The pretty interrupter appears to realize she's not welcome and gives me a peculiar glance with tired, blood-shot eyes on her way out of the room, her curly black hair bouncing behind her. I recall what Erik said about illness having no place in the Prism.

What was that all about then?

A man follows the girl out, a tall and lanky type. As he climbs the stairs, his arms swinging back and forth, I notice something familiar on the inside of his wrist — a tattoo of a "V" in thick black ink, much like the one I'd seen on Hulk's wrist.

Another coincidence?

After the doors shuts, the tension in Robert's face seems to soften. "If you're interested in some fun facts," he says, "Johanna Billings teaches a course on Prism mythology. There are those who believe that the great pyramids were built in tribute to the Prism by those who had seen it. The pyramids, along with obelisks, sprouted up all over the world like secret tributes signaling other Wakers that they were not alone. Pyramids have been found underwater, buried under sand and rock, and across continents, built by civilizations who would have had no knowledge of each another.

"And what sits atop an obelisk if not a pyramid. Or is it a Prism? Is that the true metaphor?"

He walks back to the podium and puts his hands into the pocket of his slacks. He eyes the room once more, as if memorizing the individual faces before he finally settles on mine yet again. "I don't want to spoil Johanna's class," he says, "so, that's all I'll reveal. Now go on, enjoy your paradise, and try not to let your heads spin too much."

CHAPTER 14

Through the Mist

My head isn't just spinning as I leave the lecture – it's close to exploding! I'm inspired, intrigued, confused. Robert raised so many more questions, and I don't know whether to be upset with or indebted to him for that.

I admire Michelangelo's exquisite masterpiece once more before leaving the Luminary, hopeful I can live up to its call.

Carpe Noctem. Seize the night…

Erik's nowhere in sight in the Luminary courtyard, and I'm surprised by how disappointed that makes me feel. Usually, I prefer being on my own. Patience isn't my strong suit, so it doesn't take long for me to give in to my curiosity and start contemplating what corner of the Prism I'll tackle next. It shouldn't be that hard. I'm a pretty good navigator, and there's tons of friendly people around I could ask for directions. *Are there info booths with maps, maybe? That would be useful.*

As I make my way between the towering oaks towards Castellum, I see a male figure heading toward the tunnels that connect to the gardens. It's uncanny: the hair, the posture…I even sense an air of entitlement about him.

Impossible! There's no way…

He saunters confidently behind a group of Wakers. I wait

for him to turn around so I can know for certain, but he disappears into the leafy tunnels before I can confirm anything.

Before I can determine if I've just seen Tristan Sarazen.

Don't be paranoid. Someone like Tristan would never find his way into the Prism…no chance…

Convinced by my brilliant deduction, I head towards the doors of Eden Hall as I try to silence Catherine's little voice in my head. My memory fills with flashbacks of alleyways…

Suddenly, I feel a hand touch my shoulder blade.

"Was it terrible without m…?"

I spin around to face him. My expression must give away my dread because Erik's worry becomes obvious. "I'm…sorry, I startled you."

I release the breath I've been holding in and feel foolish. "No. Sorry! I…just thought I saw someone earlier. It's nothing."

Erik doesn't look convinced. "You sure it's really nothing?"

"Yes, yeah…how was your morning?" I ask, curious as to where Robert sent him and trying to change the subject.

"Nothing too exciting. More important question is, how was *your* morning?" Erik grins perceptively, like he already knows my answer.

"Do you have to ask? It's like my whole life I've been reading a book with pages missing!" I admit. "I see why hearing it all once isn't enough. And why you like him – Robert. He really knows this place, doesn't he?"

"Yeah, he's always trying to help others 'embrace their potential' here. Rattles on like a broken record about it."

"Sounds like someone else I know," I tease Erik. "What do you talk about in your study group?"

Erik shrugs and answers curtly. "It's more a niche interest. I'll tell you about it one day. But for right now, what's the plan?"

I'm beginning to appreciate just how much humans rely on clocks. Damn those blasted things – it's hard without them. And the drawn-out Prism days are throwing me off completely. Feels like noon, but judging by the sun…is it mid-morning?

"Stop counting the minutes," Erik reminds me, snooping in my brain again. "Just seize the night, remember? Here's an idea…I ran into Jenna. She suggested a cruise through the Isles of Edenia. She's never been on a boat before — says she wants to 'conquer her fear of water in the safest place possible.' "

I try to downplay my extreme eagerness. "Sounds totally logical. I guess we should go then – you know, for moral support."

"Right," Erik agrees as he winks at me, "just for moral support."

* * *

"Ready?"

I'm not sure how to answer Erik as I stand next to him in front of the Edenia portal, unable to move my legs. Going through the portal seemed all well and good until I realized I had to *actually* go through the portal. It's not like there's just portals around every corner in the real world and I've had a ton of practice with this. "Maybe," I hesitate, taking a breath. "What's on the other side?"

"That depends on you. You decide where you want to end up. But I'm here if you need help deciding."

Erik offers to take my hand and I welcome having him direct the first journey. "I'm going through a portal!" I mumble. It doesn't even sound believable. My exhale is loud and procrastinating, but I know what I want, even if my body hasn't caught up to my thoughts just yet. "Lead the way!"

As we step through the entrance, the illusion of hazy chateaus and rooftops begins to fade away and is replaced by a milky white mist, similar to dry ice, only denser. I feel inexplicably weightless, as if walking on air; like if a gust of wind came along it would blow me clear away. Erik walks on unassumingly like he's taken the journey a hundred times before.

Our minute in the mist is unlike any other minute I've ever experienced — a feeling of complete vulnerability as I wait at the mercy of the portal to see where it will take me. Then, slowly the white substance begins to disperse. The cool fog slips away as we step into another realm and come face-to-face with an outstanding replica of the Parthenon.

* * *

"I'm having second thoughts about this."

Jenna's wrapped the drawstrings of her shorts so tightly around her finger that I worry the tip will become gangrenous and fall off. At least on Earth it probably would.

"Stop worrying," Fox reassures her. "If we're going to capsize and drown we might as well do it in paradise." He points to the name of our vessel: *La Fortuna.* "See, we already have luck on our side!"

"Oh, thanks, how do you say it, Captain Obvious?" Jenna huffs, unconvinced.

I notice we're still one short. "Where's Maeve?"

Three pairs of shoulders shrug. "We don't see her that often. Maybe every third or fourth Prism day?" Fox says, looking to the others for confirmation as he ties back his long black hair.

Jenna seems to think about it for a moment. "Something like that. I don't ask. We all have different situations going on. Or maybe Fox finally annoyed her to the point of no return. It's a definite possibility."

Fox just snorts, pretending to be offended, but offers Jenna a sweet teasing smile which she immediately returns.

I take a seat on the bow as the boat gathers speed and try to imprint the views of the shoreline on my memory. We join twenty other vessels on route to an island that resembles Santorini, with its brilliant white buildings and peacock-blue roofs rising out of the Prismatic like Poseidon's palace. After docking, there's time for a refreshing dip before we head off to explore the market.

"You can't take anything out of the Prism," Jenna reminds me as we venture off on our own. "I'm sure Erik already covered that. But you can keep some things in your dimension, if you want to."

Jenna talks a lot! I don't think I get many syllables in, but I do learn all about Jenna's family, and her abuela Marisol's arthritis, and the pet ferret she had when she was five that got eaten by a shark when it fell off her uncle's fishing boat. Surprisingly, she doesn't tell me what it was doing on the fishing boat, and I dare not ask.

At last, she takes a breath and I tell her I'm going to check out some of the art canvases for a while.

It's a generously sized market. By fluke, I end up browsing art next to a bistro where Erik and Fox have ended up. I spot Jenna preoccupied with some headbands at the shop across the street and decide to get as much quiet time as I can before she finds me again.

"I don't know why I drink this stuff here," I overhear Fox grumble as he sips a cup of coffee. "I don't even like it."

"Earthly habits die hard," Erik replies.

"Speaking of …maybe you'll finally break one of yours."

I don't intend to eavesdrop, but I'm not exactly doing much to stop myself. I try to stay concealed behind a large canvass and point my ear in the direction of the conversation I have no right to hear.

Fox motions to something Erik's holding. I can't see what it is, but Erik slips it into his pocket. "When will you learn that you can't fool me," Fox says. "You like her."

"Who?"

"Who do you think?"

Erik looks around uncomfortably. "Everest? Well, yeah…why wouldn't I like her."

"Don't be a smart ass."

Erik pauses a moment. "Okay, so I like her. She's interesting. We can have a real conversation."

I feel that familiar warmth creep into my cheeks.

"That's hard to find, man," Fox says. "And she seems normal. A step up from that girl Tommy introduced you to, what was her name? She always talked about herself in the third person…"

"It's not like you've had any better luck," Erik replies defensively.

Fox chuckles and lifts his rejected coffee in a toast. "Then may you end this vicious cycle for the both of us."

Erik laughs back. "Let's not get ahead of ourselves mate. She's just a friend."

"Wait, you didn't tell her about —"

"No! No."

"Good. We can't risk it."

"I know."

"And Maeve? Does she know about that?"

What does Maeve have to do with anything? I can see Erik shifting in his chair. "Not sure I need to get into that," he finally replies.

"It's always better to be upfront man," Fox warns. "The truth comes out one way or another. Don't let it come out the way that bites you."

Erik looks away. "Yeah. I know."

Feeling guilty, I put an end to my prying before my luck runs out, shamefully annoyed that I'm not privy to Erik's secrets. Satisfied the boys haven't seen me, I count 10 Mississippi's before making my approach, but just as I'm about to round the corner, Jenna reappears.

"Ok, Everest. You're turn. Tell me absolutely everything about Montmartre!"

* * *

We stay adrift on the Prismatic after leaving the island at sunset. Fox weaves boldly between the other boats – a thrill he and Erik enjoy, but Jenna not so much. He finally settles us down in perfect position to witness the sun's masterful performance from the best seats in the house.

I sneak away to the bow to take in the view and smell Erik's scent before he sits next to me, trying unsuccessfully not to let it distract me.

"Thanks for inviting me along," I tell him, feeling my pulse quickening.

Erik brings his hand to his head and fixes his windblown hair. "You don't have to keep thanking me. You're a part of the group now – if you want to be of course. No pressure."

I turn to meet his gaze. His eyes reflect the sky and bear into my own as if searching for something.

"Um…" He reaches into the pocket of his shorts and pulls out a small box. "I saw something today and thought it was meant for you. Wrapped it myself."

"Obviously!" I play along, admiring the flawless wrapping job. Was this what he was concealing from Fox earlier?

"It's just a small thing from the group — to celebrate your awakening. And don't worry," Erik assures grinning, "it didn't cost a thing!"

I retrieve the object from Erik's palm and unwrap the ribbon and paper. My mouth falls open when I lift the lid. The pendant seems to leap out from the black velvet inside – a bluish-grey trapezoid gemstone, atop which sits an iridescent opal triangle. "It's beautiful," I tell him, appreciating the resemblance to a snow-capped mountain. "So clever. Thank you. That was thoughtful of you…and everyone else."

I can't tell if Erik's cheeks flush or if it's just the sky playing tricks on my eyes.

"May I?" he asks. He takes the necklace out of the box and proceeds to fasten the chain around my neck, waiting until I've gathered my hair to one side. I can no longer deny the electricity building between us as his fingers lightly brush my skin and send those shivers shooting down my spine. I release my hair and simply smile in thanks again, meeting his gaze one more awkward time before reluctantly turning my attention back towards the horizon. The last of the sun's rays vanish far too quickly as the night inches closer.

"I think I might go lie down in the cabin," Jenna announces behind us.

"Oh, come on!" Fox pouts. "You're going to miss the stars – that's literally the best part!"

Jenna considers it for a moment, then shakes her head emphatically. "It's been fun, but I don't know if I want to be on a boat in the dark, even here. Let me know when we dock." With her fear not entirely conquered, she gestures a salute and heads below deck, leaving Fox looking a bit dejected.

As I wave to her, I glimpse something trailing in the water behind us. It looks like a half-submerged balloon. The darkness obscures it as I squint to make it out through an encroaching fog.

"What is that?" I ask the boys.

As the water carries it closer, my intrigue is replaced by shock and confusion. The balloon is the lifeless body of a dolphin, its grey skin streaked with blood, its flesh pierced with a spear.

Fox instantly puts his hand up to his lips. "Shhh! If Jenna sees she'll go ballistic!"

I can't make any sense of what I'm seeing. The perfect illusion has been shattered.

This doesn't belong here. No way this belongs here! This is supposed to be paradise...

The blood from the wound on the dolphin's head trickles and pools around the creature's glassy marble eyes. My throat feels dry. I'm confused, angry...

This isn't funny!

"Is it dead? I thought nothing bad ever happens here?" I look at Fox and Erik, waiting for an explanation.

Fox looks as stunned as I feel. "I don't know. I've never seen anything like this," he replies solemnly.

Erik looks just as defeated. He stands next to me, silent and motionless, for the first time not having all the answers.

The dolphin bobs before us for an eerie minute before finally disappearing, the Prism absorbing its body. Everything around us resets to perfect, everything except our tainted memory which seems to overshadow everything else.

We sit in uncomfortable silence the entire journey back to the marina, and make sure to keep the incident from Jenna, faking our best smiles upon docking before heading to the portal. Fox and Jenna walk ahead of us, Fox's usual tall posture diminished by his slumped shoulders.

"Are you okay?" Erik asks as we head towards the portal.

I can't get the image of the creature's blood-stained eye out of my mind. It's like it's looking right at me… "Yeah," I lie. "It's just unsettling."

"I'm sure there's an explanation."

But I can see Erik's just as unnerved as I am, and I can't shake the feeling that whatever, or whoever is responsible isn't finished. I feel fooled, and suddenly very guarded about giving up control of my body to the portal.

"Go on ahead," I tell Erik as I summon Juno. "I'll meet you at Castellum."

CHAPTER 15

Layers

I stare blankly after Juno as the night sky swallows her up, not sure what to say to Erik when he approaches me on the Avenue steps.

"Ev, you have to try and push it out of your mind for now," he warns me, tapping into my inner turmoil. "Don't let it consume you. I'm sure there's an answer for this."

I know he's right, and I try my best to tuck away the unfortunate ending to our day into that rarely visited room in my brain. For now.

Despite his preaching, Erik seems lost in thought himself. "I need to stop by Robert's dimension before I head to mine. Why don't you come along — get your mind off things?"

I nod, placing my hand on the pendant around my neck and digging the edges of the stones into my skin.

"Robert Crawford," Erik instructs the elevator. A few steps after getting off, we're standing in front of the professor's dimension. The door opens after a few knocks.

I don't know what I expected Robert's dimension to look like, but I certainty hadn't expected to find myself standing at the foot of a long winding driveway, outdoors. Paper white birch trees cast shadows across the grass. Aside from the generous acreage, everything about the property is normal, including the simple yet inviting coastal home that stands at the end of the driveway. White paddock fences carry on for miles, and I hear water folding onto a shore in the distance.

"Two of Robert's loves: horses and Cape Cod," Erik enlightens me. "He grew up in the Cape. But after Charlotte — his wife — died, he sold their home and moved to New Haven. Come to think of it, I don't think I've ever seen him create a different dimension. I don't know why."

"I do," I reply. "He doesn't care for the magical or the extravagant – he just wants to bring back his paradise lost. You can't just put a For Sale sign on the past. Life's not that simple."

The professor meets us on the porch. "Erik! Twice in one day. And…Everest?" he asks, pausing before saying my name. "Did I get that right?"

"Yes. I hope you don't mind me tagging along professor."

"Nonsense. I'm always happy to have visitors," Robert replies as he ushers us inside. "And please, 'Robert' is just fine.

"Francine and Simon are here — my children." We walk past a formal study and into a family room with tall antique bookcases. A boy sits on a sofa. Simon, I presume. He has his father's brown eyes and honey blond hair that's cut short.

"Simon!" Erik grabs his shoulder for one of those half hugs guys like to give. "Where have you been hiding?"

"I know…I keep getting sidetracked," Simon answers enthusiastically. "This place is a lot bigger than I thought!"

"You have no idea."

"I know that voice." A slim young woman enters from the kitchen. She has a different appearance – chin-length jet black hair and dark eyes. She exudes an undeniable confidence. She's dressed like a high-paid attorney from a legal drama, down to the six-inch patent leather stiletto pumps.

Erik waves to her. "Hey Francine. Just wanted to speak to your dad quickly. This is Everest. She's just awakened, second day. Everest, this is Francine and Simon."

I smile at them. "It's amazing that all three of you found this place!" I observe. "That's impressive."

Francine shrugs casually. "A happy coincidence, I guess."

"Happy?" Simon glares at his sister, his demeanor changed. "*That's* the word you come up with?"

Francine closes her eyes like she knows she's messed up, "Simon, I didn't mean…"

But Simon just mumbles something before excusing himself, then storms out of the room, clearly wounded by their exchange.

Was it something I said?

"Sorry," I begin. "I think I'm somehow to blame for that."

Francine waits until her brother's out of earshot to explain, then waves her hand. "Don't worry, you're not. Our mom passed, few years back. He's still processing it. We both awakened here shortly after her death, and he's convinced she had something to do with it."

I can appreciate Simon's guilt. Just like Paris, the Prism must feel like both a blessing and a curse to him.

Francine seems to have better coping skills than her brother. "He probably thinks I don't miss her as much," she adds, cool and composed, "because I'm adopted. Anyway, he's just overly sensitive. Give him a minute."

Just as I settle onto the couch, Robert rejoins us. "You should come by more often," he seems to plead, his eagerness divulging a longing, perhaps for the laughter and busyness of a household now empty with growing children. "These two are off on their own quite a bit. And Francine won't even let me see her dimension, can you believe it?"

Francine flips off one of her shoes and rotates her ankle. "It's called privacy, Dad. It is my own space." She turns to me. "Dads can be so overbearing, am I right?"

I just smile in response. I can't really relate but imagine a little overbearing wouldn't be so bad.

"Uh, Robert, could we chat…privately?" Erik asks impatiently. His solemn expression seems to convey some kind of urgency, because Robert quickly leads him to another room. Moments later, Simon returns, and Francine avoids any further discussion of their past. She also prevents any awkward lulls by asking me rapid-fire questions about my experience in the Prism, which I answer rather inarticulately with the same recycled adjectives I've been using for the last few days. The rest of the time I spend chatting with Simon, who enlightens me about his new-found enthusiasm for Nevar and his goal of mastering all the snowboarding hills.

"What a gorgeous necklace!" Francine exclaims at one point, leaning in to get a closer look at my pendant which I've started to play with.

"Oh…thanks. It was a gift. It's supposed to resemble a mountain."

"Ah…I see it now. You know, my –"

Before Francine can finish her train of thought, Erik and Robert return and Erik suggests we bid the Crawfords a good evening. It's clear from the creases around Robert's brow that the two men didn't have a feel-good conversation.

"Come by, anytime," Robert insists, trying to put on a happy face. "And if you ever find yourselves in New Haven, door's always open!"

I smile at him gratefully, and he smiles back, observing me with a curious expression.

As we walk back down the driveway, I ponder the irony of

a normal looking world within a completely enchanted one. It's like peeling away the layers of an onion. I find myself wanting someone to open their dimension door as we head back to the elevator just so I can peek into their imagination for a moment. But aside from the sound of our own footsteps, the hall is undisturbed.

Erik is quiet and seems far away. I try to think of a way to ease his mind the way he's been able to do for me so effortlessly, but I just end up asking another question.

"How do all these rooms become assigned?"

Erik shrugs. "Not sure. The logistics of this place get figured out behind the scenes; in an invisible realm we don't have access to."

"I see…What's your dimension like?"

"Do you want to see it?" he responds without hesitation.

I stop and stare at him. "What? Really? Now?"

"Why not? You just asked me about it, didn't you, or did I imagine that?"

Yeah, I totally did. Still, I hadn't expected an invitation. It makes me a little nervous.

But I sense Erik's demeanor and energy begin to shift, as if he's pressed 'pause' on the worries that previously preoccupied him. I nod. *Maybe we both need a distraction.*

"One of my favorite places in the world is Costa Rica," he tells me, speaking faster. "I spent a month there a few years back. I think I've done a pretty good job replicating it, but I could always use an objective opinion."

He instructs the elevator – "Erik Halvorsen" – and it occurs to me that I never asked him his full name before.

Once on Erik's floor, we walk a few doors to the right and stop in front of his name plate, and I nervously prepare to enter the private world of Erik's mind.

CHAPTER 16

Catching Stars

A thick leaf hits me in the face as I enter Erik's dimension. I move it aside to reveal swaying palms and heliconia plants flanking the entrance, their vibrant colors worthy of a postcard. It's daylight, and the sunlight breaks through the gaps in the lush jungle canopies. Erik walks a mere 30 steps before he stops at the edge of a precipice. The jungle continues along the other side, and the only thing that's standing in our way is a rickety wooden bridge rising over a 100-foot drop to a frothing teal river below.

I marvel at how real it looks and feels, furiously rubbing the delicate petals of a velvety purple plant between my fingers. It never wilts.

Once again, I'm blown away by the power to create anything – *absolutely anything* – from a plain tiny room. He really nailed it!

"Incredible," I mumble to myself. "You made all this?"

The pride on Erik's face is endearing as he looks out over the precipice, beaming like a child getting a new puppy. "Not bad, right? I can minimize the drop if you want…if heights aren't your thing," he offers.

I don't need him to change a thing. If his mind created this, then I trust him, and despite earlier events, I'm determined to trust the Prism again. Without a second thought I step onto the creaking wood. It sways and wobbles with every step. Against my better judgement I look down, yet surprisingly the drop gives me more of a rush than a fright. I place one foot in front of the next, and before I know it, I'm planting myself on solid ground again.

"Glad you don't scare easily," Erik says, getting off the bridge behind me.

"Well, we did just get here. Who knows what else you have waiting in here."

"Maybe just a T-Rex or two," Erik teases (hopefully), no doubt recalling my earlier apprehension about dinosaurs. "But you needn't worry. I just feed them dandelions."

His fascinating world expands around us as we go further in. "These are my creations," he says, pointing to a plant that resembles a small lampshade, covered in one large smooth flower petal. "They glow at night, like lanterns."

After a short walk, we come upon a small treehouse with white privacy curtains located close to a rock bed. But it's what's behind the treehouse that makes me do a double take. An enormous, spiral-like waterfall pours forcefully into a turquoise pool, creating a mist on the surface of the water.

I can't take my eyes off it. "Is that a spiral? How is that even possible?"

Erik beams again. "Actually, it's a waterslide. Never found one that was quite satisfying enough, so I designed my own. Care to try it out?"

Now? I hesitate. The waterfall looks like it could spit me out in a mangled heap of dislocated limbs – even kill me. But I can't bring myself to refuse. *It's the Prism. It's Erik's world. It's totally safe!* "How do we get up there?"

"We could hike."

"You've got about five seconds before I change my mind. You're going to have to do better than that."

"You'll do it," Erik insists with a wink. "But there is a faster way."

I follow him to the edge of the cliffside where thick tree branches begin so close to the ground, we can step onto them like stairs. The branches continue around the trunk, with similar trees climbing up the hill.

Erik steps on the first branch and pulls me up beside him. He takes hold of my waist and brings me in close to steady me, until I'm right up against his chest. I can feel his muscles tense up and hope the Prism does me a favor and hides my blushing. I can see myself in his dark pupils, our faces inches apart.

He grins. "Hope you have good balance!" I sense that he wants to say more, but instead he slowly takes my hands off his chest and places them on the trunk. He gives me a mischievous smile and steps back, just as the tree begins to move beneath my feet like a corkscrew.

"Just move with it," he says. "Like on an escalator."

The branch rises higher with each rotation. I see Erik following the rotations until he meets the next tree, leaping effortlessly from branch to branch and climbing upward. I manage to follow, finding it easier than I thought and managing not to fall off. It's a bit of an adrenaline rush, trying to accurately time my jumps to keep up with him.

"This is incredible!" I yell over the hum of the waterfall. "You actually thought of this?"

"Over a very strong drink!" he confirms.

When we reach the top, the branches stop on Erik's silent instruction. The Cost Rica of his mind continues as he leads me toward the sound of the water. Eventually, we step out into an opening where a river crashes over the edge of the cliffside.

"Ready?" Erik asks.

Ready for what, is the question.

I hesitate again, wondering if I'm being brave or foolish. *I've come this far…*

I take a seat in the loud river next to Erik just shy of the drop, where the water reaches my chest. It's pleasant, like a baby's bath, with oddly no current or resistance. I admire the breathtaking landscape set against a blanket of wool clouds and a sky the color of a robin's egg.

"When you're ready, just let go," Erik cries, the water splashing him relentlessly. He smiles reassuringly, his dimples melting away my inhibitions. "See you at the bottom!"

With those words, he lifts his arms over his head and disappears over the edge.

It's terrifying, watching him fall away and taking a bit of my security with him. I know that if I keep thinking about it, I won't follow through.

Just do it! (Deep breath). *Just let go.*

As soon as my mind gives the word the current kicks in, and it has no mercy. For a moment the world stands still as I seem to float, suspended in midair over the ridge, falling in slow motion before I hit the bend of the first spiral.

Then, everything changes.

The current jolts me again. I expect a one-way corkscrew to the bottom, but my body is being thrown in changing directions, weaving upside down in between the spiral motion as if travelling a never-ending celestial wormhole. The thrill ride takes its time before finally releasing me into the misty pool where I'm surrounded by a school of orange fish, their tails the length of a gymnast's ribbon. I watch their performance for a few moments, then finally make my way towards the light that beckons from the surface.

Erik's eagerly awaiting my review as he helps me out of the water and onto a large boulder. "Thoughts?"

I watch my clothes dry before my eyes. "I mean, if it wasn't for the possibility of whiplash and the obvious physics limitations, I'd say you should sell that to amusement parks." I take a seat next to him to gather my wits. "Wow Erik! This is all…really cool. That was something else!"

A few minutes of silence ensue as we remain contently in each other's company surrounded by the mist.

"I'm glad I could show this to you," Erik finally says.

I smile appreciatively. "Me too. Thank you, for this day. I still can't believe you created all this."

"You can have one of your own too – fill it with whatever you want."

"Right…" I should really get on this dimension creation business. "Is this how yours always looks?"

"I have a few I alternate. And if I'm ever feeling inspired, I can create something completely new."

I raise my eyebrows to challenge him. "Just like that?"

"Just like that!"

"Show me," I demand, almost rudely. "Not that I'm ready to leave here just yet, but…can you show me how it all works? That *is* your job, as magister, right?"

Erik chuckles. "Fair enough. Right…let's see…" He closes his eyes. "It helps if you limit distractions. Then, visualize what you want…just give me a minute to get there…"

I seize the opportunity to study Erik's softened handsome features in his state of meditative concentration, noticing the subtle highlights in his wavy hair and two identical freckles on the end of each of his eyebrows.

After a few moments of no obvious change, everything around us disappears. We're surrounded by darkness, but only for a split second. Then, light returns as we find ourselves in the middle of a rock valley surrounded by stone walls with orange wave-like ribbing. It's hypnotic and alien – like we've been transported to the surface of Mars, only with a brilliant blue sky as the backdrop.

"Where are we?"

"It's called The Wave," Erik tells me, his eyes still closed, "a sandstone rock formation on the border of Arizona and Utah — the result of years of erosion and migrating sand dunes during the Jurassic period."

"It's beautiful!" I marvel. "This place actually exists?"

"It does. Sadly, the Prism's Nucleus doesn't have one. But I can see it here for now, or at least what I *think* it looks like based on all my obsessive research and saved photos. It will hold me over until I get a chance to see the real thing." Erik maintains the landscape for a few seconds more. "It's going to disappear now."

"Why?"

"Because it's not where I truly want to be."

In an instant we find ourselves back at the foot of the falls.

"And that's how it works." Erik almost whispers, looking at me intensely. I'm not sure what's more thrilling — the transformation he's just shown me or whatever is happening between us. Under any other circumstances, my legs would carry me swiftly back over the rickety bridge to start my own dimension creation. But there's an encroaching intensity that's stronger than that desire, and more than anything I want to give into it. It's unlike any feeling I've ever experienced. I imagine it might be similar to the feeling astronauts get when they see Earth from outer space for the first time – an anxious weightlessness, a blissful euphoria, an unquenchable thirst to go further and deeper into the unknown.

"It's strange to be in daylight again," I observe, trying to avoid confronting my feelings.

Erik looks upward. "I thought you'd appreciate my dimension more by day. But if you prefer…"

Our surroundings dim to near pitch darkness, signaling Erik's lanterns to illuminate the jungle in hues of red and indigo. The stars in his universe glow as bright as those that reflect over the Prismatic but hang so low that it seems as though I could pluck one out of the sky. I hold up my arm to judge their distance when Erik reaches up himself. To my astonishment, he brings the swirling ball of light down to me.

"You can touch it," he says, grinning as my eyes nearly pop out of skull. "Remember, no limits."

This is beyond!

Erik carefully hands me the little globe of frantic energy. Its shape is constantly in flux, but I manage to contain it in the palm of my hand where it emits a soft warmth that tickles my core, much like the mysterious rainfall did. It's hard to let it go. After a few minutes, I reluctantly release it, allowing it to float up and rejoin the others.

"Unbelievable!" I whisper. "I must sound like a broken record."

"Don't worry, we all do."

I feel Erik's hand find my own and I look back down to face him. Our eyes lock, and I feel trapped in a bubble of frozen time I never want to escape from as I wonder how it would feel if our lips met.

He brushes the side of my face with his fingertips. "I lied earlier," he admits, glancing at the pendant he gave me. "It may have been slightly more than a welcome gift."

I'm utterly paralyzed. There's something about Erik Halvorsen…Maybe it's because I've never really been interested in anyone that way. Childhood crushes aside, there was never anyone I wanted to give my time to. No one who understood me or really saw me, no one who was so in-sync with my thoughts.

It's almost embarrassing – how much I just want to be around this person; laugh with him, listen to him…wrap myself up in the calming power of his presence.

Say something to him! Tell him you're glad he said that, tell him his hair looks nice. No, that's weird…please don't say that!

Suddenly, all of it scares me more than I ever thought it would – the idea that this could be something real, or the possibility that none of this is even real to begin with. I feel my smile slipping and release Erik's hand like a chunk of burning coal, then get up abruptly and start toward the jungle, hoping I can find my way to the exit.

"I should probably get back."

"Ev!" Erik protests, running after me. "Wait, you just got here…"

"I know. But it's getting late." I lie, moving with determination. "Thank you, for showing me this – "

"Ev!" He catches up and cuts me off before I can take another step. I stop abruptly, nearly colliding with him. "I'm sorry. If I did or said anything to upset you…"

I sigh. *It's not you. You're not the problem.* "No…" I interrupt, trying to say something that will makes sense. "Erik, this was amazing. *You* are amazing. I'm just…" I pause, trying to find the right excuse, finally settling on something that's vague enough to pass as a reason. "I'm just not used to this."

"Used to what?"

Too many thoughts float through my head. I can't seem to form a coherent response and just look away.

He finds my hand before I can escape again. "Just wait a

second, please. Look, I won't force you stay. But…I think there's something here, and I think you feel it too. And…I know it's all sudden and out of this world, and…well, we've only known each other two days – which, I mean, is really more like four or five with the time…" He pauses and takes a breath. "Anyway…I like you Ev. And I keep thinking that maybe we were brought together for a reason. I just…I can't shake that feeling."

I can barely look at him. Of course, there's something here! I want to say all of what he's said right back to him….and that he's been on my mind since the first day we met.

But is it real?

"I think I get it," Erik adds quickly. "I'm still not entirely real to you. None of this is, is it?"

How does he keep doing that? How is he so good at this mind-reading stuff?

I feel terrible for doubting him. And he's right; maybe if I was actually awake it would feel more possible.

"I'm sorry Erik. I like you too. I want it to be real." At least I can admit that much.

Neither of us say anything for an awkward moment until Erik makes a surprising offer. "What if we fix that? Come visit me in London this weekend!"

Ok, wasn't expecting that.

I laugh nervously. "I'm trying to escape like a coward and you're inviting me to London?"

Erik doesn't back down, his eyes wide and eager, like he's just made a breakthrough discovery. "It's only a train ride across the channel! I can pick you up from the station and we can just have a normal day, away from all this fantasy stuff. Just a normal day. I'll try to keep it as real as possible."

I sigh, glancing around the jungle, my way out within reach.

"Erik, I can't just go to another country, just like that." *Well, that's not entirely true.* It's not like I have a controlling sociopath in my life anymore. And Catherine's gone, not that she would care anyway.

Maybe I can? Why not, Everest? What have you got to lose?

"It'll be great!" Erik promises. "And I'll be a perfect gent. If I got in here the chances of me being a serial killer are slim, right?"

I laugh again. "I'm not worried about that."

"What do you say, then?" he asks hopefully. "If you hate me afterwards and find me completely insufferable, I promise I won't bother you about it ever again. I'll even hand over all my magister duties to someone more tolerable.

"So, would a few days in England sidetrack any important plans?"

My nervous excitement mirrors itself on Erik's face. What's the worst that could happen, I break some more lightbulbs with my uncontrollable rage and Erik discovers my deep dark secret and has me committed to a psych ward? *He wouldn't do that, right?*

"No plans," I admit timidly, taking a breath. "Okay. Sure. Why not?" *I hope I don't regret this.*

Erik hangs his head in relief, then looks up, smiling. "I guess I'll be looking up train schedules tomorrow."

I give him my phone number to memorize as we head back to the Castellum hallway. My pulse is still racing as we walk, and when our shoulders occasionally brush it sends tingles to the pit of my stomach. Every step creates more regret for not giving in to whatever almost happened. But it's too late now. I've made my choice for today.

"Goodnight," Erik says before the elevator doors separate us. He looks at me with a look of contentment, with those intense eyes I can't get enough of. "I guess for the time being,

I'll just have to settle for seeing you in my dreams."

I laugh out loud. "That line can never be cheesy anymore, can it?" I tell him as the doors begin to close. "See you tomorrow," I say before Erik disappears from my view, leaving me alone with my regrets.

CHAPTER 17

Relapse

There aren't too many people who wake up in Paris and wish they were somewhere else. Yet this morning, I find myself being one of those people, even though I feel completely euphoric. Thick clouds blanket the overcast sky, but in my impenetrable bubble its endlessly sunny. And the continuing absence of shattered glass is just icing on the cake.

I sift through thoughts of sailboats and waterfalls on my way to the bathroom, finally appreciating the meaning of "floating on air". But when I look into the mirror, all that ends abruptly.

For the first time my two worlds collide, and if there was ever any doubt in my mind over the Prism's existence, it's quashed by the inexplainable sight of Erik's pendant hanging around my neck.

How?

Erik and Jenna's words replay in my head. *You can't take anything out of the Prism...*

Then...how?

Maybe there's a loophole Erik forgot to tell me about? *I'll ask him about it later.* I clench the pendant in my grasp tightly, thoughts of Erik sneaking into my brain. I try to push them aside. Until I can verify that he's a real person, I can't get carried away. I check that the clasp is secure and continue getting dressed.

The thought of Peterson stealing my entire weekend fills me with dread, although I try not to let it overshadow what awaits me at the conclusion of the day. As I fasten my helmet and head out the door, relieved to place my hands on my old brass doorknob, my cell phone pings — incoming text from an unfamiliar number.

Good morning Ev.

It is, I type back, smiling once I realize who it is.

Erik: **See you tonight?**

Me: **I'll see how I feel**

Erik: **Intriguing... I like my odds though.**

I send a "fingers crossed" emoji and save the number, and for the duration of the morning exist contently in my bubble.

* * *

"Who gave you *that?*" Nina asks enviously, drooling over the pendant when I enter the office for day two of overtime hell. I've never cared much for shiny things or had many for that matter. Nina, on the other hand, could bathe in the stuff, the glittery proof dangling from her ears and both wrists. She leans in for a closer examination. "Definite keeper!"

"It's complicated," I say, without revealing anything. It would be impossible to explain any of it anyway. Who would even believe me?

"Is this why you and Tristan —"

"No! It's not like that. And there was never a 'me and Tristan'," I insist for the hundredth time. *Why is this so hard for people to understand?*

Nina's eyes travel past me. "Speak of the devil!"

A voice cuts through the hum of the air conditioning. "It looks like you're doing well."

It feels like someone's punched me in the stomach with an iron fist. I turn to see Tristan standing in the hall outside the break room, his hands in the pockets of his granite blue suit.

"Nina," he says coldly, without taking his eyes off me. His glare is paralyzing, and I shamefully allow him to hold me captive with it.

What is he even doing here?

"Tristan," Nina replies uncomfortably. "Didn't expect to see you here…and on a Sunday. Well, um…excuse me."

Nina mouths *Are you OK* before leaving, and I assure her I'm fine with a subtle nod. *You can handle him,* I tell myself. *Just don't shatter any glass windows or you'll definitely get fired!*

Tristan takes a step forward. "May I join you?"

I lift my chin. "I'd rather you didn't. I thought I was clear I never wanted to see you again."

He holds up his hands as if in surrender and keeps advancing. "I'm not here to upset you Everest."

"Doubtful. What other motive could you possibly have?"

"My father's looking to hire Peterson for some security issues we're having at one of the banks. He asked me to accompany him to the meeting."

"On a Sunday?"

"It's urgent. I didn't plan on running into you. I was just looking for some coffee."

"I'm pretty sure they serve specialty cappuccino in the executive boardroom, so there's really no reason for you to mingle with the commoners," I shoot back, refusing to let him win.

"I don't want to fight," Tristan insists, appearing to relinquish some of his coldness. He glances curiously at my pendant but doesn't ask about it, choosing instead to take a few more steps in my direction. "I don't expect to talk now, but hopefully, one day, we can be civil and discuss what happened."

I roll my eyes as I tuck the pendant under my shirt. "I don't need to discuss anything. And we both know the only thing that got hurt that day was your pride."

He maintains his position, then takes his hand out of his pocket. "I just want a truce, to wish you happiness, whatever that is."

Wish you happiness? Is this a joke?

It isn't like Tristan to accept defeat so graciously. *A truce?* I still don't trust him, but his uncharacteristically kind demeanor leaves a crack in my protective wall. I remind myself that hanging on to resentment will only stand in the way of my future and the Prism. Cautiously, I lean forward and accept his outstretched hand, shaking it firmly as if completing a business transaction. His cold ring rubs against my fingers. "To moving forward, and staying out of each other's way," I agree.

Then it hits me.

Suction. Heaviness. Numbness.

It's happening again! *No! How?* I must have some deeply rooted conditioned response to his presence I haven't recovered from yet.

I pull back my hand, putting an end to that dreaded sensation, then bolt past him out of the room, hopeful that this "truce" is the last chapter of our unfortunate story.

* * *

As the day drags on, I can't shake the uneasy feeling bubbling in the pit of my stomach. It's not butterflies this time – it's something more ominous and far less pleasant. I'd hoped that burying the hatchet with Tristan would have brought some closure, but our exchange has left me confused and anxious, even about the Prism.

Even about Erik.

The turbulence inside me induces a splitting migraine and nausea. And no matter how hard I resolve to snap out of it I find myself drifting back into a downward spiral.

When I enter the humid apartment, I feel extremely alone despite knowing I'm a few hours away from being anything but. Strangely, the thought of seeing the Prism again brings me little comfort. I'm drained. Hollow. Like an addict relapsing back into the darkness.

Mushy oatmeal once again.

What's so special about me? How did I get in? It's all too perfect. I don't deserve perfect.

The tears overwhelm my throat as I wallow in my weakness and devastation, feeling like an imposter that's been exposed for what she truly is. I don't know where to place my feelings, which thoughts to attach them too. My body falls hard onto my bed, and I bury my face in the pillow, weeping into it uncontrollably.

I don't deserve perfect. I don't...

CHAPTER 18

Fortunate Meetings

My cheeks feel like a cracked desert plain from the dried tears. I must have fallen asleep unintentionally. Through the brain fog, I hear my phone pinging me awake. My eyes shoot open. *There are no cellphones in the Prism! NO!*

I regard my Montmartre apartment with a sinking dread. I never went back!

"No, no, no, no, no…" I did exactly what Erik warned me not to and let my negative thoughts run wild. *Damn it! I'm such an idiot!*

The phone starts ringing again. I answer angrily without glancing at the number. "YES!"

"Hi." The voice is familiar and comforting, and some much-needed relief rushes over me, calming the flames of self-loathing.

I can barely get my thoughts together. "Erik…I don't know what happened…I think…"

"Ev, it's fine. It happens to all of us. Trust me, it won't be the last time."

I take a moment to calm down and listen. "You're not upset?" I ask after a pause, expecting to be ripped apart —

expecting the reaction Tristan would have had. Expecting my own reaction, for that matter.

"What? No, of course not. A little worried though. Is everything ok?"

I pause again, weighing how much to reveal. *No, everything is not all right. Everything is all wrong, again!* "I just had an off day, I guess." I answer vaguely. I feel terrible for letting Erik down. "I was looking forward to seeing you," I tell him and can almost feel his mood lighten from hundreds of miles away as I wait impatiently for his reply.

"I'm just glad you're okay," he says, soothing me again with his voice. "I was looking forward to seeing you too. I'll make you a deal. You work on getting back on track, and I'll plan a day for us in the Prism, to make up for lost time."

"I'll take that deal!" I reply without hesitation.

"And don't worry, you're just human. Try not to beat yourself up too much."

Easier said than done. "Thanks," I say to him, "and thanks for calling." I want more than anything to keep talking to him – the real him, on a phone in the real world. It's nice. It's normal. But it's Monday. "Sorry, I have to get going. I took the day off for this volunteer thing and I'm already late."

"That's probably exactly what you need. I'll see you tonight," Erik decides for me.

My determination returns. "I'll be there!"

"I know," he replies confidently before the call ends. I can picture him smiling as he says it.

I stare at the phone for what seems like a full minute. I guess this is how it feels, to be supported. It's a foreign feeling, long forgotten and buried with Uncle Tim and Mom. My excitement over the Prism reignites and I vow not to screw up again.

At least, not for a while.

* * *

On any other day, Rue Tournesol is probably a rarely disturbed dead-end street outside the city. But today it's alive with construction crews, ready to continue the work of yesterday's shift on a home restoration for a deserving family.

"The father was shot during a robbery, you know," I overhear one of the volunteers gossiping. "His wife couldn't keep up with the bills. She and the kids lived in that abandoned warehouse near the train yard for three months before someone found them."

"Mon Dieu!" some others exclaim.

"Kids?" I ask curiously.

"Boy and girl, twelve and eight," the volunteer tells me. "Poor souls! Can you imagine?"

The place is already looking better, but still needs a ton of work both outside and inside. It will take several volunteer shifts and a lot of contractors to get it up to living standards again.

"Attention!" The group lead calls out in French as we all gather around the run-down structure in our beat-up clothes and hard hats. "Thank you for coming today. I expect everyone to be safe. Please read the safety guidelines that were sent to you. Wear your hard hats at all times. *All times!* Remember, this is a construction zone. And once again, thank you for your time. The Vidal family deserves this. Let's make it happen for them!"

The upbeat energy is palpable. After the enthusiastic cheers die down, I check my assignment and get busy gutting the kitchen. It's a lot harder than I imagined, but I can't deny that breaking a bunch of stuff and watching it disintegrate feels extremely satisfying. Erik was right — it's exactly what I need! By lunch, the muscles in my arms burn. I'm exhausted, famished and a whole new level of sweaty. Food is generously provided by a local deli, and the hungry workers take their break around the building site, finding seating on lumber piles.

As I bite into a grilled panini, I notice a little girl in red jean shorts approaching me with a lunch of her own. She's too young to be part of the crew, but she definitely belongs on the site, judging from the pink hardhat on her head.

"Bonjour," the girl says, standing right in front of me. She has an infectious radiance. Her thick light brown hair is tied in two low pigtails and her brown eyes match the warmth of her sun-kissed olive complexion.

"Bonjour."

"Parlez-vous anglais?"

"Um, yes. Oui. I do," I reply, unable to decide which language to speak.

"I thought so," the girl says in a French accent as her eyes study my name tag. "Yours does not sound like a French name. May I sit?" She certainly isn't shy.

"Please." I scoot over to make room on the lumber pile.

"My maman was born in Manchester. She teaches me English."

"Oh, that's great! Is she helping today too? You don't look strong enough to lift lumber yourself."

"No. We just wanted to see the house. I am going to live here, with Maman and my brother."

And then it all makes sense! The girl's the right age… "I didn't realize – you're one of the Vidal children!"

"Lise." She extends her hand like a proper young lady.

I can't help staring at her, remembering her story, and realizing how much more there must be to it. "It is so nice to meet you Lise," I tell her sincerely.

"I recognize you from the Luminary class. Have you been

coming to the Prism long?"

The bread stops in my throat and I almost choke. Now I'm definitely staring! I probably look like one of those cartoons whose eyes pop out of their sockets and hang there on a slinky. *Did she just say what I think she said?*

"You were there? You've been to the Prism?" I stutter.

Lise giggles. "You look funny when you are surprised."

I quickly close my mouth and swallow my food. Of all the people I could have met today…

"Sorry," I stammer again, "I haven't met any other Wakers…that is, you know, here."

"You're the first I have met too," Lise said, "besides my brother. We are very new. There he is…Julian!" Lise cries, waving a boy over.

Julian seems shorter and skinner than the average twelve-year-old. Under his red hard hat, I see the same brown eyes and thick brown hair his sister has, minus the pig tails.

"This is Everest," Lise introduces me. "Remember, she was sitting in front of us at the Luminary."

"Hello," I greet him. He simply nods back with a shy smile and sad yet playful eyes, then lowers his gaze and wipes his palms nervously on his Star Wars t-shirt. I want to lock them both in an endless hug.

"And does your mom go too, to the Prism, I mean?" I ask, awed by the fact that they both found the place.

Lise is silent on this point, and Julian spares his sister from having to answer. "No. Not yet."

"Maman drinks sometimes, and cries a lot," Lise blurts out unexpectedly to everyone's surprise.

"Lise! *Silencieux!*" Julian cries, then eyes me questionably, apparently not as trusting as his sister, and for good reason.

"Who is she going to tell?" Lise retorts. But she looks

frazzled, like she's suddenly realized that Prism or no Prism, I'm still an unpredictable stranger. "Please don't tell anyone," she pleads. "It's been hard for her. She is better now. You won't say anything, will you?"

I nod reassuringly, trying to hide my concern. Julian removes an inhaler from his pocket and takes a few puffs. He looks much calmer afterward and some color returns to his cheeks. "Don't worry. I won't say anything," I assure them both again, placing my hands on each of their arms. "I'm sure your mom just needs some time."

Julian smiles faintly, putting the inhaler back into his pocket. "At least I don't need this in the Prism, right?"

I feel my eyes welling up and I'm suddenly incredibly ashamed of my negative spiral the night before. I have nothing to feel bad about. Nothing! *No more excuses!* There is a reason for this fortunate encounter, and part of it I'm sure is to give me a good kick in the pants.

"What do you plan on seeing next at the Luminary?" Lise asks, swallowing her last piece of baguette.

"Good question," I reply, finally gathering my emotions and grateful I could keep it together. "Not easy to decide, is it? Hey, why don't we do something together sometime? I have an awesome magister who can show us all the highlights."

"That would be nice," Julian accepts with surprising enthusiasm. "Our magister disappeared after our fourth day."

Disappeared? "That's too bad," I tell him, saddened.

The afternoon assignment has me cleaning up debris, and the foreman clears Lise and Julian to help with some of the lighter items. It gives us more time to get to know one another and the hours pass like minutes until the build day ends at six o'clock. By then, I've even made Julian laugh a few times, and he seems much more relaxed around me, though the poor kid can barely get a word in between all of Lise's chatter. I can only imagine the conversation if she and Jenna were ever in the same room...

I'm reluctant to bid the children goodbye, grateful to them for showing me the way to move forward again. Lise tells me they're being put up at the fancy Hotel Iliad by the construction company, after which I gently scold her for giving out her address so readily. I give Julian my cell number and the 20 euros I have left in my wallet, wishing I had brought more. Lise melts my heart with a bear hug before running off, her pig tails flapping behind her.

Standing idle at a red light on my way home I feel a balance again, and I'm anxious to get to sleep and live another day. *Like James Bond. Wait, that's Die Another Day. Whatever - same thing.*

As I glance in my side mirror to change lanes, a familiar sight catches my eye — a black Mercedes sedan with tinted windows, trailing two cars behind. *Does everyone own one of these? Stop being paranoid!* But it's too late for that – I'm already totally paranoid. And Nina's recent news update didn't exactly help.

I take an indirect route home, chastising myself for succumbing to irrational theories. But the sedan stays with me despite my odd turns. *Tristan! It has to be!* My impulsive side dares me to confront my pursuers at the next red light.

But what if it isn't Tristan? It could be nothing, or it could be something else – something worse. If it is, I don't want them knowing my address. And to top it off, I'm riding a scooter that's on its last legs and desperately needs new brakes. *Just stick with the metro from now on!*

At the next intersection I take my time, then speed through as the light turns red, trapping the sedan behind a tour bus. A right into the first alley brings me to a dead end. *Darn it.*

Desperate, I conceal the scooter behind a dumpster and

sneak past a cook tossing trash outside. He curses at me in Mandarin as I run into the chaotic restaurant kitchen. Once in the seating area, I make a beeline for the front door and peer through the glass. The restaurant is on the same street as the light I've trapped the sedan at, but the car's gone.

All I've got is a hunch. My curiosity wins over, and I flag down a taxi.

"Where to, Mademoiselle?" the driver asks me in French as I launch myself into the rear seat.

"For now, make a right here, please."

As the taxi rounds the corner, I find my hunch is right on the money: the sedan seems to have followed my route and is travelling just three cars ahead, moving at a snail's pace in the right lane. Luckily, it passes the alley and my concealed scooter. I remove my helmet, covering my head with the hood of my sweatshirt to disguise myself.

"Follow that black car," I instruct the driver. "But not too close. I don't want them to know."

I meet the driver's gaze in the rear-view as he studies me suspiciously. "Whatever you like. I've had stranger requests."

The Mercedes makes a left and continues slowly. After another few minutes it begins to speed up, altering its route to head in the opposite direction.

"Do you still want me to follow mademoiselle?" the driver asks.

I hesitate, nervous about where my inquisitiveness will take me, but ultimately make the only decision I can. "Oui. Merci." *Let's see where this goes…*

After crossing the Seine and making a series of turns, the sedan finally comes to a stop in front of a corner residence on Rue de Guerre. The grey brick structure takes up almost the entire block. An ugly bird statue guards the rod iron gate that allows access to the courtyard in front of the main doors, with more of the same creatures carved into the masonry work. The sides of the building wrap around the courtyard on each side, casting dark shadows on the entrance.

The Mercedes parks in a reserved angled parking space across the street, and I finally get close enough to get a look at the license plate as we pass it. I immediately recognize the bird on the sticker and pull myself away from the window a second before Hulk emerges from the driver's side. I only catch sight of the back of his head, but it's enough to make the ID – I'd recognize that scar anywhere.

"Pull over here, please," I instruct the driver, staying low as I spy out the back. Shorty punches in a code on a device mounted next to the iron gate, and the two men walk out of view, the gate shutting loudly behind them.

Slowly, it all begins to sink in – the realization that the two men who've been steadfastly posted outside my apartment weren't scoping out the real estate. They weren't chauffeurs, or tourists, or passionate admirers of the coffee at Emile's. They were there because I was there.

They already have my address.

The question is why? I feel a powerful chill, like an icy hand has run its bony fingers down my back and then reached in through my ribcage and squeezed my heart.

"What is that place?" I croak, my throat suddenly dry.

The driver glances in his side mirror. "Je ne sais pas. It looks like a private residence."

Impulsively, I open the cab door. "Turn around please, take your first right and wait for me a block down."

"Mademoiselle…" the driver calls after me, probably trying to stop me from doing something I'll regret. But I'm like a moth to a flame and shut the door mid-sentence.

The taxi passes me as I make my way towards the building with my head down. I retrieve my cell phone from my purse, start the video and pretend to speak into it while passing the courtyard which to both my relief and disappointment is deserted. The security is on the heavy side. Impenetrable gate aside, another touchpad is mounted just outside the main door, and at least six cameras overlook the street and front entrance alone. And that's just what I can see without lifting my face too high.

I can't make much of the stone bird, other than the fact that it's hideous, if it's even a bird at all. I manage to make out writing on a plaque on its chest. *Piscem vorat maior minorem.* Meaningless.

A light comes on in one of the windows, urging me to abandon my espionage. I quicken my step, making a right on *Rue de Soufrrance* where my taxi awaits to my relief. I check the video as I walk, but it's too dark and completely useless. The search engine corrects my spelling of the Latin phrase and provides a translation: *the larger fish eats the smaller.*

"Creepy." I slip the phone into my sweatshirt pocket, still no closer to figuring anything out.

I'm almost in the cab when a hand grabs my right shoulder from behind and directs me forcefully into the rear seat before I even know what hit me.

CHAPTER 19

Lucky One

Before I can react, she's getting in next to me. "I'll explain later," she whispers. "Take the next right," she instructs the driver.

Stunned, I just stare at her. She's young. Older than me, but young, with curly black hair tied into a high short ponytail. I know I've seen her once before, and her red nose and cracked lips confirm my guess.

She smiles a kind, tired smile while handing me my phone, then frowns again. "Sorry, I had to turn it off. You're being tracked," she whispers.

"What?"

"Just wait." The stranger puts a hand to her lips and remains elusive, then instructs the driver again. "Here!"

The cab pulls over and she motions me to follow. "Come on. Trust me."

After paying the driver, I get out of the cab. I'm not sure why – it's not exactly the rational thing to do. But she's another connection to the Prism in the real world – a loose thread I need to follow.

"Trust you? You just shoved me into a cab and pickpocketed me, but yeah, what the hell!" I reply sarcastically. She waits for the cab to round the corner, then leads me down an alleyway. As I follow her, I pray my dead body isn't unearthed here tomorrow.

The woman rolls aside a small dumpster to reveal a rusted door, then retrieves a key from her pocket, unlocks and pushes the door open and steps into the darkness.

"Um…hello?" I yell after her. "Am I just supposed to follow you in there like a complete idiot? What the hell is going on? Does this have anything to do with –"

The woman leaps back out from the darkness and grabs my arm. "NOT here!"

"Okay! Okay…" I say, recovering from the jolt she gave me.

"I'm not going to kill you. Just come! And keep it down!"

The sweat accumulating on my palms tells me to run. *What have I gotten myself into?* She releases my arm, and I'm a moth to a flame once again as I follow her inside.

"You can leave your helmet here," she tells me as she locks the door. "Now, you can speak."

We're in a narrow, forest green dingy tiled hallway that looks like the set of a zombie horror film from the 80s, minus the blood spatter and corpses. "Where are we?"

She walks briskly. "That's not important. These are just passages. It's where we're going that matters."

"You're not French," I notice.

"No. I'm from Oregon. American, same as you. My name's Sarah."

"Sarah what?"

"Just 'Sarah' to you.'

"Fine, 'Just Sarah', are you watching me too?"

"You figured that out, huh?" Sarah says with a smirk as she turns to look back at me. She has hazel eyes that match her skin and a nose piercing of a star. "Yes, but not like the others."

"And who are these 'others'?" I press her. "Hulk and Shorty?"

Sarah throws her head back and laughs. "Nice. I'm sure they'd love that." She pauses in the eerie hallway and appears to count the chipped tiles on the wall, then places her hands on two large square tiles and presses her body weight against them until the fake Styrofoam block falls out the other end. *Clever camouflage.* The opening is big enough for us to slide our bodies through comfortably. It's a good thing I'm not wearing my best clothes, because we emerge covered in dust and bits of foam into a murky brown hallway. Sarah reinserts the fake block before moving on.

"You sure we can be here?" I ask as I brush the dust off my top.

"Just follow."

"Okay…anyway, you were saying?" I remind her.

Sarah maintains her brisk pace. "I know who you are. Everest Cleary. Born in upstate New York. You and your mom moved to Chicago when you were two. You lived there until your mom died – my condolences by the way – then moved to Paris. Good student, supposedly going to Cambridge but not anymore because your aunt's a bitch…"

"Wait, how –"

"Don't know your dad. Your uncle's death probably messed you up a bit more. Weird sleep schedule and likes to throw stuff when mad."

I stop. Hearing only one set of footsteps, Sarah turns to look at me. She has a sympathetic gaze, and I get the sense that she pities me. "That's just the Coles Notes," she adds.

"Who the hell are you?" I demand, not willing to take another step until she comes clean. I feel completely violated. Who does this person think she is? What right does she have to any of that

information? The anger begins to simmer, and it must be either obvious or palpable because Sarah goes into damage control instantly.

"Woah, you need to relax! You don't want to draw attention to yourself right now." She raises her hands as if she's trying to calm a spooked horse. "We don't want to break any lightbulbs right now, ok?"

She knows! I take a deep breath and turn my anger down but continue to stand my ground.

Sarah seems to realize I'm not going to budge without some answers. She rolls her eyes and gives in. "Have you ever heard of the Vulturian Order?"

"What?" I answer, my throat dry again.

"Exactly. To the world, it doesn't exist. A conspiracy theorist's dream. In a nutshell, they're an invisible superpower and ancient puppet-master that dates all the way back to ancient Sumer."

Ok. That's pretty old.

"Their membership is largely unknown." Sarah continues. "They are thought to be responsible for some of the most significant events in history. And the only reason I know that is because my father's one of them. Otherwise, I'd be in the dark, just like you and the rest of the clueless world. And that's just how they like it."

You'd think after the Prism I'd redefine my criteria of what's normal or believable. Of course, everyone believes conspiracy theories to some extent. It's the reason we make so many movies about them. We all know in our gut that some part of the fiction is fact, which is what makes it all so alluring. But hearing it so definitely confirmed after the night I've just had really brings home the message.

"Sounds a bit exaggerated," I suggest.

"Well, it isn't!" Sarah retorts. "They want you to think it is though, so they can control the narrative. Anyway, long story short that's whose watching you. You and thousands of others. But you…well," Sarah glances at me with that look of pity again, "you're a hot topic these days."

"Me? Wait, if your father is one of them, are you?" I ask suspiciously.

Sarah dips her head from side to side. "Sort of. There's a few more initiations I need to go through before I'm granted full membership. I was just recruited to the Paris chapter this week – that creepy building you were stupid enough to be scoping out. You have a death wish or something?"

I shrug. "No."

"Before coming here, I was stationed at one of their compounds on assignment. Don't ask me where because they never told me, and I never saw the outside world for 90 days so I can't even begin to guess. Anyway, that's where I first saw them tracking you."

There's a lot to unpack from what Sarah's just revealed, but I need to get back to the most burning question. "Why do they care about *me?*"

Sarah takes a left turn into another murky brown hallway. *I really hope she remembers the way out.* "I'm still trying to piece it together," she says. "On the one hand, they're threatened by you, but on the other they think you're the key to something they want."

"And you're deciding to help me because, what…we're both American? Doesn't sound convincing. Why should I trust you?"

Sarah stops in her tracks and stares at me. There's a look of regret in her tired pretty eyes, like their bursting with pain. "I've gone over this moment a hundred times in my head," she tells me. "The moment I would finally give in to my conscience and try to sleep at night again." She slumps heavily against the wall and stares at her feet, averting my gaze. "My assignment required me to track people who emitted a certain frequency, a frequency the Vulturians are threatened by."

"What's a 'frequency'?"

"Energy, essentially. You and the people we track, you vibrate differently. More intensely, I guess. Do you know that?"

Sure, I know that. But until now I didn't realize anyone else did. I didn't realize that sweeping up the remnants of shattered glass didn't erase the proof of what I was – I didn't realize I could be targeted for doing something or being something that I had no name for or control over. I simply nod to Sarah in confirmation.

"Yeah, we know about the lightbulbs too. Anyway," she carries on, "they have a way of finding people like you. They call it the Arachna. It can pick up your frequencies. Every time I reported a significant one, it wouldn't be long before the Order removed the target – person – responsible for it from existence."

"You mean…"

Sarah lifts her chin, the pain more obvious as it nearly spills out of her glassy eyes. "They kill people, Everest. People like you. Except that when your readings flew off the charts there was no 'extinguished' notation on your file the next day. Instead, there was a special task force formed to keep tabs on you, watch your every move. I guess, you're the lucky one. You dodged a literal bullet."

Extinguished? "They could have killed me?" I ask, sinking against the wall from the gut-punch, feeling anything but lucky. *Hulk and Shorty…this whole time, they could have just put a bullet through my window and into my skull, just like that…*

Sarah's voice softens. "Look, I know this must be a shock. I'm sorry. I wish I didn't sound so harsh. But you need to process this later. We need to keep moving if we want to make it in time."

They want to kill me? I straighten back up and feel slightly dizzy but manage to follow Sarah.

She glances around the corridor. "We're almost there."

"Where are we going?" I stutter.

"A sort of spyglass. I found the map and key to this place in my dad's office before I left on assignment. When they recruited me to Paris, I saw my chance to do my own research. Of course, it doesn't help that I don't have full access to anything and am kind of a one-woman show right now. But at least I can spy on the Ertu himself!"

"The who?"

"Sorry. The Ertu. It's the name the Order gives their leader."

We enter an even narrower part of the corridor where we're forced to side-step to fit between the walls. "Keep it down now," Sarah warns. "If they hear us, I'm not sure we'll make it out of here!"

"Sure. Radio silence." *I can barely speak anyway.*

After about thirty more paces, Sarah puts her finger to her lips and moves aside a rectangular brass plate on the wall. There's enough room for both of us to get one eye in, our breathing heavy. I can hear my heart pounding through my chest, but what concerns me more is that I can hear Sarah's too, which means she's just as terrified as I am.

We seem to be peering through a bookshelf. The musty smell of old paper tickles my nostrils.

"She took something out!" A woman says in French. She's beyond my field of view, but there's something about her voice…The echo makes it hard to pinpoint. She's joined by others around a long oval boardroom table, the blazing hearth casting slinky shadows on the mahogany paneling. The curtains are thick and drawn, and the bookshelves seem to form a literary fortress around the room, covering most of the wall space. "A necklace," the woman elaborates. "She got it in the Prism, and it was around her neck when she left her apartment this morning."

A man chimes in. "Impossible! Do you know how many times we have tried taking things out of that place?" He adds something in rapid French that I can't quite make out.

"I saw the photos!" the invisible woman snaps. "I don't know how, but she's able to break the Prism's laws!"

Barely breathing, I bring my trembling fingers up to my neck and clench the pendant tightly.

"It's not that surprising, given the readings," the man sitting at the head of the table replies. "We knew this could be new territory." He sits stoically, like he's silently strategizing the chess pieces in his mind. He resembles a corpse, his pale skin illuminated by the frosty light of a laptop screen. I take a guess that I'm staring at the Ertu.

Hulk speaks next. "Should we eliminate her then Ertu?" His measured tone betrays an inner sadistic intention as he calmly offers up the idea of murdering me. It sends a coldness shooting through my bones. "She may be more of a wild card than we anticipated."

"No, Irra!"

Irra. So that's your name!

The Ertu rises and stands in front of an enormous stone fireplace, observing the flames that reach almost half his height. "She's continued to intensify, against all odds – the only target to show such resistance. She's capable of finding it, I'm sure of that now more than ever. We need patience, not rash action."

"As much as I love disagreeing with Irra," the invisible woman interjects, "he has a point Ertu. With respect, we can't risk her becoming more than we can handle, if she really is as powerful as you say."

"She didn't make it back last night," the Ertu points out.

How does he know that?

"Our test proved she is not unstoppable. But…" the room waits while their leader chooses his next words, "we do need her to return. *If* the Skala is indeed hidden within the Prism, she is no good to us if she can't get in."

Skala? Test? What is happening?!

"And the boy?" Irra presses. "Maybe it's time –"

"He can still prove useful," the Ertu interrupts, raising his hand to suppress Irra's eagerness, "especially now that the two have met. Perhaps it's in our favor that they were paired. We still need to know more about his little circle. We'll have our associates in London close in."

Erik! I feel sick to my stomach and pray I don't throw up. How does he fit into all of this?

The Ertu pours himself a glass of liquor and addresses his twisted associate. "Patience Irra. You'll get your chance to satisfy your thirst for blood. Continue as planned, for now. I want her every move monitored. A clue to finding the Skala could come at any time. We will find it, by the will of Parem."

"By the will of Parem." The bodies in the boardroom repeat the last words after their leader like an incantation before they begin to disperse.

Sarah replaces the brass plate and motions me to backtrack silently. When we're safely out of any possible earshot, she finds her voice. "They meet almost nightly, around the same time."

So many emotions and thoughts pulse through me, my brain feels like scrambled eggs. *Where to start?*

Finally, I settle on the first of many questions. "What's the Skala?"

"I was hoping you'd tell me. I can't seem to find anything on it, and as an initiate I don't have access to the Vulturian archives. All I know is that they want it. The Ertu especially — he wants it badly. He seems obsessed with it and thinks you're his best shot at the prize. Somehow, they think your frequency is an advantage." Sarah chuckles. "But you don't know anything either, so it looks like the joke's on them!"

Our steps echo off the walls. I stop and lean against the tiles while I allow Irra's words to haunt me. "He wanted to eliminate me."

"Try not to let that worry you."

"Easy for you to say! Your name wasn't tossed around in there. He watches my apartment and has a 'thirst for blood', remember?"

Sarah's gaze softens. "I know. And from what I hear he's a soulless monster. I don't even want to think about all the bodies he's buried."

I stare at her wide-eyed, my feeling of dread amplifying by the second. "You're not helping!"

"Sorry!" Sarah adds, grimacing over her insensitivity. "Look, I know you must be scared. But Irra and Basile won't move on you without the Ertu's order. I'll try to keep you updated if I hear anything's changed. But I don't think you have anything to worry about right now. They need you alive."

Basile must be Shorty. "And if things change? If I can't find this Skala thing and they get sick of waiting? If you can't get news to me in time? Why aren't we going to the police? They need to know this is happening!"

Sarah laughs at my apparent naivety, then sneezes, wiping her irritated nose on a used tissue she pulls from the pocket of her jeans. "You don't follow the news much, do you? Didn't you see who was sitting around that table? The Vulturians have infiltrated governments, media companies, universities, banks, Interpol, every intelligence agency... There is no going to the police, not unless you want to tip them off and get us both killed!"

Great! I nod, then continue following Sarah to the exit, feeling hopeless. We move through the fake foam wall back into the green zone. "I wish we had more time, but I don't want to overstay our welcome," Sarah informs me. "I don't know who else knows about these passageways."

"How do I reach you? You can't just leave me with this. I need to know more," I plead.

She hands me my helmet when we reach the exit. "All you need to know for now is that the Vulturians are dangerous and anonymous. Their fingerprints are on everything that matters on this planet, and at the same time they leave no trace. It's the perfect setup, so they pretty much always win. That's why you need to be careful and stay useful to them."

I take the helmet, then look at the troubled stranger, my skepticism returning. "How can I be sure I can trust you?" I ask, then notice her eyes begin to swim again.

"I still see their faces, you know," she replies, this time looking me straight in the eye. "Kids, mothers, grandfathers...I don't think I'll ever stop seeing them. This one little boy, he was four, maybe... I'm the reason these bastards knew about them. *I* fed them the intel. And I have to live with that now." She looks away, holding back the dam of tears lining her lower eyelid, then looks back at me. "I can't make you trust me Everest. You're going to have to decide for yourself if you want to. All I know is...we would have a way better shot of taking them down if we worked together. And with me on the inside, you would have a huge advantage." It's Sarah's turn to plead. "I have to do something to stop them."

I pity her. She's obviously tortured, and for good reason. "You just told me these people have existed for thousands of years and are basically unstoppable. The two of us, we're David and they're Goliath! What shot do we even have?"

"David won, didn't he?" Sarah quickly points out. "You heard them in there – there's some type of resistance, some thorn in their side and you seem to have an in." She waits for me to confirm it but I don't give her anything, refusing to say Erik's name. She seems to understand that my silence is non-negotiable on this point and continues.

"Look, I know little more than you about the Order. Even with my dad…he's a secretive guy. And even if I get full membership, I still won't get access to the juicy stuff right away. If this Prism underground knows anything, you might be able to find out something that could help us."

"What about you? I saw you, at the Luminary. *You* were able to get into the Prism."

Sarah chuckles. "Not the way you think. The Vulturians control my access. All I know is they took me somewhere blindfolded. Ten seconds later I'm being released into the most incredible world I've ever seen, only to be told I'm not welcome there, which, let me tell you was a huge letdown! But I don't know where I crossed over, and I don't think I'll be back any time soon. They just dangled a carrot Everest. They're good at that sort of thing. 'Hey, look at what you get if you stay loyal to us and do all the despicable things we tell you to do.' At the end of the day, the blindfold went back on, and I found myself back in the chapter house. At least it showed me that the Vulturians don't get in the same way as the Wakers. They're imposters Everest. They don't belong. *I* don't belong."

Deep down, among all the feelings of dread and fear and anger, I feel sympathy for Sarah. I want to stay in the dingy hallway for hours, picking her brain about everything she's seen and heard. But I can tell she's eager to leave and growing anxious.

"Your phone's bugged," she tells me. "Wait until you're far from here to turn it back on. Your house is bugged too. Cameras, listening devices…the works. Don't underestimate these people Everest. And don't do anything stupid, even in the Prism. Watch your back. I'll be in touch, I promise."

"How?"

Sarah wiggles her nose and starts to pull out another tissue. "I'll find you. Don't go looking for me. Don't even say my name. And don't show or speak of this passage to anyone! Only I can take you in, understand?"

I nod. I understand, I just don't like it. She seems to catch on to my inner rebel because her eyes narrow at me. "Don't even think it! This is not a game."

My mind turns to Erik and my stomach twists. "They know of people I'm close to."

Sarah nods. "You can keep them safe by staying valuable. And best not to say anything about the Order, yet. Now go! They'll be waiting for you at home. And please, try to act normal, like we never met."

"Right, normal," I mutter as I step out into the evening air. *That won't be hard at all.*

* * *

Thankfully, no one thought to steal my beat-up scooter. After bringing it home, I try to glance casually up and down Rue Marienne. Another car occupies the space of the Mercedes.

Probably another shift, considering Irra and Basile are busy plotting my execution at the big, haunted mansion. I feel vulnerable and shaken as I pass the car and resist the urge to look at the driver.

Vulturians. *Who knew?* I thought all this conspiracy stuff was just used to sell books and movie tickets. Yet here I am, living it. The main character in my own thriller.

Catherine's voice invites itself into my brain again. *"I told you Everest. You were so naïve Everest."* Even Aunt Michaela was onto something. How sad is that?

Inside the flat, I resist another urge – to turn the apartment upside down and rip out the bugs. That would only put a target on my back. I eye the ceilings and walls suspiciously and wonder how many cameras are pointed at me.

But I can't let my negative thoughts get the best of me again. *Not tonight! Not again!* Besides, returning to the Prism seems to be the only way I'll stay valuable and alive.

After changing and feeling incredibly exposed and violated – not knowing who might be watching me like a zoo animal, and from where – I throw my sawdust covered jeans into the hamper and make a beeline for the study, launching myself thirstily at the stack of Nat Geos. My thoughts turn to my own dimension. I can make it into my own oasis that I can escape to – my own private world where no one can enter unless I let them. Within seconds the magazines are sprawled across the floor. *Let fate decide.* I close my eyes and shuffle, then rest a hand on my final selection.

Caves. Where the Earth's mysterious past lies dormant in dark recesses, longing to be unearthed.

It's fitting, and as good a place as any to start.

CHAPTER 20

The Most Unusual Thing

R*emarkable! I actually did it!*

I sit speechless on my bed which, along with my wardrobe, bedside table and one terrace door overlooking the Nucleus is all that remain of my original dimension. I can't decide what I'm more impressed by — my creation or the fact that I've accomplished it on my first try. It manifested effortlessly before my eyes, pulled from the blueprints I sketched in my mind. Not only am I back, but I've created something – *my* something – from nothing.

The sunlight letting itself in through openings in the cave's ceiling casts white ripples across the navy-blue granite walls. Deeper into the recesses the walls lighten to a deep turquoise, beckoning me towards glaciers waiting within. Five corridors branch out from my position, all leading to a place where only my imagination has been but not yet my physical body. But the most fascinating elements are the glow worms that hang like string lights from the walls, making the entire space feel like a cosmic gateway.

I'm still in wonder of it when I hear two knocks, and that familiar tingling sensation propels my trembling body to the door. I place my hand on the doorknob, steady my nerves and pull it towards me. Erik stands there, just as I remember him. It feels like it's been weeks since I saw him last, and I'm glad I don't have to wait a minute longer. "Morning," he says softly. Our eyes stay glued to each other for a moment before I reach out to embrace him. He holds me tightly, exhaling a breath into my hair, and I feel those confusing emotions resurfacing. It takes all my strength to overcome the magnetic force pulling me in.

"I didn't have time to change," I say, glancing at my pajamas when I finally pull away, a little embarrassed.

But Erik's attention is directed at something else now. "Are those…glow worms?" He steps past me, distracted and wide-eyed. "Ev…this is brilliant! Most Wakers need months…"

I smile proudly to myself as I let him pass. "Yeah. I guess it turned out all right." I try to find clothes to change into while Erik saunters around in awe, whispering exclamations to himself as he dodges the glowing strings.

We spend a generous amount of time exploring the caves while Erik keeps repeating his earlier disbelief. The glaciers are ethereal, with white foamy waterfalls that escape through cracks in the glassy surface. We can see our skewed reflections in the mirror-like walls, the magnificent blue color leaving a lasting imprint in my mind. It's not easy to finally leave my dimension behind, having only scratched the surface. But I've got time on my side now – a second life.

There's no rush.

"I've planned our whole day!" Erik proclaims as we finally head outside. "How does Azula sound?" His gaze shifts to the pendant around my neck and the corners of his mouth lift. "You're wearing it again."

"Actually…," I lift my fingers to the pendant anxiously, "I maybe kind of never really took it off? I woke up with it, at home. It was strange…didn't you say we can't remove anything from the Prism?"

I don't know what to make of Erik's reaction. I expected some degree of surprise, but he just stares at me with a blank look, like I'm suddenly a stranger.

"Is it something I said?" I ask.

"Ev, no one has ever taken anything out of the Prism. Not even Robert, and he…believe me, we've all tried. If anyone had ever succeeded, we'd know by now. It's just not possible!" He picks up the necklace with his forefinger to inspect it. "You're sure? Of course, you're sure. Sorry."

Finally, he lets out a sigh and appears to give up, letting the pendant fall from his finger. "Right, well, we'll figure it out later. For now, we have a flight to catch."

* * *

I don't think I'll ever tire of the thrill of riding Juno – the calming rhythm of every wingbeat, the hot breath that escapes from her nostrils and travels back to graze my skin. Erik insisted we fly instead of portal to "get the full experience," and as I follow him out of Edenia I beat myself up a little on the inside for letting myself lose a whole Prism day.

Never again!

We pass two stone monoliths standing half a football field apart on the border of Estra. They stand there without obvious purpose, two soldier-like figures facing each other in ghostly silence, towering over the plain and making me feel incredibly insignificant. Only the mountains come close to their grandeur. As Erik guides the horses between the massive structures, I veer off course to study the intricate carvings up close— the wrinkles on their stoic faces, the armor over their tunics that appears to be from some lost, by-gone era, overlaid with brilliant emerald triangles with a small star in the center – some kind of Prism emblem I presume. The figures have no helmets or weapons, but everything about them feels protective, like they're standing guard to something that lurks in the ether, invisible to human eyes. Speaking of eyes, Juno and I could fit in one of their pupils.

"They're enormous!" I exclaim as Erik circles back to me.

"We call them the Emerald Guard. They stand on the borders of every realm," he explains.

"What for?"

"Not a clue. There's probably some obscure text on it in the Lumus, although no one's found it yet, to my knowledge anyway."

"It has to be more than a way to mark a border," I muse. "The sheer size…" Add it to the list of questions I don't have the answers to.

Erik guides us over rice fields, a replica of Zhangjiajie Forest, and the rainbow mountains, and I long to set down on every one of them. But my magister's smile tells me to have patience — that I'll see it all in good time. He flies on, refusing to deviate from our course and teasing me mercilessly. Eventually, we pass between another set of monoliths – this time covered in circular emeralds – and head towards the turquoise coast of Azula.

Erik delivers! The day is nothing short of spectacular. After exploring reefs and taking on tumultuous waves, we leave the pristine beaches on a sailboat and head northward to a string of islands that resemble a pastel painting — as if an artist reached down from the heavens and swirled the silky white sand with the turquoise water like a melted sundae.

"How many times have you been to each of the realms?" I ask Erik as we take in the view.

"All more than once — some more than others. I still haven't seen it all."

"Do you have a favorite?"

He thinks for a moment. "A few." The sun highlights the subtle streaks in his brown hair. "It's impossible to choose just one."

"Will you show me?" I ask, resting my head on his bare shoulder comfortably, as if already knowing him a lifetime.

"Every corner," he promises, running a finger over the inside of my palm as the boat rocks us back and forth.

I could stay with him like this forever. There's no pressure, nothing but sky, water, and the smell of the sea on our skin. It's the perfect moment.

But leave it to my stupid brain to get in the way.

I sit up, that anxious guilt poking at my insides as I recall the disaster I was the night before. "I think it's finally starting to hit me, how I don't have to be limited anymore." I look out at the paradise that stretches around me. "But its bittersweet. So many can't experience this. It just doesn't seem fair Erik. Why us? Why me? I'm no different than the next person. You should see how volatile I can get when I let my anger get the best of me."

"Thanks for the warning." Erik pretends to move away and I playful shove him.

"I'm serious!"

"Look, clearly the Prism thinks you should be here," he replies, moving closer again. "And it's up to everyone to find their own way."

"But what about those who live in deplorable conditions, who've suffered unspeakable tragedies?"

"History is full of people who experienced tragedy and injustice and went on to accomplish incredible things, even change the course of humanity for the better," Erik insists.

"And people from impoverished countries awaken here every day, while many from the first world remain shut out, gambling away their inheritances in the world's fanciest casinos and trying other ineffective ways to fill a void."

"Yeah, I know, but —"

Erik continues passionately, his face flushed now. "And how many use their misfortunes as crutches and excuses? That's *their* choice!" He throws aside his shirt in frustration, visibly agitated for the first time since our meeting. He runs his hands anxiously through his hair as if wanting to rip it out and I realize I've just hit a major nerve.

"Look, you're not wrong," he continues, softening. "In an ideal world, everyone should see the Prism. I just…I think we have a lot more power to change and evolve than society lets us believe. Even if we're born into something, we have our minds, we have our will. So, getting in, maybe it's a just reward rather than an undeserved privilege." He shrugs his shoulders. "Or maybe I'm just good at rationalizing things to avoid feeling guilty myself. I don't know. I guess…I just don't think we should have to apologize for the good things we have. It doesn't make us any less deserving, so long as we do good with it. You can't carry the burden of the entire world on your shoulders Ev. It's ok to be present in the moment and enjoy your blessings."

I reach for his hand to comfort him, trying to ease whatever weighs on his heart. He makes a lot of sense, and I know deep down that he's right — that there's nothing wrong with simply feeling blessed and grateful and trying to pay it all forward.

But I'm still convinced something else is keeping more of humanity from finding the Prism, and I can't even begin to conceive of what that could be. For the moment I drop the subject, not wanting to rub salt in Erik's wounds.

Erik's vulnerability brings to mind other concerns I haven't been able to push aside. "Is London safe?" I ask, very suspiciously.

Erik's brows come together. "Um…I guess so, I mean, it's as safe as any big city I suppose. That's a rather odd question. Why do you ask?"

Fix this! Don't be weird. "You know, since I'm coming to visit…just want to make sure there's nothing I need to worry about."

"Let's see…there's some swindlers that like to target tourists so steer clear of those…and I mentioned that I have a crazy roommate. That's probably the scariest part. Am I missing something?"

I give him my best attempt at a reassuring smile. I can't tell him about Sarah, even though I desperately want to. I can't tell him about the Vulturians and their sinister dealings, or that they've got Erik on their radar, because what if that puts him in more danger. All I can do is try to read his body language, which seems to be that of a person who has no idea they're being watched by a powerful secret order. "You're not missing anything," I lie. "Just being my nosy self."

As I fill Erik in on meeting Julian and Lise, an iconic horizon comes into view. Awestruck yet again, I leap from my seat.

"*Bora Borealis?* Are you serious?"

"The one and only!" Erik steers the boat to the side for an unobstructed view. "Well, I guess now there's two of them, or infinite numbers perhaps, if there really are parallel universes."

I can't take my eyes off the water. It's like a shade of blue I'm seeing for the first time, even more mesmerizing than the shade of my dimension glaciers.

Erik brings the boat to a halt in the still clear water, then comes to sit next to me. "Can I see it, if you don't mind?" he asks, motioning to my neck. I snap out of my daydream and unfasten the clasp, then place the necklace in his palm and observe him as he studies it.

"It's looks so normal," he mutters, rotating the tiny object and holding it up to the diminishing light, "and yet it's done the most unusual thing." He examines it for about a minute before finally returning it to me, but I can tell he wants to put it under a microscope and dissect it methodically. "Unless it's not the necklace…" He looks at me as if he's had a sudden revelation, and I feel like he's about to divulge something.

But our mutual puzzlement is interrupted by a silent symphony of northern lights, their ethereal hues reflecting in the Prismatic, revealing how Bora Borealis got its name. We climb out of the boat and stand in silence in the warm shallow water, content with our unanswered questions for the time being. Grains of illuminated sand twinkle like stars beneath our feet and create a dramatic dance floor for the glowing pastel waves moving through the heavens, the moons and stars appearing behind them.

Nothing is keeping me from this again, I promise myself.
Nothing!

Interlude

Erik Halvorsen waited until 2:30 in the afternoon before ringing Robert on the burner. He'd only dialed the number twice before. He knew Robert was probably on his way to teach a class on the other side of the Atlantic, but that if the burner rang, he'd answer, no matter where he was.

Robert's voice came on the line after the third ring.

"The Lion roams…"

"Until it wakes again," Erik replied, completing the code phrase. "How are you?"

"Well, I just gave a lecture in Portland last night, so I'd say 'jetlagged' and 'thrilled to be home' sums it up."

"Quite right."

"So, what is it?"

Erik had fallen asleep on the boat with Everest in the Prism and never had the chance to find Robert and tell him what he'd discovered. The news couldn't wait any longer. Erik spoke slowly, deliberately, articulating every letter. "Someone has taken something out of the Vault."

Robert remained silent for a few moments. "Are you sure?" he finally asked.

"Yes."

"What was it? Have you seen it?"

"A necklace. There's nothing unusual about the object, from what I can tell. I've seen it only in the Vault. And I don't think she would lie."

"She? Your new friend?" Robert asked, careful not to give away the name.

"Yes. I trust her."

More silence as the professor tried to rationalize the information, unsuccessfully. "Okay," Robert finally replied without offering his reasons for believing Erik so readily. "No object has ever breached the Vault. We must learn if it connects to anything. I assume you spend a lot of time together?"

Erik delayed answering, uncomfortable with what he assumed Robert was asking. He hadn't planned on lying to Everest any more than he already had to.

"Keeping our eyes open won't hurt," Robert urged, sensing his hesitation.

"Right," Erik agreed. "I'll see what I can find out."

"Be careful. I've been followed at least three times here, and once out of town. I don't know why I'm not already tied up in a trunk somewhere, but our luck could run out at any moment."

"They've tailed me too," Erik admitted, "but they seem content to stay in the shadows."

"For now. Stay vigilant. We'll discuss this further at the next meeting." Robert ended the call and limped off in the direction of his waiting students, while Erik put away the burner and turned his attention to William Bartlett who had just entered his office looking smug and satisfied.

Erik leaned in and looked sternly at the boy. "So, Billy, I thought we already established that chemistry class is not the appropriate forum for spitballs."

* * *

Irra observed the angry women flicking her ponytail and reading a text message in the dimly lit lounge.

"Come on," she fumed under her breath. "There has to be some darkness to you, something I can exploit, some way to get back what should have been mine."

Irra didn't fully understand her sudden hatred for the Cleary girl, but he respected her darkness.

"You sound like a psychopath, mumbling to yourself like that," he told her as he continued to ice his knuckles.

The woman glared at him in disgust. "Everyone knows that title belongs to you," she retorted, "though I'm sure you'd welcome it as a compliment." She thought him a vile creature, classless and purely sadistic, and she was right.

"Come now! We are on the same team, for once. Don't let the number of bodies I've buried keep you from what could be a mutually satisfying partnership."

"I don't do well in partnerships."

"Irra!" one of their associates called from the lounge doorway. "The Ertu wishes to see you."

Irra couldn't hold back his smile. It wasn't every day he allowed one and it looked as if it would crack his otherwise stone-faced visage in half. "This better be good. My resume is far too impressive for baby-sitting little girls, don't you agree?"

The woman scowled and ignored him, returning her attention to her phone.

Irra made his way to the third floor and arrogantly opened the door at the West end of the hall without knocking – the only member of the Chapter who would dare be so bold. But he knew the Ertu needed his special skill set, and that allowed him some liberties.

The Ertu sat in a halo of thick smoke, smoking a cigar. He annoyed Irra, like everything else that drew breath. But the old man fed his darkness, so they played their mutually satisfying game quite well.

"I have a new assignment for you," the old man said matter-of-factly as he motioned Irra to take a seat. "You'll be happy to know it's a little more in your wheelhouse.

"The Bolivian Minister of the Environment has developed some morals at the most inconvenient time," the Ertu elaborated, "and won't allow us to build the water treatment plant as planned due to some burial site with piles of bones in it. And he's got a following, which complicates things even further."

"How many in total?"

"Seven. They're meeting to decide the matter in the morning, according to our sources. We need to buy some time before they convene a new panel. It would allow us to get things started. It is imperative that we get things started."

The Ertu handed Irra seven files, complete with photos and details.

"Seven politicians in a closed space…" Irra managed his second smile of the day. But his glee was short-lived once he realized the required optics. "It can't appear targeted."

The skeletal man coughed out the last of the smoke that filled his lungs. "I know you prefer the messier assignments, but yes, this one must look like an accident. Choose one of them to feed your addiction, if you must. But the evidence must be destroyed completely." He put out his cigar in the ash tray. "A fire is usually effective. But I'll leave the details to you."

CHAPTER 21

A Look in the Mirror

EVEREST CLEARY

"I love the sea," Erik divulges as we stand ankle deep in the Prismatic on my fourth day back. "It has the unparalleled ability to calm the soul. My brother and I…" he pauses briefly, "we loved visiting the coast in the summers. And Norway in the winters. My brother would spend days skiing up there, teaching me, or at least trying to. I don't know how we managed it – it's so brutally cold compared to England."

He seems entrenched in a distant memory again, his bright eyes cloaked in a blanket of sorrow, yet the corners of his mouth revealing a sense of nostalgic joy.

"If you still want to come to London, I could show it to you," he offers eagerly. "The coast that is. It's not that far of a drive. My parents are at the summer house for another week or so before they head back to the city."

My stomach flip-flops. *His parents?* I've just met *him*. Then again, nothing in my life moves at a normal pace anymore.

"I'd like that," I agree, trying to hide my apprehension.

Erik smiles at me and brushes another strand of hair away from my face. Once again, I feel my heart ache for more of him, but I can't bring myself to tell him.

"See you at Stella's, don't forget," he says.

We've planned an afternoon with the rest of the group in Estra, but Erik has "some things to take care of" first.

"Where are you off to?" I ask, strongly suspecting he isn't telling me something about the Prism. The whispers between him and Robert, the comments about secret theories, Sarah's mention of a resistance group, the Ertu's interest in Erik…something's up. Why won't Erik confide in me? *Doesn't he trust me?*

As expected, Erik skirts my question. "It won't take me long. You should go. Don't keep Lise and Julian waiting."

* * *

"Everest?" Maeve's voice catches my attention as I walk into Eden Hall. Her stunning hair is arranged in a tight braid that falls elegantly over her shoulder, and a dark plum dress compliments her flawless porcelain skin. I suddenly feel very ordinary in my jean shorts and sneakers.

"Hi." I try to mask my ambivalence. Maeve's given me no reason to dislike her.

"I was hoping I would run into you again," she says cheerfully. "We didn't really get a chance to chat the other day."

No, I suppose we didn't. "We should fix that," I reply, with a genuine determination to push my inner jealous voice aside.

"Up for some butter-drenched popcorn? They're screening *Roman Holiday* at the cinema. I can never pass up an old Hollywood classic."

I feel guilty for not giving her a chance. She seems sweet and undeserving of my coldness. "That's tempting! I wish I could, but I already committed to something. Another time?"

Maeve grins. "Absolutely."

"Are you coming to Estra later?" I follow-up, this time genuinely hoping she'll be there and determined not to let any negative thoughts stand in my way again.

"I'm not sure," she replies after a pause. "You're meeting at Stella's? I'll try to be there." She waves as she ascends the moving stairs, just before a boy in a Star Wars t-shirt pops into view, his little sister in tow.

"Everest!" Lise practically yells, her light brown hair gathered in her signature pigtails.

"Hey! Missed you guys!" I hug her tightly. Julian just stands there awkwardly with his shy grin but accepts my offer at a high-five. We chat briefly about the progress on their house on our way up the steps.

"They let us go by again. Maman came too! There was a very large wasp nest in the attic." Julian tells me, allowing some excitement to break through his wall. "So, what are we doing today?"

I had planned on letting the kids take the wheel and make all the decisions. "I'm just here for the company, really. This is your day! Any requests?"

"Space!" Julian pipes up first, coming more out of his shell by the second. "And battleships."

"I do love the stars!" Lise chimes in.

"Erik mentioned there was an observatory here…" I scan the levels and see something resembling a shopping mall map. "Come on!" We step off onto the fourth floor to study it.

"They have arcade games!" Julian exclaims.

Lise groans. "You can play those anywhere."

"We can do more than one thing," I remind them.

Since they're around the corner, we start at the arcades and eventually make our way to the observatory, where Julian's right eye remains glued to a telescope for the entirety of the visit. Detailed images of the moons and planets that make up the Prism's incredible sky cover the walls, making me feel small yet again.

"Look at the rings on this one!" Julian exclaims, pointing to a purple planet that resembles Saturn.

"Is Saturn your favorite planet?" I ask.

He nods to confirm, the smile slowly slipping from his face. "It was mine and my father's. He would always try to see it through our telescope. It was a very cheap telescope, so it was a little blurry and hard to see. But we did see Saturn a few times. He would love this…"

His voice trails off, and my heart almost can't take it. *Why did I ask?* I didn't mean to bring forward painful memories. Not today. Not here. Today was supposed to be about laughter and happiness and cotton candy and fun. It wasn't supposed to be about reality.

But the Prism doesn't magically erase memories, regrets, and pain. It's not some antidote to our past that scrubs away all the unfortunate events on our hard drive. As much as I might want it to work that way, it just doesn't. Life sticks with you, no matter how much you try to forget it.

"Why don't you come to Estra with me today?" I suggest, trying to lighten the mood.

"Do you mean it?" Lise exclaims. "With you? Will there be pandas?"

I laugh. I miss being a child – the simple things brought so much delight. "There better be! Otherwise, it would be kind of a rip off, don't you think?"

An unexpected shadow comes over the little girl's twinkling

eyes and she lowers them to the floor. "I thought you only came today because you felt sorry for us," she reveals in a near whisper, as if embarrassed by her own words. "A lot of people do these days. Maman says we should be careful not to get too attached, so we don't get hurt."

Her words catch me off guard. *What a hopeless belief.* How could this perfect child think such a thing?

I take her gently by the shoulders, crouch down and bring her dark pretty eyes up to my own while biting the inside of my cheek to keep my tears tucked away. "Listen to me Lise…you and your bother are incredible, and a lot more fun than a lot of grown-ups I know. I'd spend time with you over them in a heartbeat," I assure her, looking up at Julian to make sure he knows the message is also meant for him. He pulls his sad eyes away from the planets long enough to shoot me a smile. (It's more of a subtle lip-twitch, but I take it as a win.) "You need to promise me that you'll always believe that! I'm not here because I pity you. I'm here because I want to be. Look at the fun we have together!"

Of course, there's a teaspoon of pity mixed in with all the emotions I feel for these children. How could there not be? But that's not the reason they've come to instantly matter to me. There's something about them – something that makes me want to move mountains just to see a hint of joy on their faces. Maybe it's because I can appreciate their loss and their unspoken grief, or because I can relate to Julian's inability to fully trust and confide. Maybe it's because I understand Lise's mask of care-free innocence that she lets slip-off every now and then to reveal her inner torment and vulnerability. Maybe it's because I sympathize with their loneliness, or their need to grow up quickly, or not wanting to feel like someone's charity case all the time.

Maybe it's all of the above.

Perhaps my involvement is selfish because it makes me feel needed. Or maybe seeing more than my own reflection in the mirror helps me feel less lonely.

Whatever the reason, my comments seem to do some good for I see the worry in Lise's pretty face become replaced by a hopeful glow.

"Now," I say, straightening myself up, "the real question is, do *you* two want to spend the afternoon with a bunch of boring grown-ups?"

CHAPTER 22

A Theory

"I've heard a lot about you two," Erik tells Lise and Julian at Stella's when we join the group before heading out to Estra. The two kids immediately take to Erik and Fox, who entertain them with clever riddles. With every correct answer Fox orders up a new flavor of ice cream. By the time Jenna, Francine and Simon arrive, they've tried blueberry orchid, sweet chili banana, and apple cinnamon crepe.

Maeve joins us in the nick of time. "You missed out on some five-star ice cream combos," Fox boasts.

Maeve grimaces. "If they were anything like those tacos you ordered for us then I dodged a bullet."

"Everyone loved those tacos!"

"No, Fox. No," Jenna agrees with Maeve as they reflect on the apparently awful culinary experience. She wrinkles her nose in a display of disgust. "They were *no bueno*."

"Are we flying?" Maeve asks nervously, apparently afraid of horses, or heights, or a combination of the two.

"Actually," Erik says with his mischievous grin, "we had a different idea!"

* * *

"Are you joking? You know how I feel about boats!" Jenna complains as we stand in front of the dragon boat that will whisk us away to Estra. "Are you're *trying* to torture me? We might as well be sitting in the water!"

"Maeve and Francine aren't keen on portals, or flying," Erik points out. "Come on, Jenna! You're a history fanatic. These things have been around for thousands of years. I thought you'd appreciate this a little."

The dragon boat is indeed impressive, meticulously carved and painted in crimson and indigo designs.

Francine tries to lift Jenna's spirits. "It's the Prism. There's nothing to worry about."

"Says the girl who's afraid to portal!" Jenna retorts.

"It creeps me out, okay!"

"I'm an excellent swimmer. I'll save you if you fall in," Julian volunteers valiantly, lifting his chin to appear taller to Jenna. I feel a sense of pride over his adorable new-found confidence, even if Jenna doesn't.

Jenna sighs. "That's sweet. But you're ten."

"Twelve," I correct her, but Jenna just groans.

We take our seats, with Jenna insisting she be in the middle, apparently convinced she will be the last to drown in that position. Fox eagerly takes a seat at the front.

"How fast can this thing possibly…." Before Simon can complete his sentence, the boat takes off on Fox's orders, sending us jerking backward on a wild thrill ride. Fox sticks close to the scenic coastline, with its azure water and pebbly beaches lined with fuchsia bougainvillea and elegant Cyprus trees. The only thing throwing a wrench into the experience is the sound of Jenna's intermittent screams, which eventually convince Fox to slow the speed. I'm not ready for the ride to be over when we cross into Estra and pull up to the white sands of a Thai-inspired shoreline. I deduce from how spritely Jenna runs to shore while mumbling things to herself that she's had quite enough of boats for a while.

Lise and Julian waste no time interacting with a group of monkeys who are determined to get whatever we have in our pockets. The Prism seems to read my thoughts, and I look down to see a banana at my feet. One of the mischievous creatures leaps over and devours it in an instant. The peel vanishes just as quickly.

Per Fox's suggestion, we start at The Great Wall. It resembles a giant serpent, weaving from the edge of the shoreline through the surrounding Estra hillsides. Other Wakers have set down their winged transport nearby. I'm not sure what these magical creatures eat, or if they even need to, but just for the heck of it I imagine a bushel of apples for them and watch as they contently chomp away at the fruit.

While studying the passing faces I find myself feeling unsettled. If Sarah got in, there could be other Vulturians here too. I could always keep my eyes open for anyone with an obvious ailment. But if these people could stay in the shadows on Earth, they would certainly know how to stay off the radar anywhere.

"Odd place for a bushel of apples," Francine observes, walking up behind me.

"Oh," I say, pushing aside my worrying thoughts, "yeah, I just thought they might want a snack. It really is amazing, being able to manifest whatever you want. I mean, when Erik first told me I'm not sure I really believed him."

Francine turns to face me, a look of alarm on her face.

"What is it?" I ask.

"What did you just say?"

I stare at her. Then at the bushel. Then at Francine again. "Did I do something wrong?"

"Everest, we can't manifest in the Nucleus; only in our dimension, remember?"

Right! Erik did say something about that, didn't he…

But it doesn't make sense. The banana…

"How did you do that?" Francine presses me, her eyes on fire with a desire to not only know, but to have whatever ability I seem to possess. The change in her demeanor makes me uncomfortable. I don't want to draw any attention to myself in case someone's watching.

"You know what, probably a trick of the mind," I lie, playing dumb. "It must have been there the whole time. Sometimes our minds misattribute information. That's why eyewitness testimony can be so unreliable."

Please buy it!

My re-direct seems to work, and Francine's brow relaxes. "Hmmm," she mutters, "that's true." Then she turns on her heel and walks off to catch up to the others.

Keep things to yourself from now on!

I stare at the bushel again and bite my lip as I try to fill it back up with fruit. To my dismay, more apples appear, and I realize with a sinking feeling that I'm different from everyone else here in yet another way.

I try to push the thought out of my mind for the time being, determined to make the most out of my afternoon in Estra and not say anything to Erik just yet. *Keep it light and cheerful!*

It's easy to see why the Wall is 'great.' As a military tool, it's formidable and ingenious, and I can see for miles in either direction. Eventually, I catch up to Erik and Fox as they huddle over something near one of the watchtowers.

"What's going on? What are you looking at?"

Fox steps awkwardly in front of the space they're examining, trying to conceal it. "We were just admiring how the ancient Chinese…built…stuff."

That's it! I'm over it. No more secrets.

"Oh, stop it Fox!" I snap, still on edge from my near slip-up with Francine. "You're a terrible liar — both of you! What is the big deal about me seeing a rock anyway?" I push Fox out of the way and crouch beside Erik who's studying a piece of the wall. There's a melon-sized hole in it, like someone's shot a cannon straight through.

"It's nothing," Erik mumbles. "Just a hole."

I study the remainder of the wall – intact, untouched. *Why this void?* It seems like an insignificant detail, but in a world where every detail is in perfect order it begs questions. I glance at Erik, hoping he'll finally be honest with me. "It's not 'nothing', is it?"

Erik shoots a pleading look at Fox who appears to be deciding whether I'm trustworthy or not. Fox heaves an exaggerated sigh. "You'll keep this to yourself?" he asks.

"Who could I possibly tell?"

"I need a 'yes.' "

It's my turn to sigh, impatiently. "Of course, yes."

Fox guides me a few meters away before Erik begins his explanation. "Fox and I have been noticing some…inconsistencies in the Prism. Not in the dimensions – so far, those appear unaffected. Only we can control them. But the Nucleus is supposed to be stable and as close to perfect as you can get. Yes, a loose stone here and there isn't anything to panic about, but –"

"The dolphin…," I mumble to myself. I had almost forgotten about it.

Erik nods. "Just another example of some kind of disharmony, something wrong with the Nucleus."

"We've been noticing changes for the past year and a half, in all the realms," Fox adds, careful not to let anyone overhear. "In Oransen, a whole village literally vanished within hours while we were on Safari — no trace of it. Just gone!"

"But isn't the Prism always changing, always adapting to everyone's desires or whatever?" I say, hoping to be of help.

"Change has always been gradual," Erik explains. "Sudden eradications are unheard of. And dead animals floating around – I mean, that should *never* happen. Then there are the little imperfections, like this, which seem so trivial you wonder why the population would want them to exist in the first place. It doesn't make sense."

"Is Robert worried?"

Erik looks away, avoiding my prying gaze. I don't share his talent for mind-reading. "Right now, we're just gathering intel," he says. "We don't know why the Nucleus isn't repairing itself."

The Prism disposed of everything non-essential. Surely, it could fix what was broken…

"What if the Prism doesn't want to fix itself?" I think out loud. "What if it's trying to tell you something… leaving clues." *Leaving clues?* It sounded better in my head. "Never mind…I hear it. That's clearly ridiculous."

"Clues," Fox repeats. I expect him to make fun of me, but he doesn't, and neither does Erik.

"Why did that village vanish when we were there?" Erik asks, "at *that* specific moment."

"I dunno. It's a bit far-fetched," Fox says doubtfully, more serious than I've ever seen him.

"Being the group cynic doesn't really suit you," I tell him, preferring his goofier side.

"It's a theory," Erik says hopefully. "We'll run it by…Robert." He seems to want to say more, and I'm getting more skilled at recognizing his tells. I don't like being kept in the dark, but I know his allegiance to Robert and Fox came first, and I have to respect that.

My thoughts are suddenly interrupted by a deep growl coming from behind me. I turn slowly, not knowing what to expect.

"Now, don't freak out. It's just Charaka," Erik tells me calmly, trying to prevent panic. In front of me sits a full-grown female tiger, her mouth parted in a grin that showcases her fierce set of teeth. "She's harmless — the Wall's guardian, or so we call her. She won't hurt you." Erik crouches in front of the massive cat and rubs her under her scruff, eliciting grateful purrs. "I thought I told you not to sneak up on newbies, you beautiful girl!"

I eye the tiger with trepidation, remembering that in the real-world tigers eat people. But Charaka's almost neon green eyes have a hypnotizing tranquility to them.

"Come on," Erik urges. "She's a big softie."

I approach cautiously and touch the creature's back, letting my hand travel over her smooth striped coat.

"All the animals in the Prism coexist with us in harmony," Fox explains. "They won't so much as look at you funny."

"A tiger!" Julian yells, running up fearlessly. Charaka proves Fox's point as she licks Julian's face like a domesticated kitten.

"Better than the zoo, right?" Maeve says, joining with Lise. They reach out their hands to pet Charaka, but the big cat wants no part of their attention. The tiger hisses defensively and pulls back her pink lips, causing Lise to scream and Maeve to jump back and withdraw her hand from the reach of the animal's intimidating jaws.

"You good?" Fox asks Maeve as he pulls Lise back too. Maeve just nods, visibly shaken, and takes several steps back to join Lise.

Nearby, the stressed tiger paces in a circle. Erik approaches slowly and after some whispering and coaxing, soothes Charaka back to her docile self, petting her like nothing ever happened. "I've never seen any animal in the Prism react that way," he whispers, as he rejoins us. "It's not like her..."

"Another clue?" I suggest under my breath, watching the tiger lazily stroll away.

I can almost see the question marks floating in Erik's eyes. "Possibly."

CHAPTER 23

Glass Houses

Our group disperses as evening approaches, with some heading back to Castellum and others making for unexplored corners. Lise and Julian depart with Fox and Jenna, which gives me the time to make one final stop.

"You can leave if you want," I tell Erik, insincerely.

"Well, to be honest, I've been waiting all afternoon for this."

"For what?"

He seems to blush a little. "Just…spending time, just the two of us."

I'm still too much of a coward to admit how elated that makes me.

"But if you really want me to go…"

Before he can finish, I grab his hand and drag him towards Juno and Cass who are already waiting to lift us way.

The mountains loom in the distance like gods, dustings of snow softening their jagged exterior. As we soar upward to reach the top of Mount Everest, I feel my breath catch. There it stands, isolated and treacherous, yet regal. We circle the peak several times, and each time it's not enough.

I set Juno down on the summit and place my sneakers in the snow without a worry in the world about frostbite or being able to breathe at this altitude. The Prismatic waits on the horizon, the Great Wall a speck in the distance. Everything falls away as I look down from the Prism's highest point, feeling a silent call to live up to the strength behind my name and imagining what so many would give to see what I'm seeing right now. *I wonder if my father ever got the chance.*

"You just conquered Everest," Erik jokes, setting down next to me. "How does it feel?"

"Like I cheated," I admit, taking in the view and mountain air. "But it's pretty darn cool."

Unbelievably cool!

There's a serenity and silence up here that's unparalleled. I just want to build myself a den in the snow and stay a while, away from all the questions and worries and developments of the last few days. But this peak doesn't belong to me alone, and I can see other Wakers approaching in the distance for their turn at the scenic stopover.

Erik guides Cass away, and I follow reluctantly, leaving the mountain drenched in the sunset. We dismount at the foot of the mountain for one last look. As we lead the horses down a stone path surrounded by wispy reed grass, an odd sensation of deja-vu overcomes me.

"What is it?" Erik asks, noticing the look on my face.

I shiver, looking up at the mountain I left behind. "I don't know. For some reason this feels familiar. It's weird though…almost like I'm seeing it through someone else's eyes." I can't seem to shake the odd sensation and feel my pendant grow warm on my chest.

Above us, the full moon shines like a cratered lantern. "You know, it's not that crazy," Erik replies after some thought. "If we're all connected to one another through some kind of universal link, maybe you're tapping into a memory that's somehow relevant to you, even if it's not your own."

"Yeah," I reply, still unable to shake the odd feeling, "I guess that's possible."

"Listen," Erik adds, "I'm sorry I didn't tell you about what Fox and I know…about the Nucleus."

I shake my head. "You don't owe me an apology. I'm just too curious for my own good."

"That you are! But I still don't enjoy lying to you."

"Then don't," I plead, trying to see if he'll concede anything else. "It would be nice to fill in some more blanks."

Erik takes hold of my hand and seems to consider it for a moment. "I know…But I can't. Not yet, at least. I'm sorry Ev. Just trust me, okay?"

Why does everyone expect me to trust them without telling me anything first?

But I can sense Erik's turmoil. "Okay." I stare up at him, remembering that night in his dimension and again wishing it had ended differently.

I want to tell him things too, about the Vulturians, my frequency, the Skala…everything. But I stop myself, remembering Sarah's warning. *It's not the right time.*

Suddenly, my glass-house predicament becomes obvious: I'm a complete hypocrite. Out of the two of us, it seems I'm the one with the most secrets.

CHAPTER 24

Imposter

I've bid Erik another reluctant goodbye and can still smell his scent lingering on my shirt when I enter my dimension. I'm itching to transform this space again, and it would be the perfect distraction from all the feelings I don't know what to do with.

I close my eyes and envision a provincial cottage amidst rows of fragrant lavender and flowing grasses. I soar like a bird over rolling purple and green hills, focusing on every detail as it unfolds in my mind's eye. When I open my eyes, I've once again succeeded in creating an entirely new reality and marvel at how effortless and second nature it's become in such a short time.

The soothing lavender scent sooths my lungs as I sit on the wooden floorboards and watch the firewood burning in a hearth. As an orange light escapes through the open doors and blends with the setting sun, a sense of loneliness creeps over me. I'm the only inhabitant of my dimension, and for the first time since entering the Prism I find myself missing Earth.

The terrace offers me a window into the Nucleus where a dwindling number of Wakers move about the Avenue and cobblestone streets. It's as if my visit to the mountains has awakened something in me, and I restlessly yearn to be around someone or something that makes me feel alive again.

Within minutes I'm stepping onto the third floor of Eden Hall and turning into the museum entrance. I head down the Renaissance corridor, past a display case that contains a model of Leonardo da Vinci's Revolving Bridge. The ceilings of the glass cases are all open, allowing anyone to withdraw the items for a closer look.

"Jenna must live here!" I whisper to myself.

Still fascinated by the fact that I could potentially be touching something made by da Vinci himself, I place the model back with great care and continue down the corridor towards a grand hall of paintings where I deplete a generous amount of my Prism time bank. At last, my body gives the signal and I retreat contently back down the quiet corridors.

But my contentment is short-lived.

My legs turn to stone before I can make it to the descending staircase. I'm staring at a face – a face I never thought I'd see again. A face I never thought I'd see in the Prism.

His face.

Am I hallucinating for real this time?

It just isn't possible! How can he be here? Did I transcend into a regular dream? Can that even happen?

He sees me and to my dread makes his way in my direction. I'm powerless to escape, unable to free my legs of the stone my mind has encased them in.

"Everest?! You're here!"

Tristan's voice echoes sharply, each word hitting my ear drums like a jackhammer. I travel back to the alley and feel the bruises returning to my ribs.

How can you be here? You can't be here!

"I'm so glad you've found your way in!" Tristan continues. To an outside observer he probably looks thrilled for me, but I'm not fooled by his narcissism and false sincerity.

Something's wrong. *This is all wrong!*

My arms seem to still work, so I pinch myself behind my back like a child trying to awaken from a nightmare. But the image before me remains unchanged.

Finally, I manage to speak. "How…how did you get in here?"

Tristan casually steps closer, as if we're long-lost friends and nothing awkward has passed between us. "What do you mean?"

I contain my urge to push him and his smug phoniness over the banister. "Stop it! How did you do it?" I feel my blue eyes turning grey with every second he stands before me.

His temples twitch before he plasters another fake smile on his face. "Oh, I've been coming here for years. I wanted to tell you so many times but…well, you understand how impossible that would have been." He laughs unnaturally, taking another step forward. "What a relief to not have to hide it any –"

"No more lies Tristan! How?" I demand through clenched teeth.

"Everest, calm down." He holds up his hand, the fake enthusiasm in his voice vanishing. I'm not buying the act anymore and I guess his ego can't handle it.

"You know what, forget it! Just leave me the hell alone!" I force my legs free and rush past him towards the stairs. "I don't know why you're here or what you want, but you need to leave. You don't belong here!"

"And you do?" he snaps. "Because you're better than me?"

I turn to face him again, looking him dead in the eyes. "At least I don't get off on hurting people and crushing their spirit. But I do pity you and your cold heart, if you even have one!"

"I wouldn't waste your energy on pity Everest. And I don't think the Prism would look favorably on your sentiment towards me. I was only trying to be cordial. We did call a truce after all."

I turn on my heel, not wanting to give him the satisfaction of seeing just how much he's rattled me.

"I hope we can start over," he calls after me, "leave this anger behind."

How dare he? How does *he* have the audacity to lecture me about *my* anger?

But yes, I *am* angry. I'm enraged! At him. At myself for letting him rattle me. At the Prism for letting him in...

How the hell did he manage it?

I race down the moving stairs without looking back, my stifled tears backing up in my throat. The serenity of my provincial dimension doesn't match the tumultuous storm building inside me. I manifest a punching bag in a corner of the cottage and take out my frustrations on it mercilessly, each hit sending the treacherously heavy object swinging further than the last. I hit and hit and hit... On Earth, my hands would have been swollen and throbbing, but the Prism won't allow it. It's unsatisfying and I yearn to feel the pain.

Following a few moments of concentration, a desert racetrack replaces the lavender fields. No spectators, just a long, winding, and dusty road, surrounded by canyons and barren land. Nothing else in sight, except a red sports car waiting to be pushed to its limits.

I take my seat on the leather and place both hands on the wheel, depressing the gas pedal as far as it will go. The tires shriek loudly as I rip up the dirt road, sending gravel and dust flying into the air. The engine masks my screams, and I keep them coming. I push the vehicle down the track until the surroundings become a blur, releasing a little more fury with each turn and losing track of the number of laps I've completed. The anger eats at me, ripping me apart from the inside and creeping up from my stomach to warm my skull.

When I finally let the engine die, I'm relieved to feel hollow again. Whatever consumed me, it's no longer there. At least not to the same degree. I remain for some time in the idle car, unsure how to get back to where I started, my eyes fixed dead-ahead. Slowly, my pulse decelerates, and my tunnel vision expands. I bring back the lavender fields, grateful for a safe way to work out my recklessness.

But the fact remains that I have a new problem to solve: Tristan doesn't belong. I feel it in my bruised bones. And I need to make sure he doesn't return.

I just hope I don't lose the Prism in the process.

CHAPTER 25

Connect the Dots

Erik's voice is hoarse and tired when I call him the next Earth morning from a pay telephone. "Miss me already?"

He's the only one I can confide in. The only one I trust. "Did I wake you?"

"Wouldn't mind if you did."

I chuckle. "Good to know, in case I ever have burning questions at three in the morning."

"Let's not get carried away!"

I smile at Erik's never-failing ability to relieve my anxiety. I let a few moments pass, not sure where to start.

"What's on your mind?" he asks.

"You always know."

"Yeah, well…you don't hide your emotions well. You'd be a terrible poker player."

I smile to myself again, picturing Erik doing the same. "Probably." I pause again as my mood resets. *Might as well get right to it.* "I saw someone in the Prism last night, someone who wasn't supposed to be there. I don't know what to make of it," I blurt out.

It's Erik's turn to stay silent. "How do you mean? Who was it?" he finally asks.

"It was Tristan, an old acquaintance. I ran into him the night I didn't return. He's the one I cut out of my life the night I awakened. I just don't know how…my brain is about to *explode*! Of all people…Erik, if you knew him…"

"Did he hurt you?" Erik interrupts, the ease gone from his voice.

"No, not like that," I assure him. *At least, not anymore.* "He gets to me in a different way. He's not the kind of person who should have access to the Prism."

"Oh, really? I recall you sang a different tune not too long ago," Erik reminds me.

I exhale loudly, sucking up my pride. "I know. You were right. Access to the Prism should be earned. But the Tristan I know, or knew, just wasn't on track for that. Something's wrong Erik. I just feel it."

"Well," Erik offers after a moment, "I wish I could give you an explanation… I'm glad you're okay though. Maybe just try and stay away from him for now. I don't want you to get hurt, in any way."

That's it? I expected some magic solution that would ensure Tristan's instant banishment. That's all he's got?

"Ok…well, there's something else," I continue. While disappointed by Erik's response, I'm desperate to get everything off my chest. "It's strange…when we went to Estra, I think I may have manifested things in the Nucleus."

"Ev, that's impossible," Erik says through a yawn. "No one can alter the Nucleus besides the Prism itself."

"Well, I think I can too. I can show you. I don't know why or how, but I can." Erik's ensuing silence makes me wish I kept my mouth shut. "You don't believe me, do you?"

"Of course, I believe you," he reassures me. "Ev…I'm just surprised. I mean, sure, the Nucleus can read our thoughts, steer our boats…that sort of thing. But it has never listened to our desire to create matter and alter it. It only reabsorbs the energy of matter once we no longer have use for it."

"As far as you know."

"Ev, you have to be careful," Erik warns, a sense of urgency in his voice. "These…abilities you have. You can't tell anyone. We shouldn't even be discussing this over the phone. I should've known better."

Shit! That makes two of us. At least I'm on a payphone.

"Please," Erik adds, "don't draw attention to yourself."

"What's going to happen if I do?" *Just tell me!*

"I promise, I'll tell you more. Just not now."

I'm beyond annoyed. We're talking in circles, each one of us afraid to reveal too much. Maybe if we just came clean the dots would all connect. I stare suspiciously at the phone, suddenly feeling very exposed. "Fine. See you tonight," I say childishly, and hang up abruptly.

An email from Erik arrives in my inbox 30 minutes later: a ticket for the Eurostar, leaving Saturday morning at 8:45. It feels a bit like a bribe, but my mood improves at the thought of a weekend away with him – the real him. Still, my questions remain and eat at me slowly as the day drags on.

Still no word from Sarah. She's a complete ghost and I have no way of finding her. I want desperately back into that corridor to listen in on the Ertu and get some answers. Maybe my frequency has something to do with my abilities in the Prism.

Maybe, maybe, maybe… I'm sick of maybes!

Before heading to work, I call a cab and take an indirect route to the Vulturian chapter house, making sure there's no one on my tail. I wait by the alley and watch for signs of any activity, but my efforts are fruitless. Two smartly dressed middle-aged men complete what looks to be a possible drug deal, but that's about it.

It's clear Sarah doesn't want to be found. I have no choice but to keep waiting and hope that she's still alive to find me.

* * *

My worries are temporarily alleviated when one of my hall mates reveals some exciting news the next Prism morning.

"Are you coming to the festival?" the little Japanese girl asks me as she shows off her impressive futuristic metropolis made entirely of licorice. I've become friendly with a few of my hall mates now, and it's always a treat to see their dazzling dimensions.

"There's a festival?" I inquire, fishing for details.

"Not *a* festival. There's lots of those. *The* festival!"

And then it begins – the elaborate description of what is apparently the greatest three days in the history of the known Prism universe: the Senna Regale.

"And my epic surprise is ruined," Erik pouts later that day as we walk the grounds of the Climbing Gardens. "I was going to tell you this morning. I even have a related excursion planned. It involves shopping."

"Your idea of fun is going shopping with me?"

"No! Not even remotely. I would much rather take you ziplining, or to a football game."

"You mean soccer?"

Erik feigns horror and holds up his hands. "We can no longer be friends."

I give him a shove. "Fine, football. So, is this Regale really all that?"

"I can't lie, it's pretty spectacular. And we have access to garments only the rich and famous can otherwise afford. So, take advantage, my lady."

"Well, since you put it that way."

"We can go this morning. But I need to see Robert first. Will you wait for me?"

Interesting. "I think I know how that conversation's gonna go. It's not weird at all, knowing you're going to talk about me behind my back," I say a little coldly. Erik's guilty expression leaves me conflicted. "Sorry. I know. Just go."

He shoots me a grateful look. "Just be a little more patient. I'll meet you in the Forum, ok?"

As I watch him depart, I recount the myriad of emotions I felt the night before and the look of satisfaction on Tristan's smug face. *He's up to something.* The idea of seeing him again is as nauseating as the Prism will allow. I'm not even sure what I'd say to him if I saw him again. Yet despite that I find myself in the Castellum elevator, saying words I never thought I would find myself uttering in the Prism.

"Tristan Sarazen."

I wait for the elevator doors to open, but nothing happens.

"Tristan Sarazen."

Nothing.

Does he not have a dimension? But that's the only way to get in?

Except it isn't!

I suddenly realize that the truth has been staring me in the face all along. Sarah's already given me the answer.

Tristan *is* an imposter after all. "Because he's a Vulturian!"

CHAPTER 26

Nosedive

Ever see those movies when someone comes close to dying and their whole life flashes before their eyes in a rapid collage of scenes? That's also how it feels during great unveilings. Such as when you realize that you've been targeted by a murderous organization, and that seemingly unrelated events in your life were all secretly orchestrated to further that purpose.

It's all clear now – Tristan inserted himself into my life for a reason. Why else would he want to be around me when he couldn't stand me?

I'm furious at myself for being taken for a fool. *Damn it, Sarah! Where are you? You're the one Vulturian I want to run into!*

When I meet Erik in the Forum, I try to work on that poker face, unwilling to throw more at him than I already have. The Vulturian revelation will have to wait.

"So, Milan huh?"

Erik nods with enthusiasm. "Let's portal to Lake Geneva. There's a train that will take us the rest of the way."

"Can't we just portal straight there?"

"We could," he replies mysteriously, "but we don't want to!"

* * *

"Does *everything* here fly?"

Turns out Erik left out a few things about our new method of transportation, like the fact that the train doesn't exactly need tracks. The giant machine unexpectedly takes to the air seconds after departure from Lake Geneva, and heads straight for the mountain pass that will lead us to Milan Station.

Other than the large cushy seats, everything on the Sky Serpent is made of glass, and with no rails to anchor it to the ground it's free to travel wherever, and how high it pleases, occasionally at warp speed. I clutch Erik's hand as we weave in and around sharp peaks, skim the surface of the valleys and soar off cliffs, the treacherous yet magnificent mountains dwarfing us and taunting us at every turn.

"It's never a dull moment with you," I tell him as we pull into our destination, breathless from the adrenaline. "A heads up would have been nice!"

Erik just grins mischievously. "I was a little nervous you would break a window and throw me out of it after that first cliff dive. Besides, I had to make shopping somewhat interesting."

We're about to rise from our seats when the train starts to move again. "There's more?"

Erik seems equally surprised. "Not that I remember," he says, looking around as the train proceeds ever so slowly back the way it came, inching further away from the station.

Then without warning, the glass machine jerks backward and nearly vertical, launching us face-first into the seats in front and sending other passengers barreling down the aisle and into the glass car divider! It shows no signs of slowing down as it speeds upwards and backwards, eliciting panic and screams inside the car as passengers try to figure out what's happening.

This isn't fun anymore! The faces around me look shaken, eyes wide and worried as the train continues upward at full power.

Finally, it comes to a halt and jerks everyone back, then levels out to an eerily silent horizontal position.

After the shock wears off, the chatter and questions begin.

"What on earth is going on here?" Someone behind us demands as the chatter resumes. Others press their startled faces against the glass, eventually taking their seats again and waiting helplessly for the ride to resume.

"It's never done that."

"I was just on it yesterday. This didn't happen…"

"I don't like this," I whisper to Erik, noticing that for the first time I'm not spared feeling ill in the Nucleus. My stomach flips and a subtle headache begins to throb around my right temple.

"Me neither," Erik agrees. "Come on. I want to see if there's anything up ahead."

We make our way toward the sliding glass door that separates us from the first car. Those who've gathered at the front window are slowly dispersing. There's nothing to see. We're just sitting there at what feels like airliner height, waiting.

Waiting for what?

"How long are we expected to just hang out up here?" come anxious voices.

"It's never been *this* extreme," Erik mutters, his brow furrowed. "Something's changed."

I'm worried that the train's stillness is giving us a false sense of security. And just as the thought settles in my mind, I'm proven correct. The machine takes a sudden and rapid nosedive back toward the mountains below!

I reach for a railing and feel the weight of falling bodies

crushing my rib cage as we plummet, pushing me hard against the glass. The mountains come into view, and it becomes clear that we're headed for a hard hit, with no sign of stopping. One look at Erik and the truth is clear: this isn't a thrill ride, and we all know it now. The screaming gives it away – no one wished for this. The Nucleus is no longer giving us what we want. There's something else calling the shots.

Can we even die in the Prism? Would we just wake up, or would that be it — lights out?

I see Erik looking for an opening as he pulls himself free of those on top of him. "Maybe if we jump, summon our horses..."

But his pushing on the glass yields no results – there's no escape. We're in a tightly sealed and plunging glass capsule.

This isn't right! The Prism wouldn't let this happen.

"We need to stop it!" Erik cries.

"Aren't there controls?"

"No. The Prism controls it."

Wait! "Apples and bananas!" I mumble. It's a longshot, but maybe... I shut my eyes, trying to eliminate distractions just as Erik taught me, and imagine some kind of steering apparatus – anything that looks like controls...*What would controls look like?*

At first nothing. I focus harder — so hard that I feel the intensity tear through my skull. I lift my eyes to gage our distance to impact and to my disbelief find the strange contraption I imagined before me.

"Erik!"

The steering wheel and levers look like they belong on a boat, not a train. *Who cares! Just work!* I push back against the weight of the body on my back, and free my arms to take hold of the wheel while placing my foot on something resembling a brake. The wheel moves in a spherical motion.

I hear Erik's muffled voice over the loud hum of the speeding machine. "Ev…"

"Just help me!" I motion to the wheel, fighting its resistance. Erik helps me pull it up and miraculously the mammoth machine begins slowly evening out.

We're doing it!

The train's moving slower now and no longer fully vertical, and the pressure on my back starts to lessen as gravity does its job. *It's working!*

But as I do a quick calculation in my head, I realize it's not enough! We're still going too fast, and collision is inevitable. At this rate, we're going to hit solid rock at 60 miles per hour!

Maybe something to soften the blow…

As Erik and I work to slow the train further, I close my eyes again and the throbbing in my skull amplifies.

Focus…

When I open my eyes, the rocky surface of the mountains has become coated in thick layers of white powder. I let out a sigh of relief. I have no energy left, and it's the best I can do before we make the dreaded impact.

I shut my eyes as the train barrels into the snow with a thud, the car shaking violently as it tunnels its way through, eventually emerging into the daylight and sliding onto an icy clearing. Up ahead, the sudden drop-off is unmistakable – the only question is 'how high.'

No more. I'm drained from battling whatever is fighting us and have nothing more to give.

Stop! I manage to plead silently. *Just stop!*

"It's slowing down!" someone cries.

I peer outside through half-closed eyelids, the mountains no longer a blur. Then I shut my eyes again, grab Erik's hand, and wait. The Prism seconds seem to pass ever so slowly, until…

Silence. Stillness.

I allow myself to see what everyone else is seeing. Beneath me, the first ten feet of the glass train floor hangs over a 300-foot drop down the side of a steep cliff. Seconds separated us from a very different fate, whatever that would have meant in this parallel world.

Erik is gently jostling my arm. "Ev, what's happened to you?"

I must look run down. I certainly feel it. *Whatever happened to no discomfort?* I manage a faint smile. "I'm fine."

"No, you're not," he insists, helping me up. "Come on — let's get the hell off this thing!"

Wakers have already started piling out of the cars. Snow spills welcomingly into my sneakers as I place my trembling legs and feet on ground.

"Summon your horses," Erik calls to whoever will listen. "Double up if you need to. Ride to the nearby stations and tell the others."

I watch the scene unfold through a haze and a ringing in my ears. Erik leads me towards Cass and lifts me onto the mare. I let my body fall limply forward, my cheek nestled in Cass' mane. I glance at the Sky Serpent which lies motionless on the snow like an empty shell of snakeskin. I feel Erik board Cass and guide her upward until the train completely vanishes from view, the chilling scene fading behind us like a bad dream.

"Thank you," Erik says softly in my ear as we leave.

"For what?"

He pulls me closer between the reigns, his heart beating fast against my back. "I think you know."

✳ ✳ ✳

Word spreads quickly about the runaway train, and Milan Station is a scene of pure mayhem and confusion when we arrive to a crowd of concerned Wakers, including Robert Crawford.

"What happened?" he asks frantically when he sees us.

Erik shrugs and lets out an exasperated breath. "I honestly don't know. It just took off — like it wasn't under the Prism's control anymore," he answers. "Just barreled towards the ground like a bloody missile! It's like it wanted us to crash."

"But you didn't," Robert points out, looking at me with worry. "It fixed itself?"

Erik studies me with equal concern. "I'm not sure we have the train to thank for that."

Seriously, how bad do I look? Did I lose an eye or something?

"Take her back to Castellum," Robert advises Erik. "You two have been through enough for today."

"What's happened here?" a distinct low voice booms over the crowd. A broad-shouldered man with a long white braid over one shoulder is calmly making his way in our direction, Wakers parting around him like the Red Sea. He's like a slow-moving beacon of tranquility in an ocean of chaos and wears an emerald velvet robe over his clothing like he's taken a wrong turn at a wizarding convention.

"Who is *that*?" I ask.

"Jeremiah Poppin," Robert answers with displeasure. "Chair of the Imperium. Excuse me a moment."

Robert and Jeremiah eye each other like two generals facing off in battle. "I warned you this would happen Poppin," Robert fumes when Jeremiah approaches. "You *have* to take me seriously now."

I see Jeremiah shaking his head before Robert even finishes speaking, his lone feather earring swinging back and forth like a hypnotic metronome. "There isn't enough evidence Crawford."

"There isn't…are you…*this* is evidence!" Robert cries, throwing up his arms and motioning around us. "When will it be enough then? When something tragic happens?"

"I won't do what you're suggesting. It would break trust — people would lose faith —"

"There are discrete methods —"

"Enough!" Jeremiah interrupts, then lowers his voice and leans in. "This is concerning, granted. But it's a far cry from justifying the measures you'd have me implement — measures that don't belong in the Prism! And for what? Because you have a 'hunch' you won't even explain to me?"

"This is just the beginning. The…" Now it's Robert's turn to lower his voice. "The Prism *is* deteriorating, Poppin. Something has changed. You are the elected Chair of the Imperium. You need to do something!"

The Chair looks around at the shaken passengers, then turns his attention back to the desperate stare of his adversary, rubbing his chin in contemplation. "Come see me at the Imperium. We'll talk about it." He walks back the way he came with a slow even step, giving me a curious glance before leaving.

Do I not have a face anymore?!!

Robert is clearly livid.

"He'll come around," Erik reassures him, trying to break the tension.

"Will he?" Robert mumbles under his breath. "But I don't blame him. We've only given him pieces." He turns his attention to me, his expression softening, and places a comforting hand on my shoulder.

"My dear, you'd better get yourself back to your dimension. Is there anything I can do?"

I manage a smile. "Thank you, but I'll be fine."

Robert tightens his lip and nods. "Very well. Get some rest, both of you. I'm going to go track down that stubborn man." With that he smooths out his sports jacket and straightens his posture, then proceeds to push his way through the crowd in the direction of the portal.

After Robert's departure, I begin to fully grasp the gravity of what transpired, my mind replaying flashbacks. Two questions overshadow all the others: why did the Prism allow this to happen, and how did I have the power to stop it?

"I don't want to go to Castellum yet," I tell Erik.

"Ev, you really should rest."

"I'm too awake Erik. I just need to be somewhere quiet, away from all this."

Erik gives me a weak smile, then gently brushes a hair away from my eyes. "Okay," he concedes. "I know just the place."

* * *

Cass sets down on a Bavarian hilltop in view of an impressive replica of Neuschwanstein castle. The daunting mountain peaks meet the sky behind it, making the massive structure look small. We admire the breathtaking surroundings from our high vantage point, surrounded by nothing but tree covered hills and wildflowers. Erik certainly knew what I needed.

I take my time releasing consecutive breaths. "Imagine waking up to this every day."

"You should see it after a snowfall." Erik turns my chin towards him. "Enough small talk. Are you ok? I want an honest answer."

I search for some solace in Erik's eyes but can't find it.

There's no point lying to him. He'll only see right through me.

"No," I admit. "Not really. How can any of us be? The Prism is supposed to be this safe utopian haven. What happened today changes everything. I…I've just found this place, and now it feels like I'm already losing it."

Erik takes hold of my shoulders. "I know it feels a bit scary and uncertain. But it will work itself out. I'm sure there's an explanation."

"You don't know that."

But Erik looks at me sternly. "Catastrophic thinking won't bring you any closer to the answers you're looking for."

I pull out some blades of grass in annoyance and watch as new ones immediately grow in their place. "Speaking of answers, Robert and Poppin — what was that all about?"

"Poppin is a good man," Erik replies after a sigh, "a good Chair, a good Chief to his people, so I hear. But he and Robert disagree on certain things."

"Things that you can't tell me about."

Erik sighs again and leans back on his elbows. "It's not up to me Ev. If it were, you'd be the first to know. All I'll say is that Robert has been trying to get Poppin to act on the deterioration we've noticed." He pauses a moment, as if weighing the costs and benefits of divulging more. The costs apparently win.

I'm too exhausted to press him. "Let's not talk about this anymore. Tell me more about London." I'll be on another train in two days, this time jetting across the English Channel, and that makes me nervous for a whole bunch of other insecure reasons.

Strangely, it's not the train ride I fear the most, even after today. My greatest worry is that the Erik I'll meet on that day will be somehow different, and that I'll realize that all of this has just been a cruel trick of the mind. Or that Erik will realize the real Everest isn't worth his time.

"How is 'Erik of London' like?"

"Ha! Thankfully no one calls me that," Erik laughs. "I'm the same person Ev. Hope that's not too disappointing." He interlocks our fingers, but I barely have any strength left to squeeze his hand in gratitude.

"It really is beautiful here, isn't it?" I muse.

Erik nods. "That's why we can't take it for granted and we can't lose hope. It's illogical to relive the ordinary when you can experience the extraordinary."

Erik's words move me, not because of the magical setting or because his lips have said them, but because they embody what I've always known to be true in the deepest recesses of my soul. I've longed for a world where my desires are fulfilled instead of snuffed out, and I can't bear the thought of losing it.

"I know you want to stay off the subject of today," Erik tries again, "but…was it you?"

I don't know if he wants to hear the truth, or if I can even give it. "I don't know… I think so." I sigh. "Probably."

"Okay."

"I don't know why I can change the Nucleus, Erik. I'm not sure I even want to."

"Well, I'm glad you can. Who knows what would have happened today if you couldn't."

I chuckle to myself. "You know, coming here, I thought I found a place where I finally belonged. Now, having these abilities that no one else does, I feel like an outsider again."

Erik sits up and brings me in to lean on his shoulder. I let my head rest on him like a heavy bowling ball. "You're not an outsider Ev," he says. "You're right where you belong. Just trust me on that."

CHAPTER 27

Cryptic Memo

Once again, the solitude of my dimension only makes me more restless, and sleep isn't even remotely on my mind. Too much has happened today. I wish I had a switch that could turn off my brain, but just like that elusive time machine it hasn't been invented yet.

I head outside, eventually finding my way to Cascada. The waterfall valley stretches from the eastern edge of Castellum all the way to the Prism's southern boundary. As far as I know, there's nothing beyond the mountains that line the perimeter. I wonder if that's true, or if there are more alternate realities waiting beyond false borders.

The waterfalls form an endless maze and climb up the lush hillsides. It seems like the entire forest is engaged in a war of whispers from the sound of the water crashing into illuminated pools and the strangely thin birch trees being pushed around by the wind. Campfires dot the forest like lanterns, and I can hear echoes of singing and laughter that a part of me longs to join.

After some aimless strolling I come upon an older woman performing a solitary tribal-like dance around a small fire of her own. I observe her from the shelter of the trees, admiring her hypnotic movements and entranced by her mysterious chanting.

"Have you heard the legend?" the woman asks, spotting me in the shadows and motioning for me to come closer. "It is said that if someone stands at the exact right spot in Cascada, the Prism will bestow upon them a secret."

Intriguing. "What kind of secret?" I ask, inching towards the crackling fire and putting out my hands to feel its warmth.

"Now, don't you know what a secret is?" the woman laughs, shielding her long silver hair from the flames as she kneels close to me.

I grin. "Point taken. Have *you* ever heard one?"

"Not I, sadly, no. But even if I did, I couldn't tell ya. The one who hears it can never reveal it. You would find yourself mute if you tried, or suddenly unable to write a single word. And you would only remember the secret while in the Prism anyhow."

She pours me a miniature cup of a kind of tea that smells of pine needles and honey but tastes like caramel fudge. I'm not sure what it is, but the warm liquid leaves a surprisingly soothing trail as it travels down to my stomach.

"Mmm. That's…really good. Thank you. This place is just teeming with secrets, isn't it?" I note, handing her back the cup.

"That it is." The woman peers inside the cup as if reading something. "I see you are a soul tortured by a thirst for knowledge. But beware," she says, looking up at me, "knowing can be both a gift and an undoing."

Her intense gaze and ominous warning give me a faint shiver. I know I'm too curious, but until now I've never had a fortune teller warn me about it.

"I'll try to remember that," I reply, a bit unsettled.

"The tea will help you stay awake."

"Awake?"

"You feel it, don't you?" the woman says, reaching for something in the pocket of her long linen dress. "The Prism day is at an end. But the mekiza plant will give you a few more hours. See…" She places a leaf in my palm. It looks like basil, only with more jagged edges and raised green veins running over it. "A curious mind is always out of time," she adds, closing my palm around the leaf. "Make good use of the extra minutes."

Now I'm collecting magical herbs by night and speaking to apparent psychics. *What else will this day throw at me?* I thank the women and leave her to her dancing and chanting, storing the mekiza leaf in the pocket of my jeans. Then I make my way out of the valley without any secrets being revealed to me.

The confusing paths lead me into a deserted courtyard behind the Luminary. A narrow shallow pool bridges the gap between the back entrance of the Luminary and the Imperium that's carved out of the boundary rock wall. In the middle of the pool, a limestone obelisk springs upward, crowned by a gold capstone. I recall what Robert alluded to about pyramids and obelisks and can't resist the urge to slip out of my sneakers to get a closer look. I wade through the ankle-deep water, trying to make out the markings I see etched on it. The obelisk is engraved with a series of alternating symbols forming a singular line and wrapping around its four sides like a ribbon.

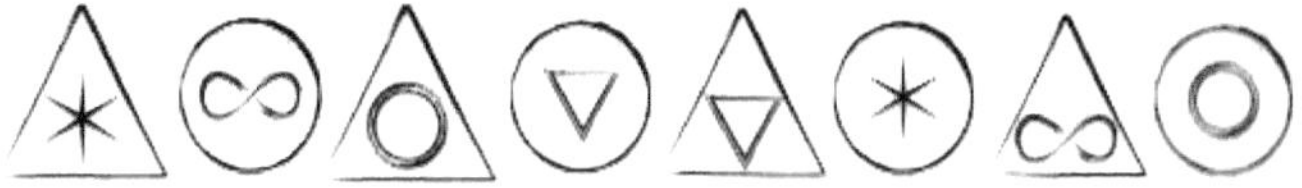

Doesn't look like hieroglyphics… I run my fingers over the carvings and feel them ripple as I circle the obelisk. They look familiar but I can't place where I've seen them…

Finally, it clicks – I've seen them carved on the armor of the emerald guards.

But what do they mean?

At last, I give up trying to decipher them, hoping as usual that Erik can provide some insight.

The charcoal exterior of the Imperium stands in stark contrast to the white limestone of the Luminary, which seems to literally glow in comparison to its counterpart across the pool. Only a small, blue light flickers in one of the Imperium's third-floor windows; the only sign of life. That song, *'one of these things is not like the other,'* starts to play in my head. Would the Council be meeting this late? Robert and Poppin maybe? Would it be terrible if I casually passed by and listened in?

Leave it alone.

Something foreign overcomes me, like a noisy gust of wind that's at my back and swishing in my ears. Before I realize it, I'm standing at the doors, sneakers in hand, without any recollection of how I got there and only a vague memory of a force having propelled me forward and something warm melting into my chest.

Just when things couldn't get any stranger, leave it to me to prove myself wrong.

The heavy Imperium doors creak loudly as I push against them. *So much for keeping a low profile.* The interior is as gloomy as the outside and eerily deserted. By Prism standards, it's rather uninspiring inside in terms of color, but the architecture is impressive, with stone columns propping up the 40-foot ceiling. The lower level houses a generous meeting chamber and a few smaller rooms, and a wide stone staircase leads from the center of the foyer to the second level, narrowing at the top and releasing onto the second-floor landing which overlooks the main level.

My stakeout of the first floor is unproductive, so I make my way to the second where I find six more rooms arranged in a semicircle around the landing.

Oddly, there's no obvious method of accessing the third floor I saw from the outside, and forcing an access point by staring up at the ceiling like a lunatic isn't working for me either, so I proceed to checking out the rooms.

The first has a gold plate on the door: *Jasmine Pollard: Archivist*. Just an office. Some sparse furniture and wooden bookcases break up all the grey, but still no obvious way of accessing a higher level. I give into my imagination and begin looking for secret compartments or passageways. But pushing against the walls gets me nowhere.

The next five rooms, including Poppin's, yield the same results.

Door number six — another office like the others. *Carmella Vieri – Physicist*, the name plate reads. She's very disorganized. Papers and nonsensical diagrams litter the floor – mostly equations and scribbles that go way over my head. I lift a small gold globe on the desk to examine it, and as soon as I remove it a ladder pops out from the ceiling, revealing access to the loft upstairs.

"Finally! Very Indiana Jones," I mutter as I pull the ladder down and place my foot on the first rung.

Carmella's loft is messier than her office. It's littered with boxes, and almost every step ends with me bumping into or stepping on something. A little window peaks out onto the courtyard, but there's no blue light or anything resembling it.

Did I imagine it? Wrong door, perhaps?

But architecturally, Carmella's loft make sense...

Something cracks under my foot again. I push some boxes aside to reveal the second half of the room, and finally find the source of the light, flickering in the corner atop a small pedestal table – a compact orb-like blue flame, raging like a perfectly contained wildfire.

That inexplicable sensation of being pulled towards something returns. I give into it, walking forward cautiously. Holding my breath, I put out my hand and let my fingertips make contact. No burn — only an unparalleled feeling of warmth and weightlessness that seems to overwhelm me from the inside out. It's even more exhilarating than the rain.

Suddenly, the flame begins to change shape, transforming itself into a series of spirals and loops in front of my eyes.

"It's not random…"

The loops take the shape of cursive writing, accompanied by a low howling sound that echoes through the room.

"Everest, you don't have much time…"

My mouth goes dry as I read the floating words. *What is this?*

"To fix the Prism and get rid of the unworthy, to give the Prism to humanity…"

The loops change shape again…

"…you must find them both and conceal them well in time.

We can help you. But the only way is through time. Listen to the whispers.

This compass —"

A loud creak and thud of the Imperium doors closing snuffs out the flame instantly. I'm no longer alone. But my worry over being discovered comes second to the panic of having lost contact with whoever was trying to reach me.

"Wait, come back...." I plead in a desperate whisper. "Who are you? *What do you want?*"

To my dismay, my pleas are fruitless, the warmth snatched from my core as if the Flame's reclaimed it. Only a trail of goose bumps remains over my skin as proof of the surreal encounter.

And an object: on the pedestal table in the Flame's place lies something round. I pick it up and open it – it looks like a locket the size of a tea saucer, hanging on a thick silver chain, the words *Carpe Noctem* engraved on the front inside a hollowed-out triangle. There's nothing on the inside, and nothing more to it.

The Flame's last words replay in my mind as I open and close the locket, hoping the clicking sound will jog a memory. "This is a compass? And, who's 'we'.... conceal them..." *Conceal what?*

Stumped, I slip the object into the pocket of my sweater, give the room one last longing look, and retreat down the ladder feeling simultaneously disappointed and exhilarated.

As I secure the ladder and return the globe back to its proper place, the sound of footsteps in the hallway outside reminds me of the other presence. I peer through the door in time to see a

figure enter the second room at the other end of the landing —
a slim woman with short hair. She emerges shortly after,
proceeding to door #3, the dimness concealing her features.

*You don't have much time…*The Flame knew someone was
coming. And if that someone is a Vulturian, I can't let them
find me here.

Only six rooms. I need to time it perfectly…I wait for the
woman to enter the fifth room, then as swiftly and as quietly as
possible make my way to the fourth. I feel my pulse in my throat
as I observe her enter Carmella's office.

As soon as she's out of view, I step out of the room and race
down the long staircase on the tips of my toes, hoping the
woman takes her time. But when I glance back, she's standing
on the landing, her face erased by the darkness. We seem to
stare at each other, like pawns across a chessboard unsure of
who should make the first move. I guess I didn't tuck the
compass away well enough because the sound of it hitting the
floor echoes loudly off the stone walls, breaking our stand-off.
It lays there, illuminated by light streaming in through the few
small windows, the echo lingering in the air.

Damn it! If she didn't know I had something before, she does
now!

My fears are promptly realized. The woman advances
quickly, descending two steps at a time. I snatch up the compass
and sprint outside toward a path for the gardens. Retreating into
a crazy maze full of giant plants isn't the best idea, and I don't
have a ball of string to mark my route (not that leaving a trail
would be wise, given my predicament). But the gardens are my
best option. I need to stay concealed, and the Luminary beacons
will soon make that impossible.

Once inside the gardens, I turn left down an alley of poppies,
hoping I don't have to go too far in. There aren't many Wakers

left at this hour. I wish there was. *I wish Erik was here.* I recall what he said about the gardens not being the best place to explore at night. *Just remember where you're going!*

After a right turn, I find a row of red hibiscus trees, their gigantic blossoms large enough to conceal a person. The flower heads have mostly closed for the night, but I manage to find one that's still open. I step inside, wrapping the thick petals tightly around myself, leaving a sliver of an opening and standing as still as possible, my breath short and shallow.

It isn't long before I see a figure approaching – the same short-hair, the facial features still hard to make out. She scrutinizes each flower, shaking the petals violently as she passes. In about six more steps she'll apply the same method to my hideout.

But as she inches closer, I feel the petals constrict around me, tighter and tighter. The woman tries to pry open the flower next to me, but it's too tightly clenched. To my relief, she appears to change her mind about the viability of the hiding spot and walks right past me to turn down another corridor.

That was insanely close!

In seconds, the petals around me begin to loosen their grip. I unravel myself, not wanting to wait around for the woman to return, then retreat the way I came, hoping I remember the way.

* * *

The compass object takes on an orange hue as I turn it over in my palm in front of my dimension fireplace.

What are you? What does all this mean?

Is this all related to the train? Was the Flame talking about the Vulturians? Are they the "unworthy?"

I wish I could relive the experience again, afraid that with the passage of time, the details of it – that unparalleled and thirst-quenching feeling of it – will slip away until it's just an obscure memory.

Time. *Conceal them both, in time.* Could it have been any vaguer?

I manifest an antique grandfather clock in front of me, the first clock I've seen in the Prism since arriving. The pendulum swings irritatingly, a reminder that with each second that passes I'm no closer to figuring anything out.

Am I being inpatient? Is the Prism telling me not to force the answers just yet, that all the pieces will fall into place at their rightful time?

Annoyed, I will the clock away and store the compass in the trinket box I find in my bedside table. I'd all but forgotten about my first Prism manifestation. Is it just a coincidence that the box is the perfect size, with barely a millimeter to spare all around?

I already know the answer.

CHAPTER 28

A Precarious Turn

With London around the corner I should be gliding on air. But instead, I navigate the metro the following morning with a troubled mind. That evening, I call Lise and Julian to check in.

"Everything is the same," Lise informs me. "We met those kids at the Prism you told us about. They're nice."

I'm glad they're making friends. But Lise's voice isn't ringing with its usual zest for life. "Is there something you want to talk about?"

"Not really," Lise replies, the melancholy now unmistakable. "It's just Maman..."

I feel my face getting flushed. *Please tell me this lady is keeping it together!* "Lise, is she drinking again?"

"No! I promise she is not. But she's just very, very sad. She cries all the time. It's just not the same without him."

Her voice cracks as she mentions her father. I just want to find her and hold her. I can't relate to the feeling of being loved by a father the way she was. But I had the love of a mother – a mother I lost far too soon. I understand the hole in her heart and how difficult it is to repair it.

I chew on my lip, angry at myself for not having the power to travel back in time and make all of Lise's worries disappear. "I lost my mom when I was not much older than Julian," I confide to her. "I know the pain you're going through. I won't pretend like it doesn't really hurt and suck. But it will get better."

That's the first lie I've told Lise, but maybe some false hope is what she needs. It sounds a lot better than *You'll learn to live with it.* No one wants to hear that.

"If you want, I could stop by today? We could go for gelato. I know a very fancy place just around the corner from where you're staying. And I mean, *fancy*!" I smile at the thought of Lise beside herself over the overwhelming selection and pink decor.

Lise lets out a giggle. "Merci, but Maman is taking us to the store to buy some school things. We'll see you at the Regale, like you said?" We'd previously agreed to attend the first day of the festival together, and I know Lise is probably counting the milliseconds and driving Julian crazy.

"Absolutely! I wouldn't miss it!"

After we hang up, I hear a knock. *I'm not expecting anyone.* I push the curtains aside and see the black sedan parked in its usual spot. *Great.*

There's no one in sight after scoping out the hallway through the peephole, so I remove the chain, grab a nearby vase and cautiously open the door. To my relief, there's no one there, but a piece of folded toilet paper lies at the foot of the threshold. I grab it and close the door promptly before reading the message:

Same place, 9pm
No tail!
Flush this.
-S

Sarah! It's about time! *Please give me something!*

I toss the note in the toilet as instructed, glancing at the clock on my way out of the bathroom.

8:23.

Plenty of time for a goose chase.

* * *

The taxi driver grins as I give him the steep fare. A roundabout route was necessary to make sure I wasn't followed. I let myself out two blocks away and go the rest of the way on foot, concealed under my hoodie and glancing behind me every so often. By the time I get to the alleyway I'm a shaking bundle of nerves. I thought I'd like espionage a lot more, but it's slightly less thrilling when it's not on TV and people are actually trying to kill you.

The dumpster is rolled aside. Before my fist connects with the door, it opens, and Sarah nearly rips my arm off as she pulls me in.

"Hi to you too!" I say, rubbing my shoulder.

"Sorry. I didn't want you lingering out there too long."

Her nose isn't red anymore, but she looks tired and spent. "Still not sleeping?" I observe.

She smirks. "What gave it away?"

My anxiety is through the roof. "So, am I finally on the hitlist?"

Sarah shakes her head to my immediate relief. "No, you can rest easy. They still need you alive. But…"

I look at her warily. "But…what?"

"The games' changed. They know you have something." Sarah eyes me from under a furrowed brow. "Everest, do you have something they might want?"

Of course! The compass. That woman saw me drop it. I remember the Flame's warning and suddenly feel uncomfortable revealing too much to Sarah. What if she's setting me up? She is technically one of them…

But my gut isn't holding up red flags and warning me to slam on the brakes. Sarah's revealed a lot already that could get her killed. That should count for something.

"I might," I reply vaguely. "I found something in the Prism yesterday, and someone really didn't want me to have it. They chased me but I lost them. I don't know who it was. This thing that they want, do you know what it is?"

"I was hoping you could tell me."

I shake my head in disappointment. "It just looks like a piece of metal." I resist the urge to tell her about the Flame. "What do they want with it?"

Sarah leans back against the wall. "The Skala. They think what you have could locate it. The Ertu's desperate to have it. He's even going to resurrect the Pledge!"

"I need a glossary at this point. The *pledge*? Why do I have a feeling I'm not going to like it."

Sarah's face tightens. "You're not! I overheard them talking about it the other night. It's got every chapter on edge. In ancient times, the Order's Supreme Hunters — the Sharurs — pledged to find the Skala within a five-year term or face all but certain death. They were brutal in their search, leaving a trail of destruction and pain in their path."

"They've been searching for it *that* long?" I roll my eyes, trying to make light of the worsening situation to alleviate my growing anxiety. "Don't these people know when to move on? What happened if they didn't find it in five years?"

"They were released into the deserts of our ancestors, to wander in disgraced solitude, the sun and the vultures eating away at their flesh and their sanity until they succumbed or survived, 'by the will of Parem.'"

Ugh. I make a face at the unpleasant imagery. "Sounds lovely."

Parem. I remember hearing that reference when we spied on the Ertu. "Who's this 'Parem' they keep talking about?"

"It's a dark force they worship – resembled by the head of a vulture and the body of an ape."

Creepy. "Well, at least they have five years. It gives us time."

Sarah laughs cynically. "You underestimate the Ertu's determination. No – this pledge is the 'expedited version'. They already chose the first Sharur – a woman. And word is, she has only four months!"

Four months? Could she be the one who chased me? "Ok. That's…a big difference – and a lot of pressure. Wouldn't want to be her."

"This isn't 1000 BC, Everest," Sarah reminds me. "They have unparalleled influence, technology, more resources than ever at their disposal.

"The membership thought the pledge long buried, a barbaric tradition of the Order's past that it had since evolved from. But now it's a reality again. They're scared, and they know the Ertu's threats are never empty. They will be ruthless Everest! I can't stress that enough."

This wasn't the news I was hoping to hear from Sarah. I slump against the wall beside her, trying to process the information and what it could mean for me, and for those around me. "Ok. Not great. Definitely not great."

I observe Sarah's bloodshot eyes with concern. They look worse than when I last saw her. "Are *you* doing okay, by the way?"

She lowers her gaze, and her face contorts like she's reliving something painful. "I'm fine."

"You don't look 'fine.' "

"It's nothing…they have me undergoing desensitization," she admits. "All members have to do it at first."

"What is that?"

Sarah straightens herself up and bites her lip, for the first time appearing visibly shaken and afraid beneath her tough exterior. "There are two kinds of Vulturians Everest: the kind who join willingly and those who are born into it. The eager volunteers are usually referred by another member. These are the sick, twisted, soulless kind – like our friend Irra. They have no compassion, no capacity to love anything except their sociopathic urges.

"The second kind, like me, are born into Vulturian families, sometimes with personality traits the Order deems…inferior: weaknesses, like empathy or compassion…or guilt."

Sarah takes a deep breath to steady her cracking voice, and I wonder if she's fighting to keep out memories she'd rather forget.

"If you're in the second group, they put you through desensitization – weeks upon weeks, sometimes months of mental torture and priming, to rid you of all the weak links. To make sure you're ready to be fully initiated. You're not supposed to remember the sessions."

I shiver at the thought of enduring whatever a desensitization would look like and look upon Sarah with pity. "Is that what happened to you?"

I can see the corner of her eye become coated with a watery veil. "Yes. Except for some reason I remember all of it. It's sickening. They don't know, of course…I've been faking it this whole time. But I don't know how much longer I can keep this up before they're onto me, or worse – before the sessions turn me…or they ask me to do something I can't come back from."

Sarah gulps hard and glances at her watch. "They're not meeting today. There's something happening in the Assembly Hall, but I'm not allowed in."

She starts to walk back to the door. "You should go Everest. Be careful. In the Prism too. They'll be watching your every move now to discover what you've found. Keep it somewhere safe."

It doesn't feel right, leaving Sarah after she's just poured out her soul – letting her return to an evil that's destroying her. "I will," I promise, "And Sarah…"

She turns back around to look at me, her eyes still glassy. "Yeah."

"I think I'll be seeing you in the Prism soon, the right way."

An unexpected smile flickers across her face and lifts the outer corners of her pretty hazel eyes. "You think so?"

"Yeah," I assure her, reaching out to squeeze her hand, "Yeah, I do."

She squeezes my hand back and nods, A silent part of me wonders if it's too late for Sarah – if she's already turned.

What if I am being played?

But her red puffy eyes give me my answer. I'll start to worry once she starts sleeping again.

Second Interlude

TARA BAHAR

It's not how I wanted to see Paris for the first time, sitting in the Assembly Hall in front of the Ertu at the pledge revival ceremony – a ceremony I thought I would never witness. An hour after getting off the plane and my fate has been all but sealed.

I hear the Ertu mumbling something about duty and power – the usual stuff I've heard him go on about when we streamed the assemblies in the Boston Chapter.

"The Eridu was prophesized by our ancestors as the key to finding the Skala and was said to hold the key that could locate its hiding place. The blue flame was to signal the Eridu's arrival. And now, we have found her. Our time has come to secure our power for the coming ages, by the will of Parem."

"By the will of Parem!" the global assembly repeats, with chapter houses around the world watching the live feed.

While most have been conditioned to reject empathy, a few new faces shift uncomfortably in their seats, probably recognizing the likely death sentence I've just received but relieved that it was me and not them.

"If you succeed," the Ertu continues, turning his attention to me, "the glory and rewards will be limitless, and the Order will be forever in your debt. If you wish to pledge your allegiance as a Sharur, raise your right hand."

If you wish? That's funny!

I feel pupils fixed on me like laser beams and I know that the choice the Ertu's given me is just an illusion. I stare at my name on the piece of paper in front of me – a name only spoken in the Order. A name no one else would ever recognize. I raise my right hand, my index and middle finger forming a "V" and read into the microphone.

"I, Tara Bahar, loyal servant of the Vulturian Order, pledge as Sharur to retrieve the Skala within four months and deliver it to the Order, by the will of Parem, or suffer the punishment of desert exile and…," I can hear my voice crack as I read the last words, "all but certain death."

One of the elders approaches me from behind and places the vulture head of Parem over me. The Ertu allows the silent observance of the ceremony to continue for a painful minute, then finally instructs, "Sharur, return."

I give the hideous headpiece back and walk with a phony look of pride on my face across the checkered floor back to my seat, trying to conceal the fear that's throbbing in my veins.

When the meeting concludes, I remain in the Assembly Hall until the last Vulturian has departed, unable to move. A few members mumble some bullshit about the "great honor" that's been bestowed on me as they pass me on their way out.

Four months! Nothing for thousands of years, and I have four months. *That's such crap!* I expected a reward for bringing the Ertu the intel about the blue flame, but this wasn't exactly what I had in mind. I suppose he didn't appreciate that I let Everest get away. I made my wager and lost the bet.

Still, I need to try. I still believe in the Order, in the inferiority of humanity. It's not over until the desert sand burns the flesh off my feet. We have Cleary, after all, and she won't elude me again. Besides, I know her weakness now.

And just think of the reward if you succeed...

Once my phone is returned to me outside the Assembly Hall, I dial it in haste, anxious to put my plan into action.

"I wasn't expecting to hear from you so soon," the voice on the other end answers. "It's been quite a day for you."

"I'm fine," I insist, brushing off my earlier anger and refocusing.

If I'm going to be a Sharur I need to think like one, embrace the ruthlessness, show no weakness of my own.

"I know how to get it," I tell the voice. "And I think you know just the person for the job. Let's meet for a drink in an hour."

CHAPTER 29

Missing Pages

EVEREST CLEARY

My bed sits atop a flat rock that juts out over a precipice, Mount Everest squarely in my sights and nothing living for miles. Just grey and snow as I try to recreate the sense of de-ja-vu I experienced in Estra inside my dimension. For some reason, I feel it holds the key to something. I imagine a cold wind slicing through my hair, hoping it will slap some sense into me, jog something….

But it's pointless. The same questions float in the Flame's writing in front of me, then fade, unanswered.

I will the wind away and let my gaze rest on the bedside table. Was it all a daydream stemming from some subconscious desire for danger in an otherwise utopian existence?

But when I retrieve the box from the drawer and lift the lid the compass stares back at me, as perplexing as the night before.

Images of vultures and pledges fill my head….it all sounds so unbelievable. *What if I'm legitimately crazy? Is everyone here crazy? Is this all some crazy delusion of an ill mind? Are we all in some high-tech mental hospital, kept docile by hallucinogens and a virtual reality matrix?*

"I just need some normalcy," I try to convince myself, storing the compass away.

I've imagined all sorts of things about the library, and with Erik "looking into things" for Robert this morning, I have the perfect excuse to finally indulge my inner book worm and visit the Lumus.

The Lumus occupies the ninth and topmost floor of the Luminary, the halls outside overlaid with mosaics depicting the Earth's ages. Four sets of wooden double doors stand around the landing that overlooks the inner courtyard, each carved with the Prism emblem and small raised dots that ripple under my fingertips like brail.

I glance up at the Michelangelo, the dome now closer than ever, the blue galaxy even more compelling and mysterious. I watch the planets and stars engage in their fluid dance around the ceiling.

"It's something else, isn't it?"

The voice belongs to a man in his thirties, wearing retro red eyeglasses, a buttoned blue dress shirt and converse sneakers, his black hair thinning on the sides. He extends his hand enthusiastically. "I'm Gill Bennex. I'm one of the volunteer librarians. I love books!"

I almost giggle at his endearing, almost child-like candor as he beams at me while impatiently shifting his weight from one foot to another.

"Pleased to meet you Gill," I reply, shaking his hand and taking an immediate liking to him. "I guess if anyone knew anything about that painting it would be you."

"Most definitely." He beams. "What do you want to know?"

How much time do you have? "How was Michelangelo able to create this here? I thought no one could change the Nucleus?"

"Ah yes! Fair question," he answers, unaware of my true

motive for the inquiry. "Most people don't realize that the Luminary has different laws then the rest of the Nucleus. Because it's supposed to be a place of ideas and learning, it allows for some innovation and change to take place within its walls."

"I see…Just within the walls of the Luminary though?"

"As far as we know. I mean…there have been rumors of others who were able to change the Nucleus in the past – Wakers with unique abilities." Gill purses his lip as he tries to think of more details to add. "But I don't know their names. It's not on record, if it's even true at all."

Pity. It would be nice to find the others. I can't be the only one…

I give the masterpiece another aching glance. "That's okay. I didn't come for that today. It's my first time here actually. Any ideas on where I should start?"

Gill's face lights up. "Ah yes! I remember my first time. Mind blown!" Gill exclaims, imitating an exploding skull.

"I want to find something on ancient history," I tell him. *And Vulturians.*

"I see we share an interest. North side. I've read quite a bit in that section."

"I'm sure you have Gill," I reply, not doubting him for a second. "I'm sure you have."

"Go on in — it's easy to navigate. Well…" a sly grin spreads across his face, "…sort of. The Lumus really is the most incredible collection in the known universe. And no holds!" He adds, almost skipping off.

I take Gill's advice and proceed through the North door, and am not the least bit disappointed by what lays on the other side.

Gill called it — mind blown!

Royal blue velvet drapes hang over the tall gothic arched

windows, and various sizes of energy orbs float under the ceiling, intertwining to form intricate suspended chandeliers. The bookcases climb 20 or more floors, the exact magnitude of the Lumus a clever illusion concealed from the outside. Platform-like contraptions fly about like hovercrafts, whisking people away to any book or section they choose without the need for ladders.

But the most intriguing part of it is that people often disappear into the stacks as if swallowed up by them, then subsequently emerge with books in hand from wherever they've just travelled to.

The Ancient History section is beyond vast. I step onto a platform hovering nearby, knowing exactly how to work it by now. After picking a point of interest I'm off, gliding effortlessly towards my destination. Space contorts around me as I cross into what seems to be another plane, and I'm no longer able to see where I've come in from as the access point closes.

I pass texts on Rome, Mesopotamia, Atlantis…

"Stop!" The platform obeys instantly. I reach toward the book entitled *Atlantis: Where It Was, Where It Went*. Intrigued, I remove it from the shelf only to find that an identical copy has taken its place. *No holds indeed!*

Nothing on Vulturians to my disappointment, even though I'm saying that cursed name over and again in my mind, trying to will it to find me. I let the platform carry me around the perimeter of the library, passing by various collections and rare first editions. At every turn the Lumus expands, but the text I'm searching for still eludes me.

This isn't working.

I set down close to Gill and a chatty older lady who's passionately psychoanalyzing a dialogue between Heathcliff and Kathy from *Wuthering Heights*. As I dismount the platform, I accidentally kick something to the floor. A book lays at my feet; I must have knocked it off a shelf without realizing. *Ancient Artifacts of Aeonia*. I've never heard of it before, but then again, I haven't heard of a lot of things apparently. *Could be interesting.* Two books is a good start.

Erik's waiting for me at my dimension door when I get back. "You've been busy!"

I hold up the books. "Got carried away. That place…"

"Yeah, you don't even feel the time slip in there. I was wondering when you'd make your first visit. Anything good?"

I shrug. "I'll let you know. What about you? Solve any mysteries today?"

Erik frowns. "No. Not my day. Would have much rather spent it with you. But tomorrow we can make up for it," he says, referencing our time in London. "Not to mention the Regale this afternoon."

Ah yes. The Regale. I smile, trying to shift gears and focus my energy on something positive and exciting – something not associated with Vulturians in any way. "Right. Can't wait to finally see what all the fuss is about."

* * *

The nightmare with the Sky Serpent interfered with my plan to pick out a dress for the Regale, but I knew my dimension wouldn't fail me. As I stare at my reflection in the mirror, the warm champagne gown I've chosen complimenting my summer glow, I have to admit that I clean up pretty good. The delicate pearl embroidery on the bodice reminds me of a whimsical woven painting and the layered chiffon skirt cascades ethereally to the floor. I pin my hair in a half updo, then allow my dimension to fix the disaster I've created and come up with something a little more polished.

"That'll have to do," I whisper, satisfied with the outcome. Content with simply having something to wear for the occasion, I bolt out of my dimension toward the elevator.

The Forum is full of Wakers already lining up for the Senna portal – some dressed up in formal attire, others in costume in tribute to Senna's many attractions. I spot Erik waiting on the edge of the sixth step on the Avenue wearing a beige suit over a crisp white shirt that's unbuttoned just enough to send a small rush of blood to my head.

He smiles when he sees me, then spins me around when I approach. "You look sensational!"

I blush, however much the Prism will allow. "Thanks. You look nice yourself." I see Erik's blue eyes light up and feel that magnetism pulling me into his orbit again. I'm getting increasingly tired of resisting it. I squeeze his hand and impulsively open my mouth to say something, even though I have no idea what will come out of it.

At that moment, Julian approaches stealthily in a very grown-up navy-blue suit, saving me from myself.

"Look at you!" I say, grateful for the interruption. "A gentleman in the making."

"Very smart," Erik agrees, letting go of my hand to shake Julian's, the boy beaming up at him like he's trying to impress an older brother.

"Thanks. There's this girl I kind of want to talk to," Julian admits, his cheeks turning a little pink. *That's how mine must look like!*

"Woah, woah! Tell us more," Erik insists. "This is important information."

Julian's becoming another person before my eyes. He's

evolved so much from that shy boy I first met at the building site.

"We met the other day, at one of the Cascada bonfires," Julian elaborates. "She's a year older than me…but I'm taller! That's okay, right?"

"Of course! Just be yourself," I encourage him with a wink. "I'm sure she'll love your company. And…where is your spirited other half?"

A cloud of peach tulle taps me on the shoulder. I turn to see Lise who looks like a flower plucked right out of the Climbing Gardens, and she has zero interest in greetings or small talk.

"How are we getting there?" the wide-eyed girl asks, bursting with anticipation. "Would it be fastest to portal?"

"Haven't I taught you anything?" Erik replies. "Where's your sense of adventure? Besides, with that line-up, it might be fastest to fly anyway." He points to the flood of Wakers spilling out of Castellum as they await their turn to go through the Senna portal.

"We don't have horses yet," Julian reminds us.

Erik waves his hand. "No matter. You'll ride with us. Come on."

We mount Cass and Juno at the foot of the Avenue, Erik and I taking a sibling each. "Hope you don't mind if we take the scenic route," Erik says as he and Julian begin their departure. He shoots me that irresistible teasing grin of his. "See you in another world," he adds with a wink.

I sigh. "Yet another one?"

Agora falls away as we navigate what look like cotton ball highways in the sky. After an indiscernible amount of time, Erik leaves the cloud paths behind and descends towards the jagged precipices of a massive canyon. We weave in and around the rock walls and emerge into a barren dessert. When we reach the cusp of the last sand dune, I realize we're in Oransen, the Pyramids jutting out on the horizon. I follow Erik's gaze and look behind me toward an approaching thunder: a herd of antelope is right on our heels. But instead of getting out of the way, Erik guides Cass downward.

I follow suit until we're just a few feet off the shaking ground, in perfect position for collision with the antlered beasts. But the herd separates, flanking us on both sides. The dust from their pounding hoofbeats swirls around us like a miniature sandstorm, and I can feel the air from their nostrils grazing my skin. Being in their presence is surreal, and I reach out to run my hand down the slope of their smooth backs as they pass us. It sure beats taking the portal!

Erik veers away again. "We're almost there," he calls, pointing in the direction of the two emerald covered monoliths that guard the border on the horizon.

Senna awaits. I wonder how close it will come to what I've envisioned and hope I'm wrong in every possible way.

Surprise me, I dare the awaiting realm. *Blow me away. Leave me speechless!*

CHAPTER 30

Four-letter Word

"Julian, pinch me. Someone…" Lise gasps as we tread air at the Senna border, surrounded by sand dunes. I've gotten my wish – I can't bring myself to say a thing.

"Look, there…a flying carpet!" Julian shouts. Another one zips by us toward a grand Sultan's palace.

"Come on! No sense watching from the sidelines," Erik urges like it's just any other day.

We set Cass and Juno down on the dusty path that leads to an ancient middle eastern city. Vibrantly colored tents and caravans of camels spread through the surrounding desert. To the north, the landscape changes to rolling hillsides covered in rich shades of green. The distant tops of castle towers peek out between the hills, marking the boundary to a new world. It's hard to decide where to look. As soon as I settle my eyes on something I'm instantly distracted by something else.

The Sultan's palace is stupendous. "I've never seen more gold in my life!" I exclaim as we take a quick tour. I'm surprised they're not serving gold plated figs! The throne room features dancers and acrobats – Lise is so engrossed in the performance she almost doesn't see us start to leave. To think all this was pulled and formed from the collective mind…

"This is just the beginning," Erik says. "Head north for hobbits and elves, dozens of castles… East is the more futuristic stuff…"

"Cool!" Julian exclaims.

Erik clasps his hands together and looks to each of us. "So, where to first?"

Please don't say dinosaurs…

"Dinosaurs!" Julian insists to my dismay.

"And rollercoasters," Lise adds. "I've never been on one before."

"Are you sure that's a good idea? Swings make you sick, remember?" Julian reminds his sister.

But Lise has her mind made up. "This is the Prism. It's different here!"

It was, I think to myself, remembering the train. But I dare not dash Lise's belief.

"All right, all right!" Erik replies, trying to mediate the requests. "One thing at a time. We'll get to it all. Just…maybe not all today."

* * *

How will I answer when Nina asks me on Monday how my weekend was? *Oh, nothing special…you know, hung out with some elves, saw a wizard turn a rock into an elephant, ran with a friendly velociraptor…flying carpets, flying horses…* Somehow, I doubt she would ever speak to me again. She might even commit me herself.

Two weeks ago, I was a character in a very different story, or rather a prisoner in it. And now I find myself part of a world where anything is possible, just as that mysterious note had promised. What are the odds…

We've done everything on the children's list and more, and the whole time I wondered why I waited so long to see Senna. I know where I'll be spending most of my Prism time for the next little while. Even with the longer days, our afternoon has passed far too quickly.

The evening brings with it a magnificent borealis sky in celebration of the Regale Gala, a masquerade held at the Spectrum Palace, the main stronghold of Senna, right on the coast. After parting ways with the siblings at another amusement park (because the two previous ones were apparently not enough for Lise), Erik and I head to the Spectrum and climb the white marble steps with other smartly dressed guests, picking out fancy masks before entering.

"What about a Toucan?" Erik teases. "Because you're so nosy."

"You're hilarious."

He picks out a dragon for himself and hands me a lioness instead. "For someone beautiful, strong and fearless."

I smile and grab it from him playfully. "Better."

Fox's AI's serve bubbly liquids and navigate the narrow spaces between the glamourous guests, masterfully balancing platters of scrumptious edibles that constantly replenish themselves like the books in the Lumus.

"Everest!" I hear Jenna yell from across the dance floor. She looks in her element dancing with Fox. At least the two of them aren't at each other's throats for a change. *I had a feeling that was an all an act.* She's picked a gazelle mask, while Fox settled on something a little more obvious.

"A fox? Shocking choice!" Erik teases him.

"It's the best animal, obviously," Fox boasts. "See ya'll later!" He whisks Jenna off for some more vigorous dancing to a swing number, and I marvel at how good they both happen to be at swing. Not at all what I imagined Fox to be into in his spare time.

A slower, more manageable tempo comes on next. "Would you join me?" Erik asks shyly.

"You know how to waltz? Is the whole world taking ballroom lessons in their spare time?"

Erik laughs. "God no! The Prism makes it easy. Just don't get any ideas for the real world," he warns, leading me to the floor. "I have no moves, other than the humiliating ones."

He puts his hand on my waist and pulls me closer. The music starts, and I find the dancing to be surprisingly effortless, as if someone else has control of my feet. Fox's new talent makes more sense now.

What's even more effortless is how it feels to be wrapped up in Erik's arms – the synchronized rhythm of our breathing, his calming energy which at the same time fills me with butterflies. I'm relieved I don't have to worry about my feet. I can just focus on Erik and the orchestra and this perfect, uncomplicated moment.

"What are you thinking about?" he asks, his warm breath hitting my neck.

That I don't want this dance to end. That I don't want you to let me go. That I just want everything to be this easy all the time.

"Nothing," I reply, "this is…nice." *That was weak.* Why can't I ever find the right words with him? What am I so afraid of?

Before I can rectify my response, our perfect moment is interrupted by the sound of a cynical laugh that seems to encircle me like an inferno I can't escape.

He's here! Tristan is here.

I spin my head in all directions but can't figure out which mask belongs to him. I hear it again, eluding me, taunting me. I sense a sinister ugly energy claw its way into my throat and slither down to my stomach – an energy that has no place in the Prism. For a moment think I spot a vulture mask in between the dancing guests; furrowed hideous eyes and a blood-stained beak.

Would he be so arrogant as to wear it? Am I hallucinating this time for real?

My mind is racing. I can't keep up the dancing any longer and break free from Erik.

"I'm sorry, I just need a minute," I tell him as I run off.

I need to get out of here.

Flashbacks of alleyways return as I push through the crowd aimlessly.

Screw Tristan. This is my paradise! Why does he have to be here!

"Everest!" A hand grabs at me and I prepare a fist, ready to punch Tristan's smug face.

"Woah! Relax! It's me." Sarah's curly brown hair peaks out from behind a llama. "Nice choice," she says, pointing to my mask.

I allow myself to breathe again. "Sarah! What are you doing here?" I ask, lowering my arm. "They let you back in?"

"Apparently. Another carrot. They sure picked the right day. This place is unreal!"

"Sarah…I –"

"And did you see the food?" she adds, admiring the passing food trays before turning her attention back to me. "Anyway, listen, things have changed."

"*Again?*" I can't keep up anymore. "What now?" I groan, still looking around me for signs of *him*.

"They've discovered something about that object you found," she whispers. "They think it's some kind of a compass."

Shit! They're not supposed to know that. How do they know that?

"And…they think it's enough to find the Skala, whatever it is," Sarah continues.

I look past the mask cut outs into Sarah's eyes, trying to read between the lines. "What are you saying?"

Her pupils dart around the room. "Once they have the compass, they may not need you anymore. They can't risk having you around to stand in their way, not with your frequency. Everest, you can't let them get their hands on that thing! It's the only thing keeping you alive. Tell me you hid it somewhere safe?"

"There you are. Why did you run off like that?" Erik's voice asks behind me.

I turn to face him, the music suddenly unbearably loud. "I…just recognized a friend. This is…"

I turn back around but she's gone, a ghost yet again. *No surprise there.* "Never mind."

Erik studies me with worry. "Ev, what's going on? You look petrified!"

I look around the room again, trying to process the situation and the gravity of Sarah's revelation. "I need to get out of here," I say to him rudely without waiting for his response.

"Ev…what…"

I run out the back doors, freeing myself of the mask and throwing it into some bushes, and don't stop until I've arrived at the edge of the Prismatic. I toss my sandals aside, letting sand spill over my bare feet. Abandoned boats bob on the water as Wakers celebrate all over Senna. Suddenly, I'm filled with regret and embarrassment. Erik deserves someone truly fearless, not a coward who runs away at every opportunity.

"Why does it seem like from the first day we met you're always running away from me?" Erik asks softly, approaching nearby but giving me some space.

I bite my lip nervously, thankful that he's found me and surprised he hasn't given up yet. He's right – I've been running scared since we first met. But I'm no longer just running from ambiguous, intangible feelings or insecurities. I'm being hunted now, by something very real. And yet I still can't bring myself to tell the one person I feel safest with because telling him could put him in danger too.

An enticing version of Atlantis floats off the Senna coast but exploring the illuminated pyramids and the maze of canals that connect it to the mainland will have to wait for another day. Dusk is slowly veiling the Prism's northern border.

"What's beyond it?" I ask, avoiding Erik's question. "The mountain boundaries…suppose you climb the perimeter all the way to the top, where would you end up?"

Maybe somewhere they could never find us…

"I'm not sure you would ever reach the stop," Erik replies. "At least I never did when I tried. The Prism just put more rock in my path."

"So, there's no escape from here? No way to travel anywhere else?"

"Escape? Why would you need to escape?" he asks.

"Just…is there more?" I press.

"There's always Earth."

I sigh. "That's not what I mean."

Erik grins. "I know. You want to know it all, don't you? Always wondering, always on to the next thing. It's what I love most about you."

He comes closer and stands in front of me, his eyes bright and hopeful, wondering if I picked up on that weighted four-letter word he's just dropped.

Yeah, I heard it.

Do I accept it, reject it, pretend it didn't happen?

"I've loved you from that first day Everest," he tells me, whether I'm ready to hear it or not, "when you took off running into the Prismatic." He chuckles a little to himself as he runs his hand through his hair. "Some would call that foreshadowing…Anyway," he whispers, gently taking hold of my hands, "I just thought you should know…before you run off somewhere I can't find you."

My heart is screaming at me to say it back, trying to let itself feel worthy of it. Even the Prism can't keep the lightheadedness at bay. "Who knew all it would take was me acting like a crazy person to capture your heart," I tell him.

He brings his hand to my face and brushes my cheek. "How many times do I have to tell you – there's nothing wrong with a little crazy."

"Erik –"

"Look," he interrupts, before I can say another word, "I don't know what's got you so spooked…why you're looking for escape routes out of paradise. But I'm in whatever this thing is between us, and I feel like you want to be in this with me. I just can't figure out why you're holding back."

It's my turn to brush my hand over his cheek just as the skies open and the rain falls, amplifying my emotions and covering us with that exhilarating blanket of serenity before relinquishing its hold and fading away. It's both satisfying and gone too soon. It's the definition of perfect timing.

It's exactly what I need to find my courage.

"I love you too Erik," I admit, unwilling to deny it any longer. I exhale deeply and close my eyes, relieved that I can finally be honest, not just with Erik but mostly with myself. "I should have said it sooner. I guess," I lower my eyes, trying to articulate the right reason for once, "…lately I've felt like everything was falling apart around me, like I was just…a huge misunderstood inconvenience. And then I came here and met you, and…you just…see me. You make everything so easy."

I look up at him, a weight gone from my chest. "I guess I've been scared that I'll figure out a way to mess this up, or that this will all…vanish."

Erik steps closer and lifts my chin, his eyes like a pool of still water I want to surrender myself to. He pulls me closer by my waist, sending shivers up my back as he brings my lips to his. I feel my heart decelerate and my inhibitions melt away as I kiss him back, finally giving into that intense desire that's haunted me.

There's something so pure about us. So light and forgiving. It's more than insane attraction, goosebumps, and intoxicating gazes. It's more than the Prism and the magic that comes with it. He's like a part of my skin. We understand each other. Ours is a bond I can't put into words, and it's more than those four letters could ever capture.

And now it's finally ours – ours to hold in our hands and mold into something real.

He leaves me wanting when he pulls away. "No one is messing anything up," he assures me, bringing his hand to rest on my hair. "I'm here for the highs and lows. You just need to decide if you are." He kisses me again, his lips soft and addictive.

I smile at him when he pulls away, still dizzy from it all, trying to let my heart accept that it can be loved for what it is – crazy frequencies, murderous enemies, absentee fathers and all the rest of it. Trying to accept that someone like Erik could want someone as complicated as me.

"I am," I tell him, meaning every word and yearning for more of him as I brush my fingers through his soft hair. This time, I'm the one who pulls him in. He meets my intensity, kissing me back harder this time. *Why did I wait so long for this? Why did I waste so much time?*

I stare at his face when we pull apart, remembering our first fateful meeting in the Forum. So much has changed since then.

"No more running then?" he asks, as I rest my head contently on his chest.

"No more running," I promise, with a touch of guilt. "But…there are a few things I should tell you."

* * *

I start a fire in the hearth and enclose us in a cozier cottage, the cold expanse of the mountains feeling a little too isolating.

"It's supposed to be a compass. Does it mean anything to you?"

Erik scrutinizes the compass – rotates it, flips it open, does all the usual things one would do when examining an oversized locket that's supposed to be something it looks nothing like. "Nope. Strangest compass I've ever seen. Where did you find this?"

"The Imperium. Long story…"

I plop myself on the bed, deflated. I can't keep the truth from him any longer. If we're going to take this next step together, we need to trust each other first.

"I haven't been completely honest with you about some things Erik." I pause, then decide to start with the most important stuff. The talking flame and shattering glass can wait. *Baby steps.* "You're being watched."

Erik returns the object to the trinket box and puts his hands in his pockets, seemingly unfazed. "I know."

I straighten up. *"You know?"*

Erik remains very stoic as we lock eyes and study each other.

"They've been at it for some time. The question is, how do you know?"

I try to figure out if he's suspicious of me or if he thinks I'm the enemy. But his demeanor is unchanged and hard to read. "I can't tell you that," I say, lowering my gaze, unwilling to unmask Sarah just yet. "But my source is good. They're watching me too, and apparently the only reason they haven't killed me yet is because I have this compass, or whatever it is. As long as it remains hidden, I stay alive…Which brings me to my next question: how safe is it in here?"

Erik glances around my dimension and shrugs. "As far as I know, no one can get into your dimension except you and whoever you allow. Ev, who do you think is after you?"

"I don't know," I lie. "But I worry that by being around me you'll be in danger too. Clearly you already are! We should put off London. It's too risky –"

"No –"

"Erik…"

"Ev, these people…they clearly still need me for something too, if I'm still alive, right? As long as we both stay useful, we shouldn't have anything to worry about. And wouldn't we be safer together?"

I can feel my eyebrows almost touching in puzzlement. "Why are you so okay with me giving you half-truths?" I ask him. *Why aren't you more surprised.*

"Because I've been doing the same. But no more," he promises. "When we return to the Prism tomorrow, I'll bring you to see Robert. He'll tell you everything. And while we're at it, maybe he can tell us more about this compass or…whatever it is. For now, I'm not going to stop living my life." He sits next to me and takes my hand, intertwining our fingers tightly. "I don't care who these people are, I won't let them ruin this for us. So, I'll be at the train station tomorrow, but I'll understand if you feel you can't be there."

I consider my options – I could either spend the weekend in Paris in a state of complete paranoia, or with Erik in a state of complete paranoia. At least with the latter, we would have each other.

"All right," I agree. "I'm in." I smile at him, determined not to worry about the Vulturians until I absolutely have to.

I lean in and kiss him, imprinting the softness of his lips and the warmth of his hands into my mind. Then I let my head rest on his shoulder as we silently stare into the hearth, content and tortured in our own way about what lies ahead.

CHAPTER 31

Earthly Strangers

I awake in my apartment at 5:14 in the morning. The last thing I remember is staring into the fire with Erik in the Prism. I smile foolishly to myself, silently wishing there had been more to recall, but relieved that I don't have to tip-toe around my feelings anymore. I stare at the ceiling, replaying the Regale and everything that happened, relieved that we can be honest and move forward. And there's no better next step than seeing the real Erik in the real world.

The morning hours drag, but by 7:32 I'm out the door and running down the stairs, too impatient to wait for the elevator. I take the back exit onto a main street a few blocks away, catching my reflection in the still dark window of a storefront. My long hair which usually hangs down over my shoulders is tied back and hidden under the hood of a sweatshirt, my eyes concealed by the dark lenses of the sunglasses I don't yet need. Given recent events, I won't spare precautions. From this point on, I need to be smarter, faster, practically invisible. They probably know where I'm going, but that doesn't mean I have to make things easy for them.

I've packed sparingly but taken what I need, including the

photo of Mom and me from Six Flags which I've tucked into my passport holder. My phone, my headphones, a camera (since I plan to keep my phone off), a change of clothes, some snacks for the trip…

Everything else I need is waiting in London.

I find a seat at Garde du Norde in view of the train schedule and look around for anyone suspicious with a small knot in my stomach. As I walk to the platform for boarding, I recount the terror of my last train experience. What are the odds of something like that happening again?

It's just a train. *Millions of people take trains.*

Onboard, a young father sits across from me with his son. *Is he one of them, planted here with a kid — the perfect cover?* As the duo engage in a humorous conversation about the Queen's Guard and whether they're allowed to pee, I begin to feel more at ease and convince myself I'm being ridiculous.

My phone vibrates. It's Erik.

"Are you on board?"

I fake my best groggy voice. "On board for what?"

"Very funny. You're a terrible liar, and apparently a terrible actress."

"Wow! I'm not even across the Channel yet and you've already insulted me twice."

"I think one of those was a compliment," Erik defends himself.

"You know, I may just change my mind and spend the weekend –"

"Doing something incredibly boring and wishing you were with me instead," Erik finishes for me. "It's going to be fine."

For the first time I don't believe him, and a nagging feeling in my gut tells me I'm walking into something that's going to end badly. It's not just Catherine's voice anymore. It's mine.

The train begins to move. It's too late to turn back now. I smile weakly, hoping no one is listening in on the conversation. "I'll see you in a few hours," I tell Erik before powering down the phone.

* * *

St. Pancras station is an impressive example of Victorian architecture. After a few minutes of admiration, I find the nearest washroom and quickly change into fresh clothes, let my hair hang loose and put the shades away. We went over most of the trip details in the Prism, and Erik's instructed me to meet him at "The Meeting Place."

"But *what* meeting place?" I had asked in confusion.

Erik just chuckled in response. "You'll figure it out."

"Oh yes, 'The Meeting Place'," a passing security guard explains. "Most people refer to it as the 'Lover's Statue.' " He points in the direction of a bronze statue of two lovers embracing, its static presence bringing a sense of serenity to the constant chaos that surrounds it.

My stomach flip flops as I look around for Erik. After some anxious scanning I glimpse his wavy brown hair, his head turning in all directions, just as mine is. Our eyes meet, and the corners of Erik's mouth begin to turn upwards as we see each other for the first time as two Earthly strangers.

Just breathe, I remind myself as we both begin making our way through the crowd of tourists and commuters. Our eyes remain locked, as if we're afraid that if one of us so much as blinks the other will disappear. At last, he's right in front of me and it's as if the whole universe pauses for a moment; as if all the people stop moving, all the second hands of all the clocks stop ticking – until Erik's widening smile moves time again and lights up the lines around his eyes that I love so much. My bag falls like a rock off my shoulder, freeing my arms to embrace him tightly.

I just hold him, feeling the vibrations from my heart against his chest. "It's really you," I whisper, reluctantly pulling away and discerning my reflection in those familiar eyes. He touches my cheek gently, then pulls me in with both hands to kiss me. The feeling is just as I remember it, and any doubt I previously harbored over the authenticity of our connection is instantly obliterated. I kiss him back between nervous laughter, not sure how to act or what to say, and not wanting to stop.

"I can't believe it's the real you!" I tell him again, looking him over and weaving my fingers through the waves in his hair. He wears a light green t-shirt that sets off his subtle tan and a pair of faded jeans, and looks exactly as I remember him, down to those elusive dimples.

"I told you – same old boring me," he says with a humble shrug.

"Well, 'boring' is looking pretty good these days."

He smiles, then lifts me slightly off the ground for another kiss and embrace. "I'm so glad you made it," he whispers in my ear before setting me down, his warm breath lingering on my neck. We just stand there for a few satisfying moments in each other's arms.

"Speaking of boring, I hope this train ride was less eventful than your last. I'm sorry, Ev, I didn't even think to ask if –"

"It was fine," I assure him, staring at him like a crazy stalker, still in disbelief that I'm actually in London and that the last week wasn't a psychotic break after all.

"Have you eaten?" He asks, taking my hand. "I'm starving! I could go for an English breakfast. Eggs, sausage, some mushrooms…"

"Well, since I'm in England I give you carte blanche to feed me the most British thing you can think of."

"I'll hold you to that. I know a great place, only a short walk from here."

We head for the exit, stealing looks like love-struck teenagers. Outside, I breathe in my first lung-full of London air as we step out onto the sidewalk – it's sticky and hot and smells of exhaust fumes and fried food from the street vendor. Not much different than Paris.

"You're going to have a great time in Jolly Ol' England," Erik says over the chatter of passing pedestrians. "And speaking of jolly, I should warn you my mum is the definition of the word. You don't mind if we visit the country for a bit, do you? I just thought it would be a nice break from all the city stuff and keep us off the radar of any unwanted company. But we can absolutely do something else, anything really."

I can't deny it; the prospect of meeting Erik's family scares me for my own insecure reasons. But to see where Erik comes from – where his memories live – is worth a little awkwardness.

"Let's do it! Carte blanche, remember?"

CHAPTER 32

Black Sheep

After breakfast and a packed afternoon of sightseeing, we're on our way to the country in Erik's old red Vauxhall Corsa. He takes a longer route to show me the Sussex coastline. It's lovely, and I would have been content to just sit on the beach and watch the tide roll in with him for the remainder of the day.

"Do you see anyone?" he asks me. We've both been checking the mirrors compulsively.

I shake my head. No sign of a tail. But then again, there could be a tracker somewhere in the car for all we know. If what Sarah says is true, there's no escaping these people. My only comfort is knowing the compass is safe in the Prism, which means they need us alive.

Finally, we come upon the summer house: a brick structure with yellow shutters and a welcoming garden now blooming with the last of the summer's pastel perennials. As I walk up the porch steps my insecurities get the best of me. What will I say when they ask about my family — when I tell them I live in Paris thanks to my uncle's charity, that my father didn't stick around, that my mother and my uncle died, that my aunts are both antisocial weirdos, and that I somehow lost my mother's hard-earned money and can no longer go to college? Might as well mention that I can shatter glass with my mind and get it all out in the open!

Erik's on to me in seconds. "It's not too late to get back in the car."

I try to shake it off. "Sorry, I'm just a little nervous. You probably have this amazing family. My life isn't so…picture perfect."

Erik bursts out laughing. "Oh, we're far from perfect! You'll marvel at the dysfunction soon enough." He gives me a quick kiss. "They'll love you, Ev. Just be yourself."

The yellow door swings open before we have a chance to knock, and a pretty lady of average height — her greying blonde hair tied back in a short ponytail at the base of her neck — stands before us, beaming as if it's Christmas morning.

"I heard your laugh, Erik! It's so good to see you!" The woman attacks Erik with a smothering embrace and plants a loud smooch on his cheek. "You look thin. You're not eating. Is that strange roommate of yours eating all your food?"

"I'm eating just fine," Erik says, kissing her back. "I've missed you. Mum, this is Everest. I told you she'd be coming."

"Yes, of course dear! Hello!"

Before I know it, I'm being smothered too. It's rather nice. Reminds me of how Mom used to hug me when I'd get home from summer camp. Catherine was never very affectionate. Mom was always the odd one out in the family when it came to showing her feelings.

"Aren't you a pretty sight!" the woman says as she leads me inside. "It's so nice to have another female around here. Come on in!"

Her jovial disposition is the perfect antidote for my anxiety. "Thank you for having me Mrs. Halvorsen. Your country is very beautiful. Erik showed me some of the highlights of London this morning. But it's just gorgeous out here!"

"Please, just Rhonwen. And thank you. We do quite like it here. It's so peaceful. And where are you from, dear?"

"Uh, across the Channel actually. Paris."

"Why, aren't you lucky!" Rhonwen gushes. "I'm itching to holiday there. It's been some time since we've been back. Maybe you can convince my homebody of a husband to finally go with me."

Erik trails behind and imitates his mother talking a lot with his mouth and hands.

"I can see you in the mirror Erik. Yes, I know I jabber," Rhonwen says, not at all offended.

Erik grimaces, apparently having forgotten about the mirror. "You know I miss your jabbering Mum," he assures her.

"Food will be ready soon. I hope you like chicken tikka," our hostess says as we enter a quaint pastel green kitchen.

I've never heard of chicken tikka but smile politely. "Can I help with anything?"

"My goodness, no! Just make yourself at home. Erik, Tanner should be here shortly."

Erik's step slows and his face tightens. "You invited him?"

Rhonwen turns to look at her son, hand on hip. "What is it with you two?"

Erik shakes his head. "Nothing. That's great. Um…where's Sheldon?"

"With your father on the terrace."

"Who's Sheldon?" I ask Erik as I follow him outside.

"My dad's best friend. The two of them are inseparable."

Mr. Halvorsen sits outside reading a magazine in a large, cushioned patio chair, a spotted terrier at his feet.

"Sheldon!" Erik cries as the dog runs toward him like a

tornado, apparently very fond of his prodigal two-legged sibling. "Yes, yes…I know you think I came back just for you!" He rubs the dog's tummy in between jumps and licks.

"He only greets you like that," Erik's father says, getting up slowly. He has the same dense head of hair he's passed onto his son, with streaks of grey.

"That's only because he rarely sees me these days. You'll always be his favorite Dad." The two men exchanged a short embrace. "Everest, this is my father, Martin."

Martin extends his hand and offers a kind smile as he looks at me over his spectacles. "Erik mentioned you would be joining us. Lovely meeting you."

"Thank you for having me. Erik speaks so fondly of you all. He's never mentioned Sheldon though," I add, petting the energetic pup who's now climbing my leg like a maniac.

"Don't say that too loudly!" Erik whispers. "Sheldon will be cross with me."

"Everest. What a unique name," Martin muses.

"My mother said my father was a climber. One of his aspirations was to conquer Everest,"

"And did he?"

Here we go. "I'm not sure. I never met him."

"Well, it's a strong name. I'm sure you're a worthy recipient." To my relief, Martin doesn't appear too fussed about the details, and that's that.

Rhonwen pops her head outside. "Tanner isn't with you?"

"We haven't seen him," Erik replies, his face tensing up again.

"Well, no matter. He can eat when he arrives. Come in before the food gets cold."

It turns out that while Rhonwen looks like someone off the pages of an English cooking magazine – right down to the vintage apron around her waist – that impression doesn't quite translate onto the plate. Not that I mind. The company makes up for it, and even Sheldon's taken to me. Or maybe he's just a clever opportunist hoping to exploit the new visitor for scraps. The conversation flows easily, with the most awkward part being Erik's unexpected coughing fit.

"That was delicious Rhonwen. Thank you," I say as I help her clear the plates.

"Liar!" Martin playfully calls me out when his wife is out of ear shot. "We all know she hasn't touched a saltshaker in years. It was bloody awful. It always is!"

"She sure had a heavy hand with the pepper today though," Erik adds, still clearing his throat. Martin and Erik snicker under their breaths, trying to hold in their laughter.

I stare at them, not sure if I should laugh myself. "Well, why don't you say anything?"

"Oh, we can't," Erik insists. "She would be gutted! And luckily, Dad usually cooks. Mum just likes to experiment on the guests with exotic recipes. We usually tell people to fill up before they get here but leave room for dessert. She's more of a baker, really."

He's right; it was worth enduring the entrée to get a taste of Rhonwen's chocolate soufflé. The divine flavor is still teasing my taste buds when the front door opens and closes loudly, giving everyone a jolt.

"Ah! That must be my other son," Rhonwen says with a hint of annoyance.

We sit in awkward silence waiting on the mysterious presence to enter. Tanner walks in completely unapologetic for being an hour and a half late. He's slightly taller and skinner than Erik, with his father's brown eyes and his mother's lighter hair. His skin is sickly pale and eyes bloodshot, and his clothes look like they've been slept in for a week and could use a proper wash.

Erik greets his older brother with less enthusiasm than I expected. "Tanner," he says, giving a nod from across the table. "How are things?"

"The same," Tanner replies rudely without looking at his sibling. He motions to me. "Who's this?"

"Um, Everest," Erik says. "Everest, this is my brother, Tanner."

Tanner eyes me with disdain. "Huh, things must be serious for you to meet the folks."

I smile politely, but he doesn't return the gesture. "It's nice to meet you. Erik's told me stories of how you spent your summers here," I add.

"Must have been old stories," Tanner replies coldly.

So much for trying to ease the tension.

"I kept food warm for you," Rhonwen interjects.

"I already ate."

"I see. Well, at least have some soufflé. It's your favorite," the mother insists with a sense of desperation.

"All right." Tanner returns shortly from the kitchen with the dessert, making no effort to hide his misery. He's clearly irked that he has to tolerate us. "So, where did you meet?" he asks Erik without looking up, gesticulating to us both with a spoon.

I notice Erik clenching his jaw – it looks like something's eating at his cheeks from the inside. "Actually, we met just recently, at a restaurant called The Prism. Come to think of it, you might know it."

Tanner stops chewing and lets his spoon sink into the soufflé. You could hear a pin drop in the room if it wasn't for Sheldon panting under the table, with the two brothers now engaged in some sort of telepathic warfare.

"I've heard of it – too bad it's so difficult to get a reservation," Tanner replies, lifting his chin and staring at Erik.

What are they doing?

"It just takes a little effort," Erik retorts.

"Well, I've certainly never heard of it," Rhonwen adds, the hidden meaning of the conversation understandably lost on her. "Is it in London?"

"It's more of a members-only thing," Tanner fills in, still staring Erik down coldly. "I think I'll finish this outside," he says, rising abruptly from his seat and taking his dessert to the terrace. Erik barely waits two seconds before pushing his own chair back and storming out after his brother.

"Not again…Erik! Martin, do something!" Rhonwen pleads. "Every time…" she cries, throwing up her arms and storming off to the kitchen. "Just one peaceful family meal. Just one! I don't ask for much."

"Let them be," Martin replies, calmly sipping his tea. "There is nothing we can say that will fix what is broken between those two. And they are obviously not going to tell us what that is. When they're ready to figure it out, they will."

I can see Erik gesticulating at Tanner outside and excuse myself. The shouting becomes more audible when I open the terrace doors.

I've never seen Erik in such a state. "We've all had it, Tanner! It's not our fault! Why do you have to punish us all the bloody time?"

"Don't you dare judge me! You have no idea what it's like — you don't live with this every day!" He lifts his right pant leg just enough to reveal a prosthetic, then notices me standing by the door.

"I…just wanted to see if everything was okay," I mumble, half-truthfully. The other reason is just curiosity.

Tanner releases his pant leg and turns his raging eyes back towards his brother. "Ask your boyfriend. He seems to have everything figured out. How nice that you get to visit paradise together. Too bad all of us aren't so lucky."

"It's your own doing you can't go back," Erik retorts. "*You* choose to be miserable and feel sorry for yourself, drowning your self-pity in bottles of pills and scotch. I think you actually get off on it, making us all walk on eggshells. How's it all working out for you, by the way?"

"Why don't you get off your high horse and fuck off!" Tanner snaps and starts walking back toward the house.

"Don't you think this has gone on long enough? We need to talk about this!" Erik calls after him.

"No," Tanner replies, scowling at me as he passes, "only you do."

"Bloody hell Tanner!" Erik cries in exasperation as his brother disappears inside. "I'm just trying to help you!" He kicks a plastic chair across the lawn and crouches on the spot, burying his head in his hands from frustration.

I can hear Rhonwen chastising Tanner. That's followed closely by a door slamming loudly and something falling inside.

I approach Erik slowly, finally starting to appreciate his turmoil and all the things he said to me in the Prism, the pieces coming together.

"I'm fine," he says before I can ask.

"Ok. Don't let this get to you," I urge, hoping to provide some comfort, but knowing it's just one of those things people say when they feel completely helpless.

"Yeah," Erik concedes, faking a smile. "Right. I'm sorry. Come on."

Once inside, Rhonwen leads me off. "House rules — whoever doesn't cook cleans. Let's put our feet up and chat."

We sink into two armchairs in the living room. Almost every space on the wall is occupied with a family photograph or a painting, or wallpaper. I try to make out the ones of Erik, curious about his childhood. There's a photo of him and Tanner beside a small Cessna airplane with what looks like a young Martin. And a lot of beach photos, I assume from their summers here. There's also a lot of photos of the boys skiing, and a display cabinet filled with trophies.

"I'm sorry you had to see that dear," Rhonwen apologizes. "Tanner he…" She takes a minute and swallows hard. "There was a car accident, you see, about eight months ago. He's not the same. I wish you could have known him before. He and Erik were like two peas in a pod…" Rhonwen's cool blue eyes begin to glisten, and she puts an index finger up to her nose. "He was a superb skier, you know. Trained a lot in Norway with my in-laws. Was even being scouted for the Olympics. But the accident took his leg. It changed him – on the inside too. He's just so angry at everything now."

She heaves a deep sigh, her eyes very glossy now. "It breaks my heart, not knowing how to help my boy."

My heart goes out to Rhonwen as she sits slumped from the weight of the impossible burden she's placed on herself. "I don't think that saving him is up to you," I say, trying to comfort her. "And from what I see in Erik, you're doing all the right things."

Rhonwen lifts her chin. "You have a kind soul," she whispers, rubbing the side of her palm over her eyes. "I can see that. You know, we really are quite fun most of the time."

We hear Erik and Martin singing in the kitchen – something about a frog, a turkey, and a pirate ship. Random, but very Erik.

I can't help laughing, imagining how much fun they must have had over the years. "I have no doubt you are!"

* * *

After leaving the summer house and escaping from Rhonwen's twelfth hug, Erik and I roll past the Sussex countryside without saying a single word for a good twenty minutes. Erik looks so far away I wonder if he even realizes I'm in the car with him. Finally, I can't take it anymore.

"Your family is really great."

Silence.

"Sheldon really missed you. I thought he would rip your arm off at the door to keep you from leaving. Of course, Tanner was a little interesting, but everyone gets to have a bad day, right?"

More silence.

I recall something Erik had said on our first day in the Prism, about being a magister once before. *They don't come here anymore.* The sadness on his face when he spoke of Nevar…the pieces start to fall into place.

"Your mom told me about the accident. You were Tanner's magister, weren't you?"

Erik exhales a long breath. "I was going to explain. It's complicated. I didn't think he'd be here." He pauses and bites the inside of his cheeks. It's a trick I use to hold back tears, and I know he's trying to hold back his emotions just the same. "I don't mean to sound harsh, but I'm just tired of fighting for him when he refuses to fight for himself. I can't get through to him, Ev. He just won't let me help."

He manages a smile and takes hold of my hand. "But I'm fine, I promise. Let's not let it ruin the weekend. We can talk about all this another time."

I hate seeing him this way. I know it's not who he wants to be. I squeeze his hand tightly, recalling how worried I was about my own complicated life. It's like Jenna said: we all have our stuff.

I look out the window at the fenced in pastures and wildflowers that line the side of the road. "All my life, I wanted to see the world," I tell him. "Then I find the Prism – limitless, perfect. Everything I ever wanted at my fingertips."

"But…" Erik says, sensing I have more to say after my pause.

I focus on the fields blanketed with tall wild grasses. "But this world is equally magnificent," I finish, "in its own imperfect, messy and chaotic way, isn't it? It's like you said – you can only take perfect for so long. Challenges make us feel alive, give us something to fight for, and Earth has enough to keep us busy for a while." I squeeze his hand again. "Maybe Tanner's your challenge right now. One of these days, you will get through to him and it will all be worth it."

Erik gives me a slow nod and returns the hand squeeze. "Well, I suppose I can't argue with my own brilliance," he teases. "You're right though, this world is pretty great, despite everything."

I'm glad he's starting to sound like himself again. "It's weird sitting on the wrong side as a passenger," I note, moving on to another topic. "Why do you Brits have to complicate everything?"

"Um, that *is* the right side! This is how cars are meant to be driven," Erik insists proudly. "Just like you're meant to measure in centimeters and Celsius."

"Right, just like it's called 'football,' " I tease, throwing in the air quotes.

Erik's smile finally breaks through. "You're on thin ice Clearly."

CHAPTER 33

Raining Glass

"So, this is the girl! Erik, nicely done," Tommy Castlemore says as he looks us over in Erik's flat. Turns out both Erik and Rhonwen were right – Erik's roommate is both strange and eccentric. As soon as we step through the door, Tommy's in our face, decked out in a short black leather jacket with more zippers than it needs. His jet-black hair is styled with excessive gel. I can't quite figure out how the red scarf fits in, but he makes it work somehow.

"Welcome to our humble abode Ms…." He begins to bow but pauses and glances up from his brow. "Sorry, I forgot her name mate."

"Everest," Erik reminds him.

"Ms Everest! Wait…like the mountain?" Tommy asks skeptically. "Are you sure? I thought it was Eleanor, or something."

"It's Everest," I confirm.

"You're certain?"

Erik rolls his eyes. "I think she would know her own name, Tommy."

"See, I just…I was so sure it was Eleanor…"

"No," Erik corrects, "Eleanor's the girl you went out with two weeks ago who, your words, 'smelled like a vanilla factory exploded and irritated your sinuses.' What would you do without me to do all your remembering?" Erik points his nose up to the ceiling. "Speaking of smells…is something burning?"

Tommy's eyes grow wide. He darts into the kitchen and returns in a few seconds with a sheepish grin. "Not anymore!"

Erik rolls his eyes a second time as he puts down our bags. "It's a miracle I'm not homeless yet."

"Erik did promise I'd be entertained," I tell Tommy, finally appreciating Erik's warnings.

"My mate is a wise man. I always aim to entertain. Drinks? Sit. Eat. Music?" Tommy spins dramatically and turns on the stereo on his way to the liquor cabinet where he busies himself with various bottles. The smell of the red cocktail he brings back nearly knocks me off my seat.

"What is this?" I whisper to Erik, setting it aside after Tommy's out of sight again.

"I've learned not to ask, but I wouldn't drink it. His uncle brought a bottle of some strong stuff from India, and he's been improvising with it a lot."

"Tonight, we party!" Tommy announces, making an appearance again. "I have a new date, Stacy. I want to take her to Achilles. It's a smashing club, Everest, just rocking. Lots of live music, new artists — cool stuff!"

Erik glances at me. I can tell he's trying not to laugh at Tommy's dramatic air drumming. "It's up to you? We don't have to go."

I had hoped for some alone time with Erik, but Tommy's so excited I can't bear to let him down. Nightclubs have never really been my scene, but seeing the London night life might be fun. "Sure, sounds great. Although, I think I need to build up a lot more energy if I'm going to keep up with Tommy over here."

"Oh, don't worry yourself with that," Tommy says. "Nobody can keep up with me! It'll be fun! You'll like Tracey."

"Stacey," Erik corrects again, setting his own drink aside after taste-testing and grimacing. "That is bloody awful!"

Tommy adjusts his scarf as he makes for the door. "I'll be back in half an hour, then we can go. Don't trash the apartment, right?"

And just like that he's gone, like a cheesy magician at a carnival.

I immediately burst out laughing. "*Wow!* You weren't kidding," I say to Erik, still recovering from the whirlwind encounter. "He is something else. In a good way though."

"Yeah. He's something. He grows on you, believe it or not. Listen, if you'd rather not go —"

"It's fine. Let's seize the night while we're still breathing, right? And after that we can go back to doing normal things."

"That don't involve alternate realities and near-death experiences?"

"Something like that."

He leans in to kiss me, the smell of his cologne quickening my pulse. He feels so real, even more real than the Prism Erik. I try to imprint the details of his face again — his elusive dimples, the intricacies of his voice, the occasional freckle on his arms, the small birthmark on the side of his neck.

"I have to admit, I'm kind of relieved," I tell him. "I wasn't sure what to expect. But you're still you."

He blushes. "I'd be lying if I said I wasn't a little relieved myself. I was half-expecting you to cancel the whole thing."

"And…," I ask nervously, "does this weekend meet expectations?"

"Exceeds. Definitely exceeds." His voice drifts as he pulls me closer. I bury myself in his embrace, feeling safe and almost understood.

There are still a few things I'm holding back. They'll be time for all that. I just want one more uncomplicated night, and then all cards on the table.

*　*　*

By some miracle, Tommy manages to persuade the bouncer to let us in ahead of the stupendously long line at the club, much to the dissatisfaction of those already waiting.

"I'm convinced Tommy has a black book on every bouncer in the city," Erik shouts over the music as we enter. "I've never had to wait in a line with him once!"

"You'll be far less embarrassed if you stick with me," Tommy advises me, leaning in so I can hear him. "I only bring Erik along to make myself look better. It's quite awful to watch really. Picture a tuna fish. Now picture it awkwardly flailing around on the shore. Now picture Erik's face on the tuna fish. Do you see where I'm going with this?"

"I'm not *that* bad," Erik defends himself. "And why a tuna fish of all things?"

A decent indie band takes the stage, and the maroon-haired singer has no trouble pumping up the crowd with his animated personality. Tommy's love life is slightly complicated by the existence of Stacey's boyfriend, who happens to be twice Tommy's size and looks like he not only pumps iron but eats it whole. After saving Tommy from what would have likely been an unpleasant fate, we head to the dance floor, where Erik's moves prove to be far less humiliating than I expected.

By the end of the night, Tommy isn't as drunk as I imagined

he would be, and surprisingly still in one piece, having wisely given up on finding love for the night. We manage to convince him to turn in early.

"It's going to be strange, not seeing you every day," I tell Erik as the three of us leave the club shortly after midnight, Tommy trailing behind and reciting poetry to himself.

Erik wraps his arm around my shoulders. "What if I told you I was thinking about visiting Paris next weekend? That is, if that would be all right with a certain someone I would be depending on for room and board."

I pull him dramatically into a kiss. "Did I ever tell you that I love you?"

"You may have mentioned it."

It suddenly seems quieter than normal. "Wait, where's Tommy?" I ask, glancing back.

"Wasn't he right on our tail?" Erik asks. But Tommy's nowhere in sight. "Tell me he didn't go back after that girl. He's hopeless!"

We head back in the direction of the club again, passing an alley on our way. You'd think by now I would have had enough of alleys, but I'm drawn to something in it. The three men are barely noticeable under the grimy dim light bulb as they crouch over a body near the back exit of the club, their fists resting on the abdomen of the person lying on the ground.

"Is it just me or does that look totally creepy?" I ask Erik, who seems to have noticed it too.

"Yeah…it's dodgy all right," he mumbles, charting a course for the men. "Wait here."

"Erik…"

"I'm just going to check it out," he assures me. I disregard the instruction and follow him, the energy around me shifting with each step until a layer of sweat covers my palms. The stench of urine and sewage escape from an overturned trash bin, its contents covered with a slithering sheet of maggots.

Erik's pendant seems to burn against my chest, like it's signaling me to turn back.

I ignore it.

"Is everything all right here?" Erik calls out.

Three hooded heads turn to look at him, their faces concealed. "Everything's just fine," one of them answers in a Scottish accent. "Just had a little too much to drink."

A leg begins to move, urging Erik to take a step closer. "I have some first aid training. Maybe I can help or call someone."

"Why don't you just move along. This doesn't concern you," the biggest of the three men replies as he rises to his feet, standing at least a head taller than Erik.

The body moves again, this time enough to roll over and reveal a red scarf trailing on the pavement.

"Tommy!" I cry, running toward him. Tommy's eyes stare through me like I'm an apparition.

"What have you done to him?" Erik yells, storming up to the men. But the biggest of the men reacts quickly and punches Erik hard in the stomach.

I stop in my tracks as Erik hits the ground hard in front of me.

"Need a girl to fight your battles?" the man sneers as I help Erik back to his feet.

"What about these two?" one of the other men suggests. "Maybe we can get something out of 'em?"

Erik holds up his hands while massaging his sore stomach. "We don't have anything. Just a few pounds. Honest. You can have all of it. Just…let us help our friend."

The tall man laughs. "It's not money we'll be takin' from ya."

Erik and I exchange a puzzled glance. *What else could they possibly want?* The men have us encircled now, blocking our exit to the street.

"This isn't looking good for us," Erik whispers, trying to shield me. "And I just quit the gym." He lunges at the leader and strikes him in the jaw. But one of the other thugs hits Erik on the back with a plank of lumber, knocking him to the ground.

Thanks. I lift the plank and return the favor, bringing it down hard on one of the men's necks. But as I'm gearing up for a second swing, a hand squeezes my shoulder tightly and pushes me aside like a rag doll onto the sticky pavement.

I hear Erik take another hit as I gather myself. A sense of déjà-vu overcomes me, accompanied by a rage I remember feeling not that long ago in an alley much like this one. I can no longer contain it, and finally let out a scream that rips through my throat. As I raise my hand instinctively to stop the plank that's now inches away from Erik's head, a body-jerking burst of energy escapes from my body and travels in the direction of the three men, striking them down like dominos and leaving a warmth trickling down my spine. The earth shakes for a moment and fragments of glass rain down from shattering windows.

I stare at the scene, dumbfounded and breathless. Forget lightbulbs – that was small time.

What the hell did I just do?!

Two of the men roll about in pain, holding their heads, while the third lies motionless. I see Erik getting up a few feet away, staring at me in bewilderment and holding his own head. I can't hear what he's saying over the ringing in my ears. *Ev, are you okay?* I see him mouth the words as he stumbles toward me before he becomes audible again.

"…okay?"

"What happened?" I mumble, massaging my throat.

"Something incredible," Erik says, helping me up. "Come on, we have to get out of here before they come 'round."

He approaches the motionless thug and searches him, pulling car keys out of his jacket pocket. The man's wrist lies facing up, revealing a familiar tattoo of the letter "V".

The same one Irra has.

The same one I thought I might have seen that day at the Luminary…

These thugs are Vulturians! What the hell?

Erik sees it too. "Damn it," he mumbles.

I jerk my head to stare at him. "You know what this is?"

He purses his lips and nods, then goes to get Tommy as I continue staring at the body. A familiar granite band catches my attention on the man's finger, and I remove it from his hand to get a better look...

"Ev, we gotta go!" Erik yells, getting in the way of my investigation. I slip the ring into my pocket, then help Erik pull Tommy's limp body off the pavement and drag it towards the street.

"He's in no shape to walk," I point out.

"That's why we need a car," Erik says, trying the key fob when we come upon the road. The lights flash on a black sedan 20 feet away. *Do these people drive anything else?*

Erik seems more composed than I am. "Get in the back with Tommy," he instructs. "We won't have long before they're onto us. The car's probably trackable. We just need to get far enough away and ditch it."

"What's wrong with him?" I ask, trying to snap Tommy out of it. But my tapping and shaking isn't very effective. I catch sight of Erik's eyes in the rear-view mirror. Clouded. Focused. He revs the engine before two gunshots hit the car.

"Shit!" I cry.

The tires shriek as we pull away. *Why would they shoot?* I'm supposed to be safe so long as I have the compass.

Unless they don't know who we are…

"You alright?" Erik cries as I check the seats and Tommy for bullet holes.

"Yeah…I think so."

"Damn it!" Erik hits the steering wheel hard with his hand, then appears to take a breath to calm himself. "Ok, I know a lot just happened, but let's keep it together. Can you do that for me? Ev?"

I nod. "You know who they are, the Vulturians," I ask him. It's all become clear – we have the same enemy now.

His jaw clenches. "Yes. But they might as well not exist to the rest of the world. So how do *you* know about them?"

"It's a long story."

Tommy starts to move next to me. "See if he'll tell you anything," Erik suggests.

"Hey, hey, Tommy…what happened Tommy? Can you hear me?" I ask, shoving him. He's almost unrecognizable from the energetic person I met earlier. "What did those guys want?"

Something registers behind the vacant stare. "Rings…" he mutters at the rate of a sloth.

"Rings?"

"They grabbed me, brought me…put their hands on…me…" He gets distracted by a smudge on the window. "Weird. I think…I'm going to throw up…"

I retrieve my find from my pocket and show it to Tommy, hoping he can control his nausea until we're out of the car. "This ring? Is it this…" I flip the interior light on. Studying it from mere inches away I realize I've seen it many times before, on the hands of a Vulturian I know all too well. "Well, I'll be…"

"What?" Erik asks.

As I hold the granite band, I let my index finger tap that familiar cloudy stone. Sure enough, I feel it again – that sensation I thought I'd never have to experience again. Heaviness, suction… The same "V", the same granite, the same etchings, and crest. Every time he touched my hand…that 'truce'…

"Son of a bitch!" Had he been somehow affecting my mind, my emotions, with *this?*

The car makes a hard left and I hear Tommy try to vomit.

"Felt tired," Tommy continues, as if talking to himself. "Everything was heavy. I just wanted to bloody die!" Tommy starts to wail. "My life is such crap!"

"Whoa Tommy, stop that," I say, slapping him gently on the cheek. "Hey! Look at me!"

"Be careful!" Erik warns me. "We don't know what that thing does!"

I scrutinize the ring with hatred, convinced of its evil. "Actually, I think I know exactly what it does." *Just how many of these things are out there?*

A hard impact on the right back bumper pushes us into the path of an oncoming bus which Erik narrowly misses.

"Crazy bastards!" Erik screams.

So much for getting some distance. My stomach is in my throat as I realize that one unlucky turn, one dead end and we're probably done.

I look behind me. A dark blue sedan this time. "What's our plan?"

"I don't know, I haven't exactly been in a car chase before," Erik replies. He pushes hard on the gas to avoid a red light. But our pursuers push their luck and nearly collide with an intersecting cyclist to stay on our tail.

"Can you do what you did, back in that alley?" Erik asks with a sense of pleading.

I look at my hands. I couldn't even figure out how to control the light bulbs. "I don't know. I don't know how I do it!"

"Look, Ev, I know what I'm asking of you," Erik says, eyes focused on the road, "to harness a power that's alien to you, that probably terrifies you…But it's saved us once already. Try to trust it."

Trust it? *I don't even understand it!*

I clasp my hands together to control the shaking, then inhale deeply and roll down the back window.

What if I accidentally hurt someone?

Focus!

I lean out, the sedan in my sights, and wait for something to overcome me as it did before.

Nothing. I just look like a crazy girl sticking her head out of a window, waiting to catch a bullet. Both disappointed and relieved, I sit back down beside Tommy.

"Hang on," Erik says as he makes another sharp turn.

"I don't know what I'm doing!" I mumble. Suddenly, it's a lot of pressure, being responsible for whether we get away or probably die.

"Think," Erik urges, "what made you do it in the first place? Did it ever happen before?"

The alley scene unfolds in my mind again. The energy release, the shattering glass…*the glass panel … Tristan… lightbulbs exploding…*

"Anger," I conclude, "I think it's my anger that feeds it."

"Well…I wouldn't ordinarily say this but try to get angry Ev. We're almost on empty."

Going down that ugly road is the last thing I want to do. But it looks like I have no other choice. I have to go there, even if it means I'm shut out of the Prism for it. After tonight, I wonder if I already am.

"Okay. Angry…what makes me angry. *That's easy. Let's start with all the time Tristan stole from me.* That ring…to think, a simple touch…

Touch!

I reach into my pocket and retrieve the ring again, careful not to touch the ivory-looking stone, identical in color and clarity to the one I placed my hand on when I left my apartment, every single day.

That stupid ugly doorknob…

Bastard!

I feel the anger building, my rage insurmountable. I lean my body out of the window and focus on the sedan without even considering the possibility of meeting one of their bullets. The scream that leaves my lips sounds like a muffled echo in my head, and whatever I release hits the sedan like a freight train, sending it flipping backwards and into the concrete wall of an underpass. I stare at the destruction I've created with a dry mouth, then slowly sink back into my seat as Erik speeds away.

"…rest! Talk to me!"

My ears are still ringing when the sound comes back. "I'm fine," I say, slowly sitting up.

"You did it!" Erik cries. "You actually did it!"

I did *something.* But was it worth the cost, to feel so much pain and anger?

I look at Erik in the rearview and realize with relief that my anger is no more – at least for now.

CHAPTER 34

It's Come to This

Erik's voice forms a cocoon around me as I sit in the back of the car in a brain fog, trying to process everything that's happened in the last 30 minutes.

"Hang in there," I hear Erik repeat for the tenth time. "How's Tommy?"

I glance at our passenger who seems to have slept through most of the ordeal.

"Completely out of it."

"We need a new ride," Erik decides. "Can you stay with him while I get one? I'll come right back. My flat will be too dangerous for us now. I know a place we can go but they'll track this car before we can get there."

I don't like the idea of splitting up, but he's got a point. "Ok. Yeah. Of course."

"They shouldn't be able to locate you so long as you keep your emotions in check. Can you do that?"

I raise an eyebrow and catch Erik's gaze in the mirror again.

"I'll explain later," he says, unaware that Sarah's already filled me in on frequency tracking. We really should have exchanged notes sooner...

He pulls over in front of a small park in a residential neighborhood, away from any obvious cameras. Together, we drag Tommy over to a bench in a hidden grove. "Here, take this." He places a gun in my hand, wrapped in Tommy's scarf. "I found it in the glovebox, in case you need it."

The gun feels cold, even wrapped in the fabric. Fitting, considering it's probably ripped the warmth from countless bodies.

Has it really come to this?

I don't want it. "I don't know how to use it," I tell him, trying to give it back.

"Hopefully you don't have to. Here…" He shows me how to take the safety off, careful to handle it through the scarf to avoid leaving prints. "Just don't point it in the wrong direction, and you'll be fine."

I try to give it back again, but Erik's busy ensuring Tommy doesn't tip over and fall off the bench.

"Be careful," I tell him, holding the chunk of metal awkwardly, "and don't be too long."

He kisses me, and I wrap my free hand around his neck, afraid I'm going to break it, afraid that it will be last time I embrace him.

He holds my face in his hands and places one last kiss on my forehead before running off. "I'll be right back," he promises.

I can only hope he's right.

I watch him depart from the bench, Tommy slumped onto my shoulder and breathing heavily, the gun clutched in my hand. I keep my hand off the trigger, afraid that I'll accidently pull it with my shaking fingers and shoot myself in the leg. My eyes don't leave the park entrance for what feels like an hour. I don't even remember blinking.

Finally, I see headlights in the distance. The car engine dies, and someone exits, and I ready the weapon as the figure approaches. Slowly the darkness reveals him and my breathing resumes.

Thank God!

"You alright?" Erik asks, taking the gun from me.

I shake my head, still in disbelief over everything. "Ask me later. You?"

"Right as rain. He still out?"

"Yeah. They really did a number on him. Where are we going?"

"To see an acquaintance. He'll be discrete. I've got your things."

"How? You said the apartment was too dangerous."

We pull Tommy up and begin walking. "I took a chance. They shot at us, so they may not have known who we were. There was no one at the flat when I got there. But it won't be long. I just grabbed the important stuff. I've actually had a go bag packed for weeks now."

So much for a fun, uncomplicated weekend.

We pile into the waiting hatchback. I don't ask Erik where he got it as I get into the passenger seat.

"This is all my fault. All of it," I whisper. "They want me to find it. And now I've put you in danger."

Erik glances up with puzzlement. "The compass thing? Don't you already have it?"

"No. The Skala."

"Huh?"

I fiddle with my pendant nervously. "There something else I've been keeping from you Erik. I met one of them – a Vulturian. She told me what they want me for. That's how I know about them."

"You *met* one?" Erik cries. "Ev, are you out of your mind?!"

"It's not what you think! She wants out. She's risked her life to help me."

"Or you're playing right into their hands! And why didn't you tell me this before?"

I had a feeling he'd react this way. And I don't blame him. I'd probably do the same if I was on the outside. "I trust her," I insist. "Someone followed me home one night. I managed to tail the car back to the Paris chapter house. The building had a gate with a 'V' on it, just like the tattoo we saw. But there were a ton of cameras, so I didn't stick around –"

"What were you thinking?" Erik cries again, slamming his palms against the steering wheel. "You have no idea what these people are capable of!"

"I was careful," I reply defensively. "And it's not like you were forthcoming with me about what *you* knew!"

Erik opens his mouth to say something but then quickly shuts it, not having a good enough defense prepared.

"Anyway," I go on, "that's when she found me – she took me into this secret passage behind the chapter house and we were able to spy on one of their meetings with the Ertu –"

"I've heard that word before, from Robert," Erik mutters. "It's their leader, isn't it?"

"Yes. Point is, she risked a lot to do that, and that earns her a chance. Thanks to her I found out a few things, including that they know about you and your little recon group – feel free to enlighten me about that, by the way – and also…that they have a special interest in me."

Erik's flushed face relaxes a little as he studies me. "What kind of interest?"

I take out the ring and place it on the dashboard of the car. It rolls back and forth, mocking me. "I just put the final pieces together tonight. Tristan has one just like it. Gave me a doorknob with that same stone. I can only guess it was meant to control me somehow, because of what I am – what I can do.

"What happened in the alley, it's been kind of happening for a while now," I elaborate, "since I moved to Paris. It was usually light bulbs or glassware, just shattering without explanation. I'm not exactly sure what it is, only that the Vulturians call it a 'frequency.' They think I can find this Skala because of it."

I sigh loudly, finally free of the last of my secrets. Unfortunately, I don't feel any better. Just hollowed out and tired.

We drive in silence for a few minutes before Erik speaks up. "We should have both trusted each other sooner."

Can't argue with that. "Yeah. We should have," I reply. I'm not upset with him. We both held back. We share the blame.

A light rain starts to leave tiny specks on the window. "I didn't want to bring you into the middle of something I didn't understand," I try to explain. "Being with you was so effortless. I didn't want to complicate it. You were the one thing that made any sense."

Erik pulls up to the back entrance of a pub and kills the engine. "I'm not Tristan, Ev," he says, turning to me, the hurt and frustration coming through his eyes. He places his palm on my hand and interlocks our fingers. "I'm not going to change the way I feel about you just because things get a little tough or absolutely bizarre, as is the case."

I chuckle. "Yeah. Bizarre is an understatement…I'm sorry."

"Me too. From now on, no more secrets." He touches my cheek gently, then proceeds to get out of the car. "Come on. We need to keep moving."

"We're staying at a pub?"

"No, but the car is." He hands me my bag. "We have a bit of a walk to Eaton's place. He's a family friend and a lawyer, in case we need one after tonight. We'll head for Paris in the morning."

"Paris? Is that a good idea? Won't they expect that?"

"Probably. We'll wait until the afternoon, let the heat die down. But I want to get you home. And if you really do trust this friend of yours…"

"Sarah," I finish, finally revealing her name. *Ok, now there's no more secrets.*

"Sarah. Well…maybe she can help us somehow."

"Right. Just one problem: I have no way of reaching her. She comes to me."

"Then let's hope you two have some intuitive bond you can tap into. We can't go back to your apartment either. In fact, you should make some calls, tell people you'll be out of town for a while."

It really *has* come to his.

"Here," Erik says, handing me a phone. "Only burners from now on."

"That's something you don't hear every day," I mumble, taking it from him and looking it over before putting it in my bag.

We walk in silence to Eaton's townhouse as normally as possible, Tommy underarm, our worlds rocked, and our new-found happiness shattered. Erik seems like a different person – less his upbeat self, more thoughtful. I suppose that's a good thing. We need focus and logic now.

After a few blocks we knock on the door of a brick Georgian townhouse. Eaton turns out to be shorter-than-average, middle-aged with salt and pepper hair. The minute he sees Erik's face he seems to know better than to ask questions. "Come in!" he says, looking up and down the street for anything suspicious.

"Thanks mate. It's just for one night," Erik assures him.

"For as many as you need," Eaton replies. "Your friend looks rough. Come on, get him on the couch."

The place smells nice, of bergamot and cedar. The navy-blue walls are broken up by some abstract art canvases and the furniture looks like it belongs in a posh social club. The place is immaculate, books organized by color and size and blankets folded to perfection. I'm almost afraid to touch anything.

"I'm going to call my folks," Erik says after we're all settled, "and catch up with Eaton quickly. I owe him a laugh or two for barging in like this." He smiles his serene smile as he pulls me into an embrace, but it's not enough this time.

When he leaves, I take a moment to steady myself, then dial Catherine's mobile. As expected, it goes straight to voicemail.

"Hi," I say, my voice quivering. Despite our differences, I don't want any harm to come to her. I quietly laugh to myself, realizing being hauled up in my Aunt Michaela's bunker might not be such a bad thing, given the circumstances. Maybe the crazy bat was onto something after all.

"It's me…Everest. Just wondering how things are going," I start. "I wanted to let you know I got an internship at one of Peterson's branches, in Berlin. It's sudden, so…I'll be out of town for a few weeks at least. Maybe more. I'll stay in touch and try you again." I'm careful not to reveal any details that could point to her whereabouts. "You should stay there as long as you need to. I'll be gone anyway."

I wonder how much Tristan's deceptive gift affected her. She wasn't the happiest before he came into our lives, but I'm sure it didn't help.

The next call I ponder is to Lise and Julian, but it's the middle of the night and I don't want to alarm their mother. *I'll see them in the Prism soon enough.*

I'm staring up at shadows of moving branches on the ceiling, waiting for the dreaded sound of shrieking tires and gunshots outside when Erik enters the room. He lays down next to me on top of the bedspread, placing a comforting arm across my abdomen.

"I hate not knowing what I'm up against," I tell him, pulling him close and trying to reclaim that calm we once felt around each other.

"We'll be in the Prism soon," he reminds me. "You'll get your answers then. Just try to sleep. All you need is a few minutes."

Right. *All I need is a few minutes…*

Easier said than done.

CHAPTER 35

Monster at the Gate

Gill wrinkles his nose and looks up at the stacks of books in concentration. "You mean, like healing crystals?" he asks when Erik and I inquire if he knows of any texts on supernatural stones in the Lumus.

"No." I sigh. It's impossible to accurately describe the stupid thing without giving too much away.

The library's quiet, with most Wakers already converging on Senna for the second day of festivities. We'll be meeting Robert instead and I want to come to our meeting prepared.

"Have there been any stones in the history of the real or Prism world that have been used in a supernatural way to affect humans?" Erik asks again, trying unsuccessfully to be more specific.

Gill throws up his hands. "You just rephrased your original question. You've got to give me more here."

Erik's patience is quickly wearing thin. "I wish I could mate," he says through clenched teeth, uncharacteristically agitated.

I give Gill a pat on the shoulder. "Don't mind him. Long Earth night."

The librarian grins and nods his head. "Say no more. Uh, let me think here…there's a whole section on historical artifacts. You might find what you're looking for there."

"Thanks."

"Say, why aren't you two in Senna like everyone else?" Gill asks, peering over his thick frames.

I shrug, playing off the urgency of the situation. "Same reason you're not Gill. A tortured, curious mind."

"Of course, the best kind of reason, I suppose," he says with an approving smile before briskly walking away with a bit of a waddle. "Good luck! And let me know what you find. I'm curious myself now."

Erik huffs, staring at the looming stacks of books as we step onto our platforms. "It's endless! We better get started."

A thunder-like rumble puts an abrupt stop to our search before it even begins and sends powerful shockwaves through the very foundations of the Luminary. Hardcovers rain down on us, and the energy orbs rattle and bounce off the ceiling. Wakers in mid-air struggle to keep their balance, some falling only to be scooped back-up by their loyal platforms before hitting the ground. Erik and I shield our heads as we wait for the vibrations to subside; then, as if of a single mind, guide our platforms to the nearest window.

The horizon is cloaked in an advancing darkness, the winds rapidly picking up speed and scooping up water from the nearby Cascada pools.

"We don't get storms," Erik says. "I'm going up to get a closer look."

Cass and Juno are already waiting when we step outside. Others join us in the skies over the Prismatic and face the disturbance that seems to be originating from over Senna.

"It felt like an earthquake," a girl next to us shouts. "That's impossible, right?"

Nothing is impossible anymore.

An earthquake in the Prism. If it's true it doesn't bode well. "No one wishes for the earth to break apart," I say. *Or for a train to crash.* Is the Prism destabilizing further?

"I don't think an earthquake is our biggest problem anymore," Erik observes. A dense charcoal storm cloud is approaching quickly from the north, accompanied by a fierce wind that we're completely powerless to challenge. I'm almost unable to take my eyes off it. It's hypnotizing and beautiful in a terrifying way, with thick spirals circling a menacing eye. I know we need to get out of its way, but a part of me wants to stay and see if I'll come out on the other side.

"Ev!" Erik snaps me of my momentary lapse in judgement. "We need to go!"

"Lise and Julian!" I suddenly remember. Panic grips my chest. "They're in Senna!"

"They could be anywhere!" Erik shouts. "You won't find them before this thing hits. If they're with others, they'll find shelter. We need to go!"

I look once more toward Senna, then follow him reluctantly, my concern for the children mounting. But I know he's right – I won't make it anywhere close to the realm. Juno's already pushing her strength to the limit, her wings laboriously working against the opposing force. The clouds are making up ground quickly, hiding something threatening brewing on the inside. What's caused the Prism to take such an extreme turn?

Finally, I reach the Promenade, with Erik not far behind. "Go, wait it out in safety girl," he orders Cass. "I'm going into the gardens to warn others," he says. "The tall vines may be obstructing their view of the storm."

"I'll take Cascada. Meet at the Luminary?"

"Don't take too long. Spread the word and run!"

I nod, releasing Juno and praying the Prism will protect her somehow.

I don't have much work to do. Wakers have already taken shelter in the caves. Only a few remain, and they don't need much urging as the storm cloud casts a shadow over the ground under our feet, creeping forward, inch by inch, like an eerie blanket. It's warning enough. I consider taking shelter myself, but remember that Robert is waiting, which means answers are waiting.

I can make it.

I sprint towards the path that will lead me to the Luminary, hoping to outrun the beast. But soon it's upon me – rain, followed by hail the size of mango fruit. It falls with such force that it leaves craters in the grass. I feel it clip my heels and hammer at my knuckles as I try to protect my head. A tornado-like force scoops up the water from a nearby pool creating a waterspout, the wind pulling me into the vortex. I push on, grabbing branches to propel myself forward, and finally come upon the path I've been looking for. The trees thrash about like wild hair, ready to entrap me in a web of bark and leaves, but I make it out before they get the chance. To the right, I see Erik running from the gardens towards the Luminary doors.

The hail continues to pommel the courtyard as I cross. I use the remainder of my strength to ascend the steps and pull Erik's hand toward me as he comes up behind. We launch ourselves into the safety of the Luminary and push desperately against the doors, finding to our dismay that we're no match for the storm. As the treacherous hail begins to make its way inside, another body joins us and with a great heave we secure the fortress.

CHAPTER 36

Through the Labyrinth

Gill's spectacles hang crookedly off his nose as he leans breathless against the door. "What the heck is happening out there?" he asks, fixing himself up.

"Nothing good," Erik answers, patting Gill's shoulder. "Thanks, by the way. We wouldn't have shut that door without you."

Gill nods, stunned. "I've never seen anything like that…at least, not here…"

We listen with bated breath to the chaos outside, moving cautiously away from the entrance after we check that it's secure.

"Don't open that door until this all blows over," Erik instructs Gill, taking my arm. "And thanks again mate."

I feel bad leaving Gill behind. The poor guy looks absolutely bewildered.

"This way," Erik motions, ushering me into a small unnumbered lecture hall on the first floor containing no more than 30 seats. The curtains are drawn, but there's just enough light to navigate. Erik locks the door behind us and checks it twice, then walks toward the lecture stand, which has wooden appliqués attached to the front that look like scrambled puzzle pieces. He crouches in front of it and proceeds to shift the appliques around, his hands moving fluidly to solve the puzzle. The last piece falls into place, the appliques now forming a labyrinth, and the podium beneath us glides sideways to reveal an orb-illuminated staircase that descends below the floor.

My veins nearly burst with excitement. *Forget loft ladders.* "Now this is real Indiana Jones! Is this where you sneak off to all the time?"

But there's nothing lighthearted about Erik today. "I trust you Everest," he says soberly before he leads us in. "No one can know about this place. Only a small group of us have ever been down her." He turns to face me. "Do you understand?"

His gaze is intense. I nod back. "Got it."

Our heads simultaneously jerk toward the sound of someone fidgeting with the room door lock.

"Hurry," Erik urges, stopping to turn a lever that's protruding from the stone passage, sliding shut the access point.

"What if it's Robert"?

"Then he'll know what to do. The door to the outside won't open until the podium's locked back in place and the puzzle's scrambled. Here…" He hands me a small replica of the labyrinth which he retrieves from behind a loose stone on the wall. "I'll help you memorize the sequence before you leave today. No one can get their hands on this."

I take the object, running my fingers over the pieces, and continue to follow Erik down the steps. Even with the orbs, there's no view of the bottom. Only after about 30 steps do I begin to make out an end point. We finally emerge into a long corridor that curves at the end.

"It's the same pattern as the puzzle," Erik explains. "A

labyrinth. You need to memorize all the turns perfectly or you'll get lost in one of the false corridors."

So far, this is turning out to be a high-stakes test of my memory. "What happens if I end up in a false corridor?"

"I don't know. But it's for our protection, so I assume getting stuck isn't good. If there's ever a threat, the labyrinth will reset with a new configuration. For now, we follow the pattern, and we don't stray!" Erik warns again, putting my curiosity in its place.

"Understood."

The walls are five large stones high, carved in various symbols that differ in shape and position. I refer to the map in my hand and compare it to what's in front of me, trying to keep a running mnemonic in my head. The last stone of the old corridor and the first stone of the next are always the same, marking the correct path. *Right turn, dragon to…is that a tree? Tree to…star…*

After five or six turns the labyrinth releases us into a short passage with a single door standing at the end. I try to steady my nerves as I follow Erik, the importance of being granted entry weighing on me. He gives me one more serious look before he opens the door, followed by a grin as his face softens a little.

"Well, you wanted answers," he says, opening the door and allowing me to walk in first. "Here they are."

I inhale a long breath, unsure what to expect. Inside, the stone walls continue, covered in tapestries that give the room some warmth and color. Maps, scribbled chalkboards, bookcases…on the far wall hangs an enormous mirror-like circle – at least 20 ft in diameter – only it's entirely black, without reflection. And beneath it a solemn-faced Robert Crawford sits around a large round table, Fox and Simon on one side of him. No Francine. No Jenna. No Maeve. No one else I recognize. Thirteen other faces turn to study me as I breach the threshold, likely trying to determine if I have clearance to be there.

"Welcome Everest," Robert says, greeting me with a faint smile. "We've been expecting you. I'm glad you two made it. We were worried you'd be caught in that storm."

"We were," Erik says, motioning me towards two empty seats.

Robert rises. "Everyone, meet Everest Cleary —"

The door opens behind us, and a woman rushes in, taking her seat in the last empty chair and bringing the total bodies in the room to nineteen. She must have been the one trying to get in the room.

"I know we all respect Erik and his judgement." Robert resumes, turning to Erik. "I trust you've apprised Everest of the paramount importance of secrecy?"

Erik nods decisively.

"Everest, you must keep your membership in this group in the strictest of confidence," Robert instructs me. "I need your word on that before I go any further."

It's clear from the stern look Robert imparts on me that he won't accept anything short of my complete allegiance. But at the same time, there's a silent desperation behind his eyes, almost like a personal desire which I can't quite decipher. "You have my word," I assure him.

He seems almost relieved and shuts his eyes as if he's finally received something he's long waited for. "Well, Everest, I assume you have questions."

I let out a nervous laugh. "That's an understatement."

Robert smiles again. "I suppose it is."

The nameless faces nod in agreement, having probably all

been in my shoes at one point or another, desperate for the same answers I hope to get.

First question. "What is this place?"

"This is the Citadel," Robert replies. "And we are the Sentries, selectively chosen to watch over the Prism."

"Chosen…by who?"

"We've been brought into the fold by others like us who've come before, but only if we meet certain criteria. All of us, yourself included, possess certain qualities. You see," Robert continues, "all humans are born extraordinary, a repository of unlimited potential, each one of us equally capable of realizing it.

"But life changes us. The current landscape of society, our values, our beliefs, they all affect the extent to which we can fulfill that innate potential. Through this intricate dance and the passage of time, our potential is either nurtured or chipped away. For some reason or another, the potential of those in this group has flourished to exceptional levels. I think you may know what I'm talking about?"

I wring my hands together under the table. Frequency, potential…whatever it's called, I'm still not sure how I feel about it.

"Don't be afraid of it," Robert urges, reading me like a book. "You have an unwavering belief in the light that we know is at the heart of our entire existence. It creates a force, an energy that is unwilling to be contained — that can change physical matter, affect space and time, even control elements…" Robert glances around the room. "Each of us brings to the table such an ability, or potential, as we call it, though we all manifest it slightly differently. That's why we know we can trust each other, because we trust the good that made us this way.

"You already know Simon, Fox, and Erik. Meet Petra, Liam,

Hadid, Jason, Shahina, Ethan, Hannah, …" The faces salute me one by one as Robert points them out; some regard me warmly, a few with suspicion. "…Agnes, Yoshi, Giovanni, Dan, Corinne, Izabel and Tula."

"Once, when you felt like an outsider here, I said you were right where you belonged," Erik reminds me. "Do you believe that now?"

I'm stunned, but at the same time liberated and slightly less afraid of the things I've done. I turn to look at Erik. "You too?" He simply grins, telling me all I need to know.

"The Vulturians," I look back at Robert, "they know about all of you too? They can track your frequencies, just like they can track mine?"

Robert raises a brow, no doubt wondering how I already know so much. Erik holds up his hands. "I swear, it wasn't me."

"It wasn't him," I confirm, backing Erik up.

"I thought I'd be the first to introduce you to that word," Robert admits, giving me a curious look. "But yes, they can find us, which is why you need to learn to control that potential, to stay off their radar. Or 'frequency' as you call it."

"They're term, not mine," I clarify. I shudder at the reminder that I'm living on borrowed time. "What do you know about them? What more can you tell me?"

"They're master manipulators," Erik weighs in, "and their extreme wealth – which they've amassed over thousands of years – and access to unlimited resources makes them almost unstoppable. If they want a war, they get a war. If they want a dictator, they get that too. They sit at the heads of the most powerful companies, influence almost every media outlet and what every person sees and hears."

Robert rises from his seat and begins to walk around the table, continuing with the lesson. "You see Everest, the

Vulturians were never interested in anything that we would consider good. Their very name implies it and their allegiance to their dark god, Parem. They preyed on suffering and picked up the scraps of conflict and unrest. Over the years, they migrated and created chapters in different regions. By the time the Enlightenment arrived, they had infiltrated the most elite societies and royal courts, whispering hatred and inciting bloodshed through indirect means, always in the ears of those with the power to bring their plans to fruition. Then, they silently waited for the carnage to unfold, pillaging, blackmailing, taking advantage of the opportunities that hate, greed and desperation left behind.

"And all the while, the world continued on, ignorant of the true puppet master that built its invisible empire upon the Earth's wreckage. They operated unchallenged for centuries. But the Enlightenment and the belief in human potential and education was a threat to their agenda. They wanted to keep knowledge for the few." Robert stops pacing, having made a full circle around the table back to his chair. "You'll have to give these lessons one day yourselves. Fox, take over, will you?"

Fox straightens his posture, surprised to be called upon, and takes a moment to figure out where to start.

"Ciavutti," Robert reminds him.

"Right! Thanks Bob," Fox replies, and receives a playful eye roll from Robert. "So, the Vulturians…not fans of education. All but one – the son of one of the highest-ranking members. Enzo Ciavutti. He questioned the Order's intentions and mingled with the commoners against the Order's wishes. Even fell in love with the daughter of a blacksmith who he married in secret. He tried to encourage the Order to educate the lower classes, believing that enlightenment would be best served if it reached as many minds as possible. But the Vulturians weren't interested. They wanted people to feel like victims, promote the illusion that there was more evil in the world than there actually was. They have no interest in empowerment or unity – they only pretend they do so they can further their own agenda and manipulate the emotions of the masses.

"Anyway, they murdered Ciavutti's wife in front of him and banished him, his own father disowning him for his philosophy." Fox pauses to take a drink, allowing the platinum-haired woman named Petra to step in next.

"At some point," Petra continues, with an Eastern-European accent, "Ciavutti was able to enter the Prism where he and others decided to create their own society with the goal of nurturing human potential, so the world would never again suffer through the ignorance and despair that had plagued it for millennia. They called themselves Luminarians, after the Luminary. The Vulturians heard of their work and persecuted them. Many enlightened minds — scholars, inventors, artists — vanished or were executed, including Ciavutti. His own father eventually ordered his death. The rest of the Luminarians withdrew to operate in secret."

Woah! The group has filled in some blanks about the Order that Sarah left out. Some very important blanks. This must be the kind of information she couldn't access in the Vulturian archives. *What else is contained in there?*

"Why doesn't everyone know this?" I ask. "I can't even find anything on Vulturians in the Lumus."

Robert shakes his head. "Knowledge of their existence has been passed down by word of mouth, and there are no texts we know of that speak of them. Only we and, of course, the Vulturians themselves know of the existence of the Order. The Vulturians have been successful at infiltrating authorities, publishing houses and media groups – organizations that effectively silence the truth before it even has a chance to be shared. That's how they want it, labelling anyone who challenges them as extremists or crazy conspiracy theorists. It's how they shut down discourse about their operations. They'll burn any book that refers to them. But I'm convinced there's more proof out there somewhere, perhaps in their own heavily guarded archives. We just haven't found it yet."

"Where are the Luminarians now?" I ask, captivated.

"Most were killed," Fox answers, solemnly. "Others were corrupted by the Vulturian promise of wealth and power, swayed by the Order's misguided message of human limitation and weakness. The few who escaped were forced into hiding. Once reunited in the Prism they formed the Sentry, pledging to operate as a secret agency out of the Citadel to protect the Prism from Vulturian influence."

Intriguing. "Are there any left in the Prism today?"

"Just two that we know of," Erik mutters under his breath as everyone turns to look at Robert Crawford.

CHAPTER 37

Coming Clean

Robert places a hand on his son's shoulder, taking a moment before he addresses the room.

"I'd like to think Simon and I are not the only ones, but officially, yes. My grandfather was a Luminarian, and his father before him. But ancestry doesn't matter here, only our allegiance to the Sentry. We're all Luminarians now, tasked with protecting the Prism. And I hope there will be more of us soon.

"On that note, now that Everest is up to speed, we have some pressing issues to discuss."

Robert's voice echoes off the stone ceiling. "We've known for some time that the Vulturians have infiltrated the Prism." He looks toward me and raises his hands up defensively. "We're not elitists, Everest. Don't mistake our protection of our world for entitlement. But an imbalance in the energy structure of the Prism will inevitably cause it to disintegrate. With the influx of too much negative energy, the scales will tip and the Prism can be, at the very least, significantly crippled. Entry must always be earned."

Where have I heard that before?

"You've all told me your findings," Robert adds. "Whatever

is happening outside right now is merely another example of the effect of that unwelcome presence. They're here, and it seems in increasing numbers. The question is 'why.'"

I'm the reason, I silently answer him. *And the Skala.* But I bite my tongue, for now.

"The Prism cannot exist without the resilient people of Earth," Petra adds for my benefit. "It is their imagination that allows it to take form — it feeds and nourishes the Prism, like the sun and the water nourish a plant. Remove nourishment, and the plant dies. Similarly, the Earth cannot progress without the people that come to the Prism. Remove the positive force on the Earth, and it…ah, what is the word…um…stagnates. The two are interdependent."

"Speaking of stagnation, what about our numbers?" the boy named Jason interjects. He looks like he's still in high school – maybe a few years younger than me. He slams his palm repeatedly on the table to get attention. "We need to recruit! There needs to be more of us to stand a chance against them."

The room starts to hum with concerned chatter, some heads nodding in support of Jason.

"Why *is* the Sentry so small?" I ask above the noise to Jason's point. "There must be more of us in the Prism. This can't be it."

"The problem isn't how to get the good apples," Erik answers. "It's how to keep out the bad ones."

"What, you don't trust Jenna, Maeve? What about Francine?" I turn to Robert. "Surely —"

"Assuming can be dangerous," Robert warns, looking a bit dejected. "We can't let our emotions and personal ties cloud our judgement and lead us to whisper too much into the wrong ear."

It makes sense now - why Erik kept me in the dark for so

long…It really wasn't his call to make. I realize how hard it must have been for him not have shared everything he knew, and glance at him with a touch of guilt over my previous impatience.

"As the oldest member," Robert says, "I watched many of my fellow protectors slowly vanish. Some passed on, others never returned. I feared a sinister force behind it all. I vowed to rebuild the Sentry, but carefully. You are all here because your potentials are so tangible, only a strong positive force could allow them to become amplified to such a degree." He glances at me again, like he's silently trying to convey a message only he has the legend to decode. "I knew I could trust that force – a force that makes you feel like your whole body could explode trying to contain it."

"This is all super-spiritual and kumbaya and all…but back to the main problem," Jason says impatiently, shifting in his seat. "How do we lure out the Vulturians? If we can't trust anyone because we don't know who's tainted, then we need to flush them out!"

"It's not that simple," Fox reminds Jason.

Robert nods. "We know that Vulturians are entering the Prism another way — not through Castellum. We've considered a secret census, to see who has their own dimension and who doesn't, based on the hypothesis that only true Wakers would."

Jason throws up his hands. "Then what are we waiting for?"

"Poppin is firmly against it," Robert reminds him, "for his own well-intentioned reasons, I'll admit. After all, he doesn't have all the facts."

Jason scowls. "This is a ridiculous waste of time. We shouldn't be worried about secrecy or discretion at this point, or what one man thinks. They're bringing a war to us. We have to respond!"

A woman in her thirties speaks next, her braid the color of sunlit wheat. "If we come at this too strong, we would only tip off the Vulturians and unsettle everyone. We can't risk breading fear — it would just hasten the Prism's disintegration."

"Agnes is right," Erik agrees. "The last thing people want is something resembling a military state in their paradise."

"You seem to have a lot figured out," Jason barks at Erik, "for someone whose been here a hot five minutes!"

"I've been here just as long as you mate," Erik retorts sharply. "You might want to watch your mouth!"

"I think I can help," I interject without thinking things through. "I know one of them. A girl. She's new to the Order – she approached me recently and says she wants to bring them down. She's the reason I know about them. I think she could help us."

Oops. Bad idea. Before I'm done speaking, Jason stands up abruptly and points an accusing finger at me. "You brought in a spy who's conspiring with the Order!" he yells at Erik. I'm beginning to think he's the token hot head on the team. "She could be one of them! Did that not occur to you?"

"Hold on! I'm not a spy, or the enemy," I tell him defensively.

"Prove it!"

Erik sends his chair flying back as he leans over the table and glares at Jason. "I thought I told you to watch your mouth!"

"Or what, 'mate?' "

"Enough, both of you!" Robert shouts, bringing his fist down firmly on the table. "Everest is here because *I* allowed it, and that is the last time any of you will question the allegiance of anyone in this room, am I clear, Mr. Harris?" He shoots Jason a stern look and imparts the same silent warning on Erik. "As for our dilemma of how to identify the Vulturians, I agree, we must be careful how much we reveal to the population, and the Imperium. And before we start making any claims, we need all the facts — who they are, what they're after, how they're breaching the Prism.

"Everest," Agnes says, turning to me, "this source you have…are you sure she's trustworthy?"

I look around the room at the others, searching for approval. Most of them probably share Jason's suspicions. And while I don't have warm fuzzy feelings about the guy, I'd be skeptical in his shoes too.

"She hates the Order," I reveal. "She isn't like the rest of them. And she's risked her life to help me. So yes, I think she can be useful to us. In fact, she's already proven herself."

Robert sits down. "How?"

"She helped me scout out one of their meetings through a spyglass in the Paris chapter house. Long story short, they're after something called the Skala. We haven't been able to find out what it is yet, but they think people like us can find it…specifically…"

Do I say it? Might as well…*Just rip it off like a band-aid.* "Specifically, me."

I feel like I'm in front of a jury awaiting my verdict, my dirty laundry aired out for the world. "For some reason, they think I'm capable of finding it because of my frequency, or potential, as you call it here. That's the only reason I'm apparently alive; otherwise, I would be 'extinguished.'…Again…their term."

"Extinguished…So, they *are* killing people like us," Petra says to herself, her face suddenly blanketed with sorrow.

I look around at the other faces, many of whom look as crestfallen as Petra. Even Jason shows emotion, bringing his hands to his head and leaving his seat to stand against the back wall as he processes things.

I wish I wasn't the bearer of the news. "Yeah, they are," I reply softy. "I'm sorry."

"There's been rumors," Hadid interjects. "People – Wakers – disappearing. We thought it was just coincidence. But…now…"

There's that word again. I remember what Julian had mentioned about his magister. *Disappeared…*

"Even a few of our own," Petra adds solemnly, looking at the others. "We didn't want to think the worst. But maybe we should have."

I'm hesitant to continue, but they deserve answers. "They have something called the Arachna," I elaborate. "It's some kind of tech I think that picks up our potentials. Anyone deemed to be too great a threat is eliminated. But I guess they have to allow some of us to find our way here, like you said. I think they have an algorithm that decides who stays alive and who…" I don't finish the sentence, not wanting to be insensitive. "They're watching us, at least some of us. They know about this group, although I don't think they know very much. That's probably why we're all still alive.

"But the Skala, that's what they're hungry for. Whatever it is, they've been searching for it for thousands of years and they're starting to get desperate."

I look at Robert. "Have you heard of the Skala? Do you know what it is?" But Robert remains silent, as does the rest of the group. *Wonderful.*

I decide to keep the compass to myself. I'll let Robert decide how he wants to handle that information. But then I feel something weighing down my jacket pocket. I reach inside, my fingers grazing the smooth granite, and I realize I must have subconsciously willed the Vulturian ring into the Prism.

"Um…one more thing," I add, not thrilled about placing a

greater target on my back. I drop the ring onto the table, sending it rolling toward the center.

"Would have come in handy when we were trying to describe the darn thing to Gill," Erik whispers to me.

"I didn't know I had it," I whisper back, trying not to obviously move my lips.

"What is this?" Petra asks.

"I took it off the finger of one of the Vulturians we had a run in with last night," I tell the group. "Someone I know, Tristan Sarazen, has one just like it. After he wormed his way into my life, I think he used it to manipulate me somehow." I avoid the curious eyes staring at me like I'm some kind of alien life form.

"And how exactly did you bring it in here?" Petra asks, taking her attention away from the mysterious object for a moment.

"I don't know. It's just something I can do," I admit hesitantly. As expected, Petra and the others stare at me in silence. Jason returns to the table with ire in his eyes, having just been given another reason not to trust me. He shakes his head as he takes his seat but reserves comment, choosing to go with an I-told-you-so smirk instead.

"Huh, that is new," Petra mutters after an awkward lull. "Glad you are on our side." She reaches out to touch the ring.

"Don't!" Robert and I say in unison.

I glance up at him, his forehead streaked with worry lines. "You've seen it before, you know what it does, don't you?" I venture a guess.

Robert scoops up the ring with a pen and brings it close to his eyes. "I had a feeling… I've seen it on the hands of those following me. It brushed against my skin once, and…the oddest sensation overcame me…" He continues to scrutinize it as other Wakers crowd around him.

"It is Vulturian for sure. The markings, look…" Petra points, examining the object over Robert's shoulder.

"It could be how they're getting in," Robert speculates, "by extracting the positive force from others in order to have enough of it to access the Prism artificially."

Heads nod around the table as the group considers the merits of the theory. I recount my own experience, the life-draining sensation, the effect it had on Tommy. It's certainly possible…

"But *where* are they getting in? Some kind of portal maybe…" Erik muses. "And what is it made of to give them the power to suck the light out of human beings and access other dimensions?"

"Well, it seems we have more questions now than when we first started," Robert observes. "But also some leads. Times have changed." He tucks the ring into a drawer on a nearby desk and locks it with a key he stores in his shirt pocket. "From now on, we meet daily…And work together," he adds, looking at Erik and Jason. They both roll their eyes, neither of them trying to hide their dislike for the other. "We always suspected the Vulturians could track significant energy release and distortion, but now, thanks to Everest, we know the lengths they'll go to in their quest to destroy others like us. All the more reason to keep our abilities, and the Sentry, cloak-and-dagger."

Robert walks over to the reflection-less mirror and places his hand on it. "The Eye will show us what the storm has brought about."

The darkness of the glass begins to scatter and gives way to a scene from the Luminary courtyard like a live feed. Downed branches, strewn foliage. I glimpse relief on the faces of the Sentry. "I thought it'd be worse," someone observes.

But Robert doesn't appear convinced. "The storm will return, in one form or another. Remember, your dimensions are the safest place if the Nucleus is under threat. The Vulturians can't breach them, as far as we know."

Simon addresses his father, asking the question that's on all our minds. "And what if the Nucleus falls? Will our dimensions survive? Will we ever be able to return?"

Robert keeps his gaze fixed on the eye. "I don't know. But I hope we never have to find out."

$$* * *$$

"A compass?" Robert asks curiously.

The Sentry's been dismissed. Only Erik, Fox, Robert and I remain. I've filled in Robert on the last bit of intelligence I know and hope for the best. The part about the Flame was hard to divulge. Even Erik looked at me strangely, hearing about the encounter for the first time.

"And you keep it safe, you said, in your dimension?" Robert asks me.

I nod. "Yes. Do you know what it is?"

Robert stares at the compass blankly, turning it around over and over, much like Erik did. "Nothing comes to mind."

"The Flame talked about concealing it – concealing 'them both.' Maybe…the Skala and the compass? It was so vague, and it all happened so quickly…"

Robert continues examining the compass. "And they think this can locate this Skala you speak of?"

I nod. "I'm worthless to them if they have it. They've resurrected something called 'The Pledge.' It gives a Vulturian four months to find the Skala or face certain death. Sarah, my source, told me about it. Until now, they thought I was their best chance at finding the Skala, but this compass changes everything. They've upped the stakes."

Robert gives the compass back to me, then places his hand on my shoulder. "I had hoped that when you finally arrived at the Prism things would be different for you – that you would get to experience this reality as it should be experienced, instead of running from a darkness that threatens you. I'm sorry Everest. Tell me, do they know about the other abilities you have – to bridge our two worlds, to alter the Nucleus…"

Fox looks at me wide-eyed. "Damn, Ev! How many more bombs are you gonna drop?"

"I'll fill you in later," Erik promises his friend.

"I'm sure they know I can take things in and out," I confirm for Robert, "because of the pendant Erik gave me. They've likely seen me wearing it. Don't know if they're onto the other thing yet."

"Best to keep that to yourself, just in case," Robert suggests. "I'll try to find out more about this compass…and this voice you say communicated with you. Truly remarkable! We'll reconvene tomorrow. In the meantime, Erik, try to help Everest reign in her potential so she can't be tracked."

Something Robert has said nags at me. "What did you mean earlier, when you said, '*when* I finally arrived?'" *Did he know I was coming?*

The Sentry leader blinks at me, then turns away. "I just wish things were different for you," he explains with a kind smile. "No one should experience the Prism like this."

No, that's not it. You know something. What aren't you telling me Robert Crawford?

* * *

"Julian! Julian!"

I bang my fist on the boy's dimension door until Lise finally answers it. "Oh, thank God!" I hug her, a weight lifted from my chest. When I open my eyes, Julian has joined us. I pull him in to hug him next, whether he likes it or not. "Are you hurt?"

Julian shakes his head. "We're fine. We found a place to hide when the storm hit."

Lise remains silent and buries her messy pigtails under my arm.

"I wish I had been there with you," I whisper. I hadn't protected them. They had no magister…they had no one…

"It's okay, Everest. You couldn't have known. We were fine," Julian assures. "There were lots of us."

Lise emerges from under my arm, finally ready to speak. "Why did that happen? I thought we were safe here?"

I hate myself for not being able to tell them more. "We're working on figuring that out. But you're safe in your dimensions. Remember that. And promise not to wander far for the next few days, just in case, okay?"

Lise reluctantly nods her pretty head, and I narrow my eyes at her, demanding verbal assurance. "I promise," she finally gives in.

Still, I have a feeling her little fingers are crossed behind her back, just like mine would be.

"Come on," I urge. I can't expect them to just remain in their dimensions. And we don't need to go far for a distraction. "Let's do something fun! What do you want to see next at Eden Hall? We still have a lot of Prism time left."

CHAPTER 38

In Plain Sight

I sit at Eaton's kitchen table like a concrete statue, unable to get my mind around everything. It's as if the Hoover Dam just collapsed and I'm being crushed by the weight of the descending water. My membership in the Sentry has brought with it an overwhelming amount of new information. I wish I had it all recorded to go through it again.

I recall my time with Lise and Julian in the Prism with a sense of contentment. They had wanted to watch some animated movies at Eden Hall, which turned out to be a welcome interruption from all the heavy stuff. It always surprises me how much I miss them when they're not around, especially since I'd never been around many children growing up.

Eaton's prepared a small breakfast and I thank him ten times for his hospitality. "I'm off to work," he says. "Just leave the key with the neighbor." When Erik's out of ear shot, he approaches me a final time. "My career has taught me that you shouldn't ask questions you don't want the answers to. Erik is being rather tight-lipped. But, if you ever need a lawyer, for any reason…." He drops his business card on the table before taking his leave and smiles at me kindly. "Nice to have met you Everest. Hope your friend's alright."

Tommy! I've been so preoccupied with my own problems I'd nearly forgotten. I find him still asleep and drooling slightly out one side of his mouth, hopefully getting the rest he needs and looking a lot better than I feel.

As I wait for Erik to come out of the shower, my attention turns to the TV news broadcast, which Eaton forgot to shut off in his haste to make it to the courthouse on time.

Rubble. Devastation. There's a woman's crying, her face streaked with dirt. A man covered in blood and mud speaks hysterically in Spanish to the camera above the headline. DEADLY EARTHQUAKE HITS BOLIVIA.

There are no coincidences.

Instead of walking away from the news as I usually do, I turn up the volume: "…this Bolivian city…magnitude earthquake…thousands assumed dead or missing. This tragedy has rocked the country, just days after the shocking loss of eight government officials in an electrical fire…"

The scene changes to a conference room where an older man in a suit speaks to reporters: "We have resources in place to assist the Bolivian people. The Guerin Foundation is committed to providing access to clean water, and we will work with the crisis team to ensure that the region recovers from their terrible loss."

I stare at the television screen, regressing back to my catatonic state. The man's silver hair, his pale, stoic face, those cold eyes so absent compassion. *I know you.* I read his name repeatedly to make sure I'm seeing it correctly.

Arat Sarazen.

"Son of a…"

Erik emerges from the bathroom dressed and ready, using

another towel to dry his hair. "I thought you didn't watch this stuff."

I spew out my words so quickly they barely make sense. "It's them! Ertu – it's Tristan's father! They made the quake!"

"Woah! Slow down Ev. Say that again."

I take a breath and repeat myself.

"That's Tristan's father – the president of the Guerin Foundation – that's his bank. Arat Sarazen. I knew his name from Tristan but never saw a picture of him, until now. He's the Ertu, the same man I saw with Sarah! If they're all Vulturians…" I take a seat on the sofa, pondering the web I'm starting to unravel. "He used his own son to manipulate me. The Vulturians must have caused the earthquake in Bolivia and the Prism…it could all be connected."

Erik runs his hand over the newly formed stubble on his cheeks. "I know how far their reach goes, but earthquakes…" he says doubtfully.

My eyes grow even larger when I see who's standing behind the Ertu. Hades, in the flesh. "Well, what d'ya know," I say, smirking to myself. "That's my boss, Vincent Frost." *Of course.* Why else would Tristan get me a job at Peterson. It was all right in front of my face.

The next story's up: something about a president getting too much ice cream for dessert.

"Ah yes, award-winning journalism," Erik remarks, rolling his eyes. "Distractions, from what's really going on out there."

"It's not impossible Erik," I insist, still dissecting the broadcast. "We go to a parallel world in our sleep and travel through portals. Who's to say the Vulturians can't instigate natural disasters? They have ridiculous amounts of money and access to technology we've never even heard of!"

Erik finishes dressing and comes to sit next to me. His face looks pensive as he stares at the busy art deco wallpaper. "If it's true, it's a terrifying thought," he says, mulling it over. "But at least we know what they're after now. And we have a theory and a team –"

"A very small team," I remind him, crossing my arms like a stubborn child.

"But a powerful –"

"…more like a microscopic team –"

"We're working on that! And don't forget, we have an inside man. Or woman, in this case, thanks to you. That's gold!"

Yeah. An inside woman I have no idea how to find.

Erik resumes his packing. "Tommy's cousin is coming to pick him up."

"Tommy…will he be ok? I don't feel right leaving him."

"He'll be fine, and safest far away from us. You went through the same thing he did, multiple times, and you made it out the other side. Tommy's a tough ox. I've seen him hit some lows. He'll bounce back."

Erik bought us tickets for the Eurostar using assumed names, leaving at 1:55 from St. Pancras. Hopefully an afternoon departure will throw the vultures off our trail. With baseball caps on and pupils down, we separately make the trip to the station.

As I pass the statue of the embracing lovers, I recall the feeling of finally seeing Erik for the first Earthly time and pray with each step that he's right behind me. We only had a day before everything fell apart around us – only brief moments of being ourselves, normal and carefree.

It seems like weeks ago now…

Five minutes after I arrive at the station, I see Erik push open the doors. I want to run to him and embrace him, but I can't do any of it.

Patience.

I'm starting to really hate that word.

We wait until the train is about ready to leave, board on different ends of the car seconds before the doors close, and walk to our separate facing seats five rows apart, knowing that the two-hour trip that will follow will be agonizingly anxious and lonely.

CHAPTER 39

Foolish Games

Erik carefully inspects our temporary accommodation, brushing some cobwebs off a coffee table. "How do you know about this place exactly? I mean, it's not the Ritz, but I suppose it's better than waking up to Tommy playing air guitar in his boxers."

We made it from Gare du Norde to the grounds of the Sorbonne without a tail – as far as we can tell. Staying at my apartment would be foolish. After many detours, walking blocks apart and communicating on burner phones, we've ending up in a quiet wing of the university's physics department, in a small storage space for the school's unused furniture. Tables and broken cabinets are piled up high against the walls.

I pull some boxes off a retro green velour couch. "I would come to the courtyard outside to read sometimes. Came in here once thinking it was a bathroom. The janitor hides the building key under the flowerpot outside. It's just for now, until we figure out something a little more comfortable."

Erik drops his bag onto the floor and pulls back the curtain slightly to look out the window. "It's fine by me. I've forgotten how beautiful this city is."

So have I. "I wish this was a less complicated visit for you."

"Are you kidding?" Erik replies, smiling broadly. "I'm in the most romantic city in the world with the woman I love, on an epic adventure where — depending on how the cards fall — I may live to tell a heroic tale or die an excruciating but memorable death. It's everything an adrenaline junky could ask for!"

I laugh. "Of course, you'd see it that way." He comes over and pulls me into a hug as I try to sort through my never-ending jumble of thoughts. "How do you feel about doing some surveillance?"

Erik looks down at me with a raised eyebrow. "We just got here."

"The Vulturians are probably focused on my apartment. Might as well take advantage of their guard being down."

Erik eyes me suspiciously, trying to spy in my brain again. "You want to look for Sarah, don't you?" he guesses correctly.

"She's our best chance. And it beats inhaling all the dust in here. What have we got to lose?"

"A limb or life, possibly," Erik points out, joking (but not really). He flops down on the couch, sending a blast of dust into the air. "Fine," he says, in between stifling sneezes, "but we need to be invisible. Hopefully she'll come to us before we end up on some offering pyre."

* * *

"That's one ugly statue."

"Yeah. They really picked an unfortunate mascot," I agree with Erik. "I guess money and power can't buy you everything after all."

We're carrying out our recon of the Paris chapter house

from a stairwell window in the residential building across the street.

"It looks impenetrable. It's cameras on top of cameras," Erik observes. "They're probably looking at us right now!"

"Don't even joke about that. Okay, so we wouldn't get in through the front door."

"Maybe Yoshi can help get around the security system. He's a hacking prodigy, that one."

There's always that. "I still can't believe people don't know about them."

"Because money and power *can* buy you anonymity, and keep the media off your scent," Erik reminds me. "Come on. Let's not overstay our welcome."

"Are you two out of your minds!" a voice hisses from behind us before we have a chance to gather our things. I stop in my tracks, but the fear quickly fades – the voice is familiar, and one I've been hoping to hear.

"You really don't listen to instructions well, do you?" To say Sarah looks displeased is an understatement. The only thing softening the daggers shooting from her rich brown eyes are the delicate curls that frame her face. The dark bags under her eyes tell me she's still not sleeping.

I smile at her guiltily, hopeful her anger towards me is temporary. "We were hoping to run into you."

"Hoping? You're just lucky I live in the building next door and saw you come in. I thought it was you by your walk."

"I have a walk?"

"Sort of. I'm strangely observant about that sort of thing. Anyway, your fake bob and beard won't be enough to fool them. At least figure out some better disguises."

"We were careful," I assure her, "and it's what we could manage on short notice."

Sarah crosses her arms, clearly annoyed, but eventually grins after keeping me in suspense long enough. "It's good to see you Everest. I was getting worried. They're looking for you everywhere. And the compass. When I saw you weren't at your apartment for days, I started to suspect the worst."

"They won't find the compass," I assure her.

Sarah sighs. "Then they might find something to trade for it. No one you know is safe anymore. You need to lay low. I mean it this time. How do you think the Ertu reacted when he heard about London?"

News travels fast. "I didn't mean to do that."

"And in our defense, they were trying to kill us," Erik adds.

Sarah narrows her eyes and scowls at him. "You must be Halvorsen."

"Yeah, hi." Erik replies cheerfully. He tries to extend a hand, but Sarah swings her head in my direction, arms still crossed. "Listen, you need to control yourself, or you're going to lead them right to your door! Will you tell her, please?" Sarah pleads with Erik.

I steady the vibrations in my chest and take a breath, just in case. "I hear you. But we need to get into that chapter house, Sarah. We need to know what they know about the compass. It could put everything into focus."

Sarah chuckles and finally lets her arms relax, letting them hang at her sides as she leans against the wall. "You don't think I've tried?" she whispers. "There is no way in hell you're getting in. *I* can't even get into 80% of that place."

"There *has* to be a way. Maybe there's an access point in the passages," I suggest. "Could you look at your father's blueprints again?

"Also…I need a way to reach you," I demand. "You coming to me isn't going to work anymore. If you want my help you need to have some faith in me too. We're either a team or you're on your own," I say, completely bluffing.

She stares me down. I hold the line, staring right back and trying not to blink. "Fine," she concedes to my relief and the relief of my watering eyes. She climbs down the steps to come face to face with me on the landing. "But no phones! There's a café two blocks west of the chapter house, Petite Brioche. I go there most days for lunch. If you want to get in touch with me leave a coded message in the bathroom stall closest to the window, under the toilet paper dispenser. I'll check regularly. Make sure it's flushable."

I nod in gratitude. "Right. Thanks."

"Now get out of here," she says, looking around the stairwell. "I'm already very uncomfortable with this."

"Come on," I say to Erik, gathering our things, "the metro isn't far."

Sarah shakes her head. "Don't be foolish. Cameras have facial rec. Just take a cab. And be careful Everest," she adds, managing one last smile. "Don't leave me alone in this fight."

I pull her into a hug to her surprise. She's an unlikely ally and friend, and one I'm thankful to have. "Don't worry. I wouldn't want to be on your bad side."

* * *

"Mademoiselle, you are going to make me very rich tonight," the cab driver says merrily as we lead him on a convoluted route back to the university.

"Oui, oui, je sais." At one point we've taken so many haphazard turns that I've completely lost my bearings.

When we finally reach our destination, we find the storage room a little cold. After freeing some more dust from the couch, we cover it with the blankets Erik's packed. As I lay beside him wrapped up in his arms, I desperately hope the Vulturians are keeping their distance. A loneliness comes over me at the thought of having to navigate my city like a fugitive, and anger begins to replace the loneliness as I think of everything the Order is ripping away.

"A little anger is like fuel," Erik reminds me, sensing my tension, "but too much can be a detonator. Your emotions feed your potential Ev. You heard Robert and Sarah – if your readings are too intense you could pinpoint our location."

I nod and try to keep my emotion at a low frequency, hoping I won't hear any shattering glass. "What about Lise and Julian…"

Erik shakes his head at me. "Reaching out to them now will only make them targets. I know it's hard, but the best thing you can do is stay away."

He's right, and I hate it. I hate all of it.

"This sucks!" I pout as he rubs my arm.

"Can't argue with you there."

CHAPTER 40

A Plan in Motion

The damage from the storm seems nearly restored when Erik and I walk to the Luminary the next Prism morning.

"We haven't bounced back completely," Petra observes inside the Citadel, her platinum hair tied up in a tight bun.

Robert sips from a mug with a distant look in his eyes. "Naturally, people's faith has been shaken. But we've done well, considering."

I have no appetite and stare at the fruit selection on my plate like it's a centerpiece to be viewed only.

Those that have been followed have taken the necessary precautions. Fox is roughing it out somewhere on the coast in Belize.

"I have left Prague," is all Petra reveals, maintaining her stoic composure and air of mystery.

Hadid moved his wife and three children out of Beirut to a small village after devising a story about witnessing a crime. "It was more believable than telling them I go to a place in my dreams and create things with my mind and an order of psychopaths is trying to kill me. Imagine that conversation! My wife would be very worried for me. She would call my mother and father right away, and my uncle. The whole family would be involved. Oh, it would be a mess, Robert. A real mess!"

"The important thing is we're all here and in one piece," adds Robert, who also left town with Simon.

"For now," Jason mumbles.

"Stop being such a downer Jason. I am getting very tired of it," Petra mutters.

"I'm just a realist," Jason retorts. "Sooner or later our luck will run out. We need to be prepared for that."

"We can't afford to panic, especially now," Erik reminds him. Jason mumbles something again and slouches in his chair in annoyance. *What is up with these two?*

"Erik's right," Robert agrees, rising to examine the map that's appeared on the Eye. "But so is Jason. We do need to focus on building up the population," Robert says, "and we need to use the Vulturians to do it. They clearly have a way of finding people like us. That should give us some leads for recruitment. Of course, getting them here is another matter. One step at a time…"

The map is daunting. *These potential Wakers could be anywhere.*

"Also," Robert continues, "anyone in the Prism you think would be a candidate for the Sentry, vet them and bring their name to me. The Vulturians are counting on us taking a back seat. We need to go on the offensive. We also need to control the message. The Order is skilled at distracting the public with insignificant stories and weaving lies of human limitation, all the while carrying out unspeakable acts that never make the front page. We need people to be aware."

"Won't that be counterproductive?" Agnes asks skeptically, "to release more negative news?"

"People need to know they've been fooled before they can learn to think differently," Robert explains. "But yes, things may have to get worse before they get better. Yoshi, Shahina, Ethan, I think you're already working on something to pull back the curtain a little?"

Ethan grins. "Yeah, we have some ideas. They're coming along. Do you want the technical details?"

"Will we understand them?" Simon asks.

"Probably not," Ethan admits.

"Just let us know when it's ready, or once you've hacked whatever you need to hack," Robert instructs with a grin, then returns to studying the map again. "Try to locate the Vulturian Chapters close to you. Look for their symbology. The egomaniacs display it rather proudly." He turns to face the group. "And be smart about it! These are professionals with a lot to lose. They will be paranoid and on the lookout for anyone looking for them."

Shahina interjects. "I can place a central contact directory imbedded deep in the back channels of the web that only we can access. It will keep us connected if we need to reach out."

"Is it secure?" Robert questions.

"I can make it Fort Knox if you want me to."

"She's quite brilliant," Erik whispers to me. "Got into MIT at the age of 16 – first person from her town to ever go to university. After she graduated, she went back and started a school there."

"I've already set up the page," Shahina elaborates, scribbling a web address on a chalkboard. "Access the link and add your details. Password is gelatinous potato."

Everyone around the table chuckles.

"Uh…I don't think I can spell that," teases Fox.

"Of all the combinations of words you could have come up with…" Corrine notes on behalf of everyone.

"That's the point," Shahina says defensively, getting up to

write the phrase on the chalkboard for Fox's benefit. "No one would ever guess that, and now you'll never forget it. Fort Knox, remember?"

"I don't think I'll look at mashed potatoes the same again, but…makes sense," Corinne replies, grimacing a little. "Gelatinous potato it is!"

"We need to figure out one more thing," Erik reminds us. "The rings. No matter what progress we make, it will make little difference if the Vulturians are able to counter it somehow with those things, and…whatever they do."

Petra motions to me with a curt nod of her head. "You seem to know the most about them. And you know the person who used it on you. Any chance he could tell you something?"

"Tristan?" I laugh at the hilarity of the idea. "He would never tell me anything!"

"But you know him," Petra points out, furrowing her brow slightly into one of her three facial expressions. The other two are "neutral" and "annoyed." She reminds me of a secret agent, and I imagine not much rattles her. "You know his weaknesses – you can exploit them."

"I can work on finding out more about the rings," I agree. "But I'll do it my way."

Robert taps his fingers on the table. "I can't stress enough the danger involved in this undertaking. Be very cautious." He looks directly at me, his otherwise composed voice betraying a slight shakiness. "That's all I'll ask of you today."

"For the record," Erik says as we all get up to leave, "if I ever see Sarazen, you probably won't get a chance to 'exploit his weaknesses.' "

"Trust me," I assure him, "it won't come to that. We'll find what we need some other way. *Any* other way."

"Petra, Fox, Hadid, Erik, and…Everest," Robert calls out.

"Can you stay for a minute?" Jason gives us a suspicious look before taking his leave.

"Are we sure we can trust that guy?" I ask Erik, who's noticed it too.

He rubs my arm, almost like he's trying to reassure himself. "I'm sure he's harmless. Just tense times."

We wait for the chamber to empty before Robert speaks again. "I think it would be wise if you could all help Everest practice controlling her potential. It would be paramount to her safety, and the group's." Robert turns his gaze toward me and smiles kindly, trying to alleviate the apprehension that is probably written all over my face. "If we weren't meant to have these abilities, they would never have been given to us."

I frown back at him. "So far, along with some good it's brought destruction and chaos. Every time I harness it it's because I'm angry at something. It feels like I'm using it all wrong. I'm not sure I want to revisit all of that anger again."

"Then don't make anger and hatred the source of it," Robert replies like it's just common knowledge. "Channel a different emotion, one even more potent. If the Prism trusts it, then it must be anchored to the light – it must be stronger than the anger. But only *you* decide how to release your potential. You need to find the light within yourself."

I didn't think of that…

I nod, still unsure how I'm going to go about reprogramming the alien force to make it less terrifying. How does one go about finding the light within themselves exactly? I pull Erik's pendant out from under my shirt and play with it nervously, a reflex I've recently developed that seems to calm me a little.

"Where did you get that?" Robert asks, staring at the pendant with an odd expression.

I let it fall back against my chest. "Oh, um, Erik did, actually. It was a gift. He got it in the Isles of Edenia. I thought he would have told you about it, and…how I can bring it in and out of the Prism."

Robert continues staring at it without blinking. "He did…yes," he says under his breath. "I just never saw it…until now."

"Is everything all right?" I ask.

He looks up at me with a blank expression, almost like he's seen a ghost. "It…" He seems to want to reach out to touch it but stops himself, giving it one last look before turning his back to me and addressing the group again.

"The realms will be deserted today," he adds, barely looking at us as he gathers his things with a sudden urgency, "with everyone either braving it in Senna or still on edge after the storm. Try to go somewhere unpopulated. We don't know how far the Vulturian arm extends or what they may do. If they see you –"

"Don't worry boss," Petra interjects, taking an aggressive bite of a green apple. "They won't."

CHAPTER 41

We Never Truly Die

Petra's pushed aside a bookcase that leads to another underground maze which seems to take us behind The Eye.

"Aren't we going back the way we came?" I ask.

"It's a secondary access point, in case we're ever shut out of the Luminary," Hadid explains. "Same maze, same labyrinth, but it releases into Cascada. We'll have more privacy there."

Erik urges me to take the lead to practice the turns. I've already started to memorize the labyrinth but still second guess every move.

"So, just to recap…" I say as we walk, "the Vulturians basically control the world, ensure poverty, instigate war, and puppeteer catastrophic events all to line their pockets and feed their lust for power. I can't believe people go to such extremes and cause so much suffering for such a selfish cause."

"Human potential terrifies them," Petra elaborates. "They're committed to propagating the belief that it's acceptable to be mediocre. But for them, mediocrity is not an option. They occupy only the highest of stations and use distractions to keep the public complacent – celebrities, carefully selected news stories, made-up enemies…anything that keeps humanity from becoming the best version of – Stop!"

I jump. "What?"

Petra points silently in the opposite direction.

"Oh. Right, thanks." I make a mental note of the correct pattern and refocus.

"You never told me about your potential," I say to Erik.

He smiles mysteriously. "It's nothing really. Small time compared to yours. I can collect light. I don't know why that specifically – kind of random – but I can absorb it. It's useful for starting a campfire, I guess."

"And handy for when the power goes out," Fox teases.

Erik laughs. "Yeah, that's actually happened!"

I look at Erik's hands, then make a left turn. "Does it hurt, absorbing light like that?"

He shrugs. "I've learned how to control and release it. It's fine. We adapt."

Yes, we adapt. There's no other way, is there?

Thankfully, I've made it out with just the one slip-up. Not bad, but still one too many. A door lets us out into a grotto behind one of the Cascada waterfalls. Petra pulls down a scope to scout out the area before signaling that it's safe to emerge. The translucent falling water conceals us from the rest of the valley like a sheer blue veil.

"We're in the farthest corner of Cascada," she says as we emerge into the forest. "Not many come this way."

I pace nervously. "I'm still not loving the idea of summoning that energy again."

"Give it time," Hadid assures. "The trick is to use only what you need. I can manipulate object size. When I started, I could make a stone expand to the size of a tire. Too much, I know. Now, I keep the changes small."

"Is that all you can do?"

"Mostly. Sometimes I can alter matter in different ways, but not very well. I'm still practicing. We all seem to do things a little differently –"

"*Everest!*"

A little girl's high-pitched cry brings our lesson to an end before it even begins. We all turn in the direction of the voices to see Lise and Julian emerging from the trees and bounding toward us through a patch of white daisies.

"Are you serious?" I hear Petra huff as she gapes at the children. They run up to us, all smiles.

"Wha – what are you doing here?" I ask, returning Lise's bear hug. They're not exactly dressed for a walk in the woods, with Lise sporting a tulip dress and Julian a crisp white shirt with a smart blue sweater. I know instantly that they're on their way to Senna. "I thought you two were going to stay close to Castellum for a while," I say to Lise. "Remember?"

"You still trying to impress that girl?" Erik asks Julian, squeezing his shoulder and fixing his bowtie. Julian confirms as much with a grin.

"He kissed her," Lise blurts out, "on the cheek!"

"Tattletale!" Julian cries furiously.

"You never said it was a secret," Lise defends herself.

Erik gives Julian a low five. "That's my man!" he whispers and gives him a wink.

"This has been really fun," Petra interrupts, eyeing the glen suspiciously, "but they can't be here!"

"Why not?" Lise asks immediately.

Erik crouches down to her level. "Lise, it's really important you don't tell anyone that you saw us here. Can we keep that between us?"

"Why not? What are you all doing here anyway?"

Petra rolls her eyes. "They are *children*. We can't trust them!"

"Hey!" Lise snaps at Petra, pouting, "I can keep a secret!"

"Really?" Petra challenges her, bending down to look her square in the eye. "Didn't you *just* snitch on your brother?"

Lise keeps her cool and lifts her chin defiantly, crosses her arms and leans into her left hip. "Like I said, he never said it was a secret."

I'm surprised to see Petra reveal a fourth facial expression; a half grin spreads across her chiseled face as she seems to develop a respect for the fight and spunk in her opponent. She stands up and backs away, accepting defeat, for now.

"Lise," I say to her, approaching and taking her by the shoulders, "we're just checking things out to make sure everything is back to normal. That's all. But we don't want to alarm anyone, so the less people who know the better, okay? And please, try not to go too far out today. Just today. I know how excited you are about the Regale, but there will be other festivals. I promise!"

Lise nods with downcast eyes, pretending not to be disappointed but failing miserably at it. "Okay. We will head back then."

"Can you come then?" Julian asks, hoping for Erik's company. "You said you would come with me to the observatory and teach me all about the stars, remember?"

Erik smiles regretfully. "I remember. Not this time mate, sorry. But don't worry — there will be plenty of other opportunities. I promise. I've got so many things I want to show you two. Why don't you tear up Eden Hall for me today?"

Petra's head moves from side to side like an owl as she stands watch, tapping her heel.

"Come on Julian. I'll race you back to Eden Hall," Lise says with renewed excitement as she takes off. "Bye Everest!"

Julian glances at me a final time and grins shyly before following his sister.

"How did they know to come all the way back here? I've only seen Sentry this far out," Petra muses.

Aside from the swaying towers of bark and leaves, Cascada is eerily silent. I discern an odd sensation – like something in the air has shifted. Like something else is present. That little voice pokes at my gut.

There are no coincidences.

My arms erupt in tiny goosebumps as I look after the children and think about what Petra just said.

"Lise," I call, a knot forming in my stomach as my walk turns to a run, "Lise, how did you know to find us here?"

But my realization comes too late. As Lise and Julian near the opposite end of the glen, two figures clad in black hoods emerge from the dense thicket and grab the siblings, their hands moving swiftly to their mouths to prevent their screams.

I stop in my tracks, paralyzed for a nauseating second and not wanting to accept the impossible scene unfolding before me. I don't need to see their faces to know who the intruders are, and when the shock wears off my rage forces me into a sprint. I can't even feel my legs as I race towards them, my surroundings a dizzying blur.

"No!" I scream at the intruders. But the sound leaves my mouth muffled and weak.

The hooded figures stand their ground, their grasp tightening around Julian and Lise's delicate throats. The one clutching Julian speaks. "Don't come closer!" the figure demands, his voice lifeless and raspy. I've heard it before, ordering a coffee at Emile's and casually offering to take my life. "Their lives, as a trade," he says.

Reluctantly, I obey and stop running, staring at Lise and

Julian with desperation. I can't use my potential if they're being used as human shields. I hear the others run up, and I raise my hand behind me, motioning for them to stand down.

"You and the compass for them," Irra demands.

"Fine! Just let them go!" I agree without hesitation, trying to fake assertiveness and hide the panic that's tearing me up on the inside. "Please! Just…let them go. I'll give you what you want."

Suddenly, something changes. *Something's wrong.* Irra glances at Julian who seems to fall limp in his hands, his face ashen. I see Lise struggling, biting down on the hand of her captor. But Julian seems to have no strength to fight back. I notice his face changing. The boy, whose eyes had just minutes ago sparkled at the thought of seeing the stars, seems to be disappearing before my eyes — the outline of his figure becoming blurred. The glint in his eyes diminishes like a dying ember in a fire and I see his chest fall still.

Julian's asthma!

This is the Prism? *No… not here …*

Irra removes his hand from Julian's mouth, then glances up at me from under the darkness of the hood, revealing his snake-like marble eyes and a sadistic smirk. "Oops."

"*NO!*" I charge at him as he throws Julian's body to the ground before retreating into the brush, Lise's captor leading the escape with Lise over his shoulder. I can feel my legs burning now as they dig into the dirt with a vengeance.

When I reach Julian's side my heart sinks. Only a vague afterimage of him remains. I try desperately to hold what's left of him, but my hands travel through him as if he's a mere illusion, his eyes two circular voids against the emerald grass, until eventually even they vanish, leaving nothing to see. Nothing to hold.

Nothing at all.

This can't be happening! "Julian!"

A single tear runs down my cheek. I won't allow another. I won't cry for him yet. *Maybe he just woke up…* That's it! He just woke up…

But even as I think it, I don't believe it. The Prism's changed, and maybe that means it can't protect us from our Earthly ailments and from meeting our true end. I let my devastation and guilt echo through the forest as I scream in frustration, barely aware of the others gathering who've been rendered speechless by their own astonishment.

"Lise's gone," Erik says frantically. "We followed them into the brush, but they're gone. We'll get horses and keep looking."

"Don't bother," I tell him weakly. "She's not in the Prism anymore. They've taken her out somehow. I just know it…"

Erik places a hand on my shoulder as I kneel in the space where Julian's body had last been. I turn to face him. By the gleam in his eyes, I know he's trying hard to hold it together for me and being torn up by his own guilt. I allow a second tear, then a third before I lunge at Erik, sobbing.

"Everest, I'm so sorry," Petra says softly, revealing a sympathetic side. "How did I let this happen? How did I not realize…"

I manage some choked up sounds through my sobs. "No, this is my fault," I tell her. "They're in danger because of me." When it seems I have no tears left, I wipe my face and straighten my back. "I have to go to Castellum."

"Let me take you," Erik offers.

But I push past him rudely towards a landing Juno with renewed determination. "I'm fine." *No more tears. No more.*

A loud rumble draws our attention to a rockslide barreling down the peaks that line the Prism's perimeter.

"We have to leave!" Petra yells as her own horse arrives. "The Vulturian presence is causing further deterioration."

I stare down the rockslide. Perhaps getting hit with a massive boulder will help me forget. Perhaps I'll get what I deserve. At the very least, maybe it will wake me the hell up.

Wake up and pray this day was only a dream.

I mount Juno quickly and refocus. The tree canopies begin to melt into one another as I head towards Castellum, pieces of the Prism falling apart behind me like pixels in a glitching video game. I feel my body inching off Juno's back as I lose focus, overwhelmed by regrets, what ifs and what nows. By the time I remember to reach for her mane my fingers grasp only air. I fall through the Prism's atmosphere towards the crashing water and impaling tree steeples, feeling myself being ripped apart, like pieces of a puzzle dispersing, no longer part of a whole — aimless, alone, untethered.

I land with a thud on a familiar surface, Juno's pale mane hitting me in the face.

What am I doing?

I take the mane and lift myself up. "Thanks girl," I whisper in her ear.

Get yourself together!

A new emotion starts to replace the despair — anger, intensified by an unsettling need for revenge. I don't like it, but it's the only thing preventing me from completely unravelling.

Once inside Castellum I race for the elevator, hoping somehow the children managed to escape and return to their dimensions safely.

"Julian Vidal," I instruct the elevator.

It doesn't move.

"Julian Vidal!"

Still nothing.

I stand as still as a flag on a windless day, refusing to accept it. *This must be a mistake…* "Julian…" I don't finish the name.

"Lise…Lise Vidal." Finally, motion. I breathe out a sigh of relief. *At least Lise is all right.* When I get to the door, I pound my fist like a madwoman.

"Lise, Julian! Open up! Please," I shout, resting my forehead heavily on the wood – but it doesn't give way. "Please, open up!"

The silence is unbearable – taunting and cruel. After more shouting and knocking and strange looks from passing Wakers, I peel myself away and reluctantly return to my own dimension, reality sinking in with every excruciating step. Lise is alive. But the absence of Julian's dimension terrifies me. My heart feels crushed by a massive boulder, pieces of it searching for a sliver of hope it can never catch.

Inside my dimension, I study the artificial reality with an odd disconnect and feel a growing emptiness. The mountains begin to fade followed by the sky, until all the creations of my mind are stripped away. Only the compass and my library books remain on the floor — the things I've brought into the dimension. I allow my body to join them as I fall to the floor on my knees, sobbing uncontrollably.

"You remind me of my cousin Stefanie when you cry."

My head shoots up. That voice…He's here! Right in front of me, wearing his favorite Star Wars t-shirt.

Alive!

"Julian!" I run to him and grip him so hard I worry I'll break the bones in his tiny frame. "Oh my God, you're okay!"

Julian hugs me back, something he's never done before – not like this. "Why wouldn't I be?" he says.

I let go of him and blink away the tears to see him more clearly. "What do you mean? Don't you remember?"

Then it dawns on me: this is *my* dimension — a reflection of my deepest desires and wishes. Julian's a mere manifestation of that desire.

Nothing more.

"No…none of this is real, is it?" I pull away angrily from the clever illusion. "Is this some sick joke?" I scream at my blank surroundings, hoping the Prism will intervene and just fix everything.

Fix it!

I look over this would-be Julian with doubt. "You're not really here."

But to add to my confusion, Julian's eyes dance with a kind of life only real eyes are capable of – a dance of memories and hopes; of school yard mischief and first crushes; of movies and arcade games, and everything in between. I see it all bursting through Julian's irises like an exploding star.

"Of course, I'm here," he says to me. "You should know better than to ask that."

"Julian," I whisper skeptically, "Don't mess with me. I think…I watched you die…"

"We never truly die," he replies mysteriously, casually glancing around my dimension. "I have to say, you haven't done much with the place."

"You're just a figment of my imagination! I don't have time for this. I need to wake up!" I pull hard at my hair, trying to force my thoughts out of my head, trying to bring back the nothingness.

"Everest," Julian continues, "don't limit your mind." He approaches, holding out his hand. "Think about it — can you imagine any of us not existing? I'm real Everest. Just a different kind of real — the kind of real that can never be destroyed. The same kind that you are — you just don't know it yet."

I reach out warily to take his small hand and feel a warm weightlessness, the same kind I'd experienced in Vieri's loft. The same kind I experienced in the rain. It soothes the pain in my heart, and I close my eyes to be able to feel it more intensely and let it calm my soul.

"I have to go now," Julian tells me, slowly removing his hand and ending the moment. He looks behind him — a light beckons in the distance in shades of the sea and sky, and his bare feet start on a path toward it.

I can feel his body being pulled away from me. "Julian…don't," I manage to whisper, choking back more tears and fearing that if I let him leave it will be final.

He glances back, his serene expression betraying a kind of insight he's suddenly grasped.

"Don't be afraid of what lies beyond," he says. "The universe is infinite — if you could only see it…" At last, I let go of the last finger I'm holding onto as Julian turns back towards his new path. "It's like…everything, all at once. You would love it Everest! I think I see Saturn…"

My heart aches as he takes another step towards the ethereal horizon, and I realize with despair that no matter where or when I wake up, he won't be there.

"Goodbye Everest. And thanks, for everything." He beams one last smile before stepping through the blinding threshold. As I watch him pass into what I can only hope is yet another world, I can't deny the beauty of it all.

"How about, 'see ya later'," I whisper back as the light fades and the nothingness surrounds me again. *See ya later.*

I can't look away from the spot where Julian left, hopeful that somehow, he'll reappear. Erik clears his throat from the door I've left ajar in my haste, then walks over to me.

"He was here," I mumble, hearing him approach. "He was

real. For one last moment…he was real. Did you see him? He was here…"

I feel Erik place a hand on my shoulder. His voice cracks a little when he speaks. "I know. I saw."

My body sinks to the floor. I feel like I'm floating aimlessly in the nothingness, the emptiness of the room intolerable. "Do you think we'll ever see him again?"

Erik joins me on the floor. "I know we will," he whispers, pulling me close to him. His tear lands on my arm and he quickly wipes his eyes to prevent any more. "I know we will."

But his reassurance isn't enough, and I can't face the unbearable fact of being responsible for Julian's end. I glare at the compass resting a few feet away, my anger returning. I reach for it, feeling an immense resentment for the thing that now lays in my palm. *Why did I have to find it?* My brain transmits the signal to my arm to throw the object as far away as I can, but for whatever reason I can't let it go, and grip it like a child holding a security blanket.

"I can't come back," I say to Erik as I close my hand tightly around the circular piece of metal. "I can't come back here."

"Ev don't…don't do that. Just give it some time."

"No Erik," I insist, my eyes becoming cloaked in a watery veil. "That's not the answer. Not this time." I feel Erik's arms wrap tighter around me as I bury my tear-stained face into his chest.

Not this time.

CHAPTER 42

The Problem with Closure

"Everest, keep up! They'll be closing soon!"

My mother's face appears before me as she runs ahead, weaving through a crowd. She's wearing her favorite red and white striped sweater with the flared sleeves. Her long wavy hair flows behind her, getting tussled around by the wind and catching in her long earrings. Her unique artisan bracelets dangle on her wrists like windchimes. You could always hear her coming a mile away.

I'm right on her heels, both of us giggling and trying to get one last ride in before the park closes.

"We're almost there…" she shouts, motioning for me to run faster as she smiles eagerly. "Come on…"

I know I made that rollercoaster ride, because I have a picture of it in my passport holder.

So why can't I catch up?

As I trail her, I feel like something is holding back my legs. I try desperately to move forward yet feel completely powerless, unable to complete a single stride or call out to her to wait for me. The park appears to get more crowded, the laughing faces and stuffed animal prizes obstructing my path.

"Everest…"

She runs further away, getting smaller until she's lost in the crowd of people and balloon animals.

"Everest, where are you…I'm right here Everest…"

"Mom!" I finally manage to yell, only to find that it's still dark in the storage room and Erik is still out cold next to me.

Just a dream. But it felt so real…

All of it feels real, until it isn't!

I shake off my nostalgia, then carefully move Erik's arm aside and sneak off the couch. He begins to stir. *Darn it!* I slip on my runners and tiptoe through the deserted hallway and into the courtyard, knowing Erik won't be far behind me.

Avoiding streetlamps, I flag down a taxi and plead with the driver. "Plus rapide!" It's 4:25, and the city will be waking soon for the morning rush. But for now, we drive through mostly green lights.

The Iliad Hotel stands four more blocks up ahead. I'm not stupid enough to pull up to the front doors. Besides, I have another problem – the street is lit with blue and red from the sirens of emergency vehicles parked outside. Four police cars. Two ambulances. A small crowd has formed at the main doors of the Iliad.

I pay the driver and cautiously make my way toward the hotel, stopping a block away to observe from the shadows in front of a storefront. Two detectives seem to be questioning the bell man who keeps shrugging his shoulders and gesticulating. The detectives move on to another witness – a woman sitting on the hotel steps, sobbing into the sleeve of an officer.

An older woman approaches the storefront and stands next to me. "Do you know what happened?" I ask her, fearing the answer.

She sighs as she fiddles with some keys. "Oh, it's awful!" she says rather loudly in a raspy voice. "I heard he suffocated, the little boy. The mother heard some ruckus and found him, but it was too late. Just tragic!"

The hotel doors open to let out a stretcher. No visible body, no attached IV; only a black bag with the words *Bureau du Coroner*. The distraught woman rushes toward the black bag, her heart-wrenching screams echoing down the street: *"Non! Mon fils! Laissez-moi voir mon fils!"* The officer tries unsuccessfully to console her and eventually manages to pull what I now realize is Julian's mother into the back of a police car as she pleads to see her son.

I sink to the ground, nauseated, and let my head fall heavily into my hands. Finally, I have the closure I wanted; the closure I now wish I hadn't been so eager to pursue. Because with it my last glimmer of hope has vanished.

My head begins to pound from a sudden headache that leaves me dizzy. *Suffocated.* There's no unseeing the black body bag.

He's really gone.

I feel the woman patting my shoulder. "You must have a very kind heart to be affected so."

More like a guilty conscience, I correct her silently as I watch the cars make their eerie procession away from the hotel.

"What about the girl?" I ask about Lise. "Is she alright?"

"She's alive, thank heavens. Paramedics took her a short while ago. I can't imagine – she must have been so afraid watching her brother struggle like that. I hear she was completely inconsolable and had to be heavily sedated."

My panic returns. "Heavily sedated?" *What have they done to her?*

I gasp a 'thank you' to the woman before stepping back out onto the sidewalk.

"Wait a moment, how did you know about the girl?" the woman shouts as I leave.

I cringe at the unwanted attention and begin to walk faster. But the damage is done. He rounds the corner in front of me and steps into my path — a man whose countless acts of cruelty might as well be tattooed on his face. My stomach churns furiously as I finally face him.

"How predictable you are, Ms Cleary." Irra's demonic voice stings like the venom of a viper. "So sorry we had to resort to such…extraordinary measures," he says, without the slightest ounce of sincerity. His perfectly white teeth glisten in the dark like those of an evil Cheshire cat. "Things went a bit further than planned. We were supposed to send the message and then grab the brats, and then, of course, you were going to hand over the compass…and we were all going to go about our day like nothing happened," he says jovially, then puts on a fake frown. "Sadly, we missed the asthma, you see. Wasn't in the file. But," his grin returns, "at least now we can meet properly."

"You're a *monster!*" I scream at him, my soul blackening by the second. Any intention I had of turning myself over to the Vulturians is replaced by a profound hunger for revenge and a terrifying desire to see them all lying dead in the street. "You'll pay for what you did. I'll destroy you!"

"Now, be reasonable," Irra replies calmly. "So much hatred won't allow you to return to your precious paradise, and it won't get you any closer to that sweet little girl."

Lise! "What did you do to her?" I demand.

He walks over to a waiting sedan and opens the back door. "A conversation is all we ask. She'll wake up if you comply."

"That's not happening," I reply coldly, the energy intensifying inside me. "I'd rather see you dead than see a hundred Prisms! And I'll find Lise on my own – you'll never take me to her. Besides, I don't need you." I feel the sweat accumulating on my clenched palms. "You know what I can do," I threaten. *Any second now and I'll have enough…*

"Yes, you do have quite a unique ability, and one which we would very much like to explore further," Irra replies nonchalantly. "But I'm going to guess that it only works if you're conscious enough to use it."

"What?"

An arm reaches across my chest and something sharp pricks my neck. I can see Irra looking pleased with himself from the corner of my eye. My rage returns, and I harness it to knock my attacker off balance. We hit the cement, the syringe lying within my reach, still a quarter full of milky liquid – the dose not fully administered.

"Basile, you are literally good for nothing," Irra sneers, making his way toward us as we struggle and pulling something out of his leather jacket.

I'm finished. I try to summon my potential, but my energy is tied up trying to free myself, my vision impaired as if I'm seeing the world from behind a shroud as whatever was in the syringe starts to kick in.

Just as I'm about to accept my fate, I see three streetlights turn off in rapid succession. Suddenly, Irra's sedan bursts into flames, the explosion catapulting him into a brick wall. The hot wind from the blast brushes over my skin and rolls the syringe within my reach. I stretch to grab it and stab it into Basile's neck seconds before Erik slams a bicycle pump into his forehead.

"It's amazing what people leave lying around on the street," Erik says, tossing the pump aside and helping me up. "You okay? Can you walk?"

I rub my eyes, trying to pull back the shroud. It lifts slightly, but my mind still feels blurry. "Yeah, I think so." I lean on Erik as he leads us away from the scene and the approaching sirens.

"This way," he says, turning down a side street and giving us a break at the next block.

"We need to go to the hospital!" I tell him as I catch my breath, seeing clearer now. "Lise might be there!"

"Are you serious?" Erik cries, shaking out his hands. "No! Bad idea! Ev, what don't you understand? You've already walked into one trap. They could have killed you, tortured you…"

"But they didn't!" I get it. He's angry. He warned me, and he was right. But I'm too proud to admit it just yet. "I had to find out about Julian. And now I need to know what happened to Lise. *I'm* responsible for this Erik. If it wasn't for knowing me, Lise would be up in that bed and Julian…" I can't bring myself to say it.

"You can't blame yourself," Erik says, taking me gently by my shoulders. "These people are…psychopaths. You're letting them get in your head. You're smarter than this Ev. They're counting on your guilt, and you're giving them exactly what they want!"

"Well, they're right to count on it! I'm going," I insist stubbornly, twisting away and turning on an unsteady heel. "I'll figure it out without getting caught this time."

"Ev, wait!" I look back to see Erik throwing his arms up in exasperation. "You're going to fall over before you even get there."

I commit back to my route, but Erik catches up and reaches for my arm, turning me to face him. I can no longer keep my tears inside as I try to keep a straight face, and my balance.

"Fine!" Erik concedes, wiping my watery cheeks. "Damn it! Let's just think of a plan first, okay?"

I throw my arms around his neck, grateful that I won't have

to do it alone. "Okay," I whisper. I reach for his hand, finding it almost burning to the touch. "Erik!" I say with alarm.

"It'll pass in a few hours," he assures, withdrawing his hand.

I lower my gaze, finally swallowing my pride. "Oh God, I'm sorry. Thank you – for saving me back there. I should have listened to you."

He brushes my cheek again and lifts my chin. "Just returning the favor," he whispers back. "You gave me a heart attack. At this rate, I won't live past 30."

"Well, I certainly hope you do. I can't lose you too."

Erik kisses my forehead and smiles. "Well look at that - we're on the same page again!"

We continue walking, taking unfamiliar streets until I don't even recognize where we are. A young woman passes us, and Erik unexpectedly asks for directions to the Salle St. Germaine.

"Why there?" I inquire after she tells us and departs.

"Maeve. She's not far from here and she may know how to help. And I remember her saying something about a cousin who's a doctor. Maybe she can find out about Lise."

"Are you sure we can trust her? She doesn't know anything about who we are, the Order, the Sentry…"

"I know. But no one else from the Sentry lives close to here," Erik reminds me. "We don't have to reveal everything. We just need a friend right now."

True. Some friends wouldn't hurt. "How do you know she'll even be there?"

"She once told me she's up for a promotion and gets to work at 7:00 sharp every morning, before anyone else. Let's hope she's still ambitious."

I walk the rest of the way in anxious silence clutching Erik's hand and avoiding cameras, and torturing myself with thoughts of all that I've lost and all I could still lose.

CHAPTER 43

Shattered Illusions

Maeve's eyes nearly fall out of her sockets when we sneak in through the front doors of the Salle behind her.

"Not who I expected to see this morning," she says, reaching to hug Erik and lingering a little too long for my liking. I brush off my petty jealousy. We have more pressing priorities, and Erik has a point – we need someone on our side.

"What are you both doing here? What's going on? Erik… Paris?"

"Is there somewhere we can all talk, privately?" Erik asks, looking around the grand event hall warily.

Maeve nods, eyeing us both with a perplexed expression. "Sure…yeah…Uh…follow me."

Her smooth red hair sways perfectly behind her as she leads us to the corporate part of the building, lined with vacant offices that will soon be filled with people that can under no circumstances find us here. I wince with every loud tap of Maeve's heel against the polished floors and keep my head down to avoid the cameras.

"The janitor should be gone by now. Let's chat in here," she says, ushering us inside her office. She closes the blinds and leans against her desk, arms crossed. "So, what couldn't wait until after breakfast? And should I be offended I wasn't your first call?" she adds, shoving Erik's arm, her voice assuming a higher pitch. My jealousy rears its ugly head again.

"Well, it's a long and unbelievable story," Erik replies.

"Is it?"

"It is," Erik confirms, the awkwardness palpable. "We could use your help though. And we could use a place to lay low for a few hours."

Maeve's eyebrows shoot up. "Lay low? What on Earth…did you two rob a bank or something?"

"No, it's fine. We're fine," I interrupt, trying to tame Maeve's suspicion. "The banks are all fine."

"One more thing." Erik glances at me. "We need to find out about a hospital patient. Isn't your cousin a doctor?"

Maeve nods. "Stephen – he's at St. Marguerite."

"Could you reach out to him for us, find out where our friend is?"

"Because you're in some kind of trouble?" Maeve tries to confirm again. Erik just shrugs and remains silent. I'm glad he's biting his tongue.

Surprisingly, Maeve doesn't press further and just types a text message on her phone, then crosses her arms again and tenses her lip. "What are friends for if not aiding and abetting. But one day, I want some kind of explanation." She slides off the edge of her desk, smoothing out her pencil skirt. "There might be a place you can hide out. No one will think to look for you there, at least for a few hours. What's your friend's name?"

I hesitate, but how else am I going to find out? "It's Lise. Her last name is Vidal. She's eight years old."

"Wait, *Lise*? Little Lise from the Prism?" Maeve gasps and draws her hand to her lips. "Oh…I hope she's alright!" She touches my hand to comfort me. "I suppose there's no point asking what happened. But you better give me some answers one day! I could get in a lot of trouble if someone finds out I let you in here. Come on, before someone sees you."

"What about security?" I ask.

"Don't worry. If they see you with me, they'll assume you're allowed to be here. They won't know any different."

We follow Maeve out of the corporate wing, passing a room stocked with props and mirrored vanities. "One second," I say, sneaking inside without asking permission.

"What are you doing?" Erik whispers, trying unsuccessfully to stop me.

Maeve fidgets anxiously beside him, looking at her phone every few seconds. "You really shouldn't be in there. We should get you hidden before my boss arrives."

But I'm not leaving without something specific. "I just want to have a look. I've never been backstage anywhere before."

I know Erik must think I've lost my mind. "Your timing is bloody awful Ev! Can we take the tour some other time? What could you possibly need in there?"

I emerge from behind a costume rack wearing a magician's hat. "Isn't it fabulous?" They both stare at me like I've sprouted three-heads.

"Just…put that back," Maeve orders, shifting her weight uncomfortably.

I pout, setting the hat down and leaving the room. "Lighten up a little. There's no one here."

"What's gotten into you?" Erik whispers as Maeve leads us down the hall and into a large loading area piled high with wooden crates. There're no windows, and only two dim bulbs provide light to the entire room.

Maeve runs a finger over a crate and examines the dust

pattern. "You'll be invisible here for a few hours, until shipments start arriving. I know it's a little dark and pungent…"

"It's fine. Thank you," Erik assures her. "We just need a few hours."

"Okay then. Stay in this corner. It's a blind spot. The cameras won't pick you up. I'll make myself scarce before I give you away. And I'll ask about Lise." Maeve seems more than anxious to leave us behind, making hastily for the door without so much as a goodbye.

But I'm not quite ready for her to leave just yet…

"Wait," I call after her, following closely. "Can you tell me where you got that gorgeous ring?" I motion to an oval-cut clouded stone on Maeve's right-hand, set against a familiar thin granite band.

Maeve turns around. "This?" she replies, twirling the ring around with her index finger and trying not to make eye contact. "It's just a family heirloom."

"I'll bet it is." Seeing my opportunity, I swiftly slap a pair of handcuffs on Maeve's right wrist, then swing her around to trap her left behind her back before she knows what hit her. "My uncle used to teach me this trick. Something he learned from a bounty hunter he once travelled with in South America."

"*What do you think you're doing?*" Maeve shrieks, trying to free herself.

Erik must think I've completely lost my mind. "Ev, what's going on?" he asks, looking like a deer in the headlights.

I feel something tucked into Maeve's skirt and retrieve a small pistol from underneath her blazer. Next, I locate her cell phone and power it off. From Erik's startled expression I can't figure out if he's completely confused or slowly piecing things together.

"I saw the cuffs when I took my seemingly random detour,"

I explain, then turn my attention back to Maeve. "I knew as soon as you pretended to comfort me – as soon as that ring brushed against my skin – that you were one of them. You miscalculated Maeve. That feeling is all too familiar to me."

I take a firm hold of her arm and throw her down to the floor, reining in the urge to punch her in the face. "Why don't you enlighten us – the Order, was it a birth right, or did you just choose to be despicable and cruel all on your own."

"It all makes sense now…," Erik mumbles, before Maeve can even answer. "No flying, no portals…the Prism could never read your thoughts, could it? You were there so seldom…you never even told us your last name." He runs his finger through his hair and lets his eyelids fall as he seems to recall all the red flags he had missed. "You bloody fooled all of us!"

"Did you think that if you drained the light out of me, I wouldn't be able to fight back?" I sneer at her. My swelling rage dims the room by half.

A devilish grin replaces Maeve's previously startled expression. "Very good, Everest!" she laughs. "If I could clap I would, but obviously you've prevented that. I can't believe I'm saying this, but I'm impressed. You seemed far too flighty to have any sort of decent IQ. I guess I did miscalculate some things." She raises herself to a sitting position. "Didn't think you'd notice my little tap. I figured your emotions were too shot from the death of your little friend. Clearly, you dealt with it better than I thought. I should apologize though – it really wasn't supposed to go that far. We only wanted to…hold on to them for a while."

I feel the hatred and anger suffocating me. I was afraid of it once, but now I feel myself embracing it. "Don't you dare talk about them!" I threaten, my fingernails digging into my palms.

"You killed him – *you killed an innocent child!* And for what? *What could be worth that?*"

"Oh Everest, you really should calm down. Such hostility isn't productive," Maeve continues mockingly, glancing around the room as if waiting for something to happen.

"How did the Order even know we'd be there?" Erik asks, trying to fill in the gaps. "How did they know to go to Cascada?"

Maeve smirks. "Oh, that juicy piece of intel was thanks to Tara."

I glare at her. "Who the hell is Tara?"

"Wouldn't you like to know."

"You bitch!" Without thinking I raise the pistol and point it at her, my pulse throbbing through the tip of my finger as it rests on the trigger. One slight depression and I can take from Maeve what she and the Order took from Julian. A life for a life, the scales justly balanced.

Erik approaches cautiously from the side, his hand stretched out in front of him. "Ev…put that down, okay…it's not worth it…it's not. Just give it to me, come on Ev…" He places his hand slowly on the gun.

"She deserves this!" I hiss, feeling the weight of Erik's hand pushing the gun towards the ground. *"Who is Tara?!"*

"You don't want to do this. Let go," Erik urges me again.

I resist. *She deserves this. They all do! This and so much more.*

I inhale a shaky breath and feel it travel through my body and into the tips of my fingers, taming some of my rage. Reluctantly, I release my hold, keeping my eyes fixed on my target as Erik swiftly secures the weapon. Maeve just sits grinning, probably thinking I never had the guts to do it.

She wouldn't be smiling if she knew how close I'd come.

Suddenly, I realize the magnitude of what could have

happened had Erik not intervened and wonder if my ever-darkening soul has finally taken a turn it can't come back from.

"Having trouble controlling your protégé, Erik?" Maeve smirks. "Or maybe you just can't stand the thought of her hurting me, after what we shared."

I look at Erik, my mouth going dry. *What is she saying?*

Erik takes a nervous step in Maeve's direction. "Maeve, don't do this."

Maeve chuckles triumphantly. "He didn't tell you!"

"Tell me what?" I ask.

Erik gives me a pleading glance, like he wants me to forget what I've just heard.

"Tell me what?" I demand again.

"I wanted to tell you, but…"

Not her. Anyone but her.

"Oh, I can fill in some of the blanks," Maeve offers, obviously relishing every second of the misery she's inflicting. "We spent some time together in London when I came to visit him a few months ago. It was memorable; wouldn't you say Erik?"

I continue to study Erik, hoping for a denial. But the guilt on his face is telling, and it confirms that my suspicions had been valid all along.

Erik rubs his face in frustration. "Maeve stop this! You and I…that should have never happened! I barely remember it…" He stops midsentence and glares at her, his eyes widening as he points his finger in her direction. "Wait…you used it on me, didn't you?"

"The ring?" Maeve shrugs and lets out another laugh. "It may have helped a little. But the way I remember it, you never complained."

I can't listen to any more of it. "You're disgusting!" I shout.

"We…uh…we should go," Erik urges, sounding defeated. "She probably already told them we're here."

I'm still reeling from Erik's betrayal and fighting the urge to slap the smirk off Maeve's perfect face. "We're going to destroy you, and your Order," I whisper, crouching in front of her. "But until that day comes, I'll be damned if I let you use this on anyone else." I rip the ring off her finger and slip it into my jacket pocket, its invisible toxin clenching my soul momentarily.

"Careful, you'll need all your strength if you want to get out of here," Maeve warns. "By the way, I can just get another one."

"Go ahead," I dare her, coming within an inch of her face. I stare past the heavy eyeliner into her piercing green eyes. "I'll take them all, every last one. Then I'll feed them to you and watch you choke and gasp for air until all the oxygen leaves your body." Maeve's twitching lip tells me I've succeeded in rattling her, and I step away before I'm tempted to consider some other foolish act of retribution.

"Erik," Maeve calls after us, "before you go, I should thank you for filling me in on just how special Everest's relationship was with those lovely children when we all toured Estra together. And knowing the hotel name saved us a lot of time. All that remained was an innocent hint from me on your very likely Cascada rendezvous and we had them right where we wanted them."

Before I can process the blow Maeve's just delivered, Erik drains the last light bulb, a stream of light shooting into his palm. He pulls my numb body through the door before it slams shut, leaving Maeve trapped in complete darkness. "Come on," he says, "don't listen to any more of her poison."

I wait until we're out of Maeve's sight before ripping my hand out of Erik's grasp.

"Ev…"

"Let's…just get out of here." I can't look at him as we walk back the way we came, the nauseating revelations replaying in my mind like a bad movie.

"Someone fed the Vulturians intel about the Cascada access," Erik notes, still analyzing the pieces. "Probably this 'Tara.' We need to find her. I bloody hope she's not Sentry! Do you think it's Sarah? The names sound similar…"

"No – it's not Sarah. She's the only one I can trust, apparently," I insist, unable to resist the passive aggressive jab at Erik. "And it's not like you've been the greatest judge of character!" *To hell with Tara. To hell with Maeve. To hell with them all.* "Do you think we're surrounded?" I ask, distracting myself by figuring out our escape plan and trying not to notice the pain on Erik's face. I don't want to feel bad for him right now.

Erik slows his step. "I think that's a certainty. I'm sorry, Ev. I should have never brought us here."

I refuse to engage with him, remaining focused on the task at hand. "It's too late. It's done. We just need to get out."

I stop to study the cameras at the security office, staying out of the guard's view. He doesn't seem to be paying attention to the footage at all as he works on a crossword puzzle. The cameras show obvious activity around what looks to be the loading area – at least four men. But the front appears unmanned. "Maeve must have told them we'd be in the storage area. They'll never expect us to just walk out the front door."

"What about alarms?" Erik points out.

But my recklessness has reached unparalleled heights. "Robert said to embrace our potential. Let's put it to good use."

CHAPTER 44

Crossroads

It appears Maeve deactivated the alarms when she entered the building, to my disappointment. It leaves me feeling unsatisfied and cheated; unleashing my wrath will have to wait for another day.

As we walk out of the Salle seemingly unnoticed, Erik observes a lone spotter across the street in a familiar black sedan. I ready myself, but he puts a hand on my shoulder. "You can't Ev. Start getting your emotions under control, or they *will* find you again."

Before I can argue, he sends the light shooting out of his palm and into a trash bin near the car, setting it ablaze and creating a distraction that allows us to evade detection. He pulls me out of the building and into a side street before I have time to argue, then hails the first cab.

The taxi ride back over the Seine is awkwardly silent, and I'm afraid that the minute I open my mouth I'll say something I'll regret.

Erik's the first to speak when we enter the physics building. *Very well. Let him try.* I feel my heart hardening with every second that passes, and fear that I'll build an impenetrable wall around it by the time he's finished.

"Ev, just hear me out," he pleads. "You know I love you. I would never hurt you. There was never anything between me and her," he insists. "I swear it!"

"And yet…" I sit helplessly down on the couch. They're just words. They bring no comfort.

"Ev, come on. You're not being fair. I didn't even know you then."

Yeah, I know that. I also know that if it was anyone other than Maeve my reaction would be different. Erik's past is none of my business. I can't hold it against him.

But it's the lie that hurts. That, and I'm shamefully aware that I'm using Erik as a scapegoat for my own guilt, which makes me feel guilty even more.

"She showed up in London," Erik continues. "We'd met recently in the Prism. Looking back, I guess a lot of things should have tipped me off about her…Anyway, Tanner and I had an ugly fight that morning and later that day I got a call that he was in the hospital. He had taken some tainted drugs and it just left me…hollowed out. Defeated. I felt like I had failed him – like I should have been able to save him from himself.

"I felt more self-destructive as the night went on. Truthfully, I don't even remember most of it…But she's right; I made my own choices, no matter what she may have done. If I had known who she was, if I had known I would meet you…"

I turn away toward the window. There's a small gap in the drawn curtains that reveals a sliver of light where dust particles dance like snowflakes, and I distract myself watching them float through the air.

Erik sighs heavily and sits down next to me. "I didn't return to the Prism that night, or for the next eight." He cautiously places a hand on my knee, waiting to see if I'll let him. "I just thought that if I told you about Maeve – about something that should have never been – it would stand in the way of our getting to know one another."

I feel a flutter from Erik's touch and believe him unequivocally. But no matter how much I want to push past things and forget, I can't. Apathy takes the place of my anger, and feeling nothing scares me more than anything. I rise from the couch and stand in the dusty beam of light.

"I get it," I admit, turning to face him and seeing myself in his misty eyes for the first time since the Salle. "I just wish I had heard it from you."

He hangs his head, then locks eyes with me again. "I know. From now on you will. Please, don't let this one thing define us."

"Tell me at least the part about Lise and Julian isn't true," I beg.

But again, Erik's face confirms my fear. "You know I wouldn't have shared that with her if I knew who she was, and I'll regret that for the rest of my life. But we both know the Vulturians would have figured things out from watching you. Maeve saw you with them herself. They didn't need me, Ev. Maeve just said that to hurt you, and it worked…like a bloody charm, it worked! She got exactly what she wanted today."

He comes over with a look of desperation and reaches out to embrace me, and I let my body fold into his arms. For a moment, we're back on our sailboat under the borealis sky…back in that shallow pool in the middle of the Prismatic our first day together. Back in his London flat, laughing at Tommy's antics. Back in Senna…

It feels as effortless as ever for that fleeting moment – until Julian's face enters my mind again. I begin to withdraw and feel Erik struggling to hold on for a few more seconds.

"If you need time, I'll give it to you," he pleads before

releasing me. The next move is mine, and I don't know if I can make it.

"Well…uh…you must be hungry," Erik says uncomfortably, clearing his throat. "Why don't I grab us some breakfast and give you some space."

I smile, grateful for the solitude, not the food.

"I won't be long," he promises. He glances at me with a desperate hope in his glacial eyes, then disappears into the hallway.

I hope his absence will make me realize how much I want him to stay, that the hurt will leave with him and scatter to the Paris wind. But instead, my conflicted emotions remain. I walk over to the window and watch him round the street corner towards the deli. My hands travel to my neck. The pendant brushes against my shaking fingertips, and I make the decision I never thought I'd make.

I don't have much time. Quickly, I reach for my bags, checking to make sure I have the burner phone and my passport. My hand hits something hard and circular, and I'm astonished to pull out the thing I've come to hate.

The compass.

Why? How is it here? I don't want it!

It lays on one of the books I'd taken out of the Lumus, which has somehow become tangled up in my sweater, willed out of the Prism just the same.

Whatever. I don't have the time or energy to come up with explanations. I glance at Erik's things again. The smell of his aftershave lingers on his clothing, and I bring his sweater up to my chest briefly and inhale. I'm seconds away from changing my mind, but I know I don't have it in me to pretend like the last few hours didn't happen.

It's better this way, for both of us.

I walk through the doors with my baseball cap on and my bag on my shoulder, my heart shattering with every step. As I leave the courtyard in the opposite direction of the deli, I know this could change us forever. I know he'll look for me relentlessly.

But this is my city. He won't find me unless I want him to.

And right now, I don't.

Epilogue

Twelve Prism days had passed since Everest's disappearance, although it felt much longer to Erik. He stared at the Citadel entrance with the same naive hope he had clung to since that morning in Paris, waiting for the doors to open and for her face to come into view. How he had managed to return to the Prism after everything that had happened was beyond his understanding. Nothing he could do or tell himself was able fill the void that Everest's departure had carved into his heart.

He remembered returning to the storage room to find it deserted and cold. He remembered launching the ceramic vase in frustration, leaving a hole in the drywall, then rushing out into an awakening unfamiliar city, searching through passing faces and never finding the one he wanted.

He remembered the overwhelming feeling of guilt and self-loathing. But he stifled that emotion and numbed himself, realizing where that path would take him and who would come calling if he allowed his potential to run unchecked.

The only thing that was pulling him back to the Prism was the possibility of seeing her again, inhaling the lavender scent of her hair, hearing her laugh... Had it not been for that desire, even his determination to rid the earth of the Vulturian plague wouldn't have been enough to bring him back. There are some things for which there is only one remedy.

But with each day that Everest failed to show, Erik's discouragement grew, and the void expanded. And he knew it was only a matter of time before it swallowed the last bit of hope that remained and shut him out of the Prism.

His fellow Sentries looked upon him with pity. Even Jason, who managed to reign in his criticisms. Erik hated it. He didn't want pity. He just wished he could turn back time and fix what he had ruined.

At last, Robert reluctantly made the call. "We've waited long enough Erik. We should begin," he suggested gently, his voice revealing a sorrow Erik sensed was similar to his own.

Erik turned his attention back to the group, which had already increased by two bodies. An ache filled the pit in his stomach, the Prism no longer able to suppress it.

Maybe tomorrow, he told himself. *Maybe tomorrow.*

* * *

Maeve twirled her new ring around her finger as she awaited the Ertu's arrival in his study. She liked her old ring better and scowled at the thought of Everest having it in her possession. At least it was worth it – no one had seen Everest in the Prism since the night of Julian's death. She assumed it wasn't a coincidence that she was now being invited to the Ertu's study. She hoped her efforts were enough to elevate her standing among the membership and imagined the ire on Irra's face when the Ertu made them equals.

The click of the door signaled her to rise in respect. The Ertu nodded to her as he walked to his desk, looking polished and skeletal at the same time. Blue veins showed through his thin skin, and his eyes looked like two black marbles, absent life, absent feeling. She had always thought he looked older than his years, and sicker by the day. If she had to guess, he was in his 70's, but then again, no one really knew how old he was, and no one would dare ask.

"Sit," the old man commanded through a cough before lowering himself into his cushioned chair. "It appears the rift you created between the Cleary girl and Halvorsen is still in play. No one has seen them together since."

"I don't think their partnership will be a problem for us anymore," Maeve replied confidently.

"Yes, well, the solving of one problem has created another. She still has the compass. And we can't find her, here or in the Prism."

The moment she had dreaded – the only complication of her victory. Maeve grinned nervously. "She'll be back, whether she likes it or not. She has something of mine."

The old man let his head rest on the back of his chair, placated for the time being. "Hmm…in the meantime, let's hope Halvorsen's misery destroys him and his little band of merry men."

"Pardon me Ertu, but shouldn't we be more proactive in bringing them down?" Maeve insisted, any sentiment she previously harbored for Erik now replaced by a desire to punish him. "If he and Crawford figure out what we —"

"They haven't, yet. And you should never underestimate the effectiveness of discouragement," the Ertu replied. "It's been one of our most effective tools. No one realizes the destructive power it yields to obliterate the human spirit. You've seen for yourself what a few well-placed seeds of doubt can do. From there, human beings are exceptionally talented at bringing about their own ruin."

Maybe the old man had a point, Maeve admitted silently. Now they would just have to wait for her seeds to bear fruit, and the Order would be waiting to feast off the scraps of their rotting carcasses.

"We don't want to attract too much attention," the Ertu reminded her. "Speaking of which, the children…" He tapped a pen on his desk. "The whole Paris block was lit up like a circus that night! Whose bright idea was that?"

Maeve swallowed hard. "The Sharur's, Ertu. Tara thought bargaining with their lives would force Cleary into handing over the compass, and I agreed. It was a solid plan. Irra and Basile were waiting for them in the Prism – exactly where Tara said they would be – but…"

The Ertu raised an eyebrow. "But…"

"But…the boy's asthma, it…complicated things. Something must have happened when we took hold of him. It may have caused him to awaken in a state of unconsciousness, unable to reach for his inhaler. We didn't expect it – Wakers are usually spared feeling ill in the Prism. The plan was to bring them back through the portal and then take the children from the hotel."

The asthma was sold as a "complication", but Maeve had a sneaking suspicion Irra was behind it somehow, and that he had watched with sick satisfaction as the boy gasped for his last breath. It wasn't like Irra to be unprepared. He planned for every contingency. "We only need one anyway," Maeve continued. "The girl screamed before Basile could sedate her, waking the mother. And with the boy's death…we just couldn't take her as planned. She's at the hospital now."

"Were there any hotel witnesses?"

"No. We took care of the cameras. And we have eyes on the hospital 24/7. The girl is in the psych ward, speaking of things no one believes, and heavily medicated by our people. It's just a matter of time before Cleary returns to Paris and comes back for her."

The Ertu eyed Maeve skeptically. "She'll come back all right. And when she does, I wouldn't want to be you."

Maeve resisted the urge to bite her lip nervously. She couldn't let the Ertu see that Everest had rattled her. She couldn't reveal that Everest's threats had caused her to startle from noises in the night. She saw the hunger for vengeance in the girl's eyes, and it haunted her.

"With respect," Maeve continued, "I think you overestimate her. She's not like us. I've seen how easily her emotions and conscience can be manipulated. She'll be a mess, and one we can easily manage."

"Hmm…" *Tap, tap, tap.* The Ertu's pen played a rhythmic beat on the desk that echoed off the paneled walls. "They'll be suspicious of a mole, the others," he continued, pointing out another problem.

But Maeve had prepared for this too. "There's none to be found. Tara was careful. When she first saw her brother with Erik and Robert in Cascada, she suspected he was hiding something. She traced back Simon's steps for months until she discovered that passage. Simon never saw her near the access point."

Maeve looked straight and gulped, hoping it was all enough and that she and Tara – or Francine as the rest of the world knew her – would remain in the Ertu's good graces.

The Ertu's frozen face revealed nothing. He could commend her or have her killed. It was a toss-up.

"Very well," he made up his mind. "We'll let it play out. In the meantime, since you've proven resourceful, you'll be receiving a new assignment with some additional clearance."

Maeve swallowed hard again, this time from relief. *This is it!*

She had worked tirelessly to prove her allegiance to the Order. She had compromised morals, betrayed friends, ruined the lives of those closest to her.

She had earned this.

The Ertu rose from his seat and made his way to the back-right corner of the study where he placed his hand over the mahogany paneling. A red glow emerged from behind the wood, then the wall shifted to the left, revealing a hidden passage. "Are you coming?" he said without waiting.

Maeve had always wondered what the remainder of the building housed and keenly followed through the opening and up a series of steps. Most Vulturians had access to only the first three floors which resembled more of an old-boys club.

But this was something else entirely.

The fourth floor was an eerie space – like a cross between a medieval torture chamber and the super-modern headquarters of a think tank, with the latest technology and modern furnishings spread out through several offices and red brick enclaves. The lights were kept dim and curtains drawn over the large windows for privacy, with the glow of computer monitors and a few dim lamps being the primary source of light.

"What is all this?" Maeve asked, peaking into a room with a "RESTRICTED" label next to a biohazard symbol. Compared to the rest of the floor, it was blindingly white inside, and her eyes hurt to look at it.

"The Nest," the Ertu replied, looking around with admiration. "Every chapter has one, though not all Vulturians know of it. Think of it as R&D. This is where ideas are born, seeds planted. Perhaps a small lie or rumor discretely introduced to incite unrest…or a virus perfected in one of our laboratories. Anything that allows the world to run the way we want it to."

The Ertu stopped to review a piece of paper handed to him by a woman. He gave her a nod and she went on her way. "We've amassed the greatest minds over the years: scientists, engineers, hackers, political analysts, psychologists, tactical experts..."

Maeve knew the Vulturians were powerful — she knew they held high offices and influenced governments and policies across the globe. But this was the day she would confirm they were involved in things that most people believed occurred strictly in conspiracy theories.

She was swimming with the big fish now. And while the gravity of that terrified her, it also gave her a rush like no other.

"And these experts, they all came willingly?" she asked.

As if on cue, two men pulled an unconscious body out of a room down the hall. "Willingness is a fluid state," the Ertu replied vaguely. "Use the rear access, you incompetent buffoons!" he chastised the men.

Irra emerged from behind the opened door and guided the men in the right direction, smirking at Maeve arrogantly before going back inside. *Lucky bastard already had access*, Maeve thought to herself as she scowled at him.

"Desensitization sessions," the Ertu explained to Maeve. "Not all members tolerate them well at first. But we try to fix any unpleasant residual effects."

Maeve eyed the limp body as it disappeared through the rear access door. "I don't remember going through that."

"Then it was effective."

A loud siren put a quick end to Maeve's bout of trepidation. "What's happening now?"

The Ertu waved his hand. "It's just the alert."

They entered a transparent elevator that moved up two more levels. The sixth floor was similar in layout, with one marked difference – a restricted area accessible only by biometric security scan on the South side. The red laser moved slowly across the Ertu's retina before the door unlocked.

At last, the siren ceased. "A significant frequency," the Ertu explained as they walked in.

"This is where you identify the frequencies?" Maeve asked, itching to put together the final pieces. She still didn't know exactly how the Order chose its targets. Different ranks were privy to different secrets. She was well aware that she was very young to be getting the clearance she was getting.

"The Arachna helps," the Ertu answered. "It started off as the Cyprus Project many decades ago. It monitors significant psychic energy release. That sound means we just found another one."

They entered the main control room. A map was displayed on a large screen, and a woman spoke into a telephone and inputted a set of coordinates into a computer.

"Outside of Johannesburg," the woman advised the team. She brought up the exact location on the map and the address flashed on the screen.

"Searching databases," the tech sitting next to her chimed in as he typed into his own computer. "Four possible. Male, 41, female, 23, female, 15, male 13."

"So, this 'Arachna', it's how we find them?" Maeve clarified as the techs worked away.

The Ertu held up his hand, showing off a massive stone weapon on his right ring finger. He eyed it with a hungry lust for the power it yielded. "Not exactly. The Tiamat is the true source of our power," he finally revealed, identifying the stone by its name. "The source of all darkness, the abyss that consumes all light. Through it we have the power to drain smaller frequencies when in contact with a host."

"Through these rings you give us?"

"Yes. But its power is not limited to a few rings."

Maeve eyed the stone on her own finger. "This rock, this 'Tiamat', it's part of something bigger?"

The Ertu nodded. "Much bigger. It is kept hidden, somewhere no one can find it. It detests any frequency of its antithesis - the Skala. The two were created together at the beginning of time, for opposite purposes. One for the light, and one for the darkness. Always connected to one another, always at war. For that reason, the Tiamat emits measurable vibrations in response to substantial positive frequencies which find their source of power in the Skala. The Arachna analyzes the Tiamat's response to locate the corresponding source of positive frequency with incredible accuracy. That's how we find them. Much easier than in centuries past. The beauty of technology!"

The hackers mined information from various sources to narrow the search.

"Down to two," one of the female techs updated. "Satellite images show the father entering the factory this morning. Hasn't clocked out. Older girl works at the local school. Camera feeds place her there."

"Satellite confirms two heat signatures in the residence."

The techs chatted amongst each other "Mother?"

"Deceased, 2013."

"One of the two kids, then?"

"What are the parameters?" The Ertu asked.

"Extinguishable, Ertu."

The Ertu tapped his fingers on a counter. "Figure out which one it is. If you can't, kill them both."

Maeve absorbed the activity in the room, unfazed by the Ertu's murderous orders. "And when you find them?"

"That depends," the Ertu replied. "If they're moderates or of interest to us, we monitor them. We need some of them to contribute to society, develop breakthroughs, art, music…reach the Prism and keep it alive."

"And the others?"

"Our position depends on ensuring that the status quo is not disturbed. The Tiamat's abhorrence of the positive frequency is for good reason. Those with too much of it are dangerous and need to be removed. People don't need to know what they're capable of. It can only lead to anarchy. Human beings are, for the most part, brainless idiots who wouldn't have a clue what to do with that kind of power. It is in our best interest to remove them, or keep them in their place, encourage them to feel like victims – powerless, tortured souls in need of our cures and guidance."

"Isn't that the truth," a man's voice interrupted.

Tristan Sarazen approached, smelling of an aura of superiority and expensive cologne, his assistant toting a briefcase behind him. "I've brought the contracts for the new acquisition."

"My son," the Ertu said, introducing Tristan and retrieving the briefcase.

Maeve nodded in greeting. She didn't need the introduction. All of Paris knew the Sarazens.

"We've allowed too many of them to reach the Prism," the Ertu continued. "They are becoming a nuisance, Everest Cleary most of all. The only reason she's alive is the Skala, or the compass, whichever comes first. We had to allow her to live so we could study her – to see if she was indeed the Eridu."

Tristan rolled his eyes and leaned against the brick wall. "*That* stupid theory again. What if the Skala doesn't even exist? Has anyone considered this? For all we know, it's just a myth, contrived thousands of years ago by some senile shaman high on hallucinogenic figs!"

"We need to resume surveillance on her, as soon as she's found," the Ertu continued, ignoring his son. "I'm flying in Crawford's daughter. Tara will work out of the Paris chapter with the two of you from now on. Her cover is intact. Use it. She'll be more effective on this side of the Atlantic, and I'm sure her time is precious to her," he added cruelly, referencing the minutes ticking away on his Sharur's pledge clock. "The three of you know Clearly the best. Your orders are simple: locate her, keep the Vidal girl secure and bring in Halvorsen. The more bargaining chips we have the better."

The old man pulled out a cigar from his suit jacket pocket and pointed it at the direction of the flickering red map. "Remember, if we succeed then we have them both — the Tiamat, the means with which we drain humanity of its positive force, never truly allowing it to reach its full potential; and the Skala, the only thing balancing the scales and standing in the way of our complete domination."

Maeve relished the thought of Everest meeting her end. But she noticed that Tristan didn't seem to be as enthralled with the idea, an uncomfortable expression strewn across his face. If he harbored any sentiments for the stupid girl, that would be a problem.

"I'm trusting the three of you to manage the Cleary situation," the leader said. "I'll be too preoccupied with Bolivia. Drilling into that fault line created the perfect test environment for our prototype."

"What prototype?" Maeve asked. She felt invigorated. The information she was receiving was unbelievable! It meant the Ertu trusted her, and that the respect she had worked tirelessly for had finally been earned.

But it also meant she couldn't mess up. If she revealed the Order's most important secrets, her life would end quickly and painfully.

The Ertu puffed out his chest as he proceeded to divulge the Order's new agenda.

"The Tiamat has allowed us to suppress and demoralize humanity for millennia. No guns, no force — one touch and we let their weak mind do our work for us. Imagine the large-scale implications of that reach."

Tristan shifted uncomfortably on the edge of the table, visibly irritated. "We already genetically incorporate it into food. How much larger of a scale do we really need?"

"So far we can only incorporate small doses," the Ertu reminded his son, "and not all foods tolerate the molecular structure of the Tiamat. Until recently, neither did water.

"But now, we have something promising – the pièce de résistance. Imagine, the global water supply infused with its properties, the possibilities…"

The Ertu stretched his wrinkled mouth into a broad grin as he finished the thought in his head, revealing his unnaturally white teeth. "The only remaining challenge is determining the dosage – a careful calculation we must perfect. We can't risk debilitating the entire global population and the Prism collapsing before the Skala is found."

Tristan grimaced. The old man never shied away from the inconceivable. And this was no exception. He had put the best biochemical engineers through countless desensitization sessions to win their allegiance. All for this.

The Ertu instructed a tech to pull up satellite imagery from Bolivia on the main monitor. "Once the formula is precise, we'll begin by fixing what our 'earthquake' destroyed, starting with the water delivery systems. Then we can figure out the dosage."

Images of the village hit by the pseudo-quake appeared on the screens; unsuspecting children waded in the river while women washed clothing along the shoreline, their homes in ruins behind them. They knew nothing of the psychological and spiritual assault the Vulturians had in store and the devastating pain still to come.

The more the Ertu thought about his diabolical creation, the more unstoppable he imagined himself becoming. "Close, very close…" he muttered under his breath, lighting his cigar while trying to stifle a cough. "The media will continue to feed the world our version of the truth, preoccupying them with insignificant details so they remain oblivious to our efforts. And with the resistance weakened, there is even less standing in our way. Cleary, Crawford, Halvorsen," he muttered their names with disdain through clenched teeth, "will soon be a minor inconvenience, erased from history like all the others."

"Aren't you forgetting something?" Tristan sneered. "What if your master plan is not 'the will of Parem'?"

The Ertu let out a phlegmy cough and observed the screens of data. "There is no doubt in my mind that Cleary is the Eridu," he said. "The prophecy clearly states the Eridu will find the Skala. She is bound to it by a fate she cannot escape – and that *is* the will of Parem."

While Tristan rolled his eyes a second time, never a firm believer in prophecies of any kind, the Ertu remained resolute in his own engrained belief.

"Soon," he said decisively, exhaling another charcoal cloud into the room and watching it fade with his marbly black eyes, "after thousands of years the world will finally bow to our every command – once we control every ounce of water, every human emotion, and every living soul."

Seize the night...

About the Author

Aneta Torchia has a B.Sc. in psychology and criminology and a Master's degree in criminology from the University of Toronto. Her interests include human behavior, ancient history, metaphysics, the mysteries of the universe, and the untapped potential of the human mind. She writes literary, suspense, and fantasy fiction, children's picture books, and non-fiction with a focus on societal issues and well-being.

anetatorchia.com | theprismbooks.com

It seems like just yesterday when I first sat down to write *The Prism* in December 2014. While my daughter lay sleeping beside me, I reached for a pen and notebook (I'm old fashioned that way) and in two hours outlined the plot, developed the main characters, and ignited a desire to bring *The Prism* to life. It was one of those rare moments where you don't feel the time slip, and by the end of it my hand hurt. Six months later, I had completed the first draft and had loved every minute of it! I had finally found that sought-after "happy place."

So, why did I wait until January 2023 to publish this novel? Rejections and my own perfectionism played a role, although I'm grateful they allowed me time to polish the manuscript into what it is now. But once it was ready, I still hesitated – because the main reason I pushed the brakes on publishing this book came down to one word: fear. It's a very personal thing, to expose one's work for the world to criticize and judge. I was terrified of others potentially deciding that the thing I had poured my heart into didn't make the cut. Even once I received that long-awaited offer for a book deal, I still hesitated.

One day, I was speaking to my daughter about the importance of being confident and harnessing her power. I was going on about how fear is a construct of our minds and how it stops us from finding our purpose and fulfilling our true potential. I was trying to instill in her a fearlessness to take on the world, regardless of what others thought. In that moment, I realized I had no business preaching any of it, because I had not taken my own advice. I was paralyzed by my own fear, procrastinating, and finding excuses rather than having the confidence to take a chance. I knew then that it was time to publish *The Prism*. If I wanted to set an example for my children, I had to start with myself.

My fear was ironic, because I wrote this story in part to draw attention to the negative mind states humans allow to dictate and shape their lives. I noticed that everywhere we turn, there is something, or someone telling us we are not good enough and selling us something that brings forth negative emotions. Some of that comes from family upbringings; we may grow up with insecurities and demons, struggling to hold on to a sense of self-worth. But even if we are lucky to have the most supportive of families, there are also external forces. And there are many of them.

It does not serve those in power for the entire world to be self-actualized and fulfilled. If there was no chaos, no tragedy, no crime, no war, how would those in power make their money? How would they hold on to their positions and influence? How would the news get viewers? By allowing their message of limitation and strife to be the main narrative in our lives, we set ourselves up to experience more negative emotions than we need to. This is a dangerous path that often leads to poor mental, spiritual, and physical well-being, and it will always stand in the way of our personal fulfilment.

The idea of powerful elites working against the greater good in the pursuit of selfish interests is by no means a new one. But history continues to prove the validity of these theories time and again, and it does not serve us to turn a blind eye to the forces who pull the strings behind the curtain. Those that try to take away our power will always tell us we're crazy for catching on to their schemes and plans. They will place a tin hat on anyone who tries to shine a light on the truth, and blatantly gaslight once the curtain is lifted. They will use the media, celebrities, politicians, and people of influence to do it, and sell themselves as being righteous and vitreous in the process. They will paint us as powerless victims in need of their protection to maintain the *status quo*. This book is a work of fiction which I initially wrote nearly a decade ago, but it is not hard to see some real-world examples and metaphors. As a society, we must remember to think critically and not dismiss the influence of these forces. We were given a mind so that we could use it. To go through life passive, afraid, and never questioning is a slap in the face to the intelligence that created us.

But *The Prism* is also meant to remind readers that even in the bleakest and darkest of times, when it seems we have no say at all and that everything is left up to things beyond our control, we have more power than we realize. For in every human being lies untapped potential that can burn like the brightest star. It is up to us to make change happen. We cannot rely on others, or blame the past, or demand from others rewards or outcomes that we do not deserve. We must act and have courage to face even formidable foes. We must use our thoughts and ideas and energy to move in the right direction – forward. Although life can be challenging, this should not discourage us from taking control of our own destiny. As John Green once said, "the darkest nights produce the brightest stars." I couldn't agree more! I truly believe that God, or the universe, or whatever you choose to call it is a friend to all creation and has given us the tools we need to thrive and grow. We just need to learn to use them wisely, always keep moving forward, and never let fear get in our way.

Another reason I wrote this novel is because for as long as I can remember, I've been searching for something to help me make sense of my existence and the universe in general. There is so much more to life than what we know and what we're told; so much that science has not yet discovered. So much that is intangible and not easily explained by quantitative measures. There is a powerful intelligence in everything around us, from the smallest cell to the most terrifying black hole. At the core of my being, I'm convinced that we are all connected to that intelligence, and that we have far more potential to shape our world than we realize. Believing in something greater than ourselves – and in the idea that we are all capable of attracting goodness into our lives – can be truly life changing. At times, we may feel that powerful and benevolent intelligence lurking around us in some invisible plane, at the tips of our fingers yet never fully accessible; or we may get glimpses into its existence by virtue of some unexplained spiritual or metaphysical phenomenon. It takes some faith to believe in that which we cannot see. And it takes courage not to be discouraged by those who do not have hope, faith or an open mind.

In a world that is experiencing growing rates of depression and anxiety, we need a shift. There is a spiritual deficiency in our society that tangible things cannot cure. This is a novel for the reader who believes there is more, in the spiritual and metaphysical sense – more than the tangible world we see around us. More than shallow relationships or hookups based on fleeting desires; more than endless partying with the pursuit of chasing a high that will never truly satisfy us in any meaningful way; more than fake photographs of strangers and celebrities that glorify a false utopia of shattered promises and dreams; more than the illusions we see displayed on our televisions, telling us to want things that will never truly fulfill us, or telling us that we're not good enough the way we are made. As a mother, I want that 'more' for my children and those I love. I want that 'more' for all humanity – healthy relationships, incredible memories, and highs that are reached not from things or substances, but through truly pure and meaningful ways. We all deserve that 'more'. And a world where that 'more' becomes the dominant narrative and force in our lives will no doubt be a better one.

The Prism is the first book in this three part-series, so be sure to follow-up with *Emerald Passage* and *Finding Aeonia* to see how the story ends. You can get updates on all the Prism books by visiting theluminarypress.com, theprismbooks.com or my author website, anetatorchia.com.

I hope you enjoyed reading *The Prism* as much as I enjoyed writing it, and I hope it inspires something in you as it did for me.

Sincerely and with thanks,

Aneta Torchia

Author's Playlist

Chapter 1: *My Mind & Me*, Selena Gomez

Chapter 2: *Waves*, Dean Lewis

Chapter 3: *The Memory of Trees*, Enya

Chapter 4: *Book of Days*, Enya

Chapter 5 & 6: *Shadows in Silence*, Enigma

Chapter 7: *Silence*, Delirium

Chapter 8: *Caribbean Blue*, Enya

Chapter 9: *The Shade*, Metric

Chapter 10: *Stargazing*, Kygo feat Justin Jesso

Chapter 12: *Past Life*, Arkells & Cold War Kids

Chapter 13: *Pax Deorum*, Enya

Chapter 14: *Wonderful Life*, Black

Chapter 15: *Sadness*, Enigma

Chapter 16: *Sky Full of Stars*, Coldplay

Chapter 17: *Sadness*, Yanni

Chapter 18: *Believing in You*, Cacti feat. Frigga

Chapter 19: *The Forbidden Pool, Lord of the Rings: The Two Towers*, Howard Shore

Chapter 20: *Firestone*, Kygo feat. Conrad Sewell

Chapter 21: *Walk You Home*, Karmina

Chapter 23: *Promise Me No Promises*, Landon Austin

Chapter 24: *Who Are You Really*, Mikky Ekko

Chapter 26: *Tempus Vernum*, Enya

Chapter 27: *Deora Ar Mo Chroi*, Enya

Chapter 29: *Storms in Africa*, Enya

Chapter 30: *Atlas: Heart*, Sleeping at Last

YOU MAY ALSO ENJOY

THE PRISM SERIES BOOK 2
EMERALD PASSAGE

&

THE PRISM SERIES BOOK 3
FINDING AEONIA

theluminarypress.com
info@theluminarypress.com

www.ingramcontent.com/pod-product-compliance
Lightning Source LLC
Chambersburg PA
CBHW050848210726
48290CB00004B/1141